The Game Master

The Game Master
Copyright © 2015 William Bernhardt
Published in print by Babylon Books
Electronic and audiobook editions by Kindle Press

THE GAME
MASTER

William Bernhardt

Babylon Books

Other Books by William Bernhardt

The Ben Kincaid Novels:

Primary Justice

Blind Justice

Deadly Justice

Perfect Justice

Cruel Justice

Naked Justice

Extreme Justice

Dark Justice

Silent Justice

Murder One

Criminal Intent

Death Row

Hate Crime

Capitol Murder

Capitol Threat

Capitol Conspiracy

Capitol Offense

Capitol Betrayal

Other novels:

Nemesis: The Final Case of Eliot Ness

Dark Eye

Strip Search

Double Jeopardy

The Midnight Before Christmas

The Code of Buddhood

Final Round

Nonfiction:

Story Structure: The Key to Successful Fiction

Creating Character: Bringing Your Story to Life

Perfecting Plot: Charting the Hero's Journey

Dynamic Dialogue: Letting Your Story Speak

Poetry:

The White Bird

For young readers:

Shine

The Black Sentry

Princess Alice and the Dreadful Dragon

Equal Justice: The Courage of Ada Sipuel

Edited by William Bernhardt

Legal Briefs: Stories by Today's Best Thriller Writers

Natural Suspect: A Collaborative Novel of Suspense

For Lara

"You can discover more about a person in an hour of play than in a year of conversation."

Plato

Part One

Opening Gambit

1

Las Vegas

C n smone pls help? Thy wnt 2 DELETE me!
It took Kadey twice the usual time to get that message out. Almost impossible to text when your thumbs slide across the translucent iPhone screen. Her sweaty hands could barely hold on to it. Maybe Twitter was not the best way to send a cry for help. But it was all she had at the moment. Calling the police would be futile. Calling a friend would sign their death warrant.

She doubted her tweet would reach anyone in time. She didn't expect a flash-mob rescue. Because even now, when there were so many unanswered questions, there was one fact about which she was certain.

She did not have much time left.

But she wouldn't give up. Her mother always said she was a fighter. That was her life mantra, even now. Her mother always supported her. Even when she decided against a career in mathematics to pursue something that brought her perilously close to what Mom called "the wrong side of the family." But The Platform made her an irresistibly generous offer. Computer programming for military contracts seemed like a fine idea. At the time.

Less so now.

She ducked into an alleyway, gasping for breath. She couldn't see anyone behind her, but she didn't let that delude her into believing no one was there. If she didn't do something fast, she would disappear, just like the others. She pushed her hair off her sweaty forehead, tucking it behind her ear.

She glanced over her shoulder. Something black and shadowy darted out of view. The harsh glare of a streetlamp burned her eyes.

Something had been there. Something that was not there now. Something hidden. Or hiding.

She'd been kidnapped once before, held against her will for what seemed an eternity. She would not survive it a second time. So she ran.

Did David have time to download the files? She couldn't be sure. After she heard the gunshot, she bolted. And now she raced down rain-slicked streets, breathless, every nerve on fire.

She smacked up against a chain-link fence, hoisted herself to the top, and vaulted over it. Her black turtleneck snagged on a wire twist, tearing. She hit the pavement on the other side hard, her knees slamming into her chin. Thank goodness for air shoes. An essential part of the savvy girl's burglar outfit.

She threw another glance over her shoulder. She didn't see anyone. If she could make it home, she had a chance.

She raced through another alley and emerged on Fremont Street, gritting her teeth. She could no longer hide in the shadows. Not if she wanted to get home. She would have to chance the neon glare of tourist Vegas.

They wouldn't try anything in public. With so many potential witnesses.

Would they?

She bolted out of the alley. The glitz of Vegas's newest hot spot immersed her in harsh white light, a hint of enriched ozone, the smell of money, and noise, noise, noise. Crowds spilled into the streets, loud and merry, or at least pretending to be. Alcohol could only take you so far, and she knew that, statistically speaking, most of these people were losing money they had worked hard to earn.

She turned sideways, edging her way through the crowd. Progress was difficult, but anyone following her would be slowed as well. Maybe more than she. Easier for one camel to pass through the eye of a needle than an entire caravan . . .

She knew she should focus on navigating the mass of bodies, but she paused long enough to glance behind her. In the sea of faces, one stood out from the others.

Because she'd seen it before.

Scream, she thought. Surely someone would help. Or would her cries be lost in the revelry, mistaken for one of the screams of excitement and delight? She had to get to her apartment. Then she

4

would be safe. She could get on her computer and use its encrypted line to get the word out, global. Take it viral. Stop them before—

Someone moving much too fast slammed into her from the left. She spun sideways, careening against the flow of traffic. A burly man with a sandy buzzcut and Jack Daniels cologne collided with her. She pitched forward, face first toward the pavement.

She fell on her hands, scraping them in the process. The raw skin of her palms burned from the grit. Boots and stilettoes pounded down all around her. She tucked her hands close to protect them from further damage.

Keep your head together, she told herself. Once you've made it to home plate, you're safe. But you can't rest until—

She heard a voice beside her, an urgent rasping whisper. "Don't move. Not if you want to live."

Her entire body tensed. He had her. And there wasn't a thing she could do about it. She would be deleted and—

"Take it easy. I'm a doctor. Just wanted to make sure you weren't hurt. If you aren't careful in this crowd, you'll get trampled. It's dangerous out here, especially when you aren't too steady on your feet. If you want to survive, let me help you."

"You're a doctor? Prove it."

The elderly man adjusted his eyeglasses. "How? You want to see my stethoscope?"

She tried to shift her paranoia into low gear. He was only being kind. "I'm fine."

"Probably. But you should still take it easy." He helped her sit up.

"I'll be okay." She looked around. Any interaction with this man might put him in danger. "I'm sorry. I can see that you're trying to help me. But I have to leave."

"I really don't think that's a good idea." He looked at her like she was drunk or crazy, speaking slowly as if to a child. He had no idea the danger he faced merely by attempting to assist her.

She struggled to her feet and backed away from him, navigating in reverse through the mob. She knew she wasn't handling this well, wasn't thinking clearly. But she had to get to her apartment. Once she had a locked door behind her, she'd be able to work it all out. What happened to David. What to do next.

She reached the edge of the main drag, leaving the hotels and casinos behind. Her sticky clothes clung to her like a polyethylene bag, tight and suffocating.

She swerved onto the street that led to her apartment. She could see the front door just ahead. She was going to make it.

She rounded the curve to her complex. She didn't slow until she was almost at her apartment's front door. She stopped, leaning against the wall, catching her breath, fumbling for her keys. She pushed open the door and plunged inside, slamming the door behind her, double-locking and bolting it. After ripping the books off the hall bookshelf and dumping them in a pile on the floor, she dragged the heavy case across the room and pressed it against the door. Then she shoved a towel under the crack. Let's see someone get through that, she thought. Check and mate, you bastards.

She went to her computer and opened her browser. She would blanket the Internet. Twitter, Facebook, Instagram, every bulletin board she knew. Maybe a Skype alert posted on YouTube. She would spread the word so far and wide that no amount of cover-up would be sufficient. She would stay locked up in here until she knew it was safe to emerge. She didn't care how long it took. She started typing—

"Katherine?"

She jumped out of her chair, pressing the Enter key by reflex. "How did you get in?"

Two arms reached out of the darkness and threw her to the floor, then pulled her arms back and snapped a pair of handcuffs around her wrists. She screamed and struggled but he was much too strong for her. His movements were precise and unrelenting, like a machine.

He held her down against the carpet and wrapped a large metal collar around her neck, then closed it with a heavy click. She knew she could never break it open, even if her hands were free. He attached a heavy chain to one end of the collar.

"Don't do this," she said. "Please."

"I have no choice."

He jerked the chain, dragging her across the room. She squirmed and tried to lock her legs around passing furniture. He was too fast and too strong.

"You have a choice," she said, gasping. "Everyone has a choice. Everyone has free will."

"Not in this world. But perhaps, in the next." He placed a mask over her face. She began to lose consciousness. "I must fulfill my programming."

2

*C*n smone pls help? Thy wnt 2 DELETE me!
　　Smone has to stp ths be4its 2 l8. Evythng s about 2 chng &
　　Special Agent Palmer stared at the computer monitor. "That's how it ends?"

Greenstreet nodded. "Not a letter more. And it's been twelve hours. She didn't show up for work."

"And you think . . . ?"

"They say she and David Bishop were good buddies. And you know what happened to him."

He leaned back in his chair and inhaled the swill they called coffee. His day never really started until the third mug. "You searched her apartment?"

"We did. And get this. When we arrived, the bookshelf was pressed against the front door. And there was a towel under the door. Windows shut. Took us forever to get in."

"And the girl?"

"Gone."

"How could she exit but leave the shelf leaning against the door?"

"Exactly. But that's not what disturbs me most."

"What does?"

Greenstreet pointed at the screen. "She didn't use all her characters. She was desperate for help, but she left characters unused. Why?"

Palmer shrugged. "Premature emission?"

"She would've sent a second message. She would've tweeted all night long. If she could." Greenstreet turned off the monitor. "She never got the chance."

"You think she's . . . gone?"

"Like the others. Deleted."

3

"Ladies and gentleman, let's hear it for the final two."

BB stepped in front of his opponent and spread wide his arms. Applause thundered through the exhibition area. He grinned and waved, completely overshadowing poor Druktenis. Why not? He saw no reason for modesty. Making it this far was an impressive accomplishment, even without considering everything else he'd done this year. He was minutes away from clinching an unprecedented Triple Crown.

Besides, women loved the cocky-bastard routine. They all wanted the bad boy.

He glanced up at the tall tiers of spectators encircling the playing table. Not an empty seat up there. He knew most of the rubberneckers were rooting for him. Why not acknowledge it? Humbleness would not fit well with his image as the Keith Richards of games. His esteemed predecessor, Tommy Angelo, once said, "The best way to play poker is to act like Jesus but play like the devil." BB thought he got it backwards.

He grabbed the microphone. "I just want to thank all the fans who brought me here. I couldn't have done it without your support. This is for you!"

The room erupted with cheers. He blew kisses with both hands, which provoked a tumult of squealing and delight. He raced around the periphery of the circle, slapping hands as he passed. A young woman who couldn't have been more than eighteen pressed a slip of paper into his hand. He didn't have to look to know it was her phone number.

"Can I have your autograph?"

The requests came from so many directions he couldn't identify the sources. A dozen pens materialized in his path. He dodged them and kept moving.

"Sorry, ladies. Not now. Gotta stay in the zone."

He raced on, then heard a tiny voice behind him. "But it's for my mother."

BB stopped short, pivoted, grabbed the pen. He scribbled his name across the front of the program. As he handed it back, he made eye contact. "You take care of your mother, sweetheart."

She grabbed the program and clutched it to her heart.

BB kept running until he made it to his seat. Yes, he'd managed to make every woman for miles around adore him.

Except the one he loved most. Her contempt was a gaping wound no doctor could dress.

Truth was, he liked the game, not the fame. But he had learned there were advantages to a high profile, especially when you wanted to supplement prize winnings with lucrative endorsement contracts and the sale of concessions.

The problem was, the longer he was in the spotlight, the greater the chance someone would learn his secret. And if that happened, the fifteen minutes of fame allotted to "BB" would come to a crashing halt. As if he had never existed.

Because in a very real way, he never had.

The overhead klieg lights were strong enough to make him wish he'd brought sunglasses. They made keeping his poker-faced sangfroid all the more challenging. He could not afford to squint or sweat.

A reporter jabbed a microphone into his face. "BB, I'm Emily Martinez-Smith, ESPN. Can you answer a few questions?"

She was pretty enough, in that Plasticine way most reporters were, but he preferred to prep for the game without media interference. He knew their involvement made the million-and-a-half purse possible. But he didn't appreciate anything that affected the purity of the game.

"What do you want to know?"

"Do you think you're going to win?"

"Of course I'm going to win. I'm the Game Master."

The crowd cheered.

"Gary Druktenis has been playing longer than you have."

"So had the reigning champ at the SCRABBLE nationals. So had the top-seeded North American chess player. Didn't matter. I *am* the Master."

The reporter smiled. He gave her what she wanted, and she was grateful. How grateful? he wondered. "What's next for the Master? Are there any mountains you haven't scaled yet?"

"Got my eye on the Mind Games Olympiad. I'd like to add an international title to my collection. Then I'm going after that squirrelly Russian guy who thinks he plays a better game of chess than I do."

"Rudolf Constanza? World Grandmaster for the last twelve years?"

"Yeah. Think it's time for him to take early retirement."

"You must be feeling intensely nervous right now. This is your first poker Grand Slam."

"Nervous is for people with doubts. I have no doubts about the outcome. Druktenis is going down." He tried to say it in the overblown professional-wrestler manner that would play well in a sound bite when they were looking for a pre-commercial clip.

"There's some controversy about whether poker should be considered a sport. Do you think it's a sport?"

"No. It's a game. And that's good. Games are about much more than violence and machismo. Games promote social interaction, strategic thinking, and abstract reasoning. They exercise the mind, prevent senility. Our lives can be defined as a network of interlocking games, many people playing different strategies but all hoping to win. Game-playing is a survival skill."

"You call yourself the Game Master. Not exactly modest."

"Modesty is for losers."

"Isn't calling yourself the Game Master like saying you're the Emperor of Ice Cream?"

"Games make people smarter."

"Chess, sure. Maybe SCRABBLE. But poker?"

"Every game has its own realm. Chess is about understanding strategy. SCRABBLE is about understanding language. Poker is about understanding people." He beamed. "And I'm the master of all three."

He saw the producer draw a thumb across his neck.

"One last question. What does *BB* stand for?"

"Anything you want it to, sweetheart."

12

"You sign your name Steven C. Thomas. So why do people call you BB?"

"That goes way back."

"But what does it stand for?"

He grinned. "Beautiful Baby. Better Bettor. Babe Bamboozler. You choose."

The reporter turned to face the camera. "And there you have it, ladies and gentlemen. We may not know what his name stands for, but we know what he stands for. A first-rate game. And today, one of these men will walk away with a purse worth one and a half million dollars."

A million and a half. That was real money. The largest purse ever awarded to a single winner of a competitive event. Some boxing purses were larger, but those had to be split by the boxer and manager and an army of trainers. Like the cheese in the children's song, the poker player stands alone. Many players sold percentages of their action before the tournament to insulate themselves against bad luck or bad cards, or to smooth out an erratic income flow. Not BB. For him, the game was paramount. Give someone else a piece, and soon they'd be trying to tell you whether to call or fold. His judgment had brought him this far. He'd let it take him all the way.

"And so the field has been narrowed to two contenders, Gary Druktenis of Skokie, Illinois, and Steve 'BB' Thomas of Palm Beach." The ESPN announcer stood at the head of the table, using the players as backdrops. "We'll enter the final round of the World Series of Poker right after this message."

Three minutes to plan his endgame.

Or not. Druktenis strolled over and extended his hand. "Looks like we're down to the finish line, pal. May the best man win."

BB reluctantly took his hand. He valued friends, but despised people who pretended friendship when they weren't feeling it, and Druktenis wasn't feeling it. BB was usually good at reading people. An invaluable asset for this game—but not necessarily for social bonding. "That's the way it generally works out."

"Man, you learned me during that hand last night. You saw right through my bluff."

"I had no idea what you were holding. I threw in after the second flop and hoped for the best."

13

"You're being modest. I've picked up a lot of tips watching you play."

BB doubted he had taught Druktenis anything. Druktenis was a twenty-year veteran of this game. "You have good instincts. You couldn't have won Chicago otherwise."

"I was on my home turf. Makes it easier."

"You didn't get that bracelet just for being the homie." The winners of all the qualifying events received a silver bracelet. The winner of the World Series received a gold bracelet, the poker equivalent of the Masters Tournament's green jacket. That bracelet was the most coveted prize in the game. The money was good, too, but that went into the bank. A champ could wear the gold bracelet forever. "I hope this doesn't go on too long. I'm melting under these lights."

"I don't think it will take that long," Druktenis said. "I don't think it will take long at all."

The announcer gave them the one-minute signal. Druktenis returned to his seat.

He pulled himself into his pregame meditative state. He'd learned to channel his mental energy and to focus it on one thing—the game.

A minute later, the World Series of Poker continued.

Different games were played at various qualifying events, but here in the finals, they played Texas Hold'em all the way to the end. The dealer tossed out the first hand.

Druktenis got an ace and king from different suits. BB had two non-counters. The flop was unhelpful. He folded at his first opportunity.

The second hand was equally unpromising. They were both dealt pairs, but Druktenis's was higher. BB bet for a time, hoping for help from the flop, but it didn't arrive.

The next few hands only made matters worse. Over $100,000 in chips traveled from his side of the table to Druktenis's. The problem wasn't Druktenis. The problem was the cards. Apparently he had displeased the gods of poker. In the first ten minutes, he only won two hands. At this rate, he had enough chips to last maybe half an hour. If he didn't turn the game around quickly, his dream of being the first Triple Crown winner was doomed.

The blinds went to $30,000. Druktenis raised to $90,000 from the button. BB held two tens. The dealer ripped out a rainbow flop of eight-nine-nine. Druktenis rapped on the felt tabletop twice—a check-raise.

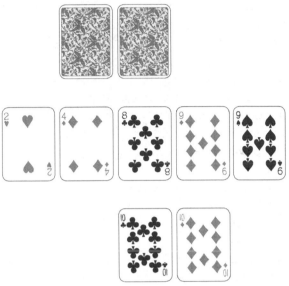

Now or never. BB bet one hundred dimes—$100,000. Druktenis raised him to $350,000. The crowd gasped.

BB did, too. But silently. If Druktenis was holding a third nine, or worse, two of them, the game was over. But he might not have bet so much if that was the case. It would be too obvious. Unless that was what he wanted BB to think.

Playing poker was a mindreading act. A player could slip into endless contemplation of what the opponent knows, what he knows you know, what he knows that you know that he knows, etc. This game required scrupulous attention to behavior, to the tiniest of details. That was why there was so much more to this game than the mere calculation of odds. Poker was not unlike the famous thought experiment with Schrödinger's cat: Observation changed the results.

"Call," he said, pushing chips forward. "And raise you another $150,000."

The audience roared. Out the corner of his eye, he saw the producer signal another cut to commercial. A second later, he felt a jolt to his shoulder. "Excuse me, sir. You'll have to come with us."

He turned to see who spoke.

The man standing behind him wore a dark suit, jacket closed, white shirt, buttoned-down collar, black tie. He didn't look like a pit boss and he certainly didn't look like he worked for ESPN.

The man tilted his head as if to show him which way to walk.

BB glanced at Druktenis. "Is this some sort of diversionary tactic?"

Druktenis appeared as baffled as he was.

BB cleared his throat. "Did you not notice the television cameras or the thousand or so people in the gallery? This is the World Series of Poker."

The man's expression remained flat. "I'm a federal agent and this is a matter of extreme urgency. Please come with me."

A federal agent? Did the man think he was cheating? "I'm not going anywhere until this game is over."

"Let me make this simple for you, sir. You have no choice." BB noticed the bulge in his jacket. "I'm prepared to use force if necessary. If you want a scene, then we'll have a scene. Or you can come quietly. But either way, you're coming."

"But—this is the World Series of Poker!"

"I don't give a damn." The man reached into his suit coat and flashed a badge. "I'm Special Agent Palmer of the FBI and I'm investigating a potential threat to national security."

"What does that have to do with me?"

"There's been a murder. Gruesome. Almost medieval." He gazed at BB levelly. "And it has your name all over it. Literally."

4

*H*e was *not the only one.*

That dangerous truth burned holes into Julian's brain. But he put it aside. He must focus his attention on the game. Emissaries of the Other could arrive at any moment.

He stared at his hands, still caked with that man's blood. Unforeseen developments required him to take steps he had not anticipated. Steps apparently no one had anticipated. Which was even more disturbing than what he had been forced to do. Everything was supposed to be worked out in advance, planned in detail, with the minutest matters taken into account. But they hadn't been. And now he was Lady Macbeth on a mountaintop, except he knew it was pointless to attempt to eradicate the damned spot. It would never come out. No matter what he did.

He had a safe vantage point that allowed him to observe the seventh floor of the neighboring building. He had watched everything that transpired since the body was discovered. He felt confident that the next few hours would unfold as planned. But he could never be totally certain. Not even the greatest oracle in the world could rest assured. Especially when the stakes were so enormous. And every move had consequences.

His eyelids ached to close. Stimulants were not allowed. Not even coffee. There was always a price to pay later. No matter. He didn't need artificial aids. The strength of his mind would keep him alert as long as necessary.

He still wore his outfit from the night before, the rapid assault shirt with saddle-shoulder design for range of movement, all-weather trousers and leather side-zip safety-toe boots. Good for running, climbing, and kicking the hell out of someone, if the game required it. A microfiber response jacket. They all came from 5.11 Tactical, the

17

American supplier that made the best clothing and gear in the world for his line of work.

He adjusted his monocular to focus on the CSI teams on the seventh floor. They would find nothing. They were not meant to find anything. The clues were for other eyes.

Just to be certain, he eavesdropped on their conversation. The night before he planted a Fortex 5000, a hypersensitive omnidirectional microphone so small it could be hidden inside the nib of a pen. Didn't even need a battery. It could be powered by induction. If it was near a power cord—and it was—it would absorb the needed energy to power itself. He could hear everything the device picked up through an app on his cell.

He adjusted the scope to scrutinize the rooftop. He detected a way to get to the other building from here. Useful. The route he had traveled last night was no longer accessible. Too many people in the way.

He did not look forward to what lay ahead. But he had a duty to perform. For the world, yes, but also for the Father.

Anything for the Father.

He understood the import of the meeting in Dubai. But it meant the Father could not be here. Even the Father could not be everywhere, could not see everything, all at once.

He was glad to be of assistance.

He was occasionally plagued with doubt. That was his great failing, his sin. But he knew this with certainty: Only one man had ever cared about him. Helped him. Saved him, after he had abandoned all hope. Saved him from the world that pushed him and beat him until he was almost utterly destroyed.

He pressed a finger against his SRAC—short-range agent communication device. Ideal for tactical exercises that required cloaked radio communications.

A voice crackled through the device. "They'll be there shortly."

"Understood."

"The game is ready?"

"As directed."

"Controls in place?"

"Of course."

"There may be more interference."

18

"I will be ready." He tapped his nylon pancake holster. "I will respond appropriately to any threats that arise."

"Good. Out."

Given the stakes, no price was too dear and any action was justified. Last night's work. Today's mission. The rigors of the game. Anything.

After all, a scientist must be rigorous.

He resumed his position and waited for the Game Master to arrive.

5

B normally processed information quickly, but this jarring interruption left his brain feeling like slow-moving sludge. "My name? On a murder? What are you talking about?"

"I'll explain everything in private. Right now, you need to come with me."

He glanced into the gallery. The spectators buzzed, wondering who the suit-coat stranger at the table might be. Twenty seconds until the commercial break ended. "I'm not going anywhere."

"I'm hoping we can keep this civil, sir."

By now, the crowd had realized something was wrong. The commercial ended and the red light on the cameras lit. The dealer waited for him to make his move.

His brain went into overdrive, performing rapid-fire calculations of odds and risk. "Can you give me five minutes?" he asked Palmer.

"No."

"One minute, then. Sixty stinking seconds."

Palmer exhaled heavily. "I suppose I can manage that."

He turned back to the game table and looked Druktenis straight in the eye. "I have a high pair. Two tens. I'm gonna win. That's why I raised."

"Is that a fact," Druktenis replied evenly. Translation: I don't believe a word you say, but I'll play your game. "I have three nines, counting the two from the flop. Sounds like you lose."

"Unless one of us is lying."

"I'm betting that's you."

"My mother told me to never tell lies. I do have two tens."

They both smiled like cobras. He detected perspiration on Druktenis's upper lip. So much was at stake. And so many were watching.

20

"You're not lying?" Druktenis asked.

"I'm not."

"Scout's honor?"

"As I live and breathe."

"Cross your heart?"

"And hope to die."

The crowd lapped it up. Laughter blended with applause. This cowboy-saloon poker game appeared headed for a showdown.

"Enough bantering," Druktenis said. "Call and raise."

"All in." Without missing a beat, he pushed his chips forward.

The gallery reacted with audible surprise. The cameras zoomed closer.

"Sure you want to do that?" Druktenis asked.

"No choice." He glanced over his shoulder at Palmer. "Apparently this is my last hand."

"Then I'll join you. We'll finish this right here and now." He pushed his chips forward. "I'm all in too."

The dealer dealt the turn card, then the river. No help for anyone

The dealer flipped over their cards.

His tens were revealed. But Druktenis had no nines to match the two from the flop.

Druktenis's lips parted. "But—"

BB's eyebrows danced. "Yes?"

"You tricked me."

"Yes."

The ESPN reporter thrust a mike between them. "What was the trick? I didn't see a trick."

Druktenis extended his hand. "Congratulations, BB. You deserve this."

"Coming from a man of your experience, that's quite a compliment." They shook hands.

The crowd exploded with cheers and applause. "Ladies and gentlemen, we have a champion," the announcer proclaimed. "The Winner of the World Series, with its 1.5 million dollar purse—and the first to capture the Triple Crown of games—the Prince of Games—"

He interrupted. "That's Game *Master*." Another enthusiastic round of cheering and clapping erupted.

Palmer tugged at his arm. "Okay, Master. Time to go."

The lead tournament official rushed forward. "Excuse me, but we have a winner's ceremony. BB will receive a trophy and a gold bracelet and a big check."

"Mail them to him."

"But the press will want photographs. Interviews."

"Sorry." Palmer flashed a badge and a don't-mess-with-me expression. The official backed off.

"I'll return as soon as I can," he said, shrugging. He grabbed Emily's microphone. "Apparently the government is so eager to claim their share of the prize winnings they're not even going to wait until I get it." The ensuing laughter helped smooth his sudden departure. Palmer led him off the stage. "Boy, you really know how to spoil a great moment."

"I'll apologize later."

"How am I going to explain why I left so abruptly?"

"You'll come up with something." The tight-lipped expression on the agent's face suggested that this man might not be his greatest fan. "Maybe you'll concoct a *Master* plan."

BB stared out the car window. Palmer hadn't said a word since they got into the agent's Ford Escort. He wasn't sure why the FBI would want to talk to him. Not because he couldn't think of anything he'd done that might get him into trouble. Because there were too many possibilities.

"You a Vegas native, Palmer?"

"Nah. East Coast. D.C."

"What are you doing in Sin City?"

"Flew out by copter this morning. Landed at Biggs." He hesitated a moment. "There have been several disappearances that may relate to an ongoing investigation. And now, an extremely puzzling murder."

"I like puzzles."

"I don't."

"Clue me in."

Palmer didn't take his eyes off the windshield. "I'd rather wait until we arrive at our destination. Then I can show you."

BB watched as the Vegas strip flew past. He loved the flamboyance of it all, the towering fountains, pirate ships, reproduction pyramids. The streets were packed with tourists, con men, and prostitutes. Shopping, gaming, and sightseeing in the middle of the desert, where there were no real sights to see. People drawn in by free drinks and buffets so they would gamble away their life savings. Disneyland for drunks and dummies.

He still loved it.

"I think you owe me something, Palmer. You yanked me away from a major conquest. Cheated me out of my chance to bask in adulation. I'm experiencing serious pokerus interruptus."

Palmer pursed his lips. Was that his version of a smile? "Most crimes are solved in the first twenty-four hours or not at all. I'm not going to waste those precious hours, especially when another life might hang the balance. Certainly not going to sit around waiting for some stupid game to end."

"Hey, the World Series of Poker is a big deal."

"So is murder."

"I never murdered anyone. Except at the card table today."

"You got lucky."

"There is an element of luck in any card game. But I beat Druktenis by outthinking him."

"Give me a break. You didn't know what he had in the hole."

"Of course I did. But that wasn't how I won. I won by making him believe I had nothing. Since he thought I had nothing, he went all in, even though he didn't have to."

"And how did you make him believe you had nothing? Mental telepathy?"

"Reverse tell."

"What, his eye twitched or something?"

"No. A player of Druktenis's experience is far too savvy to have an overt tell. He was always careful not to react to any card he drew. No facial tics, no gestures, no chatter. But since I'm a relative newcomer, it was conceivable that I might have a tell. So I made him think I did. In the early rounds, I deliberately scratched my right ear every time I bluffed. He thought it was my tell. So in the critical match, I scratched my ear when I told him I had tens. I told the truth, but he thought I was lying. And that's how I won the match."

Palmer did not appear impressed. He was sorry he'd told the story. He was a sort of magician, after all, and a magician should never reveal his tricks. When performed, they're amazing. When explained, they seem all too simple.

"So you're saying you coincidentally got your first opportunity to employ the reverse tell and win at exactly the moment I wanted to drag you away from the game table."

"No."

"So you admit you got lucky."

"I admit I could've ended the game anytime I wanted after it came down to the final two."

"And you chose not to? Just for the fun of it?"

He turned his eyes back to the window. "Druktenis is a good man. He's worked hard, put in his time. He doesn't deserve to be humiliated on national television."

Palmer made a harrumphing noise deep in his throat. "I still say you got lucky."

"Let me tell you what my mama told me many years ago. You make your own luck."

"On that subject, where's your mother now?"

"Why? Do you want to ask her about my childhood, Dr. Freud?"

24

"We had some trouble running a background check on you. Not many records in your name."

"I don't use my real name professionally."

"Or anywhere else, it would seem."

He opened a vent. Seemed way hot in this jalopy. "I try not to leave a trail. Keeps my ex-wife at bay. So getting back to the subject, what is this about? The FBI wouldn't investigate an ordinary murder."

Palmer made a hard left, turning off the main drag just before the M&M's emporium and heading south. He pulled into the lot for a large office park. "People are disappearing."

"Like in a Caesars Palace magic act?"

"Nothing nearly so entertaining. I'm taking you to the site of a top-secret, high-level Department of Defense research and development project. About a hundred people have been working here for several months. But five of them have disappeared in the last three weeks. And now one has been murdered."

"I don't see what it has to do with me. I didn't murder anyone."

"Looks like you did. And then signed your work."

"I was playing poker late last night. In front of many witnesses."

"The murders occurred after the tournament closed. And you have another connection to these crimes. This was a unique research and development project composed of two discrete groups. Scientists . . . and game designers."

"You've dragged me here because of my world-renowned gaming expertise? Look, I haven't worked on video games for about five years. And I'm doing quite well on my own, so I have no intention of—"

"You're not getting it," the agent said curtly. "I don't give a damn whether you helped increase Lara Croft's bust size." Palmer parked the car, reached into an attaché and pulled out a file. "One of those people who disappeared. The most recent one. Last night. Shortly after one of her friends was murdered." He pulled a photo out of the file. "Katherine Patricia Thomas. Your daughter."

6

The plan was in motion. The Game Master had arrived.

Julian crossed the street and raced to the far side of the building. Away from traffic. Away from the eyes of anyone who might observe. He scaled the side of the building, a sheer vertical ascent, like a rock climber working without rocks. His perfectly conditioned body glided up the wall. He jumped onto the fire escape on the third level and scurried up the ladder. That took him to the seventh floor. He grabbed the top railing of the fire escape and swung himself back and forth, gaining momentum. Then he flipped backward off the top, hit the wall with his feet, and did a back flip upward. He grabbed the corner of the roof with his bare hands. Pushing hard off his feet, he managed to propel himself onto the roof. Parkour—fun and useful. When you understood the science behind it. Wouldn't see him on those painful YouTube videos.

He tucked his assault shirt back into his trousers and crossed the roof to the skylight. Perfect. He could watch everything that transpired below without being spotted. So long as he was careful. There was too much at stake to blunder now. He'd made enough mistakes in his life.

He saw the secondary CSI fiber team finishing its work. Judging from what he heard on the Fortex, they'd found a few stray hairs and detritus. Hardly surprising, given how many people worked down there. But he'd left no traces. Nothing that could lead the authorities back to him. Or the Father.

The videographers recorded the crime scene from a multitude of angles. Eventually, they would remove the body. But it would still be there when they brought in the Game Master.

Good. That was how the game board had been designed.

He regretted what happened with Bishop. But in his infinite ingenuity, the Father had turned last night to their advantage. That was perhaps what he admired most. Adversity had once all but destroyed him. But for the Father, unforeseen adversity was a random factor soon turned to his benefit. There was a place for everything and everyone in this brave new world.

Even the Game Master. He might not know it. He might not want it.

It might kill him.

But the Game Master's role was preordained. What had begun could not be stopped.

He'd had a lifetime of experience, a lifetime of pain. But he had risen above base origins. Thanks to the Father, he had channeled his anger in a more productive direction.

His SRAC buzzed. Incoming message from Dubai.

"Is he there?"

"Yes, Father. He has arrived."

"I'll be busy for the next hour. Neopolis."

"Problems?"

"Always. I may require assistance."

"You need only ask."

"I know. We can't risk losing their support. Not quite yet."

"Understood."

"After the meeting, I'll want an update on the game."

"I will be ready."

Whatever the Father needed, he would happily provide. The Father, like the Biblical angel Gabriel, had blown the trumpet announcing the arrival of a new epoch. But there was a price. Danger. No matter. He knew the greater good would ultimately prevail. The Father would lead his people out of the Garden. The Father would guide them to a new and better future.

And he would be Michael, the angel with the flaming sword, ready to dispatch those not meant to make the journey.

7

"Kadey?' BB said. "Something happened to Kadey?"

"I'm afraid so."

He grabbed Palmer by the lapels. "You said there was a murder. Is she—"

"No. Pay attention. She isn't the victim. But she knew the victim. And now she's disappeared."

He felt a catching in this throat. "Was there—any sign of violence?"

"Some indication of struggle." Palmer brushed his hands away. "Mostly signs that she tried to keep someone out of her apartment. Ineffectively. Bookshelf was propped up against the only door."

A thousand thoughts raced through his head. He couldn't lose her. Not again. Not ever, he hoped, but especially not when she was still bitter and angry. She was his only daughter. He loved her more than he had ever loved anything in his entire life.

But he wasn't sure she knew that.

She thought he'd failed her. And to be truthful, he had not been the father he wanted to be. He could win one game after another, but he was a loser as a parent, and that loss was a dagger that pierced his heart every waking moment.

"I want to know everything you know about my daughter's disappearance. Everything."

"When we're inside."

"No, now. Any suspects?"

"Inside." Palmer paused. "I understand you and your daughter have . . . a strained relationship. Any particular reason?"

He turned his head and read the man's face. He didn't know? "How long have you been with the FBI?"

Palmer barely hesitated. "I've been on Uncle Sam's payroll for more than a decade now. Why?"

"Just wondered." Didn't exactly answer the question, did you? "Kadey disagreed with a tough call I had to make a while back. Relations have been strained ever since. I haven't seen her in—" He stopped short. "Too damn long. Who was this murder victim?"

"Man named David Bishop."

"And she knew him?"

"They worked together. And apparently were friends. She may have been present when he was killed."

"Did she leave a message? Call anyone?"

"She did leave a message." Palmer started to get out of the car, but BB grabbed his arm and yanked him back. The agent's brow slashed above eyes burning with irritation. "You do that again, poker boy, and you're going to end up with a gun in your face."

"You're not going anywhere until you tell me everything you know about my daughter."

Palmer removed the arm from his jacket. "As I said before, we can talk about it all you want. Once we get inside. If you cooperate, you'll get the information sooner." Palmer handed him an ID badge.

He clipped it to the pocket on his Hawaiian shirt. "Now I feel important." He followed Palmer toward the front doors of the building. He ached for information about Kadey, but since he couldn't force Palmer to talk, he'd have to play along. At least for now.

He could believe this building was a secret government installation, because it was just as nondescript as every other government installation he'd ever seen. Linoleum tile and cheap paper-thin plywood finish. He followed Palmer into the ancient elevator and rode to the seventh floor.

The security was more intense than the airport's. Maybe more than the White House's. He didn't just have to remove his shoes and belt. His jeans had to go, and the Hawaiian shirt, and his silver thimble Monopoly-piece pendant necklace. After he passed through the metal detector, he stood in a circular x-ray imaging chamber, the outer doors whirring around him for almost thirty seconds. Then they wanded him and patted him down.

"What's left?" he asked. "You've done everything but the prostate exam."

The gaunt inspector appeared humorless. "That won't be necessary." His nametag read KEENE.

The squint in Keene's eyes told him there was something the man was holding back. "You recognize me, don't you?"

"Saw you on television."

"You're a poker fan?"

"I despise poker. Children's game. I saw you in the SCRABBLE finals last summer."

"That was an exciting win."

"You cheated."

He recovered his cell phone and wallet. "Excuse me? I won the national championship. Fair and square."

"You played a *C* tile upside down and pretended it was a blank. You got a bingo you didn't deserve."

He didn't care what anyone thought about his looks, his clothes, his lifestyle, or even his intelligence. But he cared about games, and the one rule sacred to all gamers was that you did not cheat. Ever. "Sorry, but you're mistaken. The rules permit that maneuver. Your opponent has the right to pick up any alleged blank and flip it over to make sure it's real."

"It's not the play of an honorable man."

He remained calm. Mostly. "It's a stratagem. A *ruse de guerre*."

"It's cheating."

"My opponent was Brailling."

Keene did a double-take. "Was what?"

"Feeling the tiles in the bag. Trying to find the *X* he so desperately needed. Most tournaments use PROTILES—they're stamped, not embossed—so you can't feel the impressions of the letters. But this tournament didn't, and he was taking advantage. Now that's cheating."

Keene sniffed. "Pot calling the kettle black."

He leaned into Keene's face. "Tell you what, chumley. Why don't you stick that wand up—"

"All right, children. Move along." Palmer grabbed him by the arm. "Follow me. We've got work to do."

"Sure." He thunked Keane on the chest. "Been fun talking with you."

"Cheater," Keene murmured.

Palmer led him through thick reinforced double doors, then veered into a small office. It was cluttered and tiny and did not inspire him to seek out government work. He took the only vacant chair—the others were piled high with papers.

"I demand to know what happened to my daughter," he said, trying to sound as if he had some power in this situation, even though he knew he did not.

"I can tell you everything I know," Palmer replied. "But I'll warn you in advance, it isn't much. She was alone in her apartment last night. She shoved a bookshelf against the front door. We know she was there at 12:37 a.m., when she sent out a tweet. But when the police broke into her place this morning, she was gone."

"And the bookshelf still blocked the door?"

"Exactly. The only door. When did you last speak with her?"

He thought a moment. "I don't recall."

"You came to Vegas, where you know she lives, and didn't try to contact her?"

"I've been busy. And so is she."

Another man entered. Younger and plumper than Palmer. "This is Brian Greenstreet," Palmer explained.

No way he could be FBI. Or LVPD. Judging from the haircut, the uniform, and the deferential attitude . . .

He shook Greenstreet's hand. "Security cop?"

Palmer and Greenstreet exchanged a look. "He's a private security officer posted to this installation," Palmer explained.

Greenstreet nodded. "I gather your name is actually Steven Thomas. Mind if I ask where the BB comes from?"

"Personal eccentricity. Mind if I ask why a military installation uses private security? Why not Marines?"

"We weren't expecting trouble." Greenstreet shifted his attention to Palmer. "The forensic teams are done. We can take him in if you want."

"Good timing. If you'll follow us, please."

Together, they escorted him out of the office.

"This is the main work area," Palmer explained as they entered a spacious room that spread across most of the width of the building. "There's a specialized lab for the scientists on the floor below us. But both programmers and physicists worked here. As you can see, they preferred an open-space arrangement. No walls, no cubicles." Even cluttered with desks and chairs and the occasional file cabinet, the room was expansive. The alternating black and white parquet tile floor seemed to stretch into infinity. A skylight overhead made the usual office fluorescents unnecessary.

"Do people work here?"

"Normally. It's a crime scene at the moment. Access restricted to the forensic evidence teams and us."

They led him to the center of the room. Well before they arrived, he spotted the body sprawled on the floor.

He didn't need to ask the cause of death. The left side of the man's head was covered with blood. One eye was missing. A blood-stained sheet covered the floor beside the corpse.

His heart twisted and the air left his lungs like he'd been punched in the gut. The gore on the floor was worse than any horror film he'd ever seen, but that wasn't what left him feeling weak in the knees.

The police clearly thought the same person responsible for this mess now had his daughter.

8

Dubai Creek, Dubai, United Arab Emirates
Palazzo Versace Hotel, Penthouse

Ogilve could barely contain his impatience. So much was about to happen, so much was at stake—and he was trapped in a meeting of politicians. This must be the tenth circle of hell, the one too horrible for Dante to describe.

He shared a penthouse conference room with three of the most powerful men and women in the world. Not the ultimate decision-makers, but the ones who advised them, who were therefore in many respects far more important. He needed their continued support, so he had to tolerate the status meetings. Chun had the Far East in his fist, after all. He had to consolidate an equally powerful base in the Middle East—using the nascent Egyptian government and two others even less stable. They provided the all-important funds he needed to continue his operations—not to mention the political connections needed to sustain a clandestine underground facility half the size of a football field.

"What I'm requesting is an empirical demonstration," Prince Kussein said. "We funded your work in good faith. You tell us you've had positive results. Show us something."

"I've given you a detailed report."

"And frankly, it reads more like pulp fiction than a scientific evaluation. We require corroboration. Interpolation. Prognostication." That was Kussein. Never use a plain word if a five-syllable word was available. Did he think he was the only person who ever opened a thesaurus? Apparently he wanted to be the Gore Vidal of terrorists. "Can you get us that?"

"I suppose I could. But you might not like it."

"That's exactly what we're complaining about," Anwar Mulinak said. The former naval commander wore his full-dress uniform. Was that supposed to be intimidating? "The arrogant, superior attitude. We are your patrons. We have provided you with close to a billion dollars, not to mention the license to construct your monstrosity under the sands of our desert in complete secrecy. We deserve full access."

"And I have granted it."

"You have shut me out for the last four months."

"We had much work to do. At all my facilities, all across the globe. The results have been incredible. We've gotten what I wanted in far less time than I expected. You need to calm down." He reached for a bottle of Moët & Chandron. "Have another drink. Really. I insist."

None of them looked pleased with this response. But he noticed they drank.

"Seeing is believing," Mulinak said. "Show us something."

"Or?" He arched an eyebrow.

"You do not want to cross my government. There is no safe place for our enemies in this world."

He reached out to the snack tray, loaded with fresh hummus, kofta, olives, assorted cheeses, walnuts, and flatbread. "You assume I'm limited to this world."

That brought a profound silence to the table.

"We are gathered here for a reason." This was Rani, a lovely woman representing one of the Middle Eastern leaders. But he knew she was not actually Middle Eastern. "We call our alliance Neopolis for a reason. The battle of Neopolis represented a turning point. The moment when ancient civilization gave way to the barbarian hordes and a new world order began. Our world has reached a similar crossroads. Should we let the new world arise according to the undirected vicissitudes of chance? Or should we seize the opportunity to reimagine the world as it should be?"

She paused, giving him more time to admire her beauty. Smooth skin, more brown than olive, and an elegant cast to her face. Exquisite.

But who cared if she was beautiful? The pursuit of beauty was more dangerous than the pursuit of truth or goodness. She was the embodiment of the type who wouldn't give him the time of day, once upon a time. The kind who laughed at him. The kind who had called him Dinky. Before he met Holly.

"Yes," he said, propping his Bontoni shoes onto the table. "I agree that we should move forward. That's why you helped finance my research and build my base of operations. But that does not mean you should control it."

"We bought and paid for you!" Kussein said, slamming his fist on the table.

"No, you financed my research," he replied evenly. "No one buys me."

"If you do not give us what we want, we will dispose of you and seize your entire facility."

"You will never be able to make it work without me and you know it. Otherwise you would have done so already." He leaned forward slightly. "If you or your people move so much as a pawn against me, you may find you dislike the endgame. My strategy is one of infinite variation. Capable of alteration at any time. Impenetrable. Undefeatable." Or so he wanted them to believe.

He gazed out the bay windows to the shifting multi-colored mirror that Dubai Creek appeared to be from this height. Yesterday, he'd spent the afternoon gazing at the Persian Gulf, coveting the man-made sand islands that allowed the ridiculously wealthy to buy their own country. He loved the date palms and the eucalyptus trees punctuating the beaches. He admired the shimmering obelisk they called the Burj Khalifa above the fascinatingly complex architecture of Sheikh Zayed Road, a brilliant combination of the old world and the new, unadulterated by billboards and tacky neon lights. Minarets dotted every street, as did the shopping centers, mostly populated by tourists able to purchase without feeling constrained by the restrictions against booze or public kissing. There was a reason some people called this country "Do Buy."

Khalifa was now the tallest building on earth, though he knew it was just a matter of time until someone built something even ridiculously taller. Construction was everywhere in this city, and he supposed it would be until the money ran out. And that wouldn't happen until the world overcame its addiction to foreign oil.

Which could occur sooner than the people in this room imagined.

"I will not be treated like a child," Kussein said. "Like some infant who cannot know the secrets of the adults. I demand full disclosure."

He'd had enough of this stupidity. He'd let them play at feeling important. To believe they were kings rather than pawns. Now it was time to tell them how it was going to be.

He rose, adjusted his Armani jacket, and addressed the assemblage. "This is what you need to understand. Your dollars did not buy me. They did not buy you The Platform or any of its byproducts. All you bought was information. That is no small thing. That gives you unprecedented power. Power that is more than adequate compensation for your contributions. Given the way your masters usually throw away their money, I believe you've acquired quite a bargain."

He lowered himself over the table, hands forward. "But this project is mine to control. And my goals go far beyond this petty political bickering. Don't try to draw me into your ideologies or religions or border squabbles. I'm not remotely interested. You want to pick a target, pick a target. I'll give you what you want. But don't attempt to interfere with my work. Ever." He made eye contact with each of them, just to be sure they heard him. "Don't get in my way. Or I'll delete every one of you. Faster than you can speed-dial your mothers."

They stared at him in stunned silence.

He settled back into his chair. "All right then. Let me explain what's going to happen next."

9

B turned his head away from the blood-soaked corpse with the smashed head. "What the hell happened to him?"

"We don't know," Palmer replied.

"Will they—Kadey—"

"We don't know," Greenstreet answered. "She and several others disappeared. This guy didn't disappear, and whoever killed him made no attempt to hide the murder."

"When did this happen?"

"Last night. Around midnight."

"How did the killer get past all that security?"

"We don't know. The building was locked up tight."

"What happened to his head?"

"We don't know that exactly, either. We only know what you can see. Four deep holes. Each one equidistant from the others."

"Holes?"

"Indentations. Three inches deep. One severed the cerebral cortex. Another pierced an eyeball."

"*Holes?*"

"Like they were drilled with mathematical precision."

"How?"

"We're still waiting for more information. Now that the videographers are done, the coroner's team will take the body into custody."

"Palmer said his name was David Bishop?"

"Yes. The man worked here."

"Like Kadey." He didn't know what to say. His mind raced through conflicting thoughts and emotions. "Who was her boss?"

"The ultimate head of the project was Emerson Ogilve."

He blinked. "Dinky?"

"I gather you know him?"

"We worked together," BB explained. "Back in my game-design days. Started a company called Gen3^2 while we were still at Stanford."

"Gen3^2?"

"Everyone talked about the second generation of gaming. Dinky wanted to suggest we were already on the third—way ahead of everyone else. In fact, we were so far ahead, we were third generation—squared."

"Very modest. He's a computer programmer?"

"He studied computers but majored in biology and neural networking. How those two fit together I never understood. Or how he got into computer games. But he was a terrific dealmaker. Could talk a man out of Park Place when he was holding Boardwalk. And he could always find grants and tax deductions. Did you know there are more tax breaks for video game companies than for researchers pursuing medical developments or alternate fuels? Even though it's one of the most profitable industries in the world? Dinky collected deductions, write-offs, and credits, usually designed for other purposes in other eras, but applicable to the video game business. Other companies followed his lead."

"While law enforcement officers have to pay their own taxes. Typical. I gather you're not still working for him at this time."

"Definitely not." His eyes drifted downward. "We had a parting of the ways."

"Ugly?"

"He . . . did something I did not approve of. Could not approve of. So I walked. Left a lot of money on the table, too. But no amount of money is enough if the price is your soul."

"Something to do with the military contracts?"

"No, Dinky wasn't doing that back then. What's he cooking up for the DOD now?"

"Some kind of combat-training program."

"I'm not surprised. Video games are good for training soldiers. They improve hand-to-eye coordination. Flight simulator games can improve real-life piloting skills. First person shooters are excellent practice for snipers. Reduce reaction time. Improve targeting. Also good for language lessons and medical training."

"The military trains soldiers with video games?" Palmer asked.

"And I'll bet the demand is increasing, as warfare becomes increasingly technologically complex. Several years ago I consulted with the Marines on a game-based simulator called VBS 2. Created by two Czech brothers and the leader of an Australian heavy metal band. I made it a thousand times more robust, complex, and addictive. Added 3-D graphics. Eventually created entire virtual worlds in the VBS universe. And the bosses loved it. The perfect anodyne for shrinking military budgets. Virtual training is far less expensive than live training. And some believe, more effective. They've got military training programs that run on smartphones now. Apps." He paused. "Is that what The Platform was developing?"

"I don't know all the details," Greenstreet said. "But I know it had something to do with movement. I gather you know what a Kinect is?"

"Of course." He had one in his condo. "A video game platform with controllers that respond to movement. So the player can interact with the program by moving, rather than simply pushing buttons."

"The Platform hoped to take that to the next level. One in which the player was not just simulating the motions of a character but actually interacting with a simulated world."

"We've done that. Three-dimensional headgear. Like the Oculus Rift."

"Without the headgear. So the player doesn't stare at a screen. The screen surrounds the player. Except you can't tell it's a screen."

"You're talking about a total immersion program. Complete sensory substitution. I can see the advantages, from a training standpoint. But I would think the cost would outstrip the usefulness. You'd need some kind of four-walled chamber. Multi-dimensional image projection. Omni-directional sound. Way too complicated and expensive for the military."

"Funny thing about military budgets," Palmer commented. "They seem to be infinitely expandable, depending upon how well the person wanting the dough propagandizes an imminent threat."

"Dinky would be good at that. But I don't think he'd commit murder just to keep a military contract." His thoughts returned to the bloody remains staining the parquet floor. "So why was this man killed? And where is my daughter?"

"That's what we were hoping you could tell us."

"But this has nothing to do with me."

"Your daughter disappeared last night. Your former partner is leading the project."

"Coincidence."

"Perhaps. But I doubt if this is." Palmer lifted the cloth beside the corpse. "The deceased wrote your name, just before he died."

"In—in his blood?"

"No," Palmer replied. "In SCRABBLE tiles."

The tiles were laid out on the floor, three groups in three rows:

10

Julian watched then through the skylight, mesmerized. The rats were in the maze. Would they find the cheese? The other players had not. But perhaps this would be different. He hoped so. He knew the game was important to the Father. He knew the outcome had larger consequences, larger than he could imagine.

He had not detected any sign of the Other.

But that didn't mean he wouldn't. He did not want a repeat of last night. He must defend the game. He must defend the Father. He would do whatever was necessary.

He heard a soft shuffling sound behind him. Movement. Not on the roof. Farther away. He heard it, despite the traffic, the noise of the air conditioning unit, the city beyond.

He had been trained to hear everything.

A moment of confusion gripped him. He was not accustomed to making field decisions. He excelled at following instructions.

He pulled out his smartphone. The screen was black.

He crept back behind the air conditioning unit. His feet glided across the gravel roof without making a sound.

Something changed.

He spent more than a few moments determining what it was, sifting through the possible options. Had there been a disturbance in the air? Had he felt a tremor in his bones?

Or was something moving? Someone. Nearby.

He was not alone.

His hand darted to his holster.

He activated his SRAC. No response. Apparently the Father was busy. Dubai was probably too far away for him to be of much assistance anyway.

He pulled out his phone, opened the secure texting program and typed.

The Other is here.

He only had to wait a moment for the reply.

Activity?

Unknown.

Do not permit interference.

How do I prevent it?

Prefer low profile. But all level responses authorized.

Understood.

I need the Game Master. One way or the other.

Will take care of it.

He had never shirked his duty. He had never run from a battle. Not since the day he was reborn at the hands of the Father.

He would do what must be done.

He turned to face the intruder.

11

"I'm beginning to see why you dragged me out of that poker game," BB murmured, staring at the Scrabble tiles. "But he left off the last letter."

"He was under a fair amount of stress, I would imagine," Palmer said. "Having just had his cerebral cortex punctured. Probably had limited time, too. We're assuming he died before he finished."

"And he just happened to have a pocket SCRABBLE set on him when he was murdered?"

"Perhaps. Don't you game freaks carry them everywhere?"

"Don't be absurd. I don't." Well, not since he got the SCRABBLE app for his phone. And the chess app, the poker and bridge simulators, and the digital *New York Times* crossword puzzle. "Why would he attempt to spell my name?"

"The obvious answer would be that he was naming his killer."

Behind him, back in the corridor, he heard shuffling feet. Keene, the irritating security inspector, cleared his throat.

"Bring her in, Keene."

A few moments later he heard the clicking of heels.

"I believe you two have met before," Palmer said.

He pivoted to greet the newcomer—and froze.

"Hello, BB. Been a while, hasn't it?"

They had indeed met before. They'd been married for fifteen years. "Linden?" Her hair was a lighter color, but she looked trim and healthy. Still working out every morning and watching what she ate, it appeared.

She approached, hand extended. Really? After being married and raising a daughter? They were going to shake hands?

She pressed something into his hand. The look on her face told him he was not to look at it now. He slid it into his pocket.

Amazing that he could still read her after so many years.

"Have they told you what happened, BB?"

Even though he hadn't seen her in years, he knew she'd been under significant stress. Her hair seemed flat, as if she'd run out of time to fix it, or perhaps simply forgotten. Her makeup was sparse, almost nonexistent, and she was dressed in black. Normally, she was the only woman in the math department who could make men hover like schoolboys. "They told me Kadey disappeared. And some man was killed."

"I wish I'd been here sooner. Took me a while to catch a flight from Davis." She turned toward Palmer, all business-like. "I got a briefing at the airport. What have you learned since?"

"Not a thing."

"I want to know everything you know. This is my only child."

Palmer nodded. "Your ex said exactly the same thing."

"BB expressed actual emotions? Imagine that."

He didn't reply. He was accustomed to keeping his feelings in check, but that didn't mean he didn't have them. He was worried and the worst of it was that he didn't know what worried him most—that Kadey was dead, or that she died hating him…

But this was unproductive. He had to remain focused. Otherwise he was of no use to anyone. Maintain the poker face. Lock your emotions in a closet. And think.

"Look, Linden, we have no reason to believe she's . . . you know."

"She's not dead," Linden said flatly.

Her curt reply caught him off-guard. "And you know this because—"

"I'm her mother. And I would know if my little girl were dead." She had her own ways of suppressing emotion, he recalled. He was surprised she allowed herself to be this emotional. Because whether she admitted it or not, she didn't know Kadey was alive. No one did. This was desperate optimism masquerading as maternal instinct.

"I'm glad you came, BB," she added.

"Like there was some doubt whether I would come? She's my daughter. How could I not be here?"

She shook her head. "Let's not get into that right now." She approached Palmer. "I want to know all of it." She punctuated her no-nonsense tone with a finger jab to his shirt. "Every last detail."

"She likes to be on top," he advised. "Of everything, I mean."

"Don't start, BB."

"It's true. You always want to be in control."

"That's how you get things done. You'd know that, if you'd ever done anything."

His eyes bugged. "Do you have any idea what I've accomplished this year?"

"Right, right. Your little games."

Palmer stepped between them. "I enjoy a good family feud as much as the next guy, but time is critical. We want to interview both of you about your daughter."

He grimaced. "Perhaps it would be best to talk to us separately."

"We don't have time for—excuse the expression—playing games."

"Too bad," Linden said. "That eliminates both our specialties."

Palmer squinted. "I . . . understood you were an academic. Mathematician."

"Specializing in game theory."

Palmer whistled. "You two were a match made in heaven."

"Not so much, as it turned out. Game theory is about numbers and social science. Not cheating your way to a SCRABBLE victory."

"I did not *cheat!*"

She ignored him. "In mathematics, the word *game* refers to a strategic situation consisting of a group of players, a contained set of possible moves or strategies, and a delineation of the potential rewards for any given combination of applied strategies."

"Sounds fascinating, but—"

"Game theory posits that an individual's success depends not only upon the choices the player makes but also upon the choices of others. In the small scale, the moves of others may be unknowable. But on the large scale, mathematics makes it predictable. The principles of game theory can be used to anticipate the outcome of any strategic situation. Assuming it's possible to take into account all the variables. Where a closed set—"

Palmer cut her off. "Can you use game theory to figure out what happened to this dead man? Or your daughter?"

"No. Too many unknowns and too many variables. The human mind cannot hold them or apply them all at the same time to—"

"Then let's get back to the investigation."

Linden tucked in her chin. "I understand." She glanced at her ex. "He couldn't grasp it, either."

"We don't have time to rehash old injuries, Linden," he said. "Whatever may be lingering between us, we have to put it aside. Our focus needs to be on finding Kadey."

"Glad to see you're interested in your daughter's welfare. Finally."

His neck twisted but he remained silent. She knew what had happened, and she knew why he had done what he did. If she wanted to spend the rest of her life blaming him, he couldn't stop her.

But it still hurt.

He noticed a streak of blood on the floor.

"Bishop was moved here," he said. "He was killed somewhere else."

"Yes," Palmer replied.

"But why?" He gazed around the office area. "For that matter, the entire room seems disarranged."

"Excuse me?"

"Look around you. There's no symmetry."

"Does it offend you aesthetically?"

He moved toward the nearest desks. "Normally, in open offices like this one, the desks will be lined up in a more or less orderly fashion. All in a row, or at right angles. But not here. Everything's helter-skelter."

"It's true," Greenstreet replied. "This isn't the usual office layout. Some of these desks have been moved."

"Perhaps there was a struggle?" Palmer ventured.

BB walked the length of the room, pacing from one end to the other. Adrenaline pumped through his body, just as it did in the final stages of a game, as he approached the clincher move. Every nerve tingled. He learned a long time ago that his body liked adrenaline even better than oxytocin. Winning a hard-fought game could produce an ecstasy greater than anything else he had ever experienced.

He was onto something. He just couldn't quite isolate it.

"These desks have been moved," he said, speaking quickly, thinking aloud, "but not at random. If you play Go, the Asian strategy game, or its American derivative, Pente, you learn to see patterns in seemingly random arrangements of objects."

"This is a murder investigation," Palmer groused. "Not a game. We have to—"

He slapped his hand down on a desktop. "This is a glass bead!"

"No," Palmer said, "that is a desk."

"Today, it's a glass bead." He moved rapidly to another desk turned cater-corner to the other. "And this is a glass bead." He ran to yet another. "And this one, too." He looked up, his eyes darting. "These desks were moved. For a reason."

"I agree that they were moved," Greenstreet said. "But who cares? What difference—"

Linden interrupted. "Oh my God. Look at his eyes. Like a cocaine addict just after a snort."

"He uses cocaine?" Palmer asked.

"No. He uses puzzles. Mental challenges. That's what turns him on. Nothing else comes close."

"That must've caused a few marital difficulties."

"Don't waste the sympathy. I'm over it."

"Whose desk was this?" BB asked, returning to the first desk he'd slapped.

"Belongs to Barry Fried," Greenstreet said. "Head of the game design team."

He moved to a relocated desk on the other side of the room. "And this one?"

"His top assistant. Rita Benedict."

He raced to the north side of the room, not far from where the body was. "This one?"

"Conner Davis. New kid. Fried's errand boy."

He smiled. "Good. Very good."

Palmer pursed his lips. "If this eccentric performance is supposed to impress me, or distract me, you've failed. What the hell do you think you're doing?"

"Solving the puzzle."

"You mean the murder?"

Instead of answering, he raced to another desk. "Who sat here?"

Greenstreet replied. "The head of the physics team."

"Yes. That makes sense. Programmers and physicists. Two teams." He looked up. "The woman who sits here. Who is she?"

"How did you know it was a woman?" Palmer asked. "There's no nameplate."

"It's obvious."

"Not to me."

"There are feminine traces."

Greenstreet chuckled. "Most of these female physicists aren't that feminine."

He ran a finger across the surface of the desk, then turned the finger upward. "See that?"

Palmer looked. "Dust?"

"Look closer."

"Cocaine?"

"Keep trying, Watson."

"I give up. What is it?"

"Face powder. The woman who sits here has been putting on her makeup at work. Bit of flesh-colored makeup on the phone receiver, too, where she pressed it against the side of her face. I don't know how you missed that. Didn't you say you were with the FBI?"

Palmer squinted.

He pointed upward. "Can we get to the roof?"

Greenstreet's eyes narrowed. "We . . . could."

He raced ahead of them. "Then let's go." A moment later, he was halfway to the stairwell.

Linden arched an eyebrow. "Come on, gentlemen. The game's afoot."

When BB was far enough ahead that the FBI agents could not see, he unfolded the piece of paper Linden had pressed into his hand. It appeared to be a grocery list. Probably a scrap she found in her purse. But she'd written a message on the back.

The note was terse, but he had no problem understanding it.

THEY'RE GOING TO ARREST YOU. GET OUT OF HERE. SAVE KADEY!

12

"**B**ob!"

Senator Vogel turned slightly and saw Palmietti, his campaign manager, running toward him, a stack of papers flapping in his hands. McKay and the new pollster trailed behind him.

Palmietti arrived first, grabbing his arm and gasping between syllables. "What is this?"

The papers bounced up and down, but he managed to recognize his handwriting. "Those are rewrites of our canned debate responses. I think they might work."

"Think? Bob, we haven't tested this." Palmietti swiveled toward McKay. "Is this your work?"

McKay pressed a hand against her dress. "I didn't write this. I think it's crazy."

"It's not crazy," Vogel said. "It's honest. And it shows that I know what I'm talking about, which is something the voters need to know. That I'm so well-informed I can't boil complex issues down to minuscule sound bites."

"There's too much rattling on about foreign countries and crops and other stuff most Americans don't give a damn about. Just wave the flag and talk about the Grand Old Party. That's always worked for you in the past."

"And that's why we're trailing in the polls. Less than a week until election day, and my opponent leads by a five-point margin. If we don't try something new, we lose."

"I'm with Mitch on this one," McKay said. "The new approach is dangerous. At least let us test-drive it. Run it up the flag and see if anyone salutes."

"The debate starts in three minutes."

"Bob, this is political suicide."

He turned his attention to the new kid, the policy-wonk pollster. "What do you think?"

The kid shrugged. "I'm just shooting from my gut here, but . . . I'd vote for you."

He smiled. "That's what I needed to hear."

He started toward the stage, but Palmietti stopped him. "Bob, listen to me. I'm your campaign manager—"

"No, actually, you're not." He pointed toward the kid. "You are."

The kid's eyes widened. "I am?"

"You bet. With your instincts and my inside knowledge, we still might win this thing." He removed Palmietti's hand and started toward the stage. "Wish me luck."

Vogel shifted his weight on the stool. He hated town meetings. The constituents were too close. The questions were too random. There were no filters. They weren't even on a stage and they lacked the distancing protection of the podium. The audience sat on tiered semicircular risers. Red, white, and blue streamers dangled from the ceiling. The moderator sat at a small desk in the center with a microphone and a small stack of index cards upon which attendees had written questions. The moderator screened the questions, but neither the candidates nor their staff would see or hear them in advance.

His showboating opponent insisted that one of the preliminary debates be conducted in this down-home format. The con artist styled himself as the man of the people, the common man, the blue-collar candidate. Which was quite a stretch for a man who lived off a trust fund provided by a daddy who made his fortune brokering munitions of dubious legality. Nothing was more tiresome than a candidate who started to believe his own spin.

Time to speak. What was it again? Right. Balancing the budget, take 417.

"That's a good question," he said, addressing a slender brunette mother of four. "These are treacherous times. Which is another reason I find my opponent's policies so unwise and potentially deadly. He sat as vice president during an administration that left our military dangerously understaffed, under-equipped, and under-funded. We can't afford to take chances like that. Now don't misunderstand me. Cuts must be made. But not at the expense of national security."

"May I respond to that?" His opponent, Vice President Norman Beale, rose from his stool. He wore a blue suit and red tie—virtually a clone of President Fernandez, the man upon whose coattails he had ridden to national prominence. "May I speak in defense of this administration, the first in three decades to put us on track to a balanced budget? This is not a time for the usual saber-rattling. This is not a time when a man should try to win votes through fear tactics. This is a time for fresh thinking, bold ideas, and the courage to make them happen."

Beale's inane oratory was followed by a round of applause, the loudest of the event. He loved applause, thought it the sweetest sound known to man. When the applause was aimed in his direction. Every time the crowd clapped for him, his heart swelled. Every time they clapped for his opponent, he died a little.

The moderator read the next question.

"This comes from a farmer with a small acreage in Kansas." The farmer raised his hand. "He wants to know what you plan to do to stabilize the price of wheat and to protect farmers from the dangers posed by the current market. Vice President Beale, you have the first reply."

"Well, that's . . . that's an interesting question. I mean, a very good question. But a complex one. Many factors involved. Many."

Vogel rediscovered his smile. His opponent was floundering like a leaky dinghy.

This was why his secret advisor sent him those detailed position papers. The ones he'd rewritten into the debate notes. Hadn't seen the relevance at the time, but . . .

"If we provide subsidies to farmers, the price won't matter as much . . ." Beale continued. "We've come a long way since the Dust Bowl days . . . My father told me tales of men standing in breadlines, crops that wouldn't come, drought, hard times, especially for the common man. But we can do better, and in my administration, we will, because . . . because . . . American farmers are the breadbasket of America. Breadbasket of the world, really. We have to take care of our farmers. The important thing is that we all work together, stretch a hand across the aisle and unite to do what's best for America . . ."

He thought his worthy opponent must have set a new world record for cramming the largest number of meaningless platitudes into a two-minute response. He sensed he was not the only one relieved when the red light glowed.

Even the moderator appeared embarrassed by that mugwump of an answer. "This was not on the list of topics presented to the candidates beforehand," the moderator commented. "Perhaps we should move on to—"

"No, no," Vogel said. "I'd like to respond to that."

The moderator's arched eyebrow said, You would?

He looked directly at the farmer who submitted the question. "Forgive me, sir, but I don't think my opponent gave you much of an answer, and you deserve one. It's an important question, one that goes to the heart of the future of this nation."

He saw the man's lips purse. The Kansan probably expected more vague mumbo jumbo.

"This has been a wet year here in the United States. Wet here, but dry in Western Europe, with drought in Russia, Australia, and most of Africa. This has impacted the price of wheat. It spiked. But no one knows how long the spike will last or how far it will go, which puts farmers such as yourself in an uneasy situation. For those who catch the wave, it's a boon, but for those who need the grain, supplies may be hard to come by. Especially in the Middle East—the most dangerously unstable region of the world, but also the region where wheat is the largest dietary staple, providing cheap nutrition from bread, pasta, and couscous. We don't want to give those people another reason to hate us. We don't want to give them another reason to feel uncertain about their future, or to feel the US has them in a stranglehold."

The questioner nodded his head, his appreciation evident.

"Did you know Tunisians eat more wheat than anyone else on the planet? True. More than 478 pounds per person per year, as opposed to about 177 pounds here in the US. They have to buy more than half what they need to support their largely impoverished population. This is a prescription for disaster. Completely unsustainable. With Arab countries vulnerable to global food-price shocks, the whole world is imperiled. I'm not just talking about ensuring the flow of oil. I'm talking about avoiding armed global conflict. It's not about the Dust Bowl or breadlines or other problems of the past. It's about our future. As things stand today, war is an inevitability." He held up a finger. "Unless we act now. Unless we are led by someone who understands what's going on in the world."

He sensed everyone in the room inching forward, hanging on his words. Most of the people in this state had some agricultural connection, but he had touched upon an even larger matter that concerned everyone.

"First, I propose creating a global regulatory agency. Let them set a fair price for wheat that will remain in place for the entire season. Let them also play a role in managing supplies, ensuring that expected deliveries are not curtailed by intervening economic factors. I will also commit to global subsidies to prevent starvation in critical areas of the world. Let's be honest—this may not make me popular with some members of my own party. But being president isn't about being popular. It's about being a leader. A world riddled with rampant starvation is not safe for anyone. And I can think of no better way to spend our money than by ensuring the safety of our children. By guaranteeing them a secure and prosperous future."

The applause that ensued gave him the greatest climax of his life.

After the debate, Vogel shook hands with his opponent, a pro forma gesture for the television cameras and photographers.

To his surprise, Beale held on to his hand even after the shaking ended.

"Nice work," Beale murmured. "You continue to surprise me."

He made sure no mikes were in range. "Just doing my job."

"Your answer on that wheat-price question was brilliant. I couldn't have given a response that detailed if I'd read it off a briefing paper. You're going to see your numbers rise in the morning, damn it. How did you know that question was coming?"

"My advisor always makes me do thorough preparation."

"Give me a break. You were all over that, and wheat prices have not been an issue in this campaign, ever. Not even tangentially. Who tipped you off? Did you bribe the PBS lady? Someone on your staff boinking the chairman of the League of Women Voters?"

The corner of his lips tugged upward. "Years of political experience have given me a certain degree of foresight."

"Foresight? You must have a crystal ball."

He released Beale's hand. "No. Something much better."

13

B bolted through the door at the top of the stairwell. The roof was covered with a mixture of gravel and tar that stuck to his shoes. He felt as if he were wading through a sea of discarded bubble gum. He raced to the skylight. Peering downward, he obtained a clear aerial view of the seventh-floor office space below.

"Do you see it?" he asked, trying to quell the bubbling excitement in his voice. He knew he got overexcited sometimes. Linden had belittled him for it often enough.

Palmer glanced through the Plexiglas bubble. "So?"

"You see, but you do not observe. Look harder."

Linden joined the rubberneckers. "Office floor. Workstations. Parquet floor." There was a sudden catch in her throat. "Parquet floor."

His eyes gleaned. "Anything seem familiar?"

"Stared at it every night. When we were married."

Greenstreet squinted. "You stared at this floor?"

"No. Black and white alternating squares. From one end to the other." Her lips pursed, something between a frown and an appreciative smile. "It's a chessboard."

"Not a fan?" Palmer said. "I thought all eggheads liked chess."

"I despise chess. You would too, if you had to play him."

"Reigning American grandmaster," he reminded them.

"I could live with losing," Linden explained. "It's the gloating I couldn't bear."

"It was the losing you couldn't bear," he corrected. "The PhD couldn't handle losing to a guy who never finished college."

Greenstreet was the only one still staring at the floor. "Isn't it too large to be a chessboard?"

"It is," he said, returning to topic. "The entire floor is fourteen squares by sixteen. A chess or checkerboard is eight by eight. But that's easy to fix. Pare away the excess squares in your head. Focus on the central eight by eight."

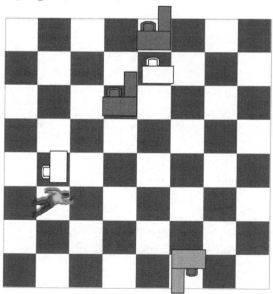

"Okay, I think I've got it. Now what?"

"Notice anything unusual?"

"All the desks you slapped are inside the central area. The so-called chessboard."

"Of course they are. The desks are markers. They tell you where the chess pieces go."

"Is he entirely sane?" Palmer asked Linden.

"Entirely?" She pondered. "He's eccentric. Obsessive. Unbelievably narcissistic, and with so little cause. But yes, probably sane. And very good at games."

"Okay," Greenstreet said, "so I imagine the center grid, and I put chess pieces on the squares with the relocated desks."

"Exactly."

"But what pieces?" He laid a hand on the nearest desk. "For instance, which piece goes on this one?"

BB made a split-second calculation, assigning colors to the desks. "Didn't you tell me that belonged to the project head?"

"Yes."

"Then he's the king. We'll make him the white king. Programmers, white. Physicists, black."

"Okay," Greenstreet continued. "So we've placed the white king. What about the assistant's desk?"

"A female second-in-command? What do you think?"

"The queen."

"Now you're getting the idea."

"And the other desk," Palmer said. "The one that belongs to the errand boy?" He snapped his fingers. "He's a pawn."

"Exactly. So is the other programmer. I saw unsorted mail on his desk. If he sorts mail, he's a pawn."

"No other programmer desks were moved. Any other white pieces?"

"No. Let's place the physicists. The black pieces. The head of the physicist team's desk was moved."

"The black king."

"But she's a woman."

"If she's the boss, she's the king."

"Then who's the queen?"

"There isn't one. That's black's problem."

"Does the corpse count as a marker?"

"I assume the body was moved for a reason."

"But there's no corpse in chess. What piece do we place there?"

"What did you tell me his name was?"

"Da—" Greenstreet released a slow smile. "David Bishop."

"Answer your question?"

"Yeah. Any other black pieces?"

"No. Black is at a disadvantage. But it still has some strength. It will be difficult for white to pin down. For most people, this board would lead to a draw."

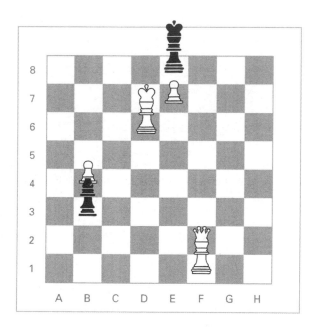

He continued. "These desks were not placed by accident, my friends. Someone arranged them with a definite purpose. To create a chess problem."

Palmer rubbed his forehead. "You expect me to believe that after committing the murder, someone rearranged the furniture to create a mind game? Who would do that? The Riddler?"

"More to the point," Linden said, "what's the goal? I've seen you work chess problems. There has to be an object. You can't come up with a solution if you don't know what you're trying to achieve."

He agreed. "We have a goal spelled out for us. Literally."

Palmer jumped in. "You mean the SCRABBLE tiles?"

"Yes."

"They spelled out your name."

"No, they misspelled my name."

"The victim didn't get all the tiles down before he bled out."

"I don't think so. Why the *Carmine*? That's not my middle name."
He moved on before anyone could ask what his middle name was.
"This message wasn't left by the victim. It was left by the killer. Or
perhaps a third party arriving after the murder."

"Because he got your middle name wrong?"

"And he omitted the terminal *S* in Thomas. And put an extra *E*
in Steven. I don't think anyone ran out of time. The misspellings are a
clue."

Palmer frowned. "Are you about to tell us Bishop was killed by
Colonel Mustard in the Conservatory?"

He ignored the agent. "Ask yourself the larger question. Why not
use pencil and paper? That would be much simpler. Why not write in
blood? That would be more dramatic. There's a laptop on the desk.
Type the message into a word processing file. Any of those
possibilities would be more efficient. So why SCRABBLE tiles?"

"You're the Game Master," Palmer growled. "You tell me."

He felt as if he were about to burst. He hated having to explain
the obvious. "What's the whole point of SCRABBLE tiles?"

No answers.

"They're designed to be moved around! Rearranged! Scrambled!
Anagrammed!" He grabbed Palmer's notepad and scribbled down the
letters. "There are many good possibilities for anagramming here."

In mere seconds, he rearranged the letters to spell:

"Or, if you prefer . . ." He rearranged the letters again:

"But there's only one correct answer." He spelled it out, using all the letters.

"Oh," Linden said. "Well. That does make more sense. It's a challenge."

14

"Ladies and gentlemen. Do we have a winner?"

This meeting finally approached the finish line, Ogilve thought, with considerable relief. He knew he'd been sleeping with the devil. Make that plural. They all had private agendas. They all had enemy lists longer than Nixon's. The desert sands he outside the penthouse window did not burn as hot as some of the grudges in this room.

Still, the outpouring of hatred that spewed the moment he opened the meeting to "nominations" astonished him.

Kussein had grudges against China. Part historic, part economic. As in, he didn't trust anyone with more money.

Mulinak favored targeting India, South Africa, Germany, and Venezuela. Rani nominated Australia.

Australia? Who had grudges against *Australia?*

He was less than astonished when, in less than an hour, they compromised by making the first target the United States of America.

"Take out the president." Kussein was nothing if not predictable. "If you cut off the head of the great snake, the rest withers and dies."

"If the president were killed by an act of terrorism, the country would descend into chaos," Rani insisted. Despite being the only female in the room—or perhaps because of it—she was one of the most forceful advocates. "Our goal is to get their attention. To give them a choice. Not to destroy them."

"I think she is right," Mulinak said, confirming Ogilve's earlier impression that the old soldier must have a crush on Rani. "If we take out the president, the entire nation goes into lockdown. DEFCON five. Positive change will become impossible. Besides, the Egyptian government still receives aid from the Americans and has a tentative diplomatic relationship. Better not to arouse them."

"Do we care if the Great Satan is aroused?" Kussein asked. "Let them suffer as they have caused so many others to suffer."

"I thought our goal was to change the world for the better," Mulinak said. "Not to start World War Three."

"You do not see the geopolitical realities. You see only the opportunity for profit."

"No, I see that targeting the president would be foolish and insane. Which perhaps explains why you favor it."

Ogilve thought this might be a good time to cut in. Before World War Three erupted in this room. "My friends, listen. This is only an opening move. A demonstration. Something to help you understand that my additional capital requirements are a worthwhile investment. The target doesn't matter—as long as it doesn't draw attention to any Gen3^2 installations."

Kussein rose. "I am not convinced that even eliminating the president is enough to justify the money we have already given you."

"Then let me offer the one thing that's better than eliminating the president."

"And that would be?"

"Controlling the president."

Silence filled the penthouse.

"Can this be achieved?" Kussein asked.

"Are we agreed that it would be a desirable goal?"

They all agreed.

"Very well. You'll have what you want in a few days. This meeting is—"

"Point of order."

Every head in the conference room turned. The new voice emerged from just outside the door.

"Good afternoon, my friends." General Chun strode into the room, a slick smile on his face.

Ogilve felt the air in his lungs turn to ice.

"Hello, Emerson. Good to see that you're well." He paused, a thin smile curling around his face. "I've missed you."

15

"Now do you believe this game was prearranged?" BB asked.

"This is . . . surprising," Agent Palmer allowed, staring at the letters.

"What surprises me," Greenstreet murmured, "is how quickly you came up with that. Almost as if—"

"As if," BB interjected, "I'm the North American SCRABBLE champion. And you're not."

"The question is, who would leave clues like this?"

"Someone who loves games."

"Yes," Palmer said, "I'll grant you that."

"You mentioned the Riddler before. As you must know, unless you had a terribly deprived childhood, the Riddler left clues because he was psychologically compelled to do so. Because deep down, he felt guilty about his crimes and wanted to be caught."

"And you think that's why the murderer left these tiles behind?"

"No."

"Then why? Why the clues? Why the desks and the SCRABBLE tiles?"

"Bread crumbs."

Linden cut in. "Getting back to the puzzle, O Great and Powerful Game Master, is it possible? Can you mate in three moves, using the chessboard setup?"

"I don't see how," Palmer said. "I know this game a little. White has more firepower, but black still has plenty of maneuvering room. This could go on for a long time."

"But this is chess, not the nuclear arms race," BB answered. "It's not about firepower. It's about strategy and position."

Linden nodded wearily. "I can see by the vivid—some might say, insane—look in your eyes that you've already found the solution. So don't be selfish. Tell."

"If the white queen makes it to black's home row, the black king is toast. The white queen is on F1, poised for the kill. So the only move black can make to protect the king is F7. Now the queen's path is blocked."

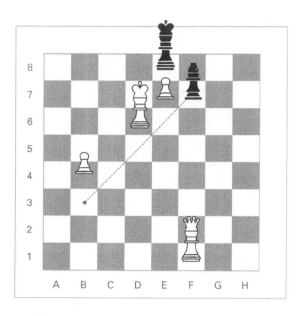

He continued. "If the queen attempts to take the bishop, the obvious move, the black king will capture it. Then the game will probably be a hopeless stalemate. At any rate, it won't end in three moves."

He drew in a deep breath. "But white does not take the bishop. Surprise! White moves to B5, cutting off the black king's last escape route. Black is powerless to prevent the inevitable. Check and mate."

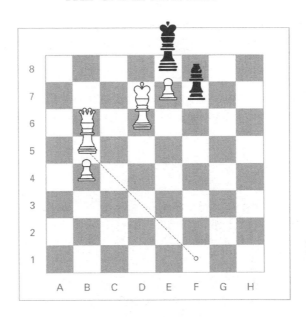

"Okay," Palmer said, "I get it. Very clever. But what's the point?"

"Let's go downstairs and take another look at the desks."

He led the way to the stairwell and opened the door for his ex. "Ladies first, Ms. Thomas."

"That's not my name anymore. Of course, it's not really your name, either."

They exchanged grimaces. As soon as she passed through, he followed her—

And slammed the door behind them. He slid the bolt through, locking it from the inside.

"Hey!" Palmer shouted. "What gives?"

He grabbed Linden's hand and led her down the stairs. "Thought we'd have a better chance of finding Kadey together. Let's get out of here." He was already halfway down the flight.

"They think you killed Bishop," she said, running as she explained.

"I know. Palmer has a tell. Several, actually. And Greenstreet isn't even trying to hide what he thinks. Guys like him always go for the easy answer. The readily available suspect."

"I overheard them talking on the radio while an officer drove me here. They think the tiles were the victim identifying his killer. And by showing how the crime scene was turned into a gigantic game, you confirmed their suspicions. Who else could construct these elaborate puzzles?"

"Why would I kill that man? I didn't even know him."

"They probably think it has something to do with Kadey. Protecting her or avenging her—the motives of a guilty father. You have to admit, it does look like something an egomaniacal Game Master might concoct."

"Maybe someone wanted to implicate me."

"Maybe so."

"Why are you helping me?"

"Because there's no one on earth better at solving puzzles than you. So even if I personally think you've lost all right to call yourself a father, you're still the best chance we have to find Kadey alive." She jumped another flight of stairs. "And you can't solve puzzles when you're behind bars."

"Sound reasoning." He exited the stairwell and raced onto the seventh-floor office area to one of the desks that was not rearranged. "This desk is on the square that represents the position the white queen takes for the final mate. The catbird seat, so to speak. Chess problems are often referenced by the clinching position."

"So?"

"So the whole puzzle was designed to draw our attention to this desk."

He glanced down. The top page of a stack of papers appeared to be covered by random numbers. Four repeating sequences of 1721 followed by a long series of zeroes and ones.

17211721172117210000000010000000000000000010000000000
00000010000000000000000010000000000000000100000000000
00000100000000000000000100000000000000001000000000000
00001000000000000000011100000000000001111000000000000
00111000000000000011011000000000000110001100000000001
10001100000000011111111000000000111111111100000001110
00001110000011100000001110001110000000001110011100000
0000011110

"Know what this is?" he asked.

"No idea."

"That's okay. I do." He shoved it into his pocket.

A second later, they heard a gunshot followed by a titanic shattering sound. Two more shots rang out after the first.

He looked up. Glass fell like raindrops.

Palmer had shot out the skylight. He was coming down the hard way.

16

One Minute Before

Palmer and Greenstreet stood at the edge of the skylight peering down.

"What are they doing?" Greenstreet asked.

"Haven't a clue. Thomas took something off that desk. He must think it's important. Why don't we find out why?" He drew his weapon. "On the count of three."

"Wait a minute," Greenstreet said, taking a giant step backward. "That must be eighteen, twenty feet down. To a very hard parquet floor."

"Where the suspect is rapidly making his escape. After seizing evidence from the crime scene."

"Couldn't we find a rope or . . . or . . . pulley or something?"

"You got one?"

"No."

"Then we're jumping."

Greenstreet's face dissolved like cotton candy on a summer day. "I—can't. I'm just a security guy."

Palmer nodded. "And that explains why." He turned back to the skylight and fired his weapon three times. The glass shattered, dropping shards of glass onto the parquet floor.

He tipped his fingers to Greenstreet. "Cowabunga."

He jumped.

17

BB rounded the corridor corner, Linden close behind. Ahead he spotted Keene, the irritating security guard who'd searched and insulted him on his way in. The guard stared at the elevator doors.

BB ducked out of sight, holding Linden back.

"Gatekeeper," he said.

"He just screens people on the way in," Linden replied. "If we stay calm, he should let us through."

"He won't. Palmer has already radioed him to stop us."

"You can't be sure of that."

"I can. I read it in his face."

"He's not even looking this way."

"Exactly."

"He's watching the elevator."

"Which makes no sense. Did he not just hear the skylight crash? Why didn't he investigate? Answer: Because Palmer told him to stay put and block our exit. I won't be able to talk my way past him."

"This is a top-level high-security secret government installation," Linden said. "The stairwells are probably already locked down. There's no other path off this floor."

"I'll think of something."

"Like what?"

He rearranged the variables in his mind. This was like a tangram, the Asian abstract reasoning puzzle. Seven pieces of different shapes, but somehow they fit together in a predetermined interlocking pattern. Palmer was one piece, the security guard was another, the elevator shaft . . .

Rearrange the pieces, he told himself. Find the combination that works.

"We don't have much time," Linden said. "If Palmer came through that skylight, he could be here—"

"Have you got something I can throw?"

Linden blinked. "Excuse me?"

"Something metal." He scanned her. No jewelry. No belt buckle. "What's in your purse?"

"Just the usual. Wallet, keys . . ."

"Give me your keys."

"No."

"Time is ticking . . ."

"Throw away your own keys!"

He gave her a long look.

Her chin dropped. "Right. How could I forget?" She complied.

He took the pitcher's stance, hands together at his chest, then stepped around the corner and hurled the keys through the metal detector.

The alarm blasted.

Keene jumped up, looking every which way at once, trying to figure out what happened.

"Very smart," Linden commented. "Now we'll never get out."

"Not that way."

"Then where are we going?"

"Back the way we came."

"That's insane."

"Which is why Palmer won't expect it."

18

Two Minutes Before

Palmer executed the standard fall technique he'd learned in Special Forces: land with bended knees, immediately roll onto your back, reverse somersault until the kinetic energy dissipates. But he jumped a little too far and his knees were a little too old. A shot of pain radiated through his left tibia on impact, and all the flipping on earth wasn't going to dissipate that.

He squatted on the floor a moment, catching his breath, gathering his strength. He radioed Keene. "Don't let anyone through." Then he called the security operations manager and ordered a complete lockdown of the building. Stairwells, doors, and windows. All controlled by computer. Once they were sealed, no one could escape.

Groaning more than a little, he pushed himself to his feet. He didn't know what stupid game Thomas thought he was playing, but this time, he'd been out-strategized. They'd learned everything there was to learn from playing with him. Now it was time to arrest him and take him in for a serious custodial interrogation. One he couldn't play his way out of, the arrogant ass.

Check and mate.

19

B B bolted through the access door onto the roof just before they heard the deadlock snap shut. Must've been triggered by an electronic signal. Probably all the locks were controlled by a computer network. They'd made it up here just in time.

He felt like the plastic rodent at the end of the Rube Goldbergesque contraption in Mouse Trap. He could run and run, but it didn't matter. Eventually, the cage would drop. Down the stairs, up the stairs, running as fast as they could. But how could he keep the cage up?

Linden bent over, catching her breath. "Nice pitch with the keys. Where'd you learn to throw like that?"

"I played baseball when I was a kid."

"Real baseball? Not Strat-O-Matic?"

He gave her a thin smile. "Didn't like it that much. Not enough strategy."

"I suppose the point was to divert everyone's attention to the elevator," Linden ventured. "How long do you think it will be before they realize it was just a set of keys?"

"Probably already have. As soon as Palmer discovers we're not on the seventh floor, he'll gather his troops and spread out through the entire building. But he won't expect us to go back to the place we just left—the farthest place from the street."

"He'll call for reinforcements."

"He already has."

"There's also that security cop pal of his."

"No worries. Greenstreet is useless."

"I wouldn't put it quite like that," Greenstreet said.

They whirled around.

Greenstreet was holding a gun.

20

Five uniformed military officers streamed through the elevator doors. Palmer had his badge out, ready to deploy them.

"Who's in charge?"

A dark-haired man in top physical condition stepped forward and saluted. "Lieutenant Michael Brogden, sir. I'm in charge."

"Were," he said flatly. "You'll take your orders from me." He didn't give the soldier a chance to argue. He didn't care whether the man thought an FBI agent could give orders to an MP. He just did it. "There are seven floors, so spread out. The doors are all locked down, but they might've already made it to another floor. They can't get out, but there are lots of places to hide. No one else is in the building, other than a security officer named Greenstreet and a floor guard named Keene. I'll tell Keene he can leave. If you find anyone else, apprehend them."

"Do you have a photograph, sir?"

He punched up the photo on his cell phone. BB from the waist up, blue Hawaiian shirt, big smile.

Brogden pursed his lips. "This shouldn't take long."

"I wouldn't think so. But he's somewhat cleverer than he looks."

"We'll find him, sir."

"I'm counting on it."

"And if he resists? Are we authorized to . . . ?" He let the question dangle.

"I doubt he'll offer any resistance."

"But if he does?"

"I'm revoking his Get Out of Jail Free card. Do what it takes. Just don't let him escape.

21

BB stared at the pudgy security officer aiming the gun at them. In his mental tangram, he'd assumed the cop stuck with the Feeb. He'd been wrong.

"Stay exactly where you are," Greenstreet said. "Palmer will be back."

"You need to let us go."

"No, I'm pretty sure I don't."

"How long have you been on the job?" He figured they had at best a few minutes before Palmer or his men found them. "One month. Two?"

"Just started last week actually. But I worked traffic in—"

"You understand that I'm being framed, right? That someone killed Bishop and took my daughter. And that she may turn up as dead as he is if I don't do something about it?"

"Talk to Palmer—"

He read the man's face as they jabbered. Why would Greenstreet have this job, at this time of his life, even though his hand jittered as he held the gun on them? "I'm talking to you. I'm asking you to do the right thing. You can be more than just another predictable law enforcement avatar."

"Don't try to get inside my head. I'm not an idiot."

"Haven't you ever wanted to be more than a security cop?"

"That doesn't . . ."

"Didn't your mother want more for you?"

"Leave my mother out of this." Greeenstreet's eye twitched. His tell.

"Of course she wanted more. She doesn't want to tell the bridge club her son is some rent-a-doofus." Pause. "She wants to tell them he was instrumental in bringing down an insidious plot threatening the security of the United States."

Linden raised an eyebrow.

"This is your chance to show her what you're made of," he continued. "Help me. Help me find my daughter."

"How is that a plot against the US?"

"Do you really think the FBI cares about the murder of one computer geek?"

"The possible kidnapping—"

"Have you not noticed that this is a top-secret military instillation?"

Greenstreet's head twitched. "I have my instructions."

"Let us go. Step aside."

"No way."

"I'm begging you. They've taken my daughter. All you have to do is—"

Before he could finish, Linden pulled an aerosol container out of her purse, held it to Greenstreet's face, and sprayed.

Greenstreet screamed. BB knocked his gun out of his hands. The security cop fell to his knees.

He swiped the man's own cuffs and chained him to the air conditioning unit. Greenstreet bellowed.

"What the hell was that?" he asked Linden.

"Pepper spray. You were taking too long."

"I almost had him talked into letting us go."

"You were taking too long."

"Well . . . thanks for the assist."

"Now I'm a felon, too. If we both go to prison, who will find Kadey?"

"That's not going to happen." He retrieved Greenstreet's weapon. "Let's get out of here."

22

Palmer got the call from Brogden not ten minutes after he was dispatched. "Reports from all floors. No one has found them."

"Look harder. They're hiding under a desk. Beneath a sofa. Playing pachisi in a pantry."

"My men are extremely experienced, sir. Well-trained. If those two people were in the building—"

"They are in the building. They had no chance to go anywhere else."

"Sir, with respect—"

"Never mind. I got a lock." A blue dot on his phone screen blipped. "Jackass looked so flattered when I pinned that ID tag on him. He didn't realize it was a GPS tracking device."

"Nice work."

Palmer punched a few more buttons. "Get ready to move your team out, Brogden. I know where he is."

Palmer and Brogden flanked the bathroom door, backs pressed against the wall, weapons at the ready. The door was closed. The readout told Palmer his quarry was inside.

He mouthed, Ready?

Brogden nodded.

He raised his right hand and counted down with his fingers. Five . . . four . . . three . . . two . . .

He smashed through the door. Brogden went right and high, he went left and low, and four other men carrying assault rifles streamed in behind them.

Keene, the elevator guard, sat on a toilet, a *Penthouse Magazine* in his lap, his pants dangling around his ankles.

Keene stared up at them, frozen stiff. "I clocked out."

Palmer pressed his fingers against his forehead. No doubt . . .

He approached the guard, carefully averting his eyes in the name of discretion, watching the readout on his smartphone. He dipped his hand into Keene's shirt pocket.

BB's ID tag.

He shook his head. "You shouldn't have called him a cheater . . ."

23

B B bounded off the bottom rung of the fire escape and landed on the pavement below. Linden followed, more gracefully and without missing a step.

He tossed her the car keys. "That's Palmer's car, the Ford Escort. You drive."

She caught the keys in midair. "You had car keys? And you made me throw mine away?"

"We need these. Your car can't be much help, since you left it back in Davis."

"And of course I'm struck driving."

"You have a license." He pulled out the numbers he had retrieved from the desk on the seventh floor. "I need to work on this puzzle. It might tell us where to find Kadey."

"How do you know it's a puzzle? Looks like gibberish to me. Maybe some kind of computer code. Ones and zeroes." She slid behind the wheel and started the car. "How did you get Palmer's car keys?"

"Picked his pocket when I accidentally on purpose crashed into him on the roof. Before I slammed the door in his face and bolted." He wiggled his fingers. "Haven't lost the old touch."

"You were already planning to steal his car?"

"I'm always play three moves ahead of my opponent. Your note told me they were planning to arrest me. And that I had to get away to save Kadey. Didn't take a genius to figure out I'd need wheels."

"Was that all you took from him?"

"Not hardly." He glanced up at the rearview mirror. "Hurry. Palmer's coming out of the building."

"But we've got his car."

"He'll find another one. Floor it.

24

Palmer commandeered Brogden's car keys. "You ride shotgun. Fire if necessary. We cannot let these people escape."

Brogden slid into the passenger seat. "You think this game freak committed the murder?"

"I think he may be guilty of more than that." Palmer started the black Impala and pulled onto the street, tires screeching. "Get the siren on the hood. He's headed for busy tourist arcas."

Brogden did as he was told. A few moments later, the siren blared.

"This car's unmarked, sir. We may attract police attention."

"We can identify ourselves." He reached into his jacket pocket. "I'll flash my ID at—"

He searched all his pockets as best he could while driving at top speed.

"What the hell happened to my badge?" His cycs narrowed as the realization dawned. "That sneaky card shark. Brogden, shoot out their damn tires."

25

Julian hoisted himself up the side of the building. He'd been hanging there for almost half an hour. Fortunately, he was in top physical condition. But half an hour was a long time, even for him. Now that the players had departed, he could return to the roof without interfering with the game.

The security officer was handcuffed to the air conditioning unit, screaming and rubbing his eyes. With a single swift gesture, Julian pinched a vital nerve near the man's carotid artery. The guard immediately lost consciousness.

He heard a barely audible shuffling of gravel behind him. "I knew it. As impossible as it seemed. I knew you were here."

She strode sideways, keeping a safe distance, dancing around him. She was dressed in black tactical clothing similar to his own. "I am your equal and opposite. If you exist, then I must also."

"Not in this game."

"There is another game. One you know nothing about."

"You might be surprised." He wondered if he should contact the Father. But what was the point? There was nothing he could do. "Are you here to kill me?"

"If necessary."

"I appreciate your honestly. I will afford you the same courtesy."

"You will attempt to kill me?"

"I will defend myself to whatever degree is necessary."

"I would expect no less." She paused. "I say that with genuine regret."

"I understand. But we are not in charge of the game."

"No. We are but tokens." She reached inside her robe and withdrew a large flail—a thick three-foot pole with a spiked metal ball swinging from the end of a short chain.

"An ancient weapon," he commented.

"An ancient Order," she replied. She lunged forward, swinging the ball before her. He ducked. The ball soared over his head.

He pivoted around, trying to stay ahead of the spiked ball. Given her background, he expected she would be fast, strong. With a dash of cruelty and the desire for power that characterized the Other.

While in Russia, he had learned *systema*, the ancient martial art of the Cossacks, with a few modern twists from the Spetsnaz—Russian military intelligence. Like many martial artists, those practicing *systema* never clenched a fist. Their primary weapon was the open hand, with the calculated occasional addition of elbows and knees. The idea was not to decimate the opponent but to wear them out. Typically, he would not touch his opponent at all until he was ready to move in for the kill, after the opponent was thoroughly exhausted.

He dodged the next swing of the flail, then feinted upward. When she raised her hands to block the nonexistent attack, he dropped to the ground and swung out his leg, thudding into her left ankle. She winced, brought the flail down like an axe. He evaded the blow, then repeated the same dropping maneuver, this time striking her right ankle. She let out a small cry and fell. He rammed his knee into her chest.

She tottered backward, but as he moved in, she unexpectedly brought the flail upward. She must have had incredibly strong forearms. He barely evaded it. A spike scraped his cheek, then dug into his shoulder. Didn't pierce the microfiber jacket.

If he'd been a second slower, he'd be dead.

He moved backward, stumbling over an exhaust pipe. He fell onto the gravel, cutting his hands.

She immediately took advantage of his vulnerable position. She sprang forward, wielding the flail in a hatchet motion. He rolled away at the last moment. When the flail thudded into the rooftop, she momentarily lost her balance. He grabbed a fistful of gravel and flung it into her face. She raised her hands to protect her eyes, too late.

He tried to stand, but the woman grabbed his boot, yanking him back down. His chin struck something metal.

The world spun around him.

"If you do not resist further, I will make your death quick," she said. "You have proven yourself valorous and worthy."

And you talk like Prince Valiant, he thought. But I suppose that comes from spending too much time in the Order. He searched the rooftop for a weapon.

A shard of Plexiglas. Near the broken skylight.

He grabbed it and jabbed it through his opponent's left leather boot.

She screamed. He jumped up, grabbed the woman by her hair and jabbed her in the throat with two extended fingers. The air rushed out of her lungs.

He wanted to spend more time reasoning with his adversary. She was misguided, but she might be persuaded to see the way of the Father. If he had time. He had gained a momentary advantage, but he could not expect it to last.

"The only way to stop me is to kill me," his opponent muttered "And you can't do it."

He looked at the jagged glass in his hand. "I could. But I don't have to. The players have left. You cannot interfere with the game."

"You mean, not here. But if you let me live, I will fulfill—"

"Your programming?"

She glared at him. "My mission."

He pulled two FlexiCuffs from his pack and tied her beside the unconscious guard. He knew she would escape, eventually. But not until he and the players were long gone.

Once her hands were secure, he searched her.

"Having a little fun?" she asked.

He ignored her. Inside her pack, he discovered a small wallet. And inside the wallet, he found an address.

His heart beat with excitement. This was the information he'd been seeking for more than a year.

Now he could take the game to them.

He touched his SRAC. The Father needed to know that the Other was actively attempting to interfere—and that Julian had discovered the means to strike directly at their heart.

No response. That was unusual. Apparently the meeting in Dubai occupied his full attention.

No matter. He typed the information into his smartphone and transmitted it. The response only took a few seconds.

Infiltrate.

THE GAME MASTER

As you wish, he thought. He'd never been to Greece before.

He jumped off the side of the roof, swinging onto the fire escape. The instrucitons did not surprise him. He just hoped he was up to it. Because at this point, they could not afford any mistakes. There were too many random factors in this game already. The next roll of the dice could change everything.

26

"Look out!" BB screamed, clutching the grip above the passenger side window.

"They're firing at us," Linden muttered.

"Sigmoid."

Linden took a hard left. Two tires bounced off the pavement. The other two squealed as if they were in pain. "Sigmoid? What does that mean?"

He shook his head. "If you'd worked those crossword puzzle books I bought you for our anniversary—"

"This is not the time, BB. What does it mean?"

"Means *swerve back and forth*. An *S*-shape. Like a coiled serpent. A moving target is harder to drill."

"Thanks." She took another sharp corner, a second too late. The Escort slammed into the curb. Both their heads hit the ceiling.

"Would you be more careful?" he said. "I'm trying to solve a puzzle. This is very complicated."

"Oh, I'm so sorry. I didn't mean for my bullet dodging to interfere with your puzzle solving."

"Just get us to the airstrip."

She glanced at the paper in his lap out the corner of her eye. "What is that thing, anyway?"

"It's code. Three-dimensional binary code."

"Can you explain what that means?"

"You're the PhD."

"In game theory, not stupid codes. When are you going to get over your infantile inferiority complex because I have college degrees and you don't?"

"Who's inferior? I don't see you solving the puzzle." He drew vertical lines perpendicular to the existing horizontal ones, creating a grid. "These numbers aren't random. They're coordinates. You notice that the first line repeats an equation over and over again. That's to get your attention. The equation gives you the size of the grid. In this case, seventeen by twenty-one. So you draw a grid that's seventeen squares across and twenty-one squares down. Three hundred fifty-seven squares total."

"The rest is binary code," he continued. "Numbers. Exactly twenty-one rows of them. One for each row of the grid. All seventeen digits long, all ones and zeroes. When those numbers are used in binary code to program a computer, they initiate a series of yes or no responses. One is yes, zero is no. Here, they indicate whether a square should be filled in or not. One means fill it in. Zero means don't."

"So it's a code that looks nothing like a code. Because it doesn't produce a written message. It produces a picture."

"Exactly. I've filled in the first two lines, working from the end backwards. I'm already seeing a pattern."

0	1	1	1	0	0	0	0	0	0	0	0	0	1	1	1	0
0	1	1	1	0	0	0	0	0	0	0	0	0	1	1	1	0
0	0	1	1	1	0	0	0	0	0	0	0	1	1	1	0	0
0	0	0	1	1	1	0	0	0	0	0	1	1	1	0	0	0
0	0	0	0	1	1	1	1	1	1	1	1	1	0	0	0	0
0	0	0	0	1	1	1	1	1	1	1	1	1	0	0	0	0
0	0	0	0	0	1	1	0	0	0	1	1	0	0	0	0	0
0	0	0	0	0	1	1	0	0	0	1	1	0	0	0	0	0
0	0	0	0	0	0	1	1	0	1	1	0	0	0	0	0	0
0	0	0	0	0	0	0	1	1	1	0	0	0	0	0	0	0
0	0	0	0	0	0	1	1	1	1	1	0	0	0	0	0	0
0	0	0	0	0	0	0	1	1	1	0	0	0	0	0	0	0
0	0	0	0	0	0	0	0	1	0	0	0	0	0	0	0	0
0	0	0	0	0	0	0	0	1	0	0	0	0	0	0	0	0
0	0	0	0	0	0	0	0	1	0	0	0	0	0	0	0	0
0	0	0	0	0	0	0	0	1	0	0	0	0	0	0	0	0
0	0	0	0	0	0	0	0	1	0	0	0	0	0	0	0	0
0	0	0	0	0	0	0	0	1	0	0	0	0	0	0	0	0
0	0	0	0	0	0	0	0	1	0	0	0	0	0	0	0	0
0	0	0	0	0	0	0	0	1	0	0	0	0	0	0	0	0
0	0	0	0	0	0	0	0	1	0	0	0	0	0	0	0	0

He continued. "Codes of this nature were devised by astronomers to send pictures into space as part of the search for extraterrestrial intelligence. They speculated that math might be a universal language for any sentient species living in this universe. The Voyager space probes contained codes that, when solved, showed erect bipedal mammals of two genders living on the third planet from the sun." He continued filling in the squares. "I think this puzzle designates a location. But someplace a little closer to home."

"You've never taken an astronomy class in your life. How do you know this?"

"I'm the Game Master, remember?"

"You keep reminding me. And everyone else you meet." Linden brought the car screeching around another corner. "There's the airstrip."

"Excellent."

"Palmer's about a block behind us. Damn. The front gates are locked."

"That's a pity."

"If we stop to open the gate, Palmer will catch us."

"And it's probably locked anyway." Still scribbling.

"So what do you think?"

"You know what I think." He glanced ahead. "I think I'm very glad this isn't my car."

"Brace yourself."

Linden smashed into the gates.

27

"They're headed for that airstrip," Brogden said. "Surely they don't think they can charter a plane. They won't even have time to buy a ticket."

"They don't have to," Palmer replied, his hands gripping the wheel so tightly his fingers were white. "They have something even better than a ticket."

"What's that?"

"My badge."

28

"We have to move quickly," BB said, tugging her out of the totaled car toward the grounded copter. "There's someone in the cockpit. The pilot, I hope. Otherwise, I'll have to fly the thing."

"Right. I'm going to let the guy who doesn't have a driver's license fly a copter."

"Stick with me and agree with everything I say."

"So we're reliving our marriage?"

He grabbed the passenger side hatch and opened it, flashing Palmer's badge. The pilot didn't move but his face registered surprise.

"Palmer sent me. We've got to medevac her out of here. Gunshot wound."

The pilot efficiently flipped the rotors on. "Understood. I'll need clearance."

"No time. She's bleeding out." He jabbed Linden in the side. She made the appropriate groaning noises. "You can get us to Vegas General in ten minutes. Radio in once we're airborne." He helped Linden into the back seat. She clutched her abdomen and howled.

The pilot was uncertain. "I still think—"

"Do you want this woman to die? Do you want her blood on your hands?"

"No . . ."

"Then get this baby into the air right now or—"

Palmer's car careened through the shattered gates. Another man leaned out the passenger side window pointing a gun.

"Okay, never mind the *ruse de guerre*." He pulled Greenstreet's gun out of the back of his jeans and pointed it at the pilot's head. "Get us into the air or you're dead."

29

"Shoot all around it!" Palmer shouted. "Scare them back down."

Brogden was already outside the car firing round after round. "Not going to happen, sir. They didn't pull back. If I disable the copter, they might be killed. Pilot included."

"A risk I'm willing to take."

"Too late. They're too far away."

"Damn!" Palmer pounded his shoe into the tarmac. "Contact McCarran Air Traffic Control. Now."

30

B B heard the rapid fire of pistols below.

The pilot blanched. "They're gonna shoot us!"

"They're just trying to scare you into landing."

"They're acting like they want to kill us."

He read the pilot's face, a short story at best. Used to following orders. Needed reassurance. "They won't kill us. Palmer doesn't want me dead, much less you."

"You don't know that."

"Think of this like a Monopoly game. We're the race car. Palmer's the shoe. I just took a ride on the Reading. Once I collect my two hundred dollars, you can roll the dice again and go anywhere you want."

"They'll track you. Grab you when we land."

"Yes, that's probably what they're thinking. So we'll have to choose the right place to land." The pilot dripped with sweat. More reassurance was required. "Don't worry. I've thought this through in advance. Just do what I tell you to do and you'll be alive an hour from now. Head south."

"I won't."

"Then I'll shoot you and fly it myself. I'm a trained chopper pilot."

Linden blinked.

"Your choice. What's it going to be?"

The pilot pushed the throttle. The copter ascended to a cruising altitude.

31

Palmer barked into his cell phone. "Did you hear what I said? There is no higher authority than me."

The crackling voice on the other end of the phone remained calm, which was supremely irritating. He supposed he should be glad the head of the air traffic controllers had a steady head on his shoulders. But right now, he wanted someone more easily budged.

"Sir, we have protocols—"

"All of which can be ignored in an emergency situation with national security concerns. And that's exactly what this is."

"Sir, we're not in radio contact—"

"I know you're not in radio contact. They're trying to stay off your radar. That's why I'm calling. Get all your airborne vessels to activate sight and radar search immediately."

"I can't guarantee—"

"They're flying over a tourist mecca. There's half a million people there. Someone will see them."

Static-filled silence. "We'll do the best we can."

"You'll find them, damn it. Or you'll answer to the Pentagon."

He snapped the phone shut and jogged into the hangar. He couldn't depend on that incompetent middle manager. Time to commandeer a ride of his own.

Run all you want, Game Master. The black rook is right behind you.

32

Ogilve stared across the conference table at his old nemesis, the man who occupied so much time in his nightmares.

"Sit down, General Chun." He pushed a champagne flute toward him. "Have a drink. My treat."

Chun did not sit, but he lifted the flute in a tiny salute. "I often think of those wonderful one hundred and twenty-seven days we spent together in my homeland, just you and me." A thin smile tugged at Chun's lips. "And your wife, of course." Pause. "And your daughter."

Stay calm, he told himself. You've come a long way in the last four years. You're not the mild-mannered geek who was so easily bullied by this man. The man who took so much. He's trying to provoke you, trying to make you feel inferior. His psychological warfare might have worked once. But now he's just a sad, brutal, pathetic obstacle.

"Are you here as a representative of your nasty government, Chun? Or just your nasty self?"

Chun took a chair on the opposite end of the table. Everyone else pulled as far away from him as possible. "Both."

"You've kept a low profile of late."

"It served my purposes."

He felt a tightening of his abdominal muscles. "I thought your nation was civilizing itself and had no further need for a blunt instrument such as yourself. Didn't I hear they were suspending their nuclear arms program?"

"That announcement was my idea. Lao Tse advised generals to lull their opponents into a false sense of security. So you can strike while they sleep."

"Whatever. Why are you here?"

Chun spread his arms magnanimously. "Because I missed you, Ogilve." He rubbed his hands together. "Are we still plotting a new world order?"

"And you aren't?"

"Not like you. Not like the dreaded Neopolis." He slapped the table, hard. "You do not seek utopia. You're a pack of malcontented lickspittles toiling in the thralls of weak and emaciated masters."

Ogilve feigned boredom. He knew nothing could possibly irritate the general more. "Again, Chun. Why are you here? Without the megalomania."

"It occurred to me that we may be working at cross purposes."

"Like that's news."

"It does not have to be so. We should be friends."

A chill creep crept down his spine. He could not stare into that man's eyes. Even now, it brought back too many horrific memories. What he did to Holly. Over and over again.

"Get to the point, Chun."

"I have worked behind the scenes as long as I can. The time has come to make my move. To rise to the forefront."

"And do what?"

"What you and your assemblage only talk about. But I will make reality."

"The same sick dream as before? The heaven-sent apocalypse?"

"You should have devoted yourself to reading more as I once suggested. It might change your opinion of me."

"That will never happen."

"Then you will perish."

"You came all this way to kill me? Surely you could've sent a flunky to do that."

"You wound me, Emerson. After all the time we've spent together, you treat me in this cold manner. Let's end this foolish feud. Join me."

"Never."

"Together we would be unstoppable."

"No."

Their eyes met across the white tabletop.

"Reconsider?"

"Never."

93

"Pity." Chun reached into his jacket pocket, took out his smartphone, and tapped a button.

Less than a second later, five assault soldiers appeared outside the bay window on descent cords. Less than a second after that, they crashed through the window.

Glass flew across the room. He dove under the table, trying to avoid injury. Mulinak ducked, but a large shard caught Kussein in the throat, impaling him.

The troops landed on their feet and aimed their machine guns.

"Last chance, Emerson."

"I have plans of my own."

"Suit yourself." Chun snapped his fingers. "Kill them."

A thunderous metallic sound followed. Three seconds later, the guns exploded. All five soldiers dropped to the floor.

Chun's lips parted, but he did not speak.

"Surprised?" Ogilve rose from the floor. "You're not nearly so clever as you think, Chun. I know you bribed my man in Paris to reveal the meeting location. And I also know your guards use Israeli TK-459s. With firing mechanisms controlled by a tiny computer chip."

"You rewrote the subroutines."

"A wireless computer virus infected the rifles the instant they entered this room. Caused the rifles to malfunction. Blow up in their faces."

"Those men will probably die."

"Better them than me."

"Who's the psychopath now, Emerson?"

Behind them, Mulinak darted out of the conference room.

"Gonna have your men kill him too, Chun?"

"For what purpose?" Chun extended his left arm to its full length. A small pistol carbine leaped out from a concealed ball and track mechanism. Chun closed his fist around the grip. "No computer chip in this one. Nothing to prevent it from firing."

"Except you."

Chun's eyes narrowed. "Do you seriously believe I won't kill you?"

"I believe that if you do, you'll never get the antidote in time."

"Antidote? Is this what you've been reduced to? Poison? The weapon of old women?"

"Which is why you didn't expect it. You were looking for an elephant when you should have been watching out for mice."

"It was in the champagne?"

"Yes."

He shoved the pistol into Ogilve's face. "Then you lose. I didn't drink the champagne."

"No. But she did."

Rani sat up straight.

"Is this true?" Chun demanded.

She nodded.

"Did you really think I would not discover that she worked for you, Chun? That she has been your faithful Mata Hari for years?"

Chun's brow creased. "Tell me how to save her."

"I will text you the antidote when I am safe. Within thirty minutes."

"I will beat it out of you now."

"Can you get it out of me in an hour? Because that's how long she has, at most, unless she gets the cure. And I think you know I won't break that quickly. Because you've tried it before."

Chun's gun wavered. "You are a complete degenerate."

"I am what you made me." He shoved Chun back, hard.

"How do I know you will text?"

"I've never lied to you, Chun. Can you say the same?"

"If you knew I was coming, why didn't you move your meeting?"

"Because I wanted you to understand something." He leaned in close. "You're not as smart as you think. You're not omniscient. You're not all-powerful. And you will never outsmart me." He placed his hand over Chun's gun and wrested it out of his hand. "Your reign of terror is over. Your days of raping and beating defenseless women are over. Your ignorant dreams of South American paradise are finished. I'm going to blow your—"

A sudden blow smashed down on his head. A trickle of sticky blood oozed down the side of his face. He batted his eyes, struggling to remain conscious.

Rani held a broken champagne bottle. "I will not allow my master to be defeated because of my stupidity."

Chun retrieved his gun.

Ogilve staggered toward the door.

"You'll never make it, you arrogant fool." Chun pulled the trigger.

Nothing happened.

"But—I loaded the gun this morning."

"Removed the bullets," Ogilve said weakly as he lurched through the doors and slammed them shut behind him. "While I was monologuing."

Ogilve entered the elevator texting. His immediate concern was that he not pass out until he was safe. Then he could call Julian and attempt to repair the damage.

He hated being dependent upon others. But he had no hope of defeating Chun. Not alone.

Come on, BB, he thought, as he watched the elevator floor numbers glide by. Do it. Before it's too late.

33

B kept his eyes glued to the copter window. He knew Palmer would call everyone he knew to track them.

"Wherever we land, the cops will be waiting for you," the pilot shouted. "What are you gonna do? Shoot your way out with that little pistol?"

"Direct confrontation is rarely the smartest approach," he replied. "Ever play Risk?"

The pilot stared at him as if he were from another planet. "What?"

"Risk. The board game. Maybe when you were in college?"

"Yeah, I've played it."

"Then you know—or I hope you know—that the smartest strategy isn't to drop right into the most desirable countries and start fighting everyone in sight. That's a rookie mistake. The smart player holes up in Australia."

"Who wants Australia?"

"Exactly. But there's only one way in. A bottleneck. An entrance that can be controlled. Territory that can be defended."

"I understand the concept," Linden shouted from the back seat. "But how does it apply to our current increasingly desperate situation?"

"We need a bottleneck," he answered, gazing out the window. "And I think I know something that would just do the trick nicely. Hoover Dam. There's only one way in."

"Then that's where the cops will wait for us."

"I don't think they can get there before us. They'll set up a barricade at the end of the bottleneck and wait. And wait. And by the time they realize we're not coming, it will be too late."

"Because we're going to stay there forever?"

"Because we'll leave the other way. The one that doesn't show up on their maps. I know a guy who lives out in the desert not far from the dam."

"Why in God's name would you know someone who lives in the desert?"

"He's a long-time colleague. His work makes it advantageous to remain out of sight."

"Drug dealer? Pimp?"

"Artist." He paused. "He's quite good at generating identity papers. Passports and such."

"You'd need someone like that in your life, wouldn't you? Given your lack of conventional ID."

"He can smuggle us out. Get us the cash we need. Then we shop for clothes and other necessaries, because neither of us can go home. Then we catch a flight."

"Did you say passports?"

"Did I not mention? I finished the puzzle." He passed her the completed grid.

```
0 1 1 1 0 0 0 0 0 0 0 0 0 1 1 1 0
0 1 1 1 0 0 0 0 0 0 0 0 0 1 1 1 0
0 0 1 1 1 0 0 0 0 0 0 0 1 1 1 0 0
0 0 0 1 1 1 0 0 0 0 0 1 1 1 0 0 0
0 0 0 0 1 1 1 1 1 1 1 1 1 0 0 0 0
0 0 0 0 1 1 1 1 1 1 1 1 1 0 0 0 0
0 0 0 0 0 1 1 0 0 0 1 1 0 0 0 0 0
0 0 0 0 0 1 1 0 0 0 1 1 0 0 0 0 0
0 0 0 0 0 0 1 1 0 1 1 0 0 0 0 0 0
0 0 0 0 0 0 0 1 1 1 0 0 0 0 0 0 0
0 0 0 0 0 0 0 1 1 1 1 0 0 0 0 0 0
0 0 0 0 0 0 0 1 1 1 0 0 0 0 0 0 0
0 0 0 0 0 0 0 0 1 0 0 0 0 0 0 0 0
0 0 0 0 0 0 0 0 1 0 0 0 0 0 0 0 0
0 0 0 0 0 0 0 0 1 0 0 0 0 0 0 0 0
0 0 0 0 0 0 0 0 1 0 0 0 0 0 0 0 0
0 0 0 0 0 0 0 0 1 0 0 0 0 0 0 0 0
0 0 0 0 0 0 0 0 1 0 0 0 0 0 0 0 0
0 0 0 0 0 0 0 0 1 0 0 0 0 0 0 0 0
0 0 0 0 0 0 0 0 1 0 0 0 0 0 0 0 0
0 0 0 0 0 0 0 0 1 0 0 0 0 0 0 0 0
```

"It's . . . a divining rod? A pitchfork? The letter *Y*? Are we going to Yemen?"

"No."

"Space Needle?"

His eyes rolled. "You're holding it upside-down."

She reversed it.

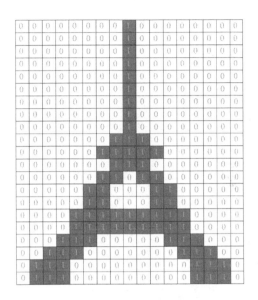

Her lips parted. "We're going to—"

He placed his hand over her mouth. "Don't say it." He tilted his head toward the pilot. "We don't want anyone following us."

The pilot turned his head. "It would be useful if I knew where we were going."

BB offered a wry smile. "Just get us near Hoover Dam. I'll take it from there."

His cell phone buzzed. He pulled it out of his pocket.

This was not a call. It was a messaged photograph.

Kadey was tied up, arms behind her back. A gag divided her face. Her clothes were ripped.

She looked terrified.

A text came with the photo. *The countdown starts now. 100 hours until she's permanently deleted.*

A moment later, a second text arrived.

Your move.

He put the phone away before Linden could see the images. "We don't have much time." He stared off into the clouds. "But we will find her, Linden. We have to."

Part Two

Every Move Has
Consequences

34

The White House, Situation Room
Washington, D.C.

President Fernandez sat with his eyes glued to the digital display on the satellite surveillance feed. The green screen reloaded on a second-to-second basis, but the fundamentals remained the same. The *X*s represented the Korean People's Army. And the *O*s, his military advisors assured him, represented the greatest threat to the stability of the free world. And for that matter, the stability of the unfree world.

"So if I understand this correctly, Chun has assembled a secret army," Fernandez said. "An army that the leader of the official army doesn't know about. That's not particularly surprising. North Korea is brutal, violent, and chaotic. The president is a puppet, which is just as well, because he's a spoiled brat and a madman. If I lived in North Korea, I'd want my own army, too."

"The question is, why now." Fernandez's chief of staff, Ross Blake, slid a leather-bound report across the long conference table. Blake was no military expert, but he had an innate pragmatism that Fernandez had found invaluable throughout his years in office. "Traditionally, military leaders don't assemble private armies just so they sleep better at night."

"You think he's planning a coup."

"We don't think he's planning to unseat Kim Jr., if that's what you mean." Blake ran his hand across his completely bald scalp. "The cult of personality attached to that family goes back decades. But Kim is largely a figurehead, at least when it comes to foreign policy. The head of the military, General Yoon, has both authority and the means to back it up. The two have a practical working agreement. Kim has a free hand in domestic matters, when his health permits him to leave his bedroom. Yoon runs the international show."

"And that's what concerns us."

The chairman of the joint chiefs of staff, Gordon Decker, obscured his view of the satellite feed. "Our intel says Chun's secret army troops are loyal, committed, and entirely invisible to Yoon."

"What's the point of that?"

"There's only one possible answer, sir. Chun wants Yoon's job."

"He's going to overthrow his immediate superior?"

"You don't assemble a secret army and then hope your boss dies of old age." Decker was a military and political expert, and he had a wonderful gift for cutting to the heart of the matter. Fernandez could tolerate his gruff attitude in exchange for being told directly and convincingly what he needed to do. The secretary of state was on her way to the White House from Lebanon, but in the meantime, he felt secure with Decker.

"I suppose not." Fernandez leaned back in his padded chair, his hand pressed against his forehead. Thank God for advisors. Foreign policy made his head hurt. He put on a good show, but he knew he wasn't up to the challenge of global geopolitics. Some people enjoyed this business, a real-world version of Diplomacy. But he didn't. He liked giving speeches, shaking hands. He liked looking out into a crowd and seeing people cheering him. But he never wanted lives depending on him. Much less, God forbid, the fate of nations. "What do we care, ultimately? So there's a new man at the head of the army. Haven't we just replaced one loose cannon with another?"

Decker shook his head, making his jowls quiver. "Better the devil you know, Mr. President."

"And you have questions about Chun?"

"Big ones. We don't know enough about him. He came from humble origins. He's been heavily involved with Korea's military research, some of which is cutting edge and seriously unconventional. And now, after more than twenty years of dutiful service, he wants to take over. Why?"

"I give up. Why?"

"We don't know. But we're concerned that . . . there might be a reason."

"There's no *might* here," Blake said, cutting in. "There is a reason. We just don't know what it is."

"Our worst fear," Decker continued, "is that Chun's got something. A weapon, perhaps. Something that he thinks gives him power. Especially if he's got an army backing it up."

"He won't do anything Kim doesn't approve."

"We don't know that, sir. He's been at odds with his government before. And he's been overheard by intelligence officers expressing a desire for change."

"Change in North Korea could only be for the better."

"I don't agree." Blake cut back into the conversation. "This is the undiscovered country—from whose bourn no traveler returns."

Fernandez hated it when Blake showed off. "What's the worst that could possibly happen?"

"The worst is that he could take a dangerously unstable nuclear nation and make it even more dangerous and unstable. That he could use his army and weaponry to affect not just his nation but the entire world. That he might have a private agenda."

Fernandez shrugged. "I still don't see why this is occupying so much of our time. We do have an actual war or two, you know."

"Yes. Those are the conflicts we know. We worry about the ones we don't know."

"The North Koreans are pip-squeaks."

"Forgive me for saying so, Mr. President, but it's usually the pip-squeaks that end up causing the big problems. Austria-Hungary wasn't exactly a world power. Neither was Germany at that time. But they brought the whole world to war. Was Troy the greatest power of the ancient world? No, but they had a lot of committed friends. Right now, Russia is dangerously unstable. China is wealthy but buried in people. The Middle East is controlled by religion and fury. And North Korea—well, who knows?"

"They won't do anything China doesn't want them to do."

"Perhaps," Decker said, "but what might China want them to do? They've been aggressively pushing at India's borders ever since the skirmish of '62. They've been fighting for control of the North Indian Ocean. India signed an alliance treaty with Vietnam to explore oil deposits in the Nam Con Son basin. So China signed a military and economic development treaty with Pakistan. And we sent troops to

Australia. China sent troops to the Andaman Islands. And so it goes until finally the whole world is shooting at one another."

"What do you want me to do?"

"Today? Nothing. But we should watch this situation carefully. And when the time comes, we must be prepared to take action. To make decisions that may affect the shape of the world."

Exactly the kind he hated most. "Gentlemen, I'm a lame duck president. I don't need this kind of stress."

"And that's another part of the problem." Blake checked Decker out of the corner of his eye. "If Chun makes his play, the leader of the free world will have to respond. And I'd rather it was you than, well, either of your likely successors."

"You don't think much of Senator Vogel?"

"I don't know who's pulling his strings. He's got a big war chest and preternatural political savvy. But bottom line, I don't know what he wants. And that makes me nervous."

"Every time there's a major conflict, the maps get redrawn," Decker added. "The balance of power shifts. And enormous power devolves to a small number of hands." He tapped his pencil on the table. "This forthcoming election could turn out to be the most important one this country has ever seen."

"You're exaggerating. Surely." Fernandez tugged on his collar. "You've always been a gloom and doom player. This world will keep on spinning."

Blake and Decker exchanged a long look.

"Yes, the world will keep on spinning," Decker said quietly. "But who's going to be onboard to enjoy the ride?"

35

Two Days Before
Port Blair
Andaman & Nicobar Islands

General Chun pushed open the hotel suite doors. "Don't bother getting up."

Commander Singh sprang out of the oversized bed, clutching a satin sheet to his chest. Hindi was one of the few languages Chun did not speak, but he comprehended the words flowing from the man's mouth well enough to know they were not friendly.

He was at the side of the bed before Singh could move. Singh opened the drawer of the end table. A silver pistol slid forward. Singh reached for it.

Chun kicked the drawer closed. "Try that again and you die. Sit still for a moment and you live. At least for the moment."

He saw Singh's eye dart to the other side of the bed.

Rani stood there, fully dressed.

"Surprised? A good soldier learns to dress quickly. Yes, you heard me correctly. The woman you thought was a barroom trollop is in fact working for me. Which means that you are now working for me as well."

Singh lunged for him, arms extended. Chun slapped the attack down, hard. Singh crumpled to the floor.

He kicked the Indian officer in the side, breaking a rib. That should keep him down long enough to complete the conversation.

"I know you speak English, Commander, so let's both do that. I also know the Indian military has stationed you here to oversee the submarine fleet at India's battle headquarters for the Indian Ocean region. And I know how important that is. These islands are closer to

Indonesia than India, but they form a protective shield between you and China, the superpower that considers your nation a major threat."

Singh wiped blood from his face. "I do not know what you are talking about. I am here on holiday."

"Aren't we all. Listen, my friend, I don't blame you. Or India. We all know China has its eyes on your mountain states. Maybe the whole country. China is building military strength—not to mention an airbase—on the Coco Islands, just a short boat ride from India's coast. And let's be honest, China's maritime force is vastly greater than yours, or that of any other power in the region. American troops in Australia are of no real consequence. China could take anything it wants. Sensible to take precautions."

"Again, I do not know what you are talking—"

He slapped Singh across the face, knocking him backward. The Indian commander attempted to rise—

This time Rani was the one who knocked him down.

"Do not attempt another attack," the sinewy woman said. "You are as poor a fighter as you are a lover."

Chun laughed. "Insult to injury." He grabbed Singh by the hair and jerked the man's head up. "Let me be clear. I will not interfere with your work. I will not undermine India's activities, even though they clearly are not in North Korea's interest. Bring on your marine commandos—MARCOS, I think you call them? Bring on your troops, warships, airbases, docking facilities—anything you like. Make it India's hub for amphibious warfare. I will not interfere."

Singh twisted his head back and forth but could not get free. "Then what do you want?"

"When the time comes, I will call you and make a request. You have submarines at your disposal. Perhaps we will send one out. Perhaps we will alter a course. I only know this: When I make my request—you will comply."

"Are you insane? A misdirected nuclear submarine could start a world war."

"I'm counting on it."

"You're talking about the end of the world."

"The end of this world, perhaps."

"I will never betray my country."

"Commander Singh—you already have." The corners of his lips turned upward. "And I took pictures." He tossed a few glossies onto the bed.

Singh glanced at the photos, then looked at Rani.

She shrugged. "I did tell you I was complicated."

"Don't feel bad, Commander," he said. "You are not the first to fall for Rani's charms. She has admirers everywhere. But the facts remain. Photos of you frolicking with a Pakistani intelligence agent will end your career and bring disgrace to your family. You will become untouchables. Or worse. In all likelihood, someone will come in the dark of the night and kill you."

"I think you must believe you are in a Western nation, General Chun. One in which every public official is required to maintain a preposterous façade of antiquated sexual propriety. We are not so Puritan here. My commanding officer has had so many intrigues with women—"

"Not with Pakistani intelligence officers."

"So long as I kept my mouth shut—"

Rani smiled. "But there's the rub, isn't it?" She pinched her right gold earring. A staticky recording played back. In Singh's voice.

". . . and they have no idea what I might do with it. I can send those submarines anywhere. I can launch their missiles anytime I wish. I know the magic word."

"Tell it to me." Rani spoke between heaving gasps. "Nothing excites me like power. Tell me and I will do anything for you."

"It is the simplest of things," Singh's voice said. "You need only transmit this word—"

Rani pinched her earring again, shutting off the recording. "Still think your superiors will laugh this off?"

Singh collapsed onto the bed.

Chun towered over him. "Singh, you face disgrace, prison, and almost certain execution. Or you can do me this one favor. What will it be?"

Chun and Rani rode to the airport in the back of a jet-black limousine. He patted Rani's hand affectionately. "You performed well. As you always do."

"Are you certain he will comply? When the time comes?"

"There is no certainty when it comes to human behavior. But I calculate all the angles and pursue the most likely plan to achieve what we want. The jigsaw pieces fall into place."

"No one can stop you."

He drew in his breath. "There is one. As you know." His eyes turned toward the window and the untamed jungle beyond. "But we will deal with him. The world is headed toward a new epoch." He rapped on the dividing panel, signaling the driver to pull over near the Learjet awaiting him. "A new dawn. A better one. And the great glory is—I'm the only one who knows it."

36

Present Day
La Tour Eiffel
Champ de Mars, Paris

BB bisected the long queue stretching from the main ticket office, tugging Linden behind him. The immense puddle-iron lattice tower cast a shadow, protecting them from the harsh noontime sun.

"You always promised me we'd see Paris," Linden commented.

"And one day, we might," BB said. "But we don't have time to sightsee now."

"Easy for you to say. You've been here before."

"Easy for me to say because finding Kadey is my number one priority. By far."

"Kadey's still alive," she said, though the slight tremor in her voice made him wonder if she trusted her intuitions as much as she claimed. "Do you think she's been . . . hurt?"

"No. And we can make sure she isn't hurt. If we get to her in time." He strode toward a reception booth at the far end of the tower.

"What could her message mean? Saying she's going to be *deleted?*"

"I don't know." Kadey had a fine command of language. He'd played SCRABBLE with her a thousand times, and sometimes she won. If she had wanted to say *murdered*, she would've said *murdered*. Unless *deleted* was some hip new slang for it, like *offed*. But he didn't think so.

"Shouldn't we get in line with the others?" Linden asked. "If we're going up?"

"I've got a better idea. Let's have lunch."

"I spotted a crêperie down the street."

"That's not where the puzzle sent us."

Even though they'd come directly from the airport and seen little of the city, he loved it. The ambiance of Paris elated him—the sidewalk café, the Latin Quarter, the seven bridges—everything. This was the country that gave the world Mille Bornes and Abalone. How could he not love it? He adored the Eiffel Tower, like most Parisians—today, not when it was first erected. He knew that it represented a huge step forward for applied engineering. And no, the replica in Vegas was not the same.

He approached the rear elevator. "Let's lunch at the Jules Verne."

"Isn't that pricey?"

"It'll get us upstairs without standing in that line." He smiled at the maître d'. "*Bonjour.* Table for three, please."

"Three?"

"Yes. Emerson Ogilve is joining us. He asked us to secure his table."

Linden gave him a long look.

"Ah. It shall be done, monsieur."

Linden remained quiet, but only until the elevator doors closed, separating them from potentially prying ears. "How did you know Ogilve had a table here?"

"I didn't. But I did notice there was a small refrigerator in his office at the Vegas complex. With a freezer."

"Here we go again. Are you going to make me ask?"

"Ask what?"

"Yes, you are. All right, Sherlock. What does the refrigerator have to do with the Jules Verne?"

He shrugged. "Many successful CEOs have fridges in their offices. But rarely freezers. Why would they want it? An ice bin so they can chill their Scotch and sodas?"

"But Dinky had a freezer. And I'm betting you know why."

"The man loves ice cream. More than he loves money. Almost more than he loves games. Care to guess his favorite flavor?"

"Tutti-frutti?"

"Crème de lucre cinnamon crunch. And care to guess the only place in Paris that serves it?"

"The Jules Verne."

"Yup. Googled it at the airport."

"You think this ice cream fanatic took our Kadey?"

"He's involved somehow. So let's walk a mile in his shoes."

The elevator doors opened and they stepped into the richly appointed lobby of the Jules Verne. The headwaiter showed them to their table on the north end of the tower, winding through the crisp white linen-topped tables and the sea of red-backed chairs. The floor was packed but the patrons were noticeably discreet and well-behaved.

He nudged the waiter aside and pulled Linden's chair out for her.

"Always the gentleman," she said.

"No, not always," he replied. "But when it matters."

"I suppose I can't have wine."

"No."

"Pâté?"

"If you must."

"You disapprove?"

"Still haven't learned to love liver." He was already distracted by the reproduction resting against the window beside the table.

Linden ordered for him. "Do you know what that picture is?" she asked.

"Seen it before. Can't place it."

"*The School of Athens.* Famous painting by Raphael. Didn't you ever play Masterpiece?"

"Of course."

"What did you think?"

"Pretty random. Not much strategy. I tried to read the other players to figure out what their paintings were worth."

"I meant, what did you think of the painting?"

"Oh. I don't think I ever did. How did art appreciation creep into your numbers-soaked brain?"

"Art and mathematics are closely related. As are music and mathematics."

"All those overpriced Time Life books that used to clutter our bedroom were because of math?"

She didn't reply.

"Well, the painting looks good on the table. Classy. Like everything else here." He picked up her plate. "JL Coquet. Designed just for this restaurant. The silver is Paolo Viale."

She still stared at the print.

113

"Why do you find that so intriguing?"

"Compare it to the art at the other tables," Linden said.

"There is no art at the other tables." Pause. "Which is your point. Anything unusual about the painting?"

She nodded. "It's a great example of calculated perspective. Two parallel lines, not parallel to the plane of the primary image, creating a vanishing point. Perspective, you know, is all about mathematics." She pointed at the center of the painting. "The great Greek philosophers are here. The title doesn't refer to a particular college at a particular time. Raphael portrayed the entire body of knowledge known as philosophy. So we have all the greats together, even though they couldn't possibly have been in any one place at the same time. That's Plato and Aristotle being chummy as they chat their way through the center. Socrates stands beside them. Note the hemlock cup. Euclid is drawing a geometric shape with a compass. And Pythagoras—"

He lifted the print to catch the light. It was encased in protective plastic but not attached to the window. "Is that a blue dot on his hand?"

Linden took the print and squinted. "Looks like a blue star."

"I don't see a star."

"Told you to get laser keratotomy."

"Not letting anyone cut on my eyeballs, thank you very much. Is that star in the original painting?"

"I'm not sure. Hey—there's something on the back."

She flipped the print around. The back revealed a much darker work of art.

"More Raphael?" he asked.

"Far from it. Dürer. An etching. Also famous. Especially among math freaks." She pointed to the title at the bottom: *Melencolia I.*

"Fun. Is it too late to order Melencolia Two and Three?"

"Actually, that's an *I*, not a one. The *I* is short for *imagination*. He's referencing the work of a contemporary, Cornelius Agrippa, who divided melancholia into three categories. This is an illustration of *melancholia imaginativa*, which afflicts artists, philosophers, and scientists. Am I boring you?"

"No, I think it's sexy when you talk like the *Encyclopedia Britannica*."

"This etching is famous in the math world. For many reasons. Notice all the geometric references." She pointed to each as she described it. "See the compass, the protractor, the hammer, the drafting tools, all lying unused. Presumably because the subject, the grumpy angel, is suffering from melancholia—what we might call bipolar disorder. Not uncommon amongst artists and philosophers. Some have suggested that Dürer was a freemason, because the compass is a Masonic symbol, but that's absurd. The hourglass was a Masonic symbol, too, but not until the eighteenth century. This is the self-portrait of an artist and scholar experiencing the moods and depressions all geniuses suffer at one time or another."

"You're speaking from experience here?"

"I lived with you for fifteen years." She returned her attention to the etching. "The signs of depression are everywhere. In the hourglass, time is running out. The balance scales are empty. The rhombohedron is broken and bears the faint image of a human skull—a dead man."

"The angel is pouting."

"Yes, dear. The angel is pouting. But here's the most famous part of the image." She pointed to the upper right hand corner. "A magic square."

"Magic? Does it change iron into gold?"

"No. Some called it a Jupiter square, to avoid the suggestion of sorcery or alchemy. Point is, it uses all the numbers from one to sixteen, perfectly arranged so that each line, horizontal, vertical, or diagonal, adds up to the same number. Thirty-four."

"Neat. Is it good for anything?"

"No. But it's very cool."

"There are more letters and numbers at the bottom. What are they?"

BNF
GV1
229
B53
176

He squinted. He was beginning to wish he had gotten the laser keratotomy, though he would die before he'd admit it to her. These figures were arranged in a rectangle, this time three by five, but they did not appear to repeat or to add up to anything. Perhaps even more telling was the fact that they appeared to have been added to the print. Then he spotted another four by four square filled entirely with letters. He copied all the squares onto napkins.

"Curiouser and curiouser," she said. "Some of them are prime numbers—but not all. Two of them are Fibonacci numbers—but not all. Three of them are squares—but not all."

"Absolutely fascinating. But will it tell us how to save Kadey?"

"Hey, I collected the data. You're the puzzle boy. Maybe you should think about—"

"Got it."

She threw herself back into her red velvet chair. "Are you serious?"

"Yes."

"That is so irritating. Care to share your deductive trail?"

"You mean it isn't obvious?"

Her lips pursed. "No. What does it mean?"

"It means you're not getting the paté. Because we're leaving. Right now."

37

Chalcis Mausoleum
Samos, Greece

Julian could barely believe he was here.

The marble blocks forming the walls of the tomb seemed to radiate despite the near total darkness. The only source of light shone down from a single opening in the ceiling, illuminating the central icon encircled by ten robed attendants.

The image was an equilateral triangle marked with ten dots, each bearing one of the first ten numbers. The dots divided the larger triangle into many smaller ones, but a circle was superimposed over the center of the largest triangle. A tetractys.

At the north end of the vault, the leader of the assemblage stood on a raised marble block, left hand stretched toward the center. As his hand approached the light, the blue six-sided star tattooed on his palm glowed.

"What is the world?" he intoned.

"All is number," the ten replied in unison.

"Where do we find purity?"

"Numbers."

"Where do we find life?"

"Reason is immortal. All else is mortal."

"Where do we find reason?"

"By the power that gave us the tetractys, which contains the fount and root of ever-flowing nature."

"Where do numbers come from?"

"Paradise."

He watched as the leader stepped into the center of the tomb, careful to make no misstep. His recent encounter with the female emissary of the Other had given him the information he needed to find this location. It was a simple matter to fake credentials that ensured they would want him to be a member. That said, it worried him that he had been so swiftly admitted. He wanted to believe that fortune smiled on him, but experience told him that whenever something seemed too easy—

But no matter. He had his orders. And he would follow them. He would get the information the Father sought, regardless of the cost to him personally.

The hooded robes and the harshness of the overhead light obscured all facial recognition. He did not know who these people were.

But he knew *what* they were.

"We are gathered in the name of he who showed us the way, the truth, and the purity of the light. We are the *mathematikoi*. We are entrusted with the great secrets the outside world cannot know."

"*Mathematikoi*," the assemblage repeated.

"We will live as he lived, in a world of purity of our own making. We will make our bodies our sanctuaries. We will pursue the knowledge and purity of numbers."

The leader performed a series of hand gestures so quickly he could not read them. In general, he knew the purpose. Sign language for the mathematically inclined. Numbers instead of letters. The equivalent of a secret handshake.

"We practice a way of life that is pure, not dissipated, and guard against whatever incurs envy."

"Whatever incurs envy," they repeated.

"Purity strengthens the soul and helps us attain freedom from physicality. When you leave the body behind and attain to the free air, you will be an undying god, mortal no longer."

"Immortal. Like the number."

The leader's voice dropped abruptly. "What is the business of this conclave?"

"We have an acolyte, wizard." The man standing beside him, his sponsor, stepped forward. "A member of the *akousmatikoi*. A listener. Who wishes to become a learner."

"Has he met the challenges? Does he live as we chose to live?"

119

Julian cleared his throat. "I have abstained from all meats and beans. I have abjured all activities of the flesh. I did not stir the fire with iron or eat from the whole loaf. I did not eat the heart."

"That is good," the leader replied. "And what else?"

"I have told no one what I have learned while listening among you." They were all lies, especially the last one. But for the Father, he would say what he needed to say.

"Who speaks for this *akousmatikoi*?"

"We do." The answer resounded from the perimeter of the circle. He had expected one, hoped for a few others. Apparently he had made an even better impression during his interview than he expected.

"Very well. Then as it has been said, so it shall be granted. Reveal yourself."

He shed his robe. He was naked. He had shaved himself completely. No hair remained on his head or anywhere else. And his chest was alive with ink.

"Behold the secrets of the world which is not yet ready. Behold the purity of numbers. Behold paradise."

Most of the inductees, he knew, settled for a discreet tat on the side of a finger or the base of a foot. Most did not go so far as to shave their heads or eyebrows. This was intended to exemplify his dedication. To ensure his access to the information he wanted.

The centerpiece of the tattoo was the iconic right-angled triangle, with squares attached to each side, illustrating the famous theorem. Dancing around and about were other mathematical symbols, geometric shapes, and the tools of the mathematician and draftsman. The compass, the protractor, the Tsquare, the level, the lever, and many others. A magic square rested over his appendicitis scar.

"Impressive. You have learned well. There remains but one matter to be considered. What offering do you make?"

He knew this would be the most important part of the ceremony, if he hoped to succeed. He had to convince them. If he failed here, everything he had done, everything he had worked for, would be lost.

Silently, Julian walked to a perfect marble cube resting on the floor. He knelt before the cube and laid his hands upon it, fingers spread.

He saw the surprised reaction on the leader's face. With this gesture, he volunteered for the most extreme show of devotion possible. But he had to convince these people that he was one of them. No matter the cost.

Pain, however great, was fleeting. His devotion to the Father was eternal. He had often said he would do anything for the Father. Today he would prove it.

"When man first walked upon the earth," he recited, "he was without number or knowledge. He walked aimlessly in ignorance. Then he looked at his hands, and numbers were revealed to him."

"But man was imperfect," the leader responded, removing a medium-sized knife from his robe. He held the blade in the air, hovering over the smallest finger on Julian's left hand.

He continued. "Three is the trinity. Nine is the trinity cubed. Nine is perfection."

"Nine is perfection," the others intoned.

"Do you seek perfection?" the leader asked.

"We all seek perfection."

"Will you sacrifice for perfection?"

"I will sacrifice for perfection."

The leader's voice rose. "Will you sacrifice for purity?"

He hesitated only a moment before responding. "I will sacrifice for purity."

The leader slammed down the knife, cutting off his smallest finger with a single slice.

He fell backward. His head spun. He was overwhelmed with a sudden nausea.

The leader wrapped something around his finger to staunch the bleeding. Then the leader pressed a red-hot, ink-stained branding iron into his palm.

This time, he screamed. He smelled the aroma of burning flesh. His own flesh.

Consciousness waned, and he supposed it would be best not to resist. He didn't want to give them any idea how strong or resourceful he truly was. He was supposed to be a man of intellect, not a man of physical strength. He didn't want them to have any idea what he was capable of doing. Or why he was really here. Or where he was going next, just as quickly as he was able.

These people were determined to interfere with the Father's plans. That was unacceptable. They could do anything to this world they wanted. Just so they didn't disturb the next one.

38

Agent Palmer hated Paris. All the clichés were true. The locals were sullen and unfriendly. The food dripped with buttery calories. You couldn't get a soft drink with ice. There was no extradition treaty with the US. And worst of all, they insisted on speaking that funny language.

He flagged down a taxi and gave the driver his destination. He had dutifully checked in with local law enforcement upon arrival at de Gaulle. And received the predictable utmost lack of cooperation. The word *murder* did not seem to stir them at all, nor did *multiple disappearances*. And he wasn't allowed to use *threat to NATO security*.

After numerous phone conversations on both sides of the Atlantic, Palmer's boss, John Stetco, communed with his equal and opposite number at *la Sûreté*. That took time, because no one who ranked above him in the local hierarchy would deign to speak to Stetco, and Stetco wouldn't speak to anyone lower. So they had to find the police Goldilocks, the person who was just right.

Sometimes he wondered if law enforcement was filled with courageous right-minded people seeking justice or just a bunch of bitchy little girls.

Eventually someone managed to obtain clearance for Palmer to continue his investigation in France. He'd had to explain why he believed his quarry was headed for the Eiffel Tower.

One thing that smartass Game Master didn't know was that Palmer had every scrap of paper on every desk on the seventh floor photocopied before he arrived. So when BB selected one piece of paper to take, he knew it must be important. He found the copy. And eventually, they'd found someone smart enough to crack the code. Though not as quickly as BB undoubtedly had solved it.

Not much to go on. But it was all he had. BB was at the heart of this international mess. He didn't have all the details worked out yet. But he would. He'd be damned if he was going to be stumped by some egomaniacal poker player.

Thank goodness for MASINT—Measurement and Signature Intelligence. Only the feds had access in the US. MASINT instruments collected and analyzed the signatures of machinery emitting thermal energy, sound waves, velocity patterns, jet fuel exhausts—and helicopter rotor vibrations. It had allowed him to track BB's getaway copter. Not in time to prevent his escape, but in time to get an early lead on following him. Then he employed a combination of surveillance cameras and eyewitnesses to trace BB out of the dam area, into LA, and out of LAX. Never in time to stop him. But only a few steps behind.

The taxi cruised up to the curbside drop point for tourists visiting the Eiffel Tower. Palmer had one foot out the door when he spotted them.

Sunglasses? Really? Was BB's ego so large he thought a pair of glasses would disguise him?

He watched as BB and Linden jumped into a cab and sped away. Bingo.

He slid back into cab, closed the door, and—

How long had he secretly longed for a chance to say these words?

He tapped the cabbie on the shoulder. "Follow that car."

39

BB knew the Rue de Richelieu was one of the oldest streets in France. Beautiful, elegant, redolent with reminders of the Paris of another era. This was the part of the city that most visitors imagined when they heard the word *Paris*. Coin shops and currency changers abounded, but so did stone houses and elegant ornate balconies, flowers and fruit stands, street musicians. The Comédie-Française was here, and the Palais Royale, site of a residence that once belonged to the great puppet-master Cardinal Richelieu himself.

When the rue terminated in the *IIe arrondissement*, BB beheld one of the most beautiful sights in the city, one he thought surpassed even the Louvre.

The Bibliothèque Nationale. The greatest library in France. If not the modern world.

Their taxicab pulled up beside the post on the curb. BB paid the man and clambered out, Linden close behind. He led the way inside.

"Is there some reason you wouldn't tell me why we're coming here?" Linden asked. "Power trip? Thrill of the surprise? Hercule Poirot twitching his waxed moustache in the final act?"

"The taxi driver didn't need to know our business."

"The taxi driver didn't even speak English."

"Or so he wanted us to believe."

"Getting a little paranoid?"

"No. But I am getting the impression there's more going on here than we understand. And that other people are following the same clues we are. If we want to save Kadey, we need to stay ahead of everyone else."

They passed through the massive double doors into the library. The front lobby sparkled with a glistening panorama of marble tile, rococo fixtures, and gilt-framed paintings. A grand central staircase immediately drew the eye.

"Not too shabby," he murmured. "Designed by Jean-Louis Pascal. When this transitioned from royal library to public library during the first French Revolution."

Linden arched an eyebrow. "Have you been here before?"

"Yes. Research project. Wrote an article on the Siege of Paris."

"You wrote about military history?"

"The Siege of Paris is a game. Classic. Pivotal in the evolution of strategy games. Commemorates the 1870 siege and invasion of Paris by the Prussian General Moltke. The siege lasted months, destroying Parisian life and killing hundreds. So they memorialized it in a game. Go figure."

"Good game?"

"Chess variant popular in the eighteenth century. Sort of a precursor to Stratego. Many unique elements. Interesting, but too much advantage to the player who moves first. Uses a black and white board not unlike chess or checkers."

"We're not about to find a corpse on a parquet floor, are we?"

"I sincerely hope not. Excuse me."

He approached an older woman sitting at the central desk. "Steven Thomas. You'll find me on your list of authorized foreign nationals. Is that silk you're wearing?"

The woman's hands touched her scarf. She spoke English with a pronounced accent. "Yes. My late husband gave it to me."

"My mother had one just like it, God bless her soul. I think my father gave it to her."

Linden had to compel her eyes not to roll.

The woman smiled. "I wear it almost every day. Reminds me of him."

"Brings out the blue in your eyes." He smiled, started to move on, stopped. "Oh—we need a pass."

"Of course." She slid a plastic-coated library pass across the table.

He snatched it up. "*Merci beaucoup. Bonjour.*"

Linden followed him up the stairs. "She never actually looked to see if your name was on her list, did she?"

"Nope. And a darn good thing, too."

"You're lucky you got away with that."

"Not luck. Observation."

"I suppose you're going to claim you read her tell."

"That's only one form of observation. The tear on the back of her blouse that no one has told her about suggests that she lives alone. But she wears a ring. At her age, that suggests widowhood. And I could see she was lonely. Given that information, it wasn't hard to figure out the best way to obtain a pass."

"What if she had looked at her list?"

"My name would've changed. I've very good at reading upside-down."

They passed through two large open doors. The spacious main reading room was so immense he found it slightly dizzying. Flat reading tables stretched almost to infinity, one pushed up against the other, each accented with green-shaded desk lamps. A wide variety of scholars dotted the tables, immersed in their research. And around them, forming a perfect circle stretching from one side of the entry doors to the other, were the stacks. Floor to ceiling bookshelves, filled to capacity, topped with symmetrical arches and divided by blue-tinted columns. The shelves stretched upward for four flights. Light streamed in from the rose windows atop each arch.

"This library had more books than any in the world, until the twentieth century," he explained. "It's still in the top five. In the nineties, Mitterand built a larger fancier wing downtown. They call it the National Library of France. Most of the major collections were moved there. But some of the older books remained here at the Bibliothèque."

"I still don't know why you decided to come here."

"The first three letters in the grid on the etching. BNF. Bibliothèque Nationale de France."

"Okay. So now that we're here, what do we do?"

"What the message told us to do."

Linden glanced at the grid he'd copied. "Is it some kind of substitution code? A cryptogram? Another magic square?"

"Even simpler than that. Stenography in its best form."

"Sten—what?"

"Hiding something in plain sight. Like in *The Purloined Letter*. Make it so simple people miss the obvious."

Linden pursed her lips. "This sounds like a prelude to you explaining how stupid I am."

"I wouldn't have married you if you were stupid."

"Thank you."

"You're just unobservant." He pointed toward the shelves. "Look around. Don't you see it? They're everywhere."

Only a few moments passed before Linden's eyes closed with a wince. "Call numbers."

40

Ogilve tapped the LSAC transmitter, using the code that triggered its emergency response signal.

No reply.

Inexplicable. Julian was nothing if not dependable. The operative believed his debt required absolute fealty and unflagging devotion. He should know. He sculpted that mind to be exactly what he wanted it to be, with considerable care and expertise. He'd learned how it was done from one of the best.

Learned how to take a pure and guileless mind and manipulate it. Turn a free agent into a puppet. Reshape the world to your own ends.

Julian had proven his resourcefulness time and time again. The training in Russia he'd financed had paid off a thousand times over. Still, after that harrowing incident in Dubai, barely limping away from Chun's grasp at the last possible moment, he couldn't shake the feeling that some unforeseen disaster lurked around the corner.

He should have seen it coming. He should've realized that, even though Rani was poisoned, she was not immobile. Of course she would be self-sacrificing. Chun manipulated and controlled her. That entire debacle was one more reminder that his predictive power was imperfect. He needed an upgrade—and he needed it quickly.

He collapsed into his desk chair and gazed at the framed photograph just to the left of the monitor. This is for you, darling. Some men started foundations to honor a lost love. Some men built the Taj Mahal.

He chose to redesign the world. For Holly. And Lily. And all the others like them.

He removed his alligator loafers and stretched his legs under the desk. Fendi really did make the best shoes in the world, worth the price and then some, but after a long day his toes longed to breathe free.

He'd come far since the days of hand-me-down T-shirts and pre-stressed blue jeans. Sometimes he wondered if he'd lost something, left some essential part of his soul behind. The person he was meant to be.

Didn't matter. As a scientist, he didn't believe in destiny. The universe did not have a master plan any more than it had a master blueprint. The cosmos proceeded along natural paths and the only fate was the fate you created for yourself. Or for others.

He pulled the wireless keyboard for his desktop computer into his lap and pressed the transmit button. Although Alex was hundreds of miles away, they could still communicate. The encryption was impossible to break. And the speed was such that for all practical purposes he was right there in Egypt sitting at the primary console.

Game status.

One remaining player.

No surprise there. He'd anticipated that result early on, even without Alex's prognosticating assistance. *Anticipated arrival at office.*

Today. Dispatch agent to library.

He understood. He pulled out his phone and made the necessary arrangements. *Status of Other.*

Insufficient data. Continued interference certain.

Does Chun know where you are?

He will.

Anticipated arrival.

Unknown.

Before the player?

Unknown.

That could be a problem. He knew Chun would find him eventually. It was impossible to hide a power-intensive, billion-dollar enterprise forever, especially from a man with Chun's resources. *Immediate target of Other.*

A few seconds passed before the response appeared on the screen.

Supreme General.

He did a double take. He hadn't expected that response. Unfortunately, Alex didn't "show his work," as his calculus professor used to say. *Explain causation.*

Next phase of Other implementation requires greater resources. Geopolitical clout. Private army insufficient. More needed to pose international threat. Essential factors for coup present: poverty, hunger, political dissatisfaction. President preoccupied. Supreme General under attack.

Couldn't be clearer than that. *Impact on election?*

Significant. Defense insecurity favors incumbent administration. Need display of foreign policy acumen. Factors indicate civil unrest caused by disaffected extremists will lead to violent action in Manhattan.

Alex proceeded to list the most likely events. Though Alex could not precisely predict which fact pattern would occur, the result of all the scenarios was the same.

Fortune favored the prepared.

Additional factors influencing election.

Alex took a full five seconds before replying.

Strife in Middle East. Oil dependency. Economic debt. Chinese economic strength. Global depression. North Korean instability. American industry weak. Unemployment. Taxation. Avian flu. Ebola. Greenhouse effect. Climate change. Melting icecaps. Ozone layer. Japanese microcircuitry. German industrial growth. Plague. South American poverty. Hunger. Educational deficiencies in American South. Rain forest cancer cure. Population explosion. Economic turmoil makes international war inevitable.

Yes, he thought, clenching his teeth, we know all that. But more importantly—

Game objective achieved?

Cannot determine at present.

He pushed the keyboard out of his lap. So frustrating. But the reply was not surprising. He knew Alex's limitations better than anyone.

This new development in North Korea changed everything. He'd heard a ticking time bomb in the back of his mind for years now. The detonation just got a hell of a lot closer. Thank goodness the election was only a few days away.

The plan had to proceed. But faster. Everything was more important—and more urgent—than ever.

BB had no idea how important he was. He was the most important player in the game, possibly the most important player in the history of the world. Men would live or die—nations would rise or fall—based upon his actions. And the man had no clue.

BB would give him the edge he needed to fulfill his plan—but it would cost BB everything.

Well, Moses never got to enter the Promised Land either.

But the death of one egomaniacal game freak was a small price to pay when paradise hung in the balance.

41

B raced up the stairs to the third level of the Bibliotechque. Linden trailed behind him, scanning the labels on the end of each shelf.

"The cutters are wrong," he explained.

"That probably sounds more ominous than it is."

"Cutters. The first two letters in a call number should indicate a category. The second line—the cutter—narrows it to a smaller subdivision. These don't make any sense."

"This is France, BB. They're not using the Dewey Decimal System."

"No kidding. Do you know how much time I've spent in libraries? The French call number system is based on the US Library of Congress system, which is employed by most of the great libraries today." His eyes followed the labels on the shelves. "Here we are. These match." He scanned the spines of the books. "The cutter GV1 brings us to Games and Recreations. Why am I not surprised?"

He pulled the book with the matching call number from the shelf. *The Book of Games: Strategy, Tactics & History*, by John Botermans. He opened to the center. The thick, hardbound, and richly illustrated book appeared to provide details on some of the great board games throughout history. In English.

Linden looked over his shoulder. "But the last three digits aren't in the call number."

"Page number." He thumbed to the proper page. "The Siege of Paris. What do you know. Almost as if someone had read my article."

"So what do we do now? Does your pass give you checkout privileges?"

"This is a reading library. No one has checkout privileges."

"Then what do we do"

"Find a clue to where our daughter has been taken." He scanned the page. Seemed like a straight-forward explanation of the game. He had this book at home and considered it one of the best and most beautiful discussions of classic games throughout history. Though he still preferred his own work on the Siege of Paris.

He scanned the discussion. Siege was best played by three players, unlike chess and checkers. One player led the white army, one the black, and one defended the citadel—the squared-off area in the center of the board. The two armies lined up on either end of the board, much as in chess. The colored circles in the center indicated where the citadel defender could place his pieces. The lines connecting the circles indicated how they could move.

The rest of the rules seemed clear and correct. The illustrations showed how each piece moved . . .

Wait a minute.

"What is it?" Linden asked. "You've noticed something. I can tell from that high-on-myself look in your eyes."

"In this illustration. Something only someone familiar with the game would spot." He pointed to the picture in question. "Each piece has different rules governing movement, and they rules are different for attacking pieces than for defending pieces. For the defending army pieces, the general can move one square in any direction, like the king in chess."

General

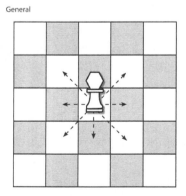

"The colonel can only move one square forward, never diagonally. Like a chess pawn, without the en passant."

Colonel

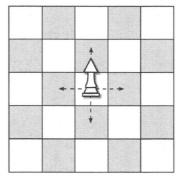

"And the soldier can only move one square at a time diagonally."

Soldier

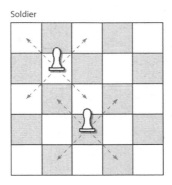

"No more than three soldiers can be on squares of the same color. Outside the citadel, a solider cannot move to a square of a different color. He must first return to the citadel—"

"I don't need a lecture on game mechanics. What's the point?"

"Look at the illustration at the bottom of the page. See how the arrow indicates the movement of the general?"

"Yeah. Three squares up or—" She stopped short. "But the general can only move one square at a time."

"Exactly." He moistened his fingertip, then lightly rubbed the blue arrow indicating the general's movement. It came off.

"Someone added that."

"For us to find."

"But what's the point?"

135

"To tell us where to go next, of course." He replaced the book on the shelf. "Let's get out of here."

"No, first you explain."

He felt a buzz in his pocket. He pulled out his phone and checked the countdown.

Only sixty-one hours left, the readout said.

Accompanied by a new photo of Kadey, looking even more desperate than before. Eyes wide and pleading. Begging him to come save her.

He could hear her voice thundering inside his head. Help me, Daddy. This time. *Help me.*

"We'll talk later. Come on." He turned toward the stairs—then froze.

"What is it?"

He nodded toward the lower level. "See any familiar faces?"

"Damn."

Agent Palmer stood on the floor below, between the reading tables.

He pushed Linden back . . .

But not quickly enough. Palmer spotted them.

He grabbed Linden's hand. "Run."

42

Palmer watched them bolt. He turned left and ran toward the side stairs between the floor-to-ceiling book stacks.

"Police," he shouted, then realized he was speaking the wrong language. Should he shout *Sûreté? Gendarme?* Perhaps the scholars in attendance had seen enough American films to grasp the meaning without translation. People were getting out of his way.

Except one. Palmer barreled around the end of the row of tables but did not see the large bespectacled man carrying a tall stack of books. At least not in time. They collided with a powerful and audible impact. Both dropped to the floor. Paper flew everywhere. Books rained down upon them. One hit Palmer in the head. It hurt.

He could see the report already. "Agent fatally injured by art history book." No, he did not want that to be the last line in his file.

He scrambled back to his feet and headed toward the stairs. Above him, he saw that BB and Linden had descended to the second level. If he took the stairs, he'd lose them.

Each of the bottom tier of shelves had gold-handled ladders to allow access to the top shelves. Palmer leaped onto the fourth rung of the nearest ladder and jumped. He grabbed the guardrail on the second level and demonstrated why he started each day with 105 sit-ups.

He swung his feet and locked them on the second floor ledge. He'd made it to the second level in fewer than five seconds.

And he was just twenty seconds away from BB and Linden.

"Stop!" he shouted, knowing perfectly well they would not. And it didn't matter. He'd just vaulted an entire library floor. He could catch a freaking poker player, not to mention his wife.

This time he had them.

43

"Hurry!"

BB pushed Linden forward so hard she almost tripped. He knew Palmer was right behind them, but the thin balcony beside the bookshelves, narrow and clogged with people and unshelved books, made it impossible to run.

He caught a glimpse inside Palmer's jacket while the man did his Spider-Man act. Palmer was packing a gun. In France, even *la Sûreté* did not carry guns.

If Palmer got them, it was Game Over. He would haul them back to the States, or at the least incarcerate them locally, and they would never find Kadey. And if they didn't, who would? Did any FBI agent know the rules to an eighteenth-century strategy game about the siege of Paris? Not likely.

He had to remain free. For Kadey's sake.

He turned and ran back toward Palmer, still hanging from the guardrail.

"What are you doing?" Linden screamed.

He grabbed a book and slammed it down on Palmer's hands. Palmer winced but did not let go of the guardrail. He pounded again, this time even harder. Palmer shuffled his hands. He slammed the book down again. But Palmer did not let go.

Tough bastard. He hated to get nasty, but he didn't see that he had any choice.

He kicked Palmer's foot off the guardrail. The agent fell sideways, his chin banging against the guardrail.

A moment later, he reared back his foot and kicked Palmer through the ornate cast-iron decoration. His foot connected with the soft part of Palmer's gut. He could see the man hurt, but he was still too stubborn to let go. Palmer would probably die of internal bleeding before he would let go.

Even though he had nothing beneath his feet, Palmer managed to pull his head over the top rail. Impressive. But unacceptable.

He reached into Palmer's jacket. The agent had no hand free to stop him. He removed Palmer's lighter.

"Don't do it," Palmer grunted.

"Sorry. No choice." He flicked the lid and lit the flame. Then he held it next to Palmer's left hand.

"You're defacing architecture that goes back centuries," Palmer grunted.

"Yes."

"You could catch the whole building on fire. The Bibliothèque could go up like the library in Alexandria."

"I think you'll let go before then." He hoped. But down on the ground floor, he saw three uniformed men enter the library. Their blue uniforms, gold buttons, and flat peaked hats told him they were gendarmes.

A librarian pointed upward. The gendarmes ran toward him.

They did not have much time.

Palmer's flesh blackened. BB pressed the lighter all the way down on the man's hand. His flesh began to bubble. It made a sickening popping sound.

Palmer still wouldn't scream. But he did finally let go.

Palmer tumbled to the ground floor with a clatter, taking the ladder with him. Books tumbled down upon him. People screamed and moved away as quickly as they could. The gendarmes raced to his side.

He grabbed Linden's arm. "Go."

44

Palmer cursed under his breath. Another reason to hate France. Their stupid libraries with their stupid little ladders.

He scrambled to his feet. A little too quickly. The room spun around him. His head hurt and his hand burned and he'd twisted an ankle in the fall.

But he still wouldn't let that damn poker player get away from him.

Hobbling on one foot, careful not to put too much weight on the damaged ankle, he sped toward the far north side of the reading room. The gendarmes tried to talk to him, but he flashed a badge and pushed them out of his way.

He'd checked the schematics of the building during the cab ride. BB would undoubtedly try to escape down one of the rear service staircases used for hauling books to the upper level shelves. From the ground floor he could escape through the rear exit. But he would have to backtrack. Palmer couldn't get there first, but he still might be able to stop him before he escaped.

If the library security staff didn't get in his way. Someone in what looked like the uniform of a museum security agent intercepted his path.

"Monsieur, *pardonnez*—"

Palmer ripped out his badge. "FBI. On detached service with the Sûreté. Move."

The library agent drank it in quickly. "But monsieur—"

"Get out of my way."

"But monsieur—"

He shoved the security agent back, hard. The man fell to the floor. A woman nearby gasped. The gendarmes rushed toward him, shouting words in that silly language he didn't understand.

Good thing those boys don't carry guns, he thought.

Yes, he would undoubtedly pay for this. But he didn't have time to waste. And he'd rather explain his actions later knowing BB was under lock and key. They wouldn't take extreme action. They thought they were chasing some low-level jerk who disturbed the peace in a public library.

He pushed through the stacks to the rear corridor, the service entrance for book transportation. This corridor would take him to the north side exit. A large flatbed pushcart rested in the hallway unattended.

He shoved off the books, pushed it like a scooter, then jumped on board.

Sprained ankle or not, he would head them off at the pass.

45

B B pulled Linden around the corner. He spotted a rear stairwell. They raced down, taking the steps three at a time, as fast as he could without falling on his face. Once they reached the ground level, they hung a sharp left and entered a service corridor.

Must be an exit around here, he mused. The books had to come in somewhere, and it wasn't through the front door.

"I think I see the way out. Probably a loading dock."

"And then what do we do?" Linden asked, huffing hard. "Hijack a truck?"

"We'll work on that when we get there."

"Why do I think this plan of yours was not brilliantly thought through?"

"Why do I think you like to complain?" He rounded another corner. "Oh yeah. Because you do."

He pumped his thighs full throttle. He'd been working with a personal trainer the past year. He was convinced that a strong body meant a strong mind, and he was determined to have the strongest mind on earth. Hadn't foreseen the possibility of library sprinting. But it proved the value of being prepared.

He reached the exit door.

Locked.

He pulled harder, clanging the handle, rattling it back and forth. Nothing. He threw himself against it. Didn't even give.

"This is bad."

"What do we do now?" Linden asked.

And at that moment, a pushcart at the far end of the hall rounded the corner and came barreling toward them.

Palmer steered the ride.

"Don't go through that door!" Palmer pulled his gun. "Freeze!"

He pushed harder on the door handle. No movement at all.
Palmer fired.

The bullet ricocheted somewhere above their heads.

"Next one hits the target, BB," Palmer shouted, speeding toward them. "I'm a very good shot."

"You want us alive," he shouted back.

"So I won't hit a vital organ."

"I have to find my daughter."

"Then you shouldn't have run."

"I'm the only one who can do it."

The cart screeched to a halt. "Don't move."

He gave the door another shove.

It opened.

An elderly man stood on the other side. "You should leave now if you care to live."

He leaped through the door, dragging Linden behind him. Palmer fired. The stranger locked the door from the outside with a key.

The gun fired again. The bullets put bulges in the metal door, but did not penetrate.

"We don't have much time," the man said with a British accent. "It won't take him long to shoot through that door."

"How do I know we can trust you?"

The man appeared irritated and impatient. He moved toward the driver's side of the sedan as he talked. "I believe your current options are rather limited."

BB hesitated.

"You can't find Kadey behind bars," Linden said. "If we don't get in that car—you're out of the game."

The elderly man gestured toward the backseat.

He glanced at the countdown on his cell phone.

They piled into the car and roared out onto the Ile de Richelieu.

46

Rani took a seat at the furthest table at the sidewalk café on the Rue de Porthos. The man in the opposite chair read today's *Le Monde*. The paper obscured his face.

Her smooth face and sculpted nose gave her a profile she knew caught men's eyes. Perhaps even the kind of profile that would cause some men to fail to exercise their best judgment.

She adjusted herself in the chair to avoid the eyes that had followed her since she entered the café. She did not want to attract attention. Except from the man she was here to see.

"How was your flight?" Chun's voice came from the other side of the newspaper.

"Adequate." She paused. "Is everything as it should be?"

"Confirmed."

"Reactions to the developments yesterday with General Yoon?"

"As expected."

"What about Ogilve?"

"He has no clue."

"He did in Dubai."

"His crystal ball has a limited range. And he has not had time to remedy the problem."

"Why are you two old foes doing this?"

"Ogilve seeks the final element necessary to complete his plans. I seek to rearrange the map. We are like chess grandmasters, each repeatedly jumping a few moves ahead of the other. And every time a piece moves, the playing field changes. No one stays ahead for long. And no one achieves their goal."

"Until someone does."

"Yes. Until someone does."

She could not miss the insinuative tone of his voice. Given what had happened recently in Pyongyang, his meaning could not be misunderstood.

"Tell me about Nevada. Your sister."

She bowed her head. "I am . . . sorry. She failed. Though I trained her myself. Though her command of ancient weaponry is unparalleled."

"There is no shame in this. Julian trained in Russia for more than a year. Perhaps she should consider more modern tactics."

"I thought—to preserve the Order—"

"I understand. But next time, she might pack a pistol, just in case."

"That is so noisy—"

"A stiletto then. As you do."

She knew her cheeks reddened and it embarrassed her. "Why do they need this Game Master?"

"I can only speculate. But I am sure it relates to Ogilve's ongoing efforts to thwart my new world order."

"But you would bring—"

He raised a hand from the paper, stopping her. "His hatred goes far back, and to be fair, is understandable." His eyes dropped for a moment. "I too have experienced the insidious means by which hardship can derange a man's logic. Ogilve does not think rationally and has not for some time." He turned a page in the paper. "And you say the game now continues here in Paris?"

"Yes. They were spotted at the Tower."

"Good. Watch them. See where the game takes him. With luck, he may lead me to Ogilve. To the location we have sought for so long."

"Of course."

"You will follow my instructions to the letter, understood? I am quite fond of you. It would grieve me to have to kill you."

"How could you even—"

"Lower your voice. Look away occasionally. Do not appear so . . . intense."

"I am speaking in whispers. No one can see my face."

"My dear Rani. Your face is not what the men in this café are staring at."

She flushed again, a reaction that infuriated her. She was a highly skilled, trained operations professional. She resented his ability to diminish her. To make her feel as if she were a foolish schoolgirl. If she didn't love him so much, she would deeply resent him. In fact, she did.

"Listen to me," she said. "I have done what was asked of me. I joined Neopolis. I consorted with the most vile people on the face of the earth."

"Rather an uppity attitude, coming from a Pakistani dictator's lickspittle."

She needed every ounce of restraint she possessed to keep from ripping his throat out with her bare hands.

"Excuse me. Can I get you something?"

Rani froze.

A waiter hovered over her right shoulder. "Sorry. I did not notice that you had joined the monsieur. What would you like?"

"Campari and orange juice."

"Of course. Is there anything else I can do for you?"

His tone suggested flirtation, despite the fact that he was at least ten years her junior. What was it about Western men? Why did they think every creature with two X chromosomes existed solely for their sexual pleasure? "No, just the—"

"It's a lovely day. And did you know there is a Renoir exhibition in—"

"Just the drink. Thank you."

The waiter skittered away. She turned back toward the newspaper. "I will do as we agreed. But I expect to be fully supported. I will not be hung out to dry. I need to know that you have my back. That you will protect me, if necessary." No response. "Do you understand me?"

The wind rustled the pages of the newspaper.

"*Do you understand me?*"

Slowly, he lowered the newspaper, and she stared into Chun's pocked face.

"Do you understand *me?*" He grabbed her by the back of the neck and raised a hand as if to strike her, stopping only inches from her beautiful face. "Not while we are in public. But later."

"You—you hate me."

"I adore you. That is why I so willingly give you what you want. What you need."

She turned her head away.

"Tonight I will claim what is mine. But for now—" His eyes narrowed. "Do as you are told."

"I . . . will."

"Good." She heard a buzzing sound from the breast pocket of his uniform.

He withdrew his cell phone and glanced at the screen. "You watch the Game Master. The endgame has now begun."

47

In the side mirror of the sedan, BB watched Palmer blast his way through the rear door. The agent looked angry enough to explode. A few seconds later, they were so far away he couldn't see the library at all.

Linden appeared rattled, but safe. He buckled his seatbelt.

Judging from the driver's accent and appearance, he was from the English upper crust. Judging from his age, he didn't normally spend his days arranging getaways.

"Care to tell me why you just saved us?"

"My employer does not wish for you to be apprehended by the authorities."

Intriguing. "If you want, you can drop us at our hotel."

"Those are not my instructions."

Beside him, he saw Linden's shoulders tense. "Where are you taking us?"

"To a private rendezvous." He seemed to be driving much faster than necessary. And heading toward the Champs Élysées.

"Sounds delightful," Linden said. "But I need a nap. And perhaps a glass of Chardonnay. Perhaps an entire bottle."

"I'm afraid I have different instructions, mademoiselle."

He eyed the man carefully, reading his face, his body language. Taut, erect posture. Crisp, no-nonsense conversation. Accustomed to taking instructions and fulfilling them. Wearing a jacket that zipped down the front, half-open. He was packing. Ex-military?

No. Spy. Or some sort of intelligence operative. But for whom?

"What if we don't care to come to this meeting?"

The driver did not attempt to threaten. There was no need. "I have my instructions."

He considered his options. He could throw the stick shift into park.

Risky. Possibly deadly.

He could attack the driver, try to grab his gun.

Risky. And stupid.

Or he could go along with this and see what was up.

Very risky.

Unless they were going where he thought they were going. Which was exactly where he planned to go next anyway. But this was not the time. Or the way. He wouldn't learn anything if he were supervised the entire time.

Linden broke the silence. "Who are we supposed to meet?"

The driver responded. "I am not authorized to answer that question at this time, mademoiselle."

"How did your employer know we would be at the library?"

Silence.

"You're not authorized to say?"

"Truth is, mademoiselle, I do not know. I'm just following instructions."

"I don't see the point of all this mystery."

"I think I do," BB said, interrupting them. "Your employer has a dramatic streak, doesn't he?"

No reaction. Except perhaps the tiniest trace of a smile.

Linden sat back, arms folded. "I'd still like to know what this is all about. Wouldn't you?"

"I already do." He glanced at the driver. "We're going to see the person who's been leading us on this merry chase, aren't we?"

No response. The driver was good at hiding his tells.

He lowered his voice. "So the question, Linden, is do we go along with this ride, or do we follow the clue we got at the Bibliothèque."

"Which is?"

He shrugged. The magician doesn't reveal his secrets. At least not until he must. "We've got to find Kadey soon or she's dead. And I think that means no social calls. Not even to the employer of the guy who snatched us from Palmer's grasp."

"I think our rescuer has plans for us."

"But following this cryptic trail of bread crumbs is the only hope we have of finding Kadey."

"You know," Linden said quietly, "the last time this happened—"

"I don't want to talk about it," he snapped.

She hesitated. "The last time—you did too little. Don't overcompensate by doing too much. If we get derailed, we won't get to her in time. They'll kill her."

He turned his head, his eyes suddenly watery. "Do you think I don't know that?" He glanced out the window. They sped down the Champs Élysées, only a few moments from the Arc de Triomphe. "But I think that means we must take charge of the situation. Make our own choices. Even if they're unpleasant ones. Starting right now."

"What did you have in mind?"

The driver took a hard left into the rotary surrounding the Arch, much too fast.

He popped open the door. "Jump."

48

Javits Center
New York City

Republican nominee Robert Vogel stepped onto the dais. No applause followed.

He felt an aching in his chest that bordered on the unbearable.

True, the candidates' representatives agreed beforehand that there would be no applause. No cheers, no boos, no laughter. The audience was carefully selected by the League of Women Voters from a pool of persons who claimed to be undecided. The so-called swing voters. Those who would decide the election, currently almost a dead heat in the polls. So there was no reason to believe they favored or disfavored him. No reason to expect to be greeted with applause.

That did not stop him from missing it. A constant craving must be fed.

He was up almost three points. But it still wasn't enough. It never seemed to be enough.

"And on your left, the Democratic candidate, Vice President Norman Beale."

The two men met in the center of the stage, smiled their fake little smiles, and shook hands. Beale towered over him by almost a foot, and he played that for all it was worth. Even wore thick-heeled shoes. Beale's broad chest and Baptist church handshake exuded confidence. Beale no doubt planned to swallow him up and eat him for breakfast. The vice president knew he had to regain lost ground while there was till time.

Beale was in for a surprise.

Almost on cue, they both turned to the crowd and offered the media-advisor-approved, one-arm-straight-up-in-the-air wave. A barrage of flashes illuminated the stage, almost blinding him. The three cameras swung from one end of the stage to the other.

The two men took their positions behind their respective podiums. How he liked the comfort of having something to stand behind. Much better than that town-meeting idiocy.

The moderator, the NBC anchor, clicked his index cards on the table in a tidy stack, then adjusted his tie. The man had terrible OCD issues, but he could run a debate without overtly taking sides, and that was all they cared about at this juncture.

"This is the third and final presidential debate, sponsored by the League of Women Voters. The candidates' representatives met in advance and agreed upon the procedures and format we will follow. Each candidate will alternate answering first. Initial responses will be limited to two minutes, with each candidate allowed a one-minute rebuttal at his discretion. The first question—"

"*Is est pro Ambiorix!*"

The unamplified cry nonetheless filled the medium-sized auditorium. Heads spun. Spectators rustled out of their seats.

He scanned the auditorium, but the stage lights made it almost impossible to gain a clear view. The Secret Service had implemented exhaustive security measures, so no one expected any trouble, but—

"*Nex ut puppet praesieo!*"

A second later, he heard a quieter but more frightening cry: "He's got a gun."

Someone raced down the nave of the auditorium, sprang off the moderator's desk, and bounced onto the small pit at the foot of the stage. He held a gun at arm's length and swung it in a wide looping arc.

The next five seconds seemed like five days.

Out the corner of his eye, Vogel saw Beale leave his podium and jump off the edge of the stage. Beale's wife left her front-row seat and ran toward him.

But Vogel moved *toward* the assassin.

The assassin's gun swung between the candidates, never stopping.

The crowd panicked. Deafening screams punctured the air. People pushed out of their seats, desperately moving away from the gunman.

Just as the gun swung their way, Beale's wife threw herself into her husband's arms. Beale did not see her. Beale was staring at the gun.

Beale wet his pants.

At the same time, Vogel raced across the stage, a stern expression on his face, a commanding tone to his voice. "Drop your weapon!"

The crowd tumbled across the aisles. No one could escape. The moderator skittered away from his desk, tripped, then fell prostrate on the floor, his face the picture of abject panic.

The gun was pointed at Beale's forehead.

Beale ducked behind his wife.

The gunman pulled the trigger.

Vogel pounced, tackling the assassin, knocking the gun out of his hand.

The bullet sailed over Beale's wife's head, pierced an American flag, and bore into the wall.

Vogel wrestled with the shooter, pinning him down with one hand.

Secret Service officers converged. They grabbed the assailant, thrust him face first to the carpet, and cuffed his hands behind his back.

Reporters converged. He heard very little of it. The adrenaline rush muddled his brain. All he was certain about was that he frequently heard the word *hero*.

He liked the sound of that very much.

Vogel was disappointed to see that he was not featured in an above-the-fold photograph on the cover of *USA Today*. That went to his worthy opponent.

The photo showed Beale cowering behind his wife's red dress, his pants stained.

That would do.

He vividly recalled the first time Ogilve had spoken to him, after virtually kidnapping him at that third-rate Iowa hotel. His Secret Service detail had disappeared and he was terrified. Could he have imagined how much his life was about to change? Or what Ogilve meant when he said they were about to change the course of the future?

"I don't understand," Vogel had said, so long ago. "What is it you want?"

Ogilve gestured toward the empty chair on the other side of his desk.

Even though he didn't want to, he sat.

"The more important question, Senator, is what you want."

"I—I don't think you kidnapped me just so you could grant me three wishes."

"You are incorrect. I've come to give you exactly what your heart most desires."

"And what would that be?"

"The presidency of the United States."

He'd pulled himself up straight, trying to evince the strength he didn't feel. "And you can deliver that to me. Like a Christmas present. Wrapped up with a bow."

"Exactly."

"What are you, some kind of marketing guru?"

"No."

"Campaign expert?"

"Never worked on one."

"Financier?"

"No. Better things than politics to spend my money on."

"Then how are you going to give me the presidency?"

"With this." Ogilve slid a flat manila envelope across his desk. "This is the speech you're going to deliver tonight to the Dallas Chamber of Commerce."

"I already have a speech."

"I know. I hacked into your laptop and read it this morning. It sucks. Nothing personal, but it's full of trite catch phrases that don't mean anything. Vague promises. Banal half-truths. The speech of a fourth-place contender. Which is exactly what you are, at the moment." Ogilve patted the envelope. "This is how you win."

He found it hard to take his eyes off the envelope. "How can you be so sure?"

"I've become very good at predictions."

"What, you read tea leaves?"

"Something even better."

"And you see me winning?"

"I see the possibility. But only if you follow instructions. This speech will touch on the primary issue of concern to the undecided demographic most likely to swing the Republican party in the next election, an issue that never appears on polls because it is subtle and subconscious, but far more important to these voters than the usual talking points. Once you've appealed to that secret majority, your rankings will increase overnight. Cable news commentators will call you viable. Big money PACs will find you attractive. Water-cooler buzz will gravitate your way. By the time the convention arrives, you'll be the surprise victor by a significant margin."

"And this critical but secret issue is—?"

"That would be telling."

"Thanks, but I think I can get to the White House on my own."

"Actually, you can't. I've worked out every possible scenario. And in each one, you lose. Indeed, in each one, you're hammered. Trounced. Humiliated." He peered across the desk. "Surely you can feel that already. Deep in your gut, where the flop sweat already oozes. You always knew you'd fail. You knew you didn't have what it takes. But you don't have to." He shoved the envelope forward again. "Your father was wrong about you. I can make you a winner. And isn't that what you've always wanted? Isn't that how you put the final nail in that old asshole's coffin? By becoming the president of the United States?"

"What do I have to give you to get this magic envelope? My immortal soul? Signed over in blood?"

"All I will ever ask is that, once you're president, you make a few critical decisions in the manner that I indicate. That's all."

"And if I don't?"

"It's your choice." He smiled. "Do you want to be president or not?"

His hands trembled as he unsealed the envelope.

Vogel stepped before the throng of reporters attending the impromptu post-assassination-attempt press conference. The Secret Service was still trying to determine how the would-be assassin, Frank

Boulder, a Latin teacher from a Wichita high school, got into the auditorium, much less with a gun. Conspiracy theories floated all over the Internet. But all anyone knew for certain was that Beale had freaked, wet himself, and used his wife as a human shield. Vogel had strode forward like a hero and brought the assassin to his knees.

This time, he didn't even have to hear the applause to know it existed.

"I just have a few preliminary words. I'm grateful that no one was hurt. I'm optimistic that the troubled soul who broke into the Javits Center will receive the treatment he so clearly needs, and that his family will not be subjected to unnecessary heartache or shame. We are none of us perfect. We need to bind together during difficult times, not split apart."

The first time he took a breath, a thousand hands shot into the air.

"Senator, is it true that President Fernandez is considering awarding you the Presidential Medal of Valor?"

"I've heard nothing of this. That would certainly be unprecedented. A sitting president giving a medal to someone who's currently after his job?" The reporters laughed. "And a candidate from the other party no less. I'm not holding my breath."

He said. Even though he knew it would happen.

"Sir, can you provide an explanation for your rapid response to the threat? Most people present had barely processed the existence of a threat. You brought the man to his knees in fewer than five seconds."

"I've been blessed with fast reflexes." He paused, adopting a more somber tone. "There were a lot of people in that auditorium, Helen. Women, even children. I couldn't let anyone get hurt."

"Did you see him coming? Did something tip you off?"

"No. I guess you could say I've got an early warning system burned into my brain."

Another hand shot up. "Polls are now showing you as the front-runner and the election is only two days away. Are you surprised?"

"I'm excited. For the future."

But surprised? No.

49

Julian knew something was about to happen.

He could feel the buzz. He could hear his fellow Pythagoreans whispering. He could see the furtive movements, just out of sight. Unfortunately, that wasn't particularly useful intel. He'd infiltrated this group, even given up a finger, so he could learn something useful.

And so far, he had nothing. Nothing except a mutilated hand and a bright blue star-shaped tattoo. Sure, he'd only been a member for a short time, but he'd hoped they would be more trusting. And talkative.

He was an experienced intelligence operative, but this assignment was tricky, and not just because he didn't speak Greek. Many of the scientists in this facility spoke other languages, at least eight that he recognized. They came from all around the world. They had their own bedroom and work facilities. The only time they were all together was during meals in the cafeteria. He had been told that there were occasionally evening ceremonies, but none had occurred since he was inducted into the *mathematikoi*.

He still did not know the name of the man he had come to know as the Leader, the man who seemed to run this operation, at least locally. But he tried to talk to him whenever possible. He found it easier to take the man seriously when he was out of the robes.

"Looks like we're on the move," Julian said casually over a cafeteria tray.

The Leader smiled. "This place is always on the move. People come and go. It's the nature of the beast. They have their own lives and work back home, and regardless of what excuse they're using to explain their absence, they can't be gone too long without arousing suspicion."

"And we don't want that."

"No. Especially now."

"Why now?" he said as casually as he could manage.

The Leader allowed himself a small smile. "Be patient. You've been accepted into our fold, but you can't expect us to reveal all our secrets the first week."

"Of course not. I was just . . . wondering if there was some way I could help."

The Leader nodded. "Ever been to North Korea?"

"Can't say that I have. Didn't know Americans were allowed to go."

"They're allowed. They're actually trying to encourage tourism. Desperate for foreign dollars."

"And that's where you're headed?"

The Leader nodded.

"I've been to Russia," Julian commented.

"What were you doing there?"

Normally, when he worked undercover, he kept his lies to a minimum. Only fibbed when necessary. When you started telling gratuitous falsehoods, before long you couldn't remember everything you'd fabricated. This was an instance, however, when he would have to lie.

"Cold fusion research. Worked with a team from the LVB. Thought it was promising. Didn't work out, though."

"Pity. What our Order could do with that. How long were you there?"

"Almost a year. Not the same as Korea. But equally unfriendly. At least when I was there. So if I can help—"

"Was your work in weaponry?" the Leader said, cutting him off.

"No. Generalized scientific research."

"Then you probably won't be called. No worries. Your time will come. In the meantime, remember—don't eat the beans."

He grinned back. "I didn't see any."

"And you never will."

That exchange was not nearly as helpful as he had hoped. But he had heard at least two words of interest: *North Korea.*

That meant Chun was on the move, in all likelihood.

And there was that other word. *Weaponry.*

Not surprising, under the circumstances.

He thought about tapping his LSAC and conveying this to the Father, but he decided not to take the risk. He'd make some excuse later to go off campus.

If Chun was initiating a major gambit, the Father needed to know. Since he was setting up an endgame of his own.

The final conflict was approaching faster than anyone had imagined.

50

"Could you drive a little faster?" BB asked.

"Still don't see why we're doing this at two in the morning," Linden grumbled.

"Because we don't want to be seen."

"Yes, I know you hate attention. That's why we jumped out of a racing car on the busiest street in the world."

"We survived, didn't we? I'd jump out of an airplane if it saved Kadey."

"But why are we here?" She parked the rental Versa in the office lot. They headed toward the front door.

"Don't you see? The illustration of The Siege of Paris. It was wrong."

"Because the general moved three squares instead of one."

"Exactly. Now think that through in your head. General three squares. General three squares."

Linden's lips parted. "Gen3$^{2.}$"

"Exactly. Ogilve's company. Which coincidentally has an office here in Paris."

They found the office on a side street just off the *Champs Elysses*. He was surprised to see there was still a fair amount of pedestrian and automobile traffic, even at this hour. City of Lights, yes, but did they never turn them off? Made it harder to avoid notice. At the same time, he suspected they might actually be less obtrusive because they were not the only people in sight.

They had spent almost an hour deciding how they should dress for this operation. Linden favored all-black. He thought that if they dressed in all-black they might as well wear serial numbers around their necks.

They settled for dark sweaters and blue jeans.

The lobby door was open, but the stairwell door was locked and the elevator button did not respond. He approached what looked like a small ATM.

"No guard in the office," he noted. He touched the Start button on the screen. A green cursor lit up on a digital LED display.

"I suppose I don't need to tell you that if you get this wrong, you'll probably set off a silent alarm and we'll have the *Surete* breathing down our necks in about ten seconds."

"The thought did occur."

"But the Great and Powerful Game Master thinks he knows all."

"Well, the Game Master thinks he has solved the puzzle."

"Duck!" Linden yanked him away from the terminal and into the shadows. He held his breath. A moment later, a uniformed gendarme passed by on the street, visible through the front doors. The officer glanced into the lobby.

"Move on," he muttered. How would he explain what they were doing here this time of night?

The gendarme shone a flashlight through the glass panes. He slowly moved it across in a broad arc.

"If the cop comes in," Linden breathed into his ear, "you grabbed me and held me here against my will."

"So I'll do time in a foreign prison for kidnapping?"

"Yes. But I'll be free."

"Very thoughtful. But since I'm the only one who can solve the puzzles, you take the dive. I'll visit you often. Really."

The gendarme stepped closer to the glass, pressing his free hand against it. Eventually he moved on.

"What was that all about?"

"Cop must've heard something," Linden replied.

"Or seen something." He returned to the display and touched it again. The green cursor lit.

"So how can you be sure you know the entry code?"

"Did you notice, as I moved the cursor across the screen, that there is only room for sixteen entries?"

"No."

"Did you notice that the numeric keypad contains letters and numbers on the buttons, like an old school telephone?"

"So?"

"Most of these digital security panels only accept numbers."

"We really don't have time for your Ellery Queen routine. How did you get the code?"

"Got it back at the Tower. Remember the Durer etching at the restaurant? Remember the two magic squares? One with all the numbers from one to—"

"Sixteen."

"Exactly. So that each side added up to thirty-four. Here. I copied it down on a napkin."

Linden took the napkin and examined it. "Okay. So?"

"The second magic square contained letters. I copied it onto another napkin."

Linden peered at it. "But this isn't really a magic square. Letters don't add up to anything."

"Obviously you haven't played Scrabble enough. Anytime I see letters that don't spell anything, I rearrange them until they do."

Linden tucked in her chin. "It's…some kind of message? A cryptogram? Letter substitution code?"

"Good ideas. But wrong."

"Computer code?"

"Excellent guess, given our background."

"But, I can tell from your patronizing expression, not correct."

"True."

"Anagram?"

"Sort of. Try looking at each letter in the order of the numbers in the other square. In other words, look at the letter in the box numbered one, then the box numbered two, and so forth."

"Okay. P, L, A, Y. That's a word. Play."

"Very good." He tapped the letters into the terminal. "Keep going."

"R, I, T, H, M…ok, we're in trouble."

"Why?"

"It's not a word."

"Not yet."

"There's no word that begins R-I-T-H-M."

"There is."

"If you think that spells rhythm, you really have been cheating at those Scrabble tournaments."

"Keep giving me the letters."

"O-M-A-C-H-I-A."

He punched in the final letters. An instant later, a light appeared on the panel. He heard a click.

The stairwell door was opened.

"It's two words," he explained. "Play Rithmomachia." He took her arm and tugged her toward the door.

"Don't tell me. It's some kind of board game?"

"The greatest game of them all."

They started up the stairs. He arrived at the top floor and opened the door. A few moments later they were in Ogilve's office. To avoid detection, he kept the lights off, but used a small flashlight he'd brought in his pack.

The office occupied the entire fifth floor. He wasn't sure if this made it a penthouse office. He knew Paris had height restrictions to prevent buildings from looming over the Eiffel Tower. Nonetheless, it had been appointed with sufficient luxury to make clear that the occupant was a Very Important Person.

Dinky had come a long way since the grunge wardrobe and the video game posters.

In a corner, he found an étagère loaded with old board games.

Behind Ogilve's desk, he spotted a framed portrait. A middle-aged man in Tudor garb.

"Sir Walter Raleigh?" he guessed.

Linden sighed. "Sir Thomas More. Saint Thomas, if you're Catholic."

He pondered. "Dinky wrote about More in school. Was always trying to get me to read some book the guy wrote. I think More was his personal hero. Must still be. Died for his faith, right?"

"And yet," Linden said, "when More was Lord Chancellor, he had many Protestants put to death."

"So he got in death what he gave in life. I suppose there's poetic justice in that."

"Did you know More gave us the word 'utopia'?"

"You never cease to amaze me with your compendium of useless knowledge, dear."

"This from the man who spent our honeymoon memorizing Scrabble words. Thomas More wrote a book in which he envisioned a complete restructuring of society. In his dream world, there was no private property—because after all, what did that concept ever give

164

mankind except something to fight over? In his utopia, there were no locks on doors—because there was no need for them. Property was kept in communal warehouses and leased out to people who needed it. Families rotated among houses every ten years, so no one consistently had anything better than anyone else. The most important jobs were in agriculture. More valued those who actually produced something of use to others. Unlike the present world, which seems to primarily reward those who produce nothing at all."

"What were you supposed to do if you didn't know how to farm?"

"In More's world, you did. Everyone took turns working the farms, in two-year shifts. Men *and* women, I might add. And if you weren't farming, you were doing something else of value. Masonry, carpentry. Metalwork."

"Sounds idyllic."

"I guess. Prisoners were bound with chains of gold."

"Why gold?"

"Because More wanted people to learn to despise it. Chains, chamberpots, anything repellent, those would be made of gold. He wanted his people to spend their lives pursuing real value. Not rocks and metals."

"I feel much the same way."

"That explains the engagement ring you gave me."

They exchanged a look.

He approached the display case to the right of Ogilve's spacious office. It contained many remnants from Ogilve's career. Magazine articles, plaques, the usual Hall of Ego stuff. An old Apple IIe console. A first-edition Risk board, a Franklin Mint Monopoly. Several other games.

All he cared about was on the bottom shelf. A game board that looked somewhat like two chessboards pressed together, with four kinds of tokens: squares, circles, pyramids, and triangles. Numbers on the tokens.

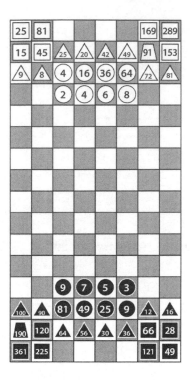

"And what might this be?" Linden asked.

"A game played for many centuries, throughout history. Rithmomachia." He paused. "Also known as the Philosopher's Game. Some people believed it contained all the secrets of the universe. Goes back to the Middle Ages. At that time, the word 'philosopher' was used as we would use 'scientist.'"

"I don't think alchemists trying to turn iron into gold qualify as scientists."

"And yet, modern chemists are able to transmute elements in some circumstances. Anyway, this game was only played by the intellectual elite, in part because it involves a lot of math. The name is Latin for 'battle of the numbers.' Others have called it 'chess for mathematicians.' The game is based on the Pythagorean theory of numbers and has been traced all the way back to ancient Byzantium. Ancients attributed it to Pythagoras himself, though we have no way of knowing who actually invented it. In some eras, it has been connected to clandestine organizations."

"That doesn't surprise me, if it came from Pythagoras," Linden said. "I studied him in school. His life was way more interesting than the average mathematician. He founded his own secret society—sort of a cult, really. Or a commune. Everyone pooled and shared resources, including, reportedly, women. They adopted ascetic practices, such as vegetarianism. And for some reason, beans were forbidden. They had secret symbols and were extremely devoted to one another—which meant secrets rarely escaped. Hard to get in—required a long probationary period. But once you were in, you were in for life."

"Sound like crazies to me. Ancient Greek Trilateral Commission."

"Who's to say? They sought serenity and self-awareness. They loved music and poetry. Practiced regular exercise. Had obsessions about numbers, but given the founder, that was probably to be expected."

"Obsessions? Such as?"

"They always met in groups of ten. They considered three, and its multiples, the height of perfection. And the square root of two was a forbidden subject which could only be discussed with members."

"The square root of two was forbidden?"

"Because it's not a rational number. So they believed its existence threatened the entire field of mathematics. Which could impact economics, commerce, politics, even religion. Could shake their world at its foundation."

"So it's a secret society formed around the square root of two."

"Many believed there was more to it than that. They believed that the true unity of quantifiable data is not manifested on earth. That the only perfection exists in numbers. So they explored the relationship between numbers and objects, numbers and natural phenomena. Some said that, through their pursuit of science and numbers, they uncovered secrets relating to creation itself. The solution to great mysteries too dangerous to be known by the world at large."

"In ancient Greece? I find that hard to believe."

"And others agree with you. But we still don't know how the Egyptians built the pyramids. Or mummified corpses. Or how Stonehenge—"

"Could we get back to the game?" He glanced uneasily at the window. "You can continue the lecture when we're not breaking the law, okay?"

"As you wish. What's the significance of the board? Another hidden message?"

He nodded. "I think so. Each of the different-shaped pieces moves in different ways. But capturing depends on the numbers. There are many different numbers and four ways to capture. So you can see, this game is already more complex than chess."

"I'll probably be sorry I asked, since I'm never likely to accomplish it, but how do you win?"

"There are eight ways to win. The first five are called 'common victories.' Those are the easiest, though still quite complex. Experienced players will only accept the 'proper victories,' which are far more difficult. They require a player to line up at least four of his pieces on his opponent's side of the board in a mathematical progression—arithmetic, geometric, or harmonic."

"Like in Boethius."

"Glad to see that math Ph.D. paying off. An arithmetic sequence exists when the same difference exists between each of the numbers."

"A geometric sequence exists when the next number in the progression is obtained by multiplying each number by the same number."

"And the harmonic sequence consists of at least three numbers that are harmonically proportionate. Meaning they follow the formula:

a/c = (b-1) (c-b)." He pointed to a series of numbers on the board. "See? It's easier to visualize than to explain."

"That seems like a much more difficult way to win than the others," Linden commented.

"It is. But in Rithmomachia, a more complicated victory is a source of pride. *Victoria Magna*—the Great Victory—only requires three pieces in an arithmetic arrangement, but no player with any self-respect would be content with that. *Victoria Major*—the Greater Victory—requires any two of the progressions. And *Victoria Excellentissima*—the Greatest of Vic—requires all three."

"So that's how a real man wins."

"Exactly. If I recall correctly, Dinky's hero Thomas More played this game. It's rumored that when he played Henry VIII—"

"And now let me remind you that the lectures can be saved for when we are not breaking the law." She glanced out the window, careful not to disturb the shutters. "I'm worried that the gendarme will return."

He flattened himself on the floor so he could view the board at eye level. "I note that these pieces are not in the starting position. When the game begins, all pieces are lined up on the edges, sort of like a modern-day game of Stratego. And four of the pieces are not where they should be. The numbers are wrong, too."

"I'll have to take your word for it."

"So I assume those are the ones I'm supposed to focus upon. Applying the math, we get four numbers: 31, 12, 29, 55."

"And they mean?"

He typed the four numbers into the Notes app on his iPhone. "Depends on how you read them. Since we're all Americans, I'm going to assume he wants to read them as you would a book. Left to right." He pursed his lips. "In the world of cryptography, four two-digit numbers could conceal enough information to describe an assassination plot. I could encode plans for building nuclear weapons in four numbers. I could—"

"But what is the message here?"

"I think—"

He heard a clicking sound.

He turned slowly.

And saw the driver standing behind them. The man who'd rescued them from the Bibliotechque.

The man who now held a gun pointed at Linden's head.

51

Twenty-four Hours Before

Chun strode into Supreme General Yoon's office. He did not prostrate himself. He did not bow. He did not even salute.

Because he had no reason to do so.

Yoon glanced up, displaying little interest. The attractive, much younger, dark-skinned woman draped across his lap occupied more of his attention. "Chun? Do we have an appointment?"

"No, General. But we need to discuss matters of vital interest to the welfare of this great nation."

Yoon's irritation could not be more apparent had he held up a sign. "Make an appointment."

"I'm here now."

Yoon pulled away from the woman nibbling on his neck. "Let me say this again, Chun, so the desires of your superior officer will be clear. Make an appointment."

He could remember a time when the slightest hint of Yoon's disapproval would have been enough to send him scrambling to make amends. But that was long ago. He was no longer the unloved boy who endured daily struggles for survival throughout the Great Famine. That world was relentlessly indifferent, even cruel, to him. He was an adult now, an adult committed to creating a better world than the one he had known.

And he was not going to let this fat brass hat stand in his path.

"I am sure your consort will not object to a brief discussion of matters of state, General Yoon. Particularly when there is pressing need."

Yoon tossed the woman off his lap. She let out a small yelp. "You presume too much, Chun. I have given you the freedom of my palace

171

because you have proved useful to me. But you are not irreplaceable."
Yoon's eyes narrowed to tiny slivers. "No one is irreplaceable."

He met Yoon's gaze directly. "I feel exactly the same way."

"I give you sixty seconds, Chun. Then I call in the General's Guard."

"This won't take nearly so long. All I want is the Device."

Yoon's chin lowered. His steady gaze evolved into a slow burn.

"We both know you have been a figurehead for years, Yoon. I run the military. And perhaps most importantly, I run the scientific research that is about to usher this great nation—though not as great as it should be—into a new era."

"These words are treason."

"These words are truth. I am willing to let you remain in your current position, so long as you do not get in my way. But our nation can no longer be content to play the role of the wild cannon, the insane unpredictable threat. We have the power to be a dominant player in world politics, provided we make the correct moves at the correct time. And so long as I am in charge of the military, we will." He paused. "But I need the Device."

"You plan to achieve this delusional world dominance by launching nuclear missiles?"

"If I must. But what is necessary at this time is that the United States believes I am capable of launching nuclear missiles. That they believe I am ready, willing, and perhaps even eager to launch nuclear missiles. For that to happen, it must become known that I have the Device. I must be seen in public with the Device. I must be photographed peering down at the Device, as if debating whether to punch in the codes that will bring the world to war in the blink of an eye."

"You are insane, Chun. Dangerous and insane."

"To the contrary, General. I am the most rational man in the room. Probably in the military complex. Because I am guided by the logical analysis of existing data. More data than you can conceive of mastering. A thousand variables. A billion. All strategically arranged like pieces on a chessboard."

"You have delusions of godhood."

"I have no delusions at all. But godhood might be increasingly accurate."

Yoon rose to his full height. Which was almost a foot lower than Chun's full height, even in his thick-heeled shoes. "This is your last chance to save yourself. Swear fealty to me. Beg my forgiveness."

"Or else?"

"I will have my Guard in here in a matter of seconds."

"Just give me the Device. If I knew where it was, I'd have already taken it. Since I don't, I need you. But my patience for games is not infinite. When I can see the end, I tend to gloss over the intermediate moves. Give me the Device."

"The Guard will cut off your balls and stuff them down your throat. Every loyal member of my Guard—"

"Is dead."

Yoon fell silent.

"Slaughtered while they slept. Nerve gas delivered by a targeted transmission field developed by my friends in Greece. Something new, though derived from the Russian BX9 gas that killed almost a thousand people in Moscow."

"You expect me to believe you have assassinated my entire Guard?"

"It matters very little whether you believe it. The fact is, they are all dead. While my private army is very much intact. So I will be assuming control of the military. And our weaponry. And I intend to use them both."

"You are talking world war. You are talking holocaust. Millions of deaths."

"Billions. The blood will run deep—for a time. But when the dust has settled and the carcasses are buried, we will see the dawn of a new age. A utopia. The likes of which few have even dreamed. And the likes of which only one man—me—has the ability and foresight to build."

"I will put you down like the rabid dog that you are!" Yoon reached into his coat pocket—and found nothing.

From behind his desk, the beautiful dark-skinned woman— Rani—glided across the room. She held Yoon's PDA in her hand.

"Looking for this?" She slapped Yoon across his face. "Get down on your knees and beg, you pathetic dog. You have always disgusted me. Now I will treat you as you deserve to be treated."

Chun leveled a gun. "I have been told by my associate that you have a certain fondness for pain, General. So what comes next may be pleasurable for you. Though I very much doubt it."

52

B smiled at the man holding the gun. "We could use a ride, my friend, but we're not ready to leave yet."

"Last time you left in such a hurry," the driver said in his clipped British accent. "Before I could say my farewells properly."

"Is that why you're here? To collect your fare?"

"I want those numbers."

"Then ask your boss. I'm sure he'll be happy to provide them to you."

"He only thinks he's my boss. Give me the numbers."

"Okay, I'll write them down for you."

"I hope you will not be offended if I say that I do not trust you. Give me your phone."

Linden's ashen face trembled. She looked as if she might pass out.

The driver pushed his gun forward, shoving Linden's head back. "Give me the phone. Or she dies in the next five seconds."

He handed the man his iPhone. "How did you find us?"

"You have never been out of my sight."

"Why did you wait this long before you intervened?"

"I wanted to make sure you obtained the desired information first."

"Why? What are you going to do with it?"

The driver slipped the phone into his shirt pocket. "Perhaps you believe I am just an ignorant chauffeur and lackey. I assure you that is not the case. I am quite intelligent. And I work for an organization that has been involved in this intrigue far longer than you."

Linden raised an eyebrow. "But apparently none of you know how to play Rithmomachia."

"I do not waste my life playing stupid games." The driver shifted his aim. "Your time is coming to an end, Game Master."

"Hey," he said, holding up his hands. "I gave you the phone. You said you'd let us go."

"No, I did not. But I will make your deaths quick and clean."

"That's decent of you."

"You have no idea what is at stake here. You play with titanic forces long in conflict that now—"

A shrill, piercingly loud alarm sounded. The driver started. The muscles in his arms and neck tensed.

The driver was only diverted a moment, but that was enough. Linden slammed a clenched fist onto his wrist, knocking the gun downward. The driver fired, but the bullet hit the carpet. Linden pivoted, swinging as she advanced. She led with her left, slamming her fist into the driver's neck. Barely an instant later, her right elbow smashed into his nose.

His hands moved to his face.

Linden knocked his hands aside, wrapping her forearm around his neck and forcing his head downward. She raised her knee with the sudden impact of a battering ram. It smashed into his already damaged nose, splintering the cartilage. Blood and flesh spurted in all directions.

Linden yanked the driver's head upward by the hair. She jammed the flat of her hand under his jaw. His head whipped backward, slamming into the wall. His eyelids fluttered for a moment. Then he crumpled to the floor.

BB stared at her, lips parted. "I am so glad I never complained about your cooking."

"Help me." Together they rolled the driver over.

He retrieved his phone from the man's pocket.

"He won't be out long, BB. I didn't hit him that hard."

"Looked pretty darn hard to me. Have things gotten a lot tougher in the math department?"

"I've been studying Shodokan Aikido." She grabbed the gun and placed it in her satchel. "Girl can't be too careful these days. Was that your cell phone making the racket?"

He nodded. "I've got a one-button app that sounds an alarm sixty seconds after being activated. Useful when meetings are boring you to death. I pushed the button before I handed it to him."

"I knew you were stalling for some reason. So I was ready to take advantage of the diversion when it occurred."

"This man is out like a rock. What did you do to him?"

"After I was sure the gun wasn't trained on you, I went after his nose. I don't care how tough your attacker is—hit him in the nose and he closes his eyes and raises his hands. It's instinctive and almost impossible to prevent. That gave me the opening to shove his head down and smash his forehead, also guaranteed to incapacitate. A blow to the jaw, properly executed, will almost always induce unconsciousness. It jolts the brain stem, which causes it to immediately terminate all non-essential functions."

"The well-educated woman's approach to kicking butt and taking names."

"Basically." She heard noise outside the door. The elevator was moving. "I think we're about to have company. Let's get out of here."

They raced into the hallway outside Ogilve's office.

The light above the elevator door lit. Following the bell chime, the doors opened.

Two gendarmes, including the man they had seen before on the street, entered the hallway.

BB grabbed Linden's hand and tugged her the opposite direction. "Run."

53

Twenty-four Hours Before

C hun was not surprised that Supreme General Yoon did not hold up well under torture. Not much effort was required. A few blows to the solar plexus with a hammer, a few removed fingernails. Rani drew pictures on his chest with her stiletto. Nothing lethal, but she made sure he felt it. She'd been toying with Yoon for some time—while he mistakenly thought he was toying with her—and she exacted her revenge with relish. Before long, Yoon revealed everything Chun needed to know to hasten the transfer of power, including the protocols and passwords controlling the air and naval fleets.

He also opened the safe where Yoon kept the digital transmitter that could launch North Korea's nuclear arsenal.

The Device.

"Fool," he muttered to the bleeding prostrate commander spread across the carpet. "This should be on your person at all times. Other leaders will only respect you if they fear you." He memorized the codes, then destroyed the notes. "With this, I can dominate them all."

He held a speedy meeting with the leaders of the various platoons in the new combined armies. Declarations were drafted declaring him the new acting Supreme General. President Kim's signature would be required to make it a permanent appointment. But the ultimate outcome was a foregone conclusion. So long as he had control, he didn't much care what his title might be.

Once they were ready, he ushered in a select member of the government-controlled news media, a slender telegenic reporter he knew he could trust to do and say what she was told to do and say. He brought her into Yoon's former office, pulled out a chair for her—

ignoring the blood smears on the carpet—and took his position on the opposite side of the desk. In the General's chair.

Not bad for a boy from a village in the valley of the Baekdu volcano region, a village so small it did not even appear on the official maps. Once he had struggled just to eat. Now he sat in the most powerful chair in the nation.

"We have obtained incontrovertible evidence of Yoon's treason. He received financial payments from representatives of the American intelligence community, whom he aided and abetted on several key occasions, weakening the Korean defense and making us vulnerable to the Americans' aggressive warmongering. Rest assured that Yoon will suffer appropriate punishment."

The reporter waved to her cameraman, signaling him to move in for a close-up.

Chun placed the Device on the desk, just before him, knowing the leaders of the superpower nations would know what it was.

"Are you declaring war on the United States?" the reporter asked.

"The United States has already declared war on us. We will do what we must to defend ourselves, not only against them, but against all hostile nations. If we are pushed, we will push back. We will protect Mother Korea."

"Do you believe Korea's allies will support your actions?"

"I know they will. The world map is changing. The actions taken in the days to come will change this world, permanently and dramatically. The transition will be difficult for some. Complex. Perhaps even bloody. But always for the greater good."

"But if the world changes so dramatically, no one can be certain of the outcome."

No one, he thought, smiling. Except me.

54

B B pulled Linden toward the stairs. He could hear the gendarmes' footsteps, much too close behind them. Once they were through the door to the stairwell, he took the driver's gun from her and fired in the general direction of the officers. They scattered. He fired a few more rounds, aiming toward the ceiling. He didn't want to harm them—but they didn't need to know that.

He bolted toward the ground floor, two steps at a time. "I bought us about ten seconds with the gun. Let's make the most of it."

"We could just tell them the truth. Dinky might not press charges."

"We broke in here a few hours after we trashed the national library. Then you practically killed a chauffeur. Oh, and I just shot at police officers." He swung himself over a railing. "I don't think we should turn ourselves in."

He knew he didn't have to remind her they were working under a deadline. He didn't have to look at his cell to know where the countdown stood. Fewer than fifty hours until his mysterious correspondent said Kadey would be killed.

A few moments later, he heard the door on the top floor open. The gendarmes were back in pursuit. He thought they might take the elevator down and head them off at the pass. They probably didn't want to risk letting the fleeing felons out of their sight. Or perhaps they split up. He had no way of knowing. And he didn't have time to investigate.

He reached the ground floor, Linden arriving only a few seconds behind him. They raced through the lobby and out into the street. Ten seconds later they were in their rented Versa.

He pushed her to the passenger side. "I'll drive."

She glared at him. "You don't know how to drive."

"I don't have a license. Doesn't mean I don't know how to drive. Nothing personal, but you're too cautious and law-abiding to drive a getaway car."

She complied. He pulled out onto the Champs Élysées. "How much lead do you think we have?"

Linden looked into the side mirror. A blue circular flash illuminated the darkness. "I'd say, roughly, none."

He floored it. "Probably not the same cops. They radioed for assistance."

"Doesn't really matter. They're all equally capable of putting us behind bars. Do the French still ship criminals to Devil's Island?"

He veered into the lane nearest the curb, almost riding up on the sidewalk. Cafés, theaters, shops, flew by. A continuous line of street lamps and horse-chestnut trees. Last time he'd been to Paris, he recalled seeing quaint Parisian eateries and eccentric boutiques, but now it all seemed to be name-designer chain stores, Gucci and Prada, Louis Vuitton and the like. Part of the global banalization, he supposed.

"Look out!" Linden shouted.

In the headlights, the Arc de Triomphe loomed ahead. He was fairly certain that if he took out a national treasure, he'd never leave the country alive. He jerked the wheel as far as it would go, making a hard right without slowing. He felt two wheels rising off the ground.

"Jesus God, slow down!" Linden shouted.

"I thought we were trying to escape."

"Kind of a Pyrrhic victory if you die in the process."

He straightened the car out and barreled down the rotary to the other side of the famous avenue. He was flanked by two police cars now, one on each side. A voice blasted from a bullhorn attached to the hood.

"*Pull over immediately.*"

"Did you hear what they said?" BB asked Linden.

"Hard to miss."

"Aren't you surprised?"

"Did you think they were chasing you for an autograph?"

"They spoke in English." He floored the accelerator. "They know who we are."

55

Ever since he left the *Bibliotechque*, Palmer had been at *Metro Surete* headquarters explaining the commotion he'd caused, and eventually monitoring all incoming reports, hoping for some information he could use.

Reports of a high-speed chase on the Champs Élysées attracted his interest. The license plate revealed that the car had been rented by an American.

The Game Master. "Show me the pictures!"

He ground his teeth together at the snail-like pace of his so-called assistant. Jean Luc, according to his name tag. The fact that he had a name tag should have told the whole story. They had assigned him a low level troll, someone no one else needed. Like sticking a pacifier into the irritating American's mouth.

He managed to keep his temper in check. Barely. Normally, when a federal agent entered a local police department, the hierarchy was immediately clear. No turf war necessary. The FBI took priority.

Should be the same here. This case had global ramifications, far greater than these functionaries understood. But he had not been able to get any attention from the DGSE—the Direction générale de la sécurité extérieure—the French equivalent of the CIA. So he was stuck in this office, working with Jean Luc and his name tag.

"I have a visual report, monsieur. No photos."

"Are you telling me there's no CCTV on the Champs Élysées? I don't believe it."

"Video? *Oui*. You said you wanted a photograph."

He felt his fingers stiffening, advancing to the choke position. He restrained himself. He was a guest in a foreign land. Murdering his assistant would be a bad idea. "Show me the video."

"Putting it on the screen . . . now."

The image was blurred and dark, but he recognized BB. He appeared to be violating about a thousand traffic laws.

His mind raced back to the dossier he'd read before he arrived in Vegas. Ogilve had an office in Paris. Off the Champs Élysées. Coincidence?

Highly unlikely.

"Get me a car. Immediately."

"I will secure a driver and—"

"Screw that. Just get me a car."

"Monsieur, I do not have authority—"

He slammed his hand down on Jean Luc's computer monitor. "Then get the authority. Right. Now."

"I'll try to—"

He reached into the man's pockets and yanked out his car keys. "If you don't have a car for me in sixty seconds, I'm taking yours."

56

Despite BB's best efforts to swerve and veer, the two police cars still bookended him. They all barreled down the street at more than eighty miles an hour. He knew that soon one of the police cars would swing in front of him and attempt to block his progress. He didn't wait for them to make the move.

He slammed on his brakes.

The police cars shot forward. When he thought his speed had decreased sufficiently, he jackknifed the car and started back up the street the way he came, narrowly avoiding a collision with oncoming traffic. He swung the car back and forth, weaving his way through the cars, dodging the stunned late-night motorists.

"I want this to end," Linden said. "I want this to end before we're both dead."

"Doing my best." He swung the car hard to the left. The famed statue of Napoleon on his horse came immediately into view, much too close. He swung away hard. Too hard. He ran up on the sidewalk and smashed through a line of café tables.

The night was shattered by chaos as a chair flew through a plate glass window.

"He captured me and held me against my will," Linden practiced. "He forced me into that car. I wanted to escape but his willpower was too strong."

"We are not going to get caught." He pulled hard to straighten out the wheel, but he was moving too fast. He pulled one way, then swung back the other. He could feel the back end of the car whipping out of line.

And the two police cars returned to his rearview mirror.

Ahead, he spotted a long semi-trailer truck backing out of the Gucci store, blocking the westbound traffic and creeping onto the other side.

"In a few seconds, that truck will totally block traffic."

"Probably why they do their unloading late at night."

The truck continued moving backward, leaving perhaps a twenty-foot opening at the far end of the street.

"BB? You can't make it in time."

"Didn't you ever play billiards? Same principle. This is a bank shot. Except with a time limit."

He swerved the car over as hard as the wheel would turn. Tires screeched. The car went up on two wheels again and felt as if were about to roll.

He shot the car down the increasingly narrow passage. The truck never stopped backing up. He passed through the opening, then swung the car to the right just before he hit a storefront. As soon as they were through, the truck completely blocked the street.

The police cars were trapped on the other side.

They'd escaped their pursuers. At least for now.

They couldn't return to their hotel room. The gendarmes would radio for assistance. Every second they remained in France they were in danger of being apprehended.

Fortunately, he had another destination in mind. And a few other identities he could employ, thanks to the passport collection in his pack. They needed to get to the airport, fast, before every cop at de Gaulle had a photo of his face.

"Feel like a red-eye flight?"

"Why not? Where are we going?"

"You don't know?"

"How many times are we going to play this game? You're just showing off. You want me to beg you to tell me what you've figured out."

"Well . . ."

"You're just as insufferable as you were when we were married."

He didn't reply. He liked to think he had matured since then. But she knew him better than anyone on earth. She'd gotten closer to him than anyone ever had.

His cell phone buzzed.

New image. Kadey was still bound and gagged like a heifer in a rodeo, but her face was pressed against something flat, like a sheet of Plexiglas. She appeared to be trapped in an extremely tight space. The blue coloring in her face suggested she was having trouble breathing.

Forty-two hours to go, according to the clock.

The text said: *Her air is finite. You are the only one who can save her.*

He sent a reply text, as he had before, but there was no response.

He slid the phone into his pocket before Linden saw it.

"Something of interest?" Linden asked.

He chose his words carefully, his eyes fixed on the road. "Let's get to the airport."

57

Rani crept down the hallway.
　　She'd waited out of sight until the two gendarmes left. A heated pursuit, she gathered. Fine. She'd let those fools play cops and robbers. What she wanted was inside that office.

She moved silently but swiftly down the corridor. She paused just outside the door to Ogilve's office. Then, in one fluid motion, she was inside.

The room was empty.

On first inspection. Then she looked down. The man she had seen earlier, the driver, was crumpled on the ground. His face looked like raw ground beef. His nose was shattered. Dark bruises circled both eyes. He looked as if he would be unconscious for some time.

She scanned the office. Hard to know what the Game Master had seen and examined, but she knew they had been here for a reason.

She slipped her thermal imaging goggles out of her pack and slid them on. Not a tool that would be approved by the Pythagoreans. But useful, nonetheless.

Three sets of footprints were visible on the floor. The Americans and the driver. She wondered which of them had taken him out. Her money was on the woman.

The footprints covered the entire office, but the intensity of the imprints indicated that they had spent most of their time beside the display case on the south wall.

But what sparked their interest?

She slid the infrared filter over the goggles, which blocked out all normal ambient light, but intensified the sensitivity to heat. She should be able to find a trace lingering even from the slightest touch.

Someone had touched the Rithmomachia board. Repeatedly.

But of course. At the Pythagorean compound, everyone loved Rithmomachia.

She adjusted the goggles to their highest setting.

Four of the pieces glowed. They had been touched recently.

She copied the numbers down on her hand. Unless she was mistaken, these numbers were a road map that would help Chun find what he had sought for so long.

She started back out of the office, crossing over the stricken driver.

He opened his swollen black eyes.

"What . . . happened? Who are you?"

If she had just moved a little more quickly. But she couldn't risk the man describing her. Or reporting her presence. Even the vaguest description might spoil everything.

The driver tried to push himself up.

"Relax," she said, pushing him back down. "You are not going anywhere. Your body, at any rate, is going nowhere. Your spirit may be embarking upon a journey."

A second later her stiletto was out. The driver raised his hands, but not nearly quickly enough. The stiletto came down hard and fast and lodged in the side of his head, severing the cerebellum. His neural synapses were disconnected so quickly he did not even have time to scream. His face froze, mouth open, in a grotesque rictus.

His muscles relaxed and he fell back to the floor, dead.

And now she needed to depart, before those gendarmes returned. She wanted to leave no indication that anyone had been here other than the Americans. Let this death be added to the ongoing tally of crimes attributed to the Game Master.

She ran the numbers through her mind. She did not know what they meant, but solving puzzles was not her specialty. Chun would know what to do. He would either determine the significance himself, or appeal to his consultant.

She was not always proud of the assignments Chun gave her. But she believed in the goal. She knew the world could not continue in its current bloody downward spiral. No one should have to suffer as she had suffered. No child should have to grow up with the brutality she had experienced on a daily basis in Pakistan. No one should have to lose her innocence as she had.

Was it possible to recapture lost innocence? Chun believed that it was. Moreover, he believed he could make it happen. For millions.

And for that, she would serve him. Would follow him to the ends of the earth. Would satisfy every vile passion the man possessed.

Would kill anyone she had to kill. Including the Game Master. Or his wife. Or their child.

Paradise could not be bought cheaply.

58

Palmer watched through high-powered infrared goggles as BB and Linden entered the airport. He had suspected they would attempt to leave the country before a formal transit blockade could be implemented.

He strode cautiously across the lobby of the airport. He did not want them to see him.

His cell phone buzzed. He glanced at the caller.

His contact at the White House.

He kept his eye trained on BB and Linden. "Yes?"

"Let them go."

He had to pause a moment. "But I could pry the information—"

"Do you understand your orders? Follow, don't apprehend."

His teeth ground together. "Understood. I'll find out where they're going and—"

"They're going to Egypt. Flying into Cairo. The Game Master just bought two tickets."

"Fine. I'll get on the same flight."

"No. You'd be spotted."

"I can stay out of sight of that stupid poker—"

"Do you seriously think you're the only person who's watching? Are you naïve enough to think we're the only people who want to know where he's going?"

He paused a moment. "Are you saying—"

"I'm saying this is big, even bigger than you initially thought. A lot of international forces are converging. We want you to be there. But we don't want you to stop the party from happening."

"Why the hell not?"

"Here's the reality, Palmer. This is bigger—and older—than you realize. And we don't know nearly enough about it. So you just became the most important man in the American intelligence community."

"Then I want a raise."

"Just do your job."

"Look, I know a hell of a lot more about this—"

"Did you know about the military coup in North Korea?"

He didn't bother responding.

"So don't try to act all wise and wonderful."

"There's been nothing on the news."

"Yet."

Out the corner of his eye, he watched BB pass through the security gates. He'd be on the plane soon. "I'd still rather be on the same flight." As he watched, he noticed a dark-skinned woman hurrying through security. Although she tried not to make it obvious, he could see that she was keeping a close eye on BB as well.

He recognized her. She shouldn't be here.

But the fact that she was changed everything.

"Maybe it's best that I wait for the next one."

"Glad you've seen the light."

"Can you tell me more about the North Korean situation?"

"We'll forward information to your cell as it comes in."

His contact ended the conversation.

He'd wait until everyone else boarded, then use his badge to get himself on before it took off. If he sat in first class, they'd never spot him. No way he was going to risk losing this trail again.

Especially now that he knew she was involved.

He put away the goggles and shoved his right hand into his pocket.

The blue star on the palm of his hand tingled.

59

B felt certain they had eluded anyone who could possibly be following them, but he kept a watchful eye out, just the same. He found their gate, then walked to a quiet corner where he could speak to Linden in whispered tones. "You okay?"

She nodded. "Nice driving, by the way. I guess your next game will be NASCAR."

He stifled a chuckle.

"So where are we going?" she asked.

"Alexandria."

"Why?"

"You mean you haven't figured out the meaning of those numbers yet?"

Linden took his phone and scanned them. "Arithmetic progression? Geometric? Harmonic? Hell, you're just torturing me because numbers are my specialty. Okay, I'll admit I don't grasp the significance of these numbers. Tell me."

"Longitude and latitude."

She slapped her forehead. "Of course. Can you place the coordinates?"

"Yes. Got a satellite GPS app on my phone." He opened it. "Push the blue button."

She did. A small map appeared. She enlarged it.

"It's an address in Alexandria?"

"More than just an address. The site of the fabled Library of Alexandria, now home of the Bibliotheca Alexandrina."

"Another library?"

He nodded. "Even older than the Bibliothèque. And also a scientific research institute."

"You know anyone there?"

"No. But I'm willing to bet Gen3^2 has an office somewhere in the neighborhood."

"Is that where they're holding Kadey?"

"I hope so." He paused. "There's more to this than just a kidnapping."

"How do you figure?"

"We've seen clues all along the way, Miss Scarlet. Kadey's just the bait."

"To involve us?"

"To involve me. Nothing personal. To involve me in something huge."

"You're saying this is some kind of complex international conspiracy, and we're being drawn into the middle of it? If so, I think we're in over our heads."

"Maybe you are. But I have excellent geopolitical strategy skills. From playing Risk. And Diplomacy. And Dungeons and Dragons."

"That really isn't funny, BB. Our daughter's life in on the line."

"No one knows that better than me." The intercom buzzed. Time to board the flight. "We should be there in seven hours."

"And then what?"

He handed his boarding pass to the attendant. "And then I take care of my daughter. That's what daddies do."

Part Three

It's How You Play the Game

60

Four Years Before
Pyongyang, North Korea

*T*he apocalypse is heaven-sent.

Those words burned in Ogilve's brain. How could he use the keyboard when he could barely stop his hands from shaking? Chun was insane, but absolutely determined to achieve his goal. Ragnarök. Götterdämmerung. The end of days.

And he had no choice but to help the madman make it happen.

Holly's life hung in the balance. And did untold others. Maybe every life on earth.

He forced his eyelids open with his fingers, fighting through his fatigue. More than one hundred days ago his status changed from research scientist to captive. He was barely a shadow of the man he'd been before this ordeal began. But he could not sleep now. Not when so much hung in the balance.

The mainframe in this laboratory had more computing power than the Fujitsu K, generally believed to be the most powerful supercomputer in the world. But he had designed this machine with an entirely different architecture. His design mirrored the neural structure of the human brain. His first microchip, the one that attracted Chun's attention, was made of 256 artificial neurons. His current microprocessors had over ten billion neurons and one hundred trillion synapses. Ordinary chips conveyed information through a single channel, limiting their speed. His design allowed each artificial neuron to have its own channel, permitting massively greater parallel processing capabilities.

But it still hadn't given Chun what he wanted. Which just made the crazy bastard crazier. And deadlier.

He heard something behind him and jumped, literally jumped, out of his chair. His heart raced.

His lab assistant had brought him a sandwich.

He pressed a hand against his chest, trying to calm himself. Not Chun. Not this time. Not yet.

"Thanks." He lifted the sandwich to his mouth, but he had no appetite.

"Can I help you input the daily data stream?" the assistant, Julian, asked. He smiled but it was forced, tentative. The smile of another captive blackmailed into service.

"Sure." The computer needed as much raw data as possible and it was impossible to predict what might be useful. Its enormous database included almost every book ever published, in print or not. Every film, newspaper, almanac, or encyclopedia, going back at least fifty years. A constant digital feed from the cable news networks. Critical and analytical works of philosophy, history, literature, art, and science. This computer was the largest repository of information the world had ever known—like the legendary Library of Alexandria in its day. "Let me warm it up first."

He tried a few preliminary inquiries, testing its ability to discern the desired response from indirect inquiry rather than explicit questions.

Ion channel opens spontaneously but closes again before it can take effect. Inconsequential blips.

Good. The computer could decipher what was wanted without an express question because the computer didn't actually answer questions. It honed in on key phrases, searched its extensive databases, identified reoccurring relational words, then ranked them in order of frequency. More like a complex Google search than an actual reply. But this processing strategy allowed programmers to create startlingly effective medical research computers.

Fruit fly used in investigations re: malaria-carrying mosquitoes find human prey.
Drosophila melanogaster.
University of Pennsylvania physicist forefront neural coding.
Vijay Balasubramanian.
Quantum game theory Nobel Prize winners.
Eight.

How are you?

The screen blipped. No words appeared for almost three seconds, an eternity for this computer.

Busy Beavers song title.

"Guess you stumped the band," Julian said.

"Happens every time. The computer can process information, but it can't answer the simplest inquiry that requires any degree of self-awareness."

"Give it time."

"You don't know how long I've been working on this." The dream of creating a sentient computer was the holy grail of neuroprogrammers. Some succeeded in creating computers that could carry on a conversation. Somewhat. The tester did not have to chat long to realize the computer only regurgitated canned words and phrases. Other programs could synthesize input into a reasonably coherent form, generating summaries of sports stats or financial reports. But that was a far cry from sentience.

"Isn't it strange?" Julian said. "It destroys us in chess. But it can't perform other tasks that seem so simple."

"That's the irony of conventional computing. Which is why I started from the ground up, with an entirely fresh approach." To the extent that a given task could be isolated and reduced to a fixed number of possibilities, it could be mastered by a conventional computer. Hence, unbeatable chess and bridge computers. Some computers could now land airplanes, control tactical weapons deployment, or decide whether to extend credit. But sentience required the ability to go beyond cataloguing and corroborating. To exercise critical and analytical skills. To *think*.

"Have to go," Julian said, checking his watch. "Duties in the animal research center."

"No problem. I'll do the feed later." He knew Chun watched that poor wretch just as closely as himself.

"Don't get discouraged, Doctor. You'll get it. I know you will. You're—" His eyes darted downward. "You're our last best hope."

And Holly's, he thought as the man departed.

He had hoped his work in neuromorphic processing might allow computers employing his radical microprocessor design to make a cognitive leap. He'd spent months exploring how brains interpret

199

subjective experience. He analyzed the brains of people with neurological disorders. He experimented with the brain mechanisms of rodents. He developed his own theory regarding the neuronal correlates of consciousness—the minimal brain mechanisms that lead to the experience of sensation. He mapped how incoming sensory signals interact with stored data—memory—to create a cohesive picture of the world. What we call consciousness.

The question was how to reproduce that in digital code. While Holly was still—

Fingers tightened around his trachea before he knew anyone was there.

"Good afternoon, Dr. Ogilve."

He gurgled his response. How did Chun do that? He hadn't even heard the man coming.

"I've been with your wife," Chun said, tightening his grip. "And I do mean I've been with your wife. She brought a startling degree of energy to the encounter. For a woman who has been beaten almost senseless. So many times."

He tried to squirm out of the chair, but Chun's right hand pinned him down while the left choked the life out of him. His brain begged for oxygen. His tongue swelled.

"She's a remarkable woman, Emerson." Like most of the North Korean power elite, Chun studied for years in the West. He thought himself a great intellectual and enjoyed flaunting his command of languages. "Most women would not have survived half so long. She continues to endure, perhaps buoyed by the hope that her spineless husband will eventually do something to end her perpetual misery."

His eyelids fluttered. He knew he would pass out soon. Followed by permanent brain damage. And death.

"Physically your wife abides, despite the punishing daily abuse. But mentally, I fear, she is not so resilient." Chun spun him around, grabbed his hair, and jerked his head back. "Even if she survives this ordeal, she will never be the same."

He knew this was true. He'd seen the daily videos. He watched the light fade from Holly's luminous eyes. That was what first attracted him to her. The incandescent sparkle, the gaiety, the kindness that led her to take pity on a hopelessly tongue-tied science geek. She brought him the only sweetness he had ever known.

Chun smoothed his uniform tunic. "Perhaps you need to see today's video."

"I do not."

"I think you do." Chun withdrew a smartphone and pressed a button.

He turned his head away. Chun jerked it back. He closed his eyes. "Open them."

"No."

"Open them or I will avulse them from their sockets."

He opened his eyes.

The beating began as it always did. A few cruel punches to places that left no marks. Her stomach. Her neck. But Chun did not stop there, because after all, he did not care whether he left a mark. He placed a knee into her back, pulled her head by the hair, and kicked out her knees. Kicked her between the legs. Punched her, repeatedly, splitting a lip that had been split so many times it never had a chance to heal. When she fell he hauled her up and smashed her face into the concrete wall. When she fell again, he kicked her in the side with heavy rubber-soled combat boots.

As she lay crumpled and motionless on the floor, Chun bent down and removed her clothing.

He struggled with all his might to look away from the video, but Chun was too strong. He tried to reach an object, any potential weapon, but nothing was within his grasp.

"Stop it. Please. Please."

"It is over." Chun clicked off the video. "If we hurt her more, she might die. And I wouldn't want that."

"Can't you see I'm doing everything I can?"

"You are not doing enough."

"I need more time. I'm on the verge of a breakthrough. I can feel it."

"We have given you too long already."

"You can't force inspiration."

Chun's smile terrified him. "In my experience, inspiration comes when people want it—or need it—most. Adrenaline doesn't simply stimulate the heart. It feeds oxygen to the brain. It stimulates the cerebral cortex." Chun looked him directly in the eyes. "I want results. And I want them now."

201

"Just don't hurt Holly any more. Please."

"Very well."

He blinked. Did Chun say what he thought?

"We will leave your wife alone." Chun punched another button on the phone. "We will hurt this one instead."

He felt as if the air had been sucked out of his lungs. He clenched his eyes shut, but Chun pried them open.

They had his daughter.

The photo on Chun's phone revealed Lily, tied up and gagged in the same room as her mother. Meaning she watched them beat her mother. And the rest of it.

He had believed Lily was safe. He thought she was at a secret location, cared for by Holly's younger sister.

"Please don't hurt her. She's so young."

Chun swiveled him around, forcing him to face the monitor. "Make this computer think."

"I'm trying. I'm—"

Chun slammed his head down on the tabletop. The keyboard skittered across the table and crashed to the floor. His skull rang like a cathedral carillon.

Think, he told himself. You need a new idea. And you need it now. You can't teach a computer to think if you can't do it yourself. This sadistic madman has the two most precious people in the world and he will destroy them—

His brain raced, addled and spasmodic, a nonlinear rainfall of images and ideas. Think! Human intelligence has reached its evolutionary limit . . . brain size is limited . . . larger models require too much energy and move too slowly . . .

Chun jerked him out of his chair, hands clutched around his throat.

Computers have no physiological limitations . . . But they do not perceive the outside world . . .

Chun slung him brutally from one wall to the other. His head felt as if it were expanding, ready to burst.

A computer can describe a scene, but it cannot observe what it sees . . . what it does not see . . .

"Wait." He brought his arms up, breaking Chun's grip. He retrieved the keyboard, stumbling over the frayed hem of his blue jeans.

"What are you doing?"

"This computer has a huge repository of visual images."

"So?"

"The integrated-information theory of consciousness suggests"— he paused and rubbed his raw throat—"that consciousness is defined by the ability to integrate incoming sensory input with stored information to create a cohesive picture of the world."

He typed at lightning speed, opening dozens of files at once. "Consciousness, therefore, can be measured by determining how much information a system contains above and beyond that processed by its component parts."

Chun's epaulets jangled. "What are you doing? Explain this to me."

He opened hundreds more files, extracting multiple images at a time. A desperate rapid video parade flashed across the overhead monitor.

"When will it think?" Chun demanded.

"It will think at the same time we all start to think. When someone asks the right question." He continued extracting images—

Incorrect input.

His head tilted to one side. The computer had responded without prior input. What did it mean?

He glanced at the overhead monitor. He'd been clicking so fast he'd inadvertently put two images on the screen at once, one superimposed over the other. A photo of an umbrella on a photo of the Sahara Desert. But the computer treated them as one composite picture.

What's wrong? he typed.

No rain in desert.

He gasped.

"You are wasting my time with foolish games," Chun said.

"I'm not wasting your time. But you're right about one thing— this is a game. A children's game. A game for sentient beings learning how to think. It's called, What's Wrong with This Picture?" He opened more files. "Games have appealed to people since the dawn of time. Because they stretch our intellect in new and unforeseen directions, thus stimulating the pleasure centers of our brains. This particular game is used by parents and teachers to motivate children to exercise the right-brain regions of the cerebral cortex. To go beyond merely assimilating information. Beyond identifying what is in a picture."

"To determining what should not be in the picture," Chun murmured.

He superimposed two more images on the screen, this time deliberately selecting them to create incongruities. An image of a reclining man floating over the Manhattan skyline.

What's wrong?

Man cannot fly without mechanical device. Unless fictional character.

He could not help but grin. The computer was doing it. Exactly what he'd been working for so long.

He needed two more images. He scanned the daily feed and drew the first two that did not correspond. A photo from the upcoming Kentucky Derby and a large wheel of Stilton. This time he framed a less direct question.

Is anything wrong?

The ones on the end do not belong.

Not the response he expected. The Kentucky Derby photo showed the three frontrunners, according to the Vegas odds makers. The ones on the end . . .

Was it referring to the horses on the far left and right?

Explain ones on end do not belong.

The response took less time than the blink of an eye.

Banner says Winners Circle. Only center horse will win.

He pulled out his smartphone. The computer's last update was inputted last night. But the race ran half an hour ago—

And the horse in the center of the photograph won.

Chun leaned in close. "What is it doing?"

His eyes went into deep focus as he studied the last response. "More than we dreamed possible. We've crossed a threshold." He typed in another inquiry.

How are you?

I am well. And yourself?

"What does it mean?" Chun whispered.

He pushed himself away, staring at the monitor. "It means your apocalypse is on its way."

61

The White House, Situation Room
Present Day

President Fernandez threw the written report down on the conference table. The cable news pundits liked to say he was a man of infinite patience. They were wrong.

He'd had all the mealy-mouthed BS he could take.

"Just give it to me straight, Blake. Who's running North Korea? And how long before they attack?"

Chief of Staff Blake glanced at Carmine Cartwright, head of the National Security Agency, who sat beside Gordon Decker, chairman of the joint chiefs of staff. Blake ran his hand across his smooth bald head. "Chun's in control of the army and the nuclear stockpile. As for the latter . . . we don't know."

"What does the coup mean?"

Blake exchanged a glance with the Amanda Knox, secretary of state, just returned from Lebanon. This fell within her province. "It means the most dangerously unstable government on the face of the earth just became significantly more unstable."

"From bad to worse?"

"More like, from worse to apocalyptic."

Fernandez fell back in his chair. "Great. Walk me through what happened."

Blake flipped through his briefing papers. "Details are still sketchy. Chun always appeared to be the loyal servant of his superior officer, Supreme General Yoon."

"What about Kim? Isn't he the president?"

Blake tilted his head to one side. "Technically, his title is *supreme leader.*"

"Supreme leader." He paused. "I like the sound of that. You think I could get Congress to change my title to supreme leader?"

"No sir. Technically, by Constitutional amendment, the former President Il-sung, the current ruler's granddaddy, was named "Eternal President" by Constitutional amendment after he died."

"They made a dead man the president?"

"That is correct."

"A zombie president."

"Well, he hasn't risen from the grave. But these titles don't matter. The man who controls the army is the man in charge."

"And that's Chun?"

"Apparently so. He used some kind of unconventional weapon to take out Yoon's private guard. Something we don't have. We can't even figure out how it was deployed."

"What else do we know about Chun?"

"He's been involved in an ongoing altercation with Emerson Ogilve for many years."

"The computer geek? The one you're using to create military simulation programs?"

"Yes."

"Bring Ogilve in. Let's talk to him."

"Haven't been able to track him down. We're not the only ones looking, either."

"He's the head of Gen3². In Vegas. Right?"

"Exactly."

"The project that suffered the disappearances."

"And the murder."

"Do we have someone looking into that?"

"In a way. We have an agent in Paris trailing another man who is somehow involved in the crimes. Steven Thomas."

"The Game Master."

"Yes."

"Watched him win the North American chess tournament. Quite the flamboyant player. But why are we following him? Do we think he might lead us to Ogilve?"

"We hope so. They worked together, so years ago. Our agent has spotted other potentially dangerous foreign operatives in the area.

Everyone seems to be converging in Egypt. Like every dangerous power in the world got invitations to a big nasty party."

"Everyone but us."

No response was necessary.

Fernandez turned to Cartwright. "So Chun is running North Korea. What are the ramifications to our national security?"

"North Korea has the bomb, sir. Don't kid yourself that they disabled them all. And now this madman has the codes. He could launch a strike against the US without blinking. He's already hinting he considers us an enemy and plans some kind of aggressive action."

"And our retaliation would turn his little country into a rock quarry."

"Maybe. Depends on who else he has lined up on his side."

"China wouldn't help him. Not if we took a forceful stance."

"I'm not so sure."

"Why would they?"

"Because of India."

"They feel threatened by India?"

Secretary Knox cut in. "Sir, do you know the doctrine of Fear of Encirclement?" She did not pause long enough for him to answer. He knew her goal was to enlighten him, not embarrass him. "India feels threatened by China, which is constantly tightening its grip in the region. The Chinese government has invested in and traded with most of India's neighbors—Nepal, Sri Lanka, Burma, other South Asian nations. Bangladesh is entirely dependent upon China for trade. China has provided nuclear technology to Pakistan, India's archrival. And China has by far the strongest maritime force in the region."

"So that's why India might feel threatened. Why would China—"

"Because India has friends. The so-called Arc of Democracies'—Japan, Australia, and the United States."

"So we have mutual détente. No war."

"Historically, sir, the fear of encirclement by a coalition of hostile powers is exactly what leads to war. Think of Germany in 1914. Or Japan in 1941. Nations become worried. Determined to break out."

"Okay, so everyone in the region is running scared. What's the upshot?"

"I don't know. There are too many variables. Too many questions we can't answer."

"Such as?"

"For years, the prevailing view has been that China uses North Korea as their angry little sock monkey. A pawn employed to take aggressive positions so they don't have to. But if we threatened North Korea, or they threatened us, would China be their ally?"

"If they let North Korea destroy us, they'd have to forgive a lot of debt."

"Which they could do without losing a night's sleep. They'd do it in a heartbeat, if it gave them control of their region. Or perhaps even the globe."

"So if it comes to war—who wins?"

"Impossible to predict. It all depends on who does what and when they do it. The right nation making the right move at the right time could end up ruling the world."

He pushed away from the table. "I think you're being a bit dramatic."

"And I think you're being naïve, with respect, sir. North Korea is at the tipping point. If they launch a nuke, and I believe this psychopath just might, all the dominos will start to fall."

"But if we can't predict the result of a world war, then Chun can't either."

"He may not care. But to be fair, his actions of late have demonstrated an astonishing prescience. What if he gets lucky again?"

He fiddled with his coffee cup. He had no answer for that one.

Blake jumped in. "Do we have any reason to think Chun might launch immediately?"

"More likely he'll wait until our election is over," Knox replied.

"So we have until the polling places close?" Fernandez asked.

"Iran didn't feel threatened by Carter, but they released the hostages as soon as Reagan was elected. North Vietnam didn't invade Saigon until Nixon resigned. Chun may think"—Blake coughed into his hand—"may think your successor will take a tougher stance on the international scene than you have. Sorry, sir, but you're a lame duck. All future decisions will be decided by your successor."

"He won't be inaugurated until—"

"But we both know that you are effectively powerless. In the eyes of the world, the president-elect is the president."

He let that sink in. "So the future of this planet may depend on the decisions made by my successor?"

"In my opinion, yes."

He blew air through his cheeks. "Thank God. At least it won't be on my watch. Let the fate of the world be decided by the next guy."

"But the polls suggest that it will be Senator Vogel."

"I'm sure Vogel's capable of making a sound independent decision." He chuckled. "The senator may be a member of the other party. But it's not as if he's working for the enemy. Right?"

62

BB loved the hustle and bustle of Egypt. No other place on earth offered such a wide array of cultural opportunities. Street markets populated almost every corner, complete with aggressive street urchins who looked like they stepped out of a Kipling story. Museums filled with treasures dotted almost every corner. The deep chambers of the great pyramids held mysteries unsolved to this very day. And the ancient Egyptians loved games. Passing though Giza without stopping to admire the work of Imhotep and the other architectural geniuses of the fourth dynasty had been absolutely painful.

But they were on a mission. And Kadey's time was counting down fast.

Eventually the bus dropped him and Linden in Alexandria. Osiris Avenue took them downtown, close to the original site of the greatest repository of learning in the ancient world. He felt smarter just being in the general vicinity.

"I think the street we want is north of here," he said.

"I notice you're not holding a map," Linden replied. "Have you been here before?"

"No. But there was a long Alexandria mission in Tomb Raider: Apocalypse."

Linden pressed her hand against her forehead. "So you're navigating by video game?"

He squirmed. "Kinda."

"I'm walking in the shoes of Lara Croft?"

"And filling them quite nicely, I might add. As to the bosom, however—"

"Could you please pull you head out of the game world and tell me what your plan might be? I know the coordinates directed us to the Bibliotheca Alexandrina. But it's a big place. What are we going to do when we get there?"

"I've got an old friend who works here. We'll start there."

"And who is this friend? The world champion of pachisi?"

They walked up the stone steps leading to the Bibliotheca. "I'm talking about Douglas Moore. The greatest research scientist alive today."

BB gasped as he stepped into Moore's office. It was barely a closet. A desk and two chairs, no wiggle room. Papers and books stacked to the ceiling. This man was thought to be in line for a Nobel Prize. And this is what the powers-that-be gave him.

"BB! How the hell are you?" Moore stretched his hand across his desk, reaching over the clutter. He wore a white lab coat. His glasses perched on the top of his head. "I see you in the news all the time."

They shook hands. "That tells me you read only the best periodicals. *Games World of Puzzles* and such." He introduced Linden.

"Delighted. Always wanted to meet the woman who tamed the wild beast."

She smiled. "Only temporarily, as it turned out."

They chatted amiably for less than a minute before he brought the conversation to a point. He explained that Kadey was missing, and in broad quick strokes painted the scenario that brought them to Alexandria.

"I am so sorry," Moore said. "I cannot imagine what I'd do if my own daughter were in danger. Do you think your girl is somewhere in Egypt?"

"I hope so. She has fewer than ten hours left. If she isn't here—she's dead."

"Can't the authorities—"

"Useless."

"I'm sorry, BB. I've heard nothing about your daughter or anyone else who might've been kidnapped."

"Do you know why anyone would want to lead us here?"

"No idea. But Dinky seems to be involved. He's funding my research, too, you know."

"Do you know anything about his Vegas project?"

"Some kind of three-dimensional immersive training program for the military, right?"

"Apparently. Kadey was working on it when she disappeared. And she's not the only one who's disappeared. And one guy was murdered."

"You suspect some kind of . . . scientific espionage?"

"I don't know what to suspect. We've been led all around the world. But so far, it hasn't led us to Kadey." He paused. "Back in the day, you were the leading authority on the creation of virtual worlds. Which is basically what Dinky is trying to do in Vegas. Is there someone who might not want his project to succeed? A rival government, perhaps?"

Moore contemplated a moment. "I suppose it's possible. But any interference is far more likely to come from the private sector."

"Such as?"

"Game companies."

Linden peered at him. "Video game industry sabotage?"

"The gaming industry is huge. Bigger than the film industry now, worldwide. Games have become more complex, more immersive. If someone could create a truly four-dimensional immersive experience, something a player could enter without the interference of a screen, it would be worth billions."

"You think it's possible?" she asked.

"I know it is. Just a matter of time. And the person who creates it is going to be the next gaming billionaire."

"So there's actually a lot at stake in Ogilve's project."

"He's letting the government finance his R and D. But if he gets it to work, he'll take it into the private sector and make a fortune. In addition to the fortune he already has. I'm sure any number of companies would lie, cheat, kidnap, and murder to get that technology first."

"Any likely suspects?"

Moore removed his glasses and polished them with his lab coat. "I wouldn't want to accuse anyone without actual knowledge."

"What firms would benefit most from the tech you're describing?"

"Well, Linden, you've worked on closed sets before, right? Applying game theory principles to economic phenomena."

"Indeed I have."

"So you know what happens when there's money to be made, but not enough for everyone."

"Ethical behavior goes out the window. The successful strategy is the one that takes into account the strategies of others, foresees it, and thwarts it. The actions of the victor will follow a predictable mathematical pattern."

"Wait a minute," BB said. "We're talking about real people. I refuse to believe their actions can be predicted by some mathematical theorem."

Linden looked at him dismissively. "That's because you spend all your time memorizing chess gambits instead of keeping up with the latest academic literature. Game theory is probably the most important field of pure research being pursued today. Game theory has been used to analyze an extensive range of human and animal behavior. It can be amazingly accurate, so long as the variables don't overwhelm the analyst."

"But they do, in real life. So it's worthless."

"That's not fair." She addressed Moore. "Is physics worthless because the laws of physics may not always apply on the subatomic scale? Or the macrospatial scale?"

"That's totally different."

"Is it? They're both about predicting behavior. And they're both making huge strides. Initially, game theorists assumed players would always behave in a manner that maximizes their success. That's called the homo economicus model. But in reality, humans are not always so logical. There are reasons for these deviations from self-interest—emotion, altruism, irrationality, and so forth. Many scholars believe they can eventually predict how actual human populations will behave when faced with anticipatable situations. In other words, these games could give us the predictive power to foresee the future."

"Wouldn't that make life boring?"

"Assuming you need surprise to float your boat. Most scientists are more enchanted with results."

"What possible results—"

"Don't you see? If you can analyze sufficient factors to predict the future, it would be a simple matter of reverse engineering—

inductive reasoning—to determine what action must be taken to produce a desired result. You could create the future of your choice."

Moore wiped his brow. "And people are scared by genetic engineering. What would you call this? Future engineering?"

"In the right hands, it could be wonderful. Society by design rather than by accident."

"I suppose that's possible," Moore said. "But calculations on this level, with so many variables, are far beyond current capabilities."

"This is a fascinating debate," BB said, checking his cell, "but we're on a timetable. A life-or-death one. The only kind of predicting that interests me is predicting where someone took my daughter. You said you're working on one of Dinky's projects. Can you tell us what the project is?"

Moore hesitated. "The research is absolutely confidential."

"My daughter's life is in danger."

"Very well." The scientist led them out the door and into the corridor. At the end of the hall, he slipped an access card through a wall scanner. The door clicked open. "Come into my mad scientist lair."

Moore's laboratory struck him as a scaled-down version of what he'd seen in Vegas. All the usual suspects were there, the Pyrex and beakers and Bunsen burners. Not to mention a lot of electronic machinery he couldn't identify.

Then he spotted something familiar. Two boxes, each bearing pointed metallic cones made of concentric circles. "Are these what I think they are?"

Moore's grin was irrepressible. "I certainly hope so."

"Particle beam generators?"

"You got it."

"How does this relate to video games?"

"It doesn't. Ogilve seems far more interested in archeology than computer games these days."

"He does?"

"Whenever he's in town, he spends his spare time out at that tomb they discovered about three miles north of here. A minor discovery, they say, but that gives him more freedom to interfere than the Egyptian government would probably permit otherwise. Since the revolution, that government has been so poor they have a hard time saying no to anyone with major money. I think Dinky is trying to do something a little more serious with his work. So am I."

"And your work is . . ."

"Adventures in transportation."

"High speed rail? Hot air balloons? Zeppelins?"

Moore shook his head. "Teleportation."

63

Senator Vogel's former pollster, now campaign manager, showed him the most wonderful chart he had ever seen.

"Polls show you winning tomorrow, sir."

"Let's hope they're right."

"They are."

"How long until the press conference?"

"Two minutes." The kid held an iPad. "You need to see this before you go in."

He took the iPad and held it at arm's length. Vanity precluded him from wearing reading glasses when he was on the campaign trail. "Trouble?"

"Chaos in Korea. New general in town."

"Could only be an improvement."

"Don't be so sure."

He played the video feed. The former chief adjutant to General Yoon had staged a military coup. The political leadership was unchanged, but Chun's absolute control of the military, coupled with the refusal of any foreign nation to intervene, appeared to concretize his control of the nation's military might. Chun's press conference was obviously intended to threaten the Western world.

"New world order?"

"Yes, sir. That's what he said."

"What does it mean?"

"That's what everyone is wondering. I think all we can be certain about is that it means he dislikes the status quo. The superpower hegemony."

"The United States of America."

"In all likelihood."

"But we could take him, right?"

The kid shrugged. "Depends upon who's holding his leash. Or what leashes he's holding. Anyway, just in case there's a question, I want you to seem on top of it. But don't go there unless you have to. It's too close to the election to stir up trouble for no good reason. Stay on message. Better economy, more jobs, lower taxes."

"No way."

"Excuse me?"

"This is the moment."

"I don't . . . follow . . ."

"The pawns are all in position, my friend. This is when the queen rides out."

Bright lights blinded Vogel as he strode to the podium. As always, he found it disorienting, dizzying, and rude. But he did not allow any of that to show.

"I have a prepared statement," he announced, pulling his script from his jacket pocket. "Then I'll take questions."

He spread the script out and smoothed it flat with his hand.

And then he looked up abruptly.

"You know what? The hell with the prepared statement." He tossed the script into a nearby waste bin. "We're in a crisis situation here. You don't need to hear some canned tripe written by a team of staffers spouting economic wishful thinking. You need to know what's happening today. You've come a long way and your time is valuable. So I won't waste it."

He heard a shout from the back of the room. "What's the crisis?"

"I'm talking about North Korea, of course."

"President Fernandez says there's no cause for concern," a reporter said.

"Yes, I know." Vogel pursed his lips. A ridge formed between his eyebrows. "That's what worries me. I fear that our leadership is . . . dangerously out of touch. This election could not come too quickly. We need change like we've never needed it before."

A woman in the front row raised her hand. He could see they did not expect to be talking about Korea and few were prepared to do so. "Isn't this just a change from one devil to another?"

"No. Yoon may have been aggressive and under-qualified, but we had no reason to believe he was unstable. The US has been able to reach various trade and arms agreements with him as chief negotiator. Chun is a madman. A bully. A violent psychopath."

The reporters scribbled furiously. He knew they rarely heard anyone speak so honestly about a foreign leader. Diplomacy typically required more gentility.

"President Fernandez believes there's no cause for concern. And I just viewed a clip in which my opponent, Vice President Beale, states that the current administration has the situation firmly under control."

He flashed the photo his campaign manager gave him. "Have you seen this photograph?"

The reporters leaned in closer.

"This was taken just minutes after the coup. Predictably, Chun has commandeered Yoon's office." He pointed to a small black box on the desk. "President Fernandez didn't mention that box. Neither did Beale. But I will. It's critical that you understand what it is. Because that little box has the power to start the next global conflict. And yes, I'm talking about World War Three."

Now they were interested. Questions flew at lightning speed. But they were all variations on "What's the box?"

"That box is a Luddivox TM-4750 transmitter. It's basically the next generation of what we used to call the nuclear football. Simply by punching an eight-digit code into that keyboard, Chun can launch a nuclear strike against a predetermined target."

"Do you have any reason to believe he will?"

He allowed himself a little visible scorn. "Do you think that box is on his desk because it matches the lamp? He's waving his saber at us. I can't even call this a veiled threat, because there's no veil. This is open, unmasked aggression."

The reporters scribbled furiously. A hundred questions came at once. He chose the one most useful to him.

"Do you have any reason to believe he's targeting the US?"

"Did you hear what he said, live and on camera? Is there anyone else who can stand in his way?" He paused, letting that sink in. "China is a Korean ally. Hard to classify Russia, but they're much closer to Korea than they are to us, politically and geographically. Same goes for Pakistan. France and the UK pose no serious obstacles. If Chun can take us out, he can dominate the world." He paused, looking directly into the camera. "And if we wait for Korea to make the first move, with all their allies lined up in formation—it will be too late."

A senior correspondent for one of the major networks pushed himself out of his chair. "Senator, all the polls have shown you significantly ahead ever since the assassination attempt. If you are elected, can we take this as a preliminary statement of your administration's foreign policy?"

"You may. I won't let anyone undermine the authority or security of the United States. I will not hesitate to take bold and decisive action to avert this threat." He stopped, his lips compressing slightly. "A threat my opponent does not appear to even know exists."

"How did you know about the box?"

"You shouldn't be running for leader of the free world if you haven't done your homework."

"Are you sending a message to General Chun?"

"No, I'm sending a message to the American people. I'm assuring them that their interests will be protected." Pause. "Chun's a bloodthirsty maniac. I won't be speaking to him at all. Unless it's via an ICBM."

Another audible stir in the gallery. A few reporters rose from their seats and headed toward the back doors, apparently so eager to phone in their scoop they couldn't wait for the end of the conference.

"How quickly can you put your plan into action?" another reporter asked.

"Immediately after I'm in office. I won't even wait for the inaugural ball." He leaned forward. "But we cannot afford to wait for January. I'm calling on President Fernandez to take immediate action against this threat. And if he would like to consult with me, I would be happy to put aside party differences and do so. I'm calling on the president to immediately deploy the Pacific fleet in a containment formation around the North Korean coast. A bottleneck. Restrict the trade lines. See if that gives Chun something to think about. I'm also calling on the president to move the necessary aircraft carriers into position so they could launch a strike that would hit Korean soil in minutes. I'm calling on him to put the PACOM on red alert status."

He drew in his breath. "Chun wants to play ball? Fine. Let's show him how the greatest nation in the history of the world plays ball."

"Does that mean you're not ruling out the possibility of a preemptive nuclear strike against North Korea?"

He looked back at the reporter with stony eyes. "I think maybe Chun did get one thing right. This is a critical turning point in world history. And if so, the United States will defend itself."

"But Senator—"

"I can't predict the future. But I can be ready for it. Prepared. Because the truth is, no one knows what's coming next."

No one, he thought. Except me.

64

B B did a double take. "Teleportation? As in, 'Beam me up, Scotty?'"

Dr. Moore fingered his glasses. "Actually, that's a fantastic misnomer."

"Because teleportation is impossible?"

"No, because Captain Kirk never said that. Not in any of the seventy-nine episodes of the original *Star Trek*."

Linden cut in. "You've done it, haven't you? Transported mass from one location to another."

Moore nodded. "I wasn't the first. Japanese researchers first transported subatomic particles a few years ago. I've reproduced their work here. I can send a subatomic particle from this radiating point"—he touched the box on the left—"to this one." He touched the box on the right. "The particle leaves point A and appears at point B a fraction of a second later. Without crossing the space in between."

"How can you tell?"

"We use radium tracking to follow the transit of the particles."

"But it doesn't happen instantaneously."

"No. And frankly, we're not sure why. But there seems to be a time delay proportionate to the distance covered."

"That's fascinating," Linden remarked.

"Yes, but unfortunately, there isn't much practical application for transporting subatomic particles. We need to carry larger payloads."

"Like people?"

"That would be useful. If a little scary."

"But you think it's possible?"

"We've proved that it is. But we need way more processing power. Taking into account the Bekenstein bound—that's the upper limit on entropy—we've calculated that the number of information bits required to transport and recreate an adult human would be ten to the forty-fifth power, multiplied by two to the one hundred and fiftieth power." He tapped a finger against the number written on a standing board.

$$2.0057742 \times 10^{45} \text{ bits}$$

BB sighed. "Is there any chance you can explain this in a way that could be understood by someone whose primary contact with math is memorizing the odds of various poker hands?"

"I can try. My team is taking a different approach from the researchers in Japan. We're using the Bose-Einstein condensate as our theoretical conduction basis."

"Thank you for making it so clear. How does that differ from what the Japanese crew is doing?"

"This is not true quantum teleportation. All that business about trying to open wormholes and poking people through them—that's way risky. And not just to the people being transported. Maybe to the whole world. You thought the atomic bomb was dangerous? Wait until people start messing around with ruptures in the fabric of space-time. We're nowhere near ready to handle that."

A thought occurred to BB. "So you could aim your teleportation beam at someone and they would be . . ."

"Deleted," Linden supplied, giving him a meaningful look.

Moore agreed. "That is theoretically possible."

"But does everyone share your feelings about the dangers? People have been known to start projects with enormous potential hazards."

"I don't see anyone in the public sector going for this. It's too far out. The more theoretical your work becomes, the less likely anyone is to pay for it. Governments always want results. Yesterday. You got a new weapon, money will flow. You got something that can only improve the quality of life—money is hard to find."

"Seems to me," Linden said, "this could be used as a weapon. Transporting troops and munitions. Supplies. Or perhaps, transporting enemy troops away from the battlefield."

"I hope they don't twig onto that. I prefer being financed by Dinky to being financed by any government."

He pondered. "Dinky must have some reason for paying for this."

Moore shrugged. "Perhaps it relates to his excavation project. But how?"

"I don't know. I think maybe we should go out there and ask him. Thank you for your help, but—"

His cell phone vibrated. He didn't want to look, but he forced himself.

The photo showed Kadey, still bound and gagged. Her eyes wide, pleading. She appeared terrified.

A sharp serrated knife lay across her throat.

5:14 hours. Then she dies.

65

J ulian pulled the hood of the robe over his head as he strode between the marble pillars into the ceremonial room. This was his first appearance in the secret ceremony since his initiation. He hoped this meeting would give him the information he needed.

He passed several other hooded figures along the way. Each time, he raised his hand, palm outward, revealing the blue star. They did the same in response.

"The numbers be with you."

"And also with you."

"All is reason."

"All is reason."

He proceeded to the ceremonial chamber.

He still had the LSAC sewn into his inner ear. He and the Father remained in contact. The game proceeded according to plan, despite the accelerated pace of changing world events. All the pawns circled one another, but no one had an advantage. Yet. That was why he was here. To learn what he could to tip the balance.

He took his position in the central chamber.

"What is the world?" the leader intoned.

"All is number," they replied in unison.

"Where do we find purity?"

"In numbers."

"Where do we find life?"

"Reason is immortal. All else is mortal."

"Where do we find death?"

His lips parted—then froze. This was not part of the liturgy.

The leader repeated himself. "Where do we find death?"

His looked up to find the others staring at him.

They knew. His cover was blown. He reached toward his boot—

The switchblade was not inside the false heel.

A hand clamped around his throat. Another pair of arms hooked through his, pulling his arms back.

The leader stepped down from the raised platform in the center of the chamber, removing his hood as he walked. It was not the usual Leader.

It was General Chun.

"Good afternoon, Mr. Ainsbury. Or should I call you Julian? Whatever pleases you." Chun smiled. "So good to see you again. After so many years. It seems this is reunion week for me."

He didn't say a word. He couldn't think of a word worth saying.

"Are you in communications with Dr. Ogilve? If so, please give him my regards. When last we met, he departed without giving me the chance to bid him au revoir."

He struggled against his captors, but they held him tight. They had prepared this in advance. There were three strong men behind him, each holding fast. He wasn't going anywhere.

Chun thrust a finger into his left ear. The violation of his body sent chills coursing through him. Chun's face was so close he could smell the man's fetid breath.

"I can feel the transmitter, even if I cannot extract it. Without tools. Later I will rip it from your flesh. But first, I want to greet my old research companion." Chun raised his voice, bellowing into his ear. "Hello, Emerson. I have your old lab assistant. And soon I will have you."

Chun grabbed him by the jaw. "Was there an answer? What did Ogilve say?"

He did not respond.

Chun slapped him hard across the face. "What did he say?"

No response.

Chun clenched his fist and hit him. Something tore inside.

Julian extended his tongue to catch the blood trickling from the corner of his mouth. "He said for you to rot in hell like the bastard you are. He says if you hurt me he will do five times worse to you."

"That does not sound like the Emerson I remember. He's not there, is he? He is quite busy at the moment, I believe. And so he has left you alone. To die."

"He wouldn't do that. You're the killer. He's the savior."

"I'm afraid I do not remember him as fondly as you. I spent many happy times with his newlywed bride, though. Over and over again. I think I had her more times than he did. And then there was the daughter. That was choice grade-A meat, let me tell you."

He felt his stomach churn. This man was insane. And venomous. Willing to do anything to get what he wanted. There was nothing he could say that could possibly help, so he remained silent.

"This is the most humorous part of the story. Your Emerson, who thinks he is so good at games? So good at predicting the future? I finessed him. I played the card that led you straight into my trap."

"What are you talking about?"

"This society. The Pythagoreans. Yes, it was useful for recruiting scientists. Programmers. And others. Nothing inflates the intellectual mind more surely than the belief that they have received some special distinction. Why else would academics toil so, squabbling and working for such meager rewards, an endowed chair, an occasional sabbatical? I needed men of science to counter Ogilve's work. So I created a secret society. Dropped hints and clues throughout the scientific world. Made it seem so elitist and desirable. And before long, I had a better team of devoted researchers than I could have bought with all the money in the world."

"Why are you telling me this?" It was more than just a point of curiosity. The fact that Chun was willing to reveal so much suggested that the general did not think he would ever have the opportunity to repeat it.

"Because my little society attracted an unexpected bonus. You. Emerson's right-hand man. You managed to defeat my sweet Rani's sister. But not me. No one defeats me." Chun leaned in closer. "Once again I have the best possible leverage over you, Emerson. The leverage of controlling those you care about."

"I'm an employee. Nothing more. The Father cares nothing about me."

"I doubt that. And even if it is true, is Ogilve willing to sit idly in his hiding place playing his little games while I torture you? Day after day after day, always taking you to the brink of death, but never quite extinguishing you? That's what you have in your future, my friend. Beating. Branding. Rape by instrumentation. That's how we will fill your days. From now until the time either you or Emerson gives me what I want."

Julian felt his throat tightening. His devotion to the Father was unconditional—but he had never considered the possibility of brutal, sadistic torture. Inflicted repeatedly. "I would sooner die than let you anywhere near the Father."

"But I don't want to be anywhere near him. You see, my demands are so small. So reasonable." Chun grabbed him by his hair and jerked his head backward. "All he has to do is pull the damn plug."

A second later, he felt a knee sliding between his legs, straight up toward his groin. Even though he braced himself, he could not prevent the cry from escaping his lips. Sweat poured from his temples. The hand on his throat clenched harder. And then, just as the wave of pain crested, Chun hammered him again.

His knees buckled. But for the men holding him up, he would've fallen.

"Hear this, Emerson." Chun growled into his ear. "We are coming for you. You have no idea how many. My people are everywhere. In every key government in the world. And now I have every weapon known to man, and a few known only to us. I am coming for you. And your pathetic acolyte will tell me where you are."

"I will tell you nothing," he said.

Chun smashed a fist into his face. "You will tell me where your master and his toys are hidden. You can tell me now, or you can suffer inhuman, indescribable pain first. But you will tell me." He punched him again, even harder than before. "And then, Emerson, we will come for you. And we will destroy you. And then the future will begin."

66

Palmer watched BB and Linden through his high-powered binoculars as they left the Bibliotheca.

Being an authorized agent of the White House had both advantages and disadvantages. True, his hands were tied and he was not supposed to apprehend, much less eliminate, his quarry. True, he'd heard dark rumblings about North Korea and threats to global stability that gave even an old hand like him the chills.

Just when it looked as if this conflict might be coming to a conclusion, it escalated. Something big was happening.

He remembered when they first called him, pulling him off his CIA mission in Pakistan. Something was going down in Greece. Who could care? he'd wondered. Greece was about as threatening as Liechtenstein. Maybe less so. But there was some weird cult draining top scientists from all around the world. And there might be ties to Korea. So he'd gone undercover . . .

And when that trail, after several chutes and ladders, led to Vegas, he'd gone there as well. Posing as an FBI agent. Acting as if all he cared about was the murder of David Bishop.

Acting. So much acting.

If something big was about to happen, he would not give up his only lead. His bosses wanted to know where these two were going—so he would find out. One way or the other, he was bound to learn something. They had come to this laboratory for a reason. And this was not their final destination.

He would give them a little more rope. As long as they didn't know he was nipping at their heels, there was no hurry.

This had been an intriguing chase, but it was coming to an end.

67

B huddled behind a large orange and black construction crane, waiting for night to fall.

"How many guards?" Linden asked.

"I only see one."

She pulled up on his shoulders, craning to get a better view. "I would expect Dinky to have more security. Even for a minor excavation."

"Maybe he's not expecting trouble. He didn't have that much security in Paris."

And this time it looked even easier. And that was the part that concerned him most.

The excavation site was not hard to find. This part of the desert, only about three miles north of Alexandria, was dotted with construction cranes and other equipment. In the center lay a canopied declension that must be the entrance to the lower level of the underground tomb. A makeshift hand-operated elevator appeared to take people below. That elevator entrance was where the guard was posted.

What interested him most was the kind of equipment he saw, and the materials on site. He was no expert, but he'd worked on a construction crew one summer while in college and he knew a little about the subject. What he saw was concrete, cinder blocks, paneling, and all kinds of computer equipment.

Dinky wasn't excavating anything. He was building something.

What could possibly be so important, so precious, that you would want to hide it underground?

And why had every clue they'd encountered in this long insane drama brought him here?

"The Egyptians built some astonishing stone structures," he said. "The Sphinx. The Giza pyramids."

"The power of squares," Linden replied.

"Shouldn't that be cubes? Triangles? Pyramids?"

"No. I'm talking about numerical squares. Square roots, numbers multiplied to the power of two. Despite the triangular appearance of pyramids—which actually have four sides, not three—Egyptians were obsessed with squares. They believed squares to be the source of all power—even that of life itself. Which makes sense. Squares are the fundamental building block for all higher mathematics. So what's our plan?"

"I don't have one."

"I thought you were the master strategist."

"Not accustomed to breaking into underground digs. We have no tools."

"Poor planning on your part. What would you like to have?"

"A gun would be nice. Since the guard appears to have one."

"You would have no idea what to do with a gun."

True enough. But he still thought holding one might be useful. Or at least comforting. "Ok, perhaps a grenade. Something to create a diversion."

"I can create a diversion," she said. "I'll lure him off with my feminine charm. You conk him over the head when he's not looking."

"I'm having a hard time seeing this working." The security guard rose from his chair and walked toward a small trailer about fifty feet to the west. "Or we could wait until the guard leaves."

"What's he doing?"

"Don't know. Bathroom break, maybe? He's been out there a couple of hours. And I have a hunch his thermos is filled with something more refreshing than coffee. Especially given the desert heat."

The guard snapped the trailer door behind him.

"Formulated a plan yet?" she asked.

"The usual one. Run."

He leaped out from behind the crane and raced across the desert expanse toward the underground elevator. His sneakers sank into the sand, but he still managed to make good time. Linden stayed right behind him. In fact, he suspected she could pass him if she wanted,

231

but she was kind enough to let him think he was the more athletic member of the team.

He'd almost reached the elevator when he heard the report of the rifle.

"Duck!" He grabbed Linden and threw her down to the sand. The bullet smashed somewhere over their heads. He started to rise, then heard several other rifles fire behind him. He fell back, covering her with his body.

"Seems Dinky's little operation was better guarded than we realized."

"What do we do?"

"I don't think we have a choice. If we go backward, we get captured."

"If we go forward, we might get dead."

"Think of it like you're playing Sorry. You know there's a good chance you'll get tagged if you move your token forward. But it's the only way to win the game."

More rifle reports. "That's the stupidest—"

"Kadey."

She sighed. "Yes. Kadey."

They grasped one another's hands and dove toward the elevator. Something like a thousand rifles fired behind them.

68

Julian did not know how long he had dangled by the neck from the ceiling, naked, bleeding, completely vulnerable. But he knew he would not survive it much longer.

Physically, he could not be overcome. The rigors of his childhood, the agony of captivity, his *systema* training, had left him indomitable. Yes, they could hurt him. They could burn him. They could inflict all manner of torture. But he would never give in.

Mentally, he was vulnerable. Everyone was, ultimately. They had given him drugs. He did not know what they were, but he had seen the syringe enter his arm. Had felt the cold liquid gurgle through his veins. His head swam and he lost his focus, the single quality he considered most important to his effectiveness. His head swirled with a giddiness unrelated to the torture.

The noose around his neck burned. It dug into his flesh, inching ever closer to the trachea. He was suspended by a simple block-and-tackle arrangement in a small storage unit. Closed off from the world where no one could see him, no one could hear him. While they interrogated him, one man pulled him up and down, choking and asphyxiating him. First they jerked him into the air by his neck. Then they dropped him to the ground like dead weight. More than once he had thought his neck would snap. Blood and sweat crusted his skin so much he felt as if he were wearing an alien skin.

When they left to "retrieve sharper implements," they tied the end of the rope to a hook on the wall, leaving him suspended with his feet almost touching the floor.

But not quite.

The pain was excruciating. Every breath was a dearly purchased torment.

But he had not told them anything. He had not given up the Father. He had not betrayed the game. He kept his promise.

The door opened. Chun was the first in, followed by two other professional psychopaths.

"We're back," Chun announced. "I hope you've not been bored in our absence?"

He remained silent.

"Are you still feeling manly?" Chun laughed. "Soon you will not be a man at all." Chun clutched his exposed genitals, gripping far too tightly. "I could squeeze the manhood out of you right now. And I would enjoy it."

His lips tightened. "I think you enjoy having an excuse to hold a man's package."

Chun laughed again, but squeezed all the harder.

He gritted his teeth, determined not to give Chun the satisfaction of screaming.

"Your ability to reproduce has come to an end, my former lab assistant. So glad there won't be another generation of you to contend with."

A sudden wave of pain shot through him like an unbearable, omnidirectional bolt of lightning. His entire body spasmed, rippling back and forth as if he had been Tasered from within. Even after Chun removed his hand, the pain did not subside. He whipped back and forth, dangling from the rope.

Chun picked up a towel and wiped his hands. "In truth, I often think reproduction is overrated. Immortality does not come from offspring. Immortality comes from power. The power to leave your mark. The power to reshape the world in your own image."

Julian gasped in short, desperate breaths. As if the pain were not bad enough, his inability to breathe made this unbearable.

"I will be honest with you," Chun said. "I am impressed. Not many occasions arise these days when I say that. And I've had to persuade a good many people to provide information to me over the years. I haven't come to my current place in the world by being genteel. Twenty years ago you would not have recognized me. I was weak, helpless, emaciated. Abandoned. But I overcame that by finding strength within myself. A need to be better than I was. Not many people have this, I think. The world is filled with too many poseurs, parvenus, and pretenders. Too much bark, too little bite. But you interest me. You have come far since those days in North Korea when you washed Ogilve's test tubes. I honor your resilience."

He spoke through gritted, blood-smeared teeth. "A torturer knows nothing of honor."

"Does a spy? You lied your way into my organization. You used subterfuge to obtain information for your cruel master, a man who wants nothing but revenge, who is willing to inflict misery and unhappiness on billions if it gives him petty satisfaction."

"That's not true. He is the Father and—"

"He is Captain Ahab, a cripple who uses vengeance to avoid confronting his own culpability."

"You know nothing of the Father. Or what he wants."

"Then why don't you tell me what he wants?"

He bit his lips shut. He had allowed himself to be baited.

Chun flung his head back with extreme violence. He felt something tear inside his throat.

"Amazing the things you can find at the drugstore. For less than thirty euros." He reached into the bag and withdrew a canister. "Hair spray. Old school. Aerosol can. Would not appear to be a deadly weapon."

Chun sprayed it directly into his face.

Julian winced, closed his eyes. But it still burned. His eyes watered, trying to sooth the hurt. Chun kept spraying and no matter how tightly he clenched his eyelids, it leaked through.

Eventually he screamed.

"So you begin to see the potential for weaponized hair spray. Good. But I have hardly scratched the surface." He reached into the bag again, pulled out a Bic Lighter.

"You know, when I had your master—apologies, 'the Father'— under my control for one hundred twenty-seven days, he was not so resilient as you. Problem was, I did not have the freedom to torture him. I needed more than information. I needed productivity. Any extreme pain would've eradicated his ability to work. So I had to torture others—or to make him believe that I had. I had to make his adrenaline surge. I had to create a scenario in which he *wanted* to produce for me so badly it was virtually impossible that he would fail. The greatest developments come from the highly motivated."

Chun sighed. "But how do I motivate you? You care nothing for yourself. I do not currently possess the only man you care about—indeed, I want you to give him up. You have no wife, no children, no family, no lover. You are a hard man to reach."

Chun's eyes narrowed, just barely.

"Ogilve reached you. By orchestrating your escape. But no one else has. No one before or since. That is what makes my task so challenging. That is what forces me to go places I do not wish to go, to do things that go against my nature. You think I am a cruel, sadistic man. I am not. I have known cruelty. I have suffered great pain. But that has left me with nothing but love in my heart. Love for all humanity, flawed though it may be. That has left me determined to conceive a plan. A plan to eliminate pain. To make the world a better place. And now, when I am so close to making it a reality, I see myself thwarted by what? By a man with no plan at all. By a man motivated by only the basest of emotions—the desire to obstruct the plans of others. Am I to let something so petty prevent salvation for so many?"

Chun lit the Bic. "You will talk now. Or I will burn you. Starting with your male member."

Julian clenched his eyes shut.

"You can stop this. Simply tell me what I want to know."

"I will not."

"You will. Eventually."

"I will never betray the Father. Or Alex."

"You—" Chun halted. "Alex?"

He choked. What had he done?

"Ogilve calls his machine Alex?" Chun began to laugh.

And that sound gave him more chills than anything that had happened before.

"Release him." The accomplice lowered the rope.

He fell in a heap on the hard concrete floor, barely conscious.

"He calls the computer Alex." Chun pulled out his smartphone, punching buttons furiously. "And Rani followed the Game Master to Egypt before she lost him at the Bibliotheca. This tells me everything I need to know. It is not an easy thing to hide something so immense as . . ." Chun's lips curled. "Alex."

Tears rushed to his eyes. Had he fought so hard to resist—only to betray the Father inadvertently?

"It all becomes clear now," Chun said. "I know where your Father is. And his little toy. We can be there in a matter of hours. With a small army."

Chun fired off a few texts. "Julian, you have just become the most valuable pawn in the service of the black king."

69

Palmer watched from his sandy summit as BB and his ex dived down the elevator shaft. He was impressed that they had progressed so far, given their utter guilelessness and total lack of advance planning. Perhaps the blunderer's way was best after all.

But it was also becoming clear that they were following a path.

He'd kept his distance the whole time he followed them from the Bibliotheca. Saw Rani, too, but managed to stay out of her sight. She seemed to have lost the scent, probably when BB played his switcheroo game with the transit buses.

So BB suspected he was being followed. His trick had worked well enough to fool the Pakistani Mata Hari. But not him. From this high dune he could see everything surrounding the Gen3^2 so-called excavation. He did not believe for a minute that they were excavating a tomb. He'd seen construction sites before. This wasn't one.

The snipers stopped shooting as soon as the elevator doors closed and BB and Linden were out of view. The guard never returned to his post.

This was not a true security force, either. This was a mock-up. An attempt to create the illusion of difficulty and danger. While all along, the mastermind behind this operation wanted BB to come inside. Posting a guard was almost laying out the welcome mat.

As with so many games, the more players, the more complex the strategy. This game was about to have a player they had not anticipated.

Using his cell, he contacted his Interpol connection, who patched him through to the proper authorities in the Egyptian national cultural authority. There was no record of any new tomb discoveries. In fact, they scoffed at the notion that Egypt would let an American undertake an excavation, should such a project exist.

This cover didn't pass the first level of scrutiny. Though Ogilve must have well-placed friends in the Egyptian government, even if the cover was a transparent façade.

He called his contact at the White House on a secure line.

The response was immediate and direct. "Do not confront any Egyptian or North Korean representatives."

"Then how can I get anything done?"

"Your cover is that you're chasing a fugitive from justice, someone wanted for a murder on American soil. Stick to that. Follow him. If necessary, apprehend him. You've reached his ultimate destination."

"I don't know that."

"We do. We've tapped into heat and energy readings. This is the place."

"So I should back off?"

"Chun has been on television basically threatening to use nukes against the United States, or anyone else that makes him unhappy. NORAD is on red alert. The president is contemplating a formal response. In the meantime, any intel you can gather will be worth its weight in plutonium."

"So you want me to go in?"

"I want you to learn anything you can."

"What am I authorized to do?"

"Anything it takes."

"Anything?"

"You heard me."

"This Game Master already knows too much. He could be a threat to national security. Possibly international security."

There was a pause. "Anything."

"Understood."

If this was ground zero for an act of North Korean aggression, or even something worse, he wasn't going to sit on the sidelines.

He wrapped a length of cord around his waist and then tied it to a grappling hook. He would follow after the sun set, as soon as he was sure it was safe.

BB might be the world's best at playing games. But someone else was playing the Game Master. Which made him all the more certain his previous opinion was correct.

This was one game BB was not likely to survive.

70

The elevator doors opened.

BB stepped out. Linden followed.

Before they could react, the elevator doors closed behind them. They heard the engine churn into action. The cage rose. He wasn't sure how far they had descended. He guessed the equivalent of eight floors, but it was hard to tell since the elevator had no intermediate stops.

"Guess we're not going back any time soon," Linden observed.

He agreed. "That's not the way this game is played."

The room was a white box. Almost a perfect cube, but he sensed it was somewhat longer than tall. The room was featureless, only stark white walls and a carpetless tile floor.

He spotted a closed door on the opposite side of the room, almost invisible because it was white and knobless, a diagram on the wall near the door, and a keypad.

"Looks like one of those rooms in Portal," he commented.

"Did Dinky design that game?"

"No, but I'll bet he played it." He pondered a moment. "Do you suppose we're going to find one of those portal-creating guns in here? Because that would be cool. Maybe we're going to transport instantaneously from one room to the next."

"Try to get your head out of games and back to reality."

"Dr. Moore is working on teleportation."

"Of subatomic particles. Not people." Linden examined the keypad. "Same design as the one in Dinky's office in Paris."

"Because it came from the same company. And the same person."

"Very likely. What do you suppose we're supposed to do with it?"

241

"That I don't know." He surveyed the room. Other than the diagram on the wall, nothing stood out. "If this is a game of Clue, I'm holding no cards."

"It's bound to be a game. Everything else has been."

"Funny you should say that." He scrutinized the diagram on the wall. It displayed an elongated rectangle divided into thirty squares, three rows of ten squares each. Distinctive Egyptian markings dotted some of the squares.

He brushed his hand against the diagram. Perfectly smooth. No buttons.

"What is it?"

"A Senet board. Game played in ancient Egypt. A precursor of backgammon. Except that the squares are numbered. The ancient Egyptians never did that."

"I remember reading that the Egyptians were the first to put numbers to widespread practical use. They had a complete system of written numbers well known even to the illiterate. They invented the zero—a brilliant conceptual leap. It's one thing to envision quantities—they're everywhere. It took a big-brained soul to conceive of the absence of quantity. To quantify nothingness."

"Fascinating."

"The base of the great pyramid is a square whose perimeter is equal to the circumference of a circle with a radius equal to the height of the pyramid. Ultimately, it all comes down to math. Mathematical ratios. Because the Egyptians believed numbers brought luck and victory."

"Okay, now you're starting to sound like a PhD."

"About time you noticed." She examined the diagram. "Surely we weren't brought here just so you could play Senet."

"I suspect there's more to it."

"This room is giving me claustrophobia. Way too white for my taste. I'm going to see if I can make the elevator return. I don't see any point in—"

An abrupt whirring noise sounded. Like a hydraulic engine churning into play. A few moments later, the floor shook.

He crouched down, pressing one hand against the floor. Was this an underground earthquake?

The wall before him began to rise.

242

The unseen engine was not shaking the floor. It lifted part of the wall. Uncoupling it from the floor. What he had initially identified as a door was not a door. More like a curtain. It rose slowly, crinkling like a Venetian blind, revealing a translucent acrylic panel behind it.

His pulse raced, and he didn't know why. "This is what in the gaming world they call the big reveal."

"Meaning?"

"We've reached the boss level." His voice dropped. "Which is not necessarily good news."

"What do you suppose is waiting for us on the other side? Lady or the tiger?"

"Or both. A big surprise."

"Darth is really Luke's father."

"That one's been used."

"Gandalf will return, after a costume change."

"Hope this surprise is as pleasant."

By the time the wall rose half the height of the door, he could see two knees pressed against the other side of the acrylic barrier. He bent down to get a better look.

"No." He pounded on the acrylic surface. "Oh my God. Oh my God."

Kadey was on the other side. She looked much as she had in the last photo sent to his phone. She was gagged and her hands were tied behind her back, connected to another rope restraining her feet. Hog-tied. Like a twice steer at the rodeo.

She looked terrified. But she was alive.

She stared at him with pleading eyes. He knew she recognized him.

Her eyes quickly darted to her mother.

She expected her mother to save her. If she was to be saved at all. Some wounds never healed.

He had never felt so frustrated in his entire life—at least not since the last time his daughter was in danger. And he'd failed to save her.

Kadey was kidnapped on the last day of her junior year of high school. The FBI explained that the news stories about him—and the large purses he'd won—made him a target. They didn't have to tell him how slender the chances were that she would be recovered alive.

Instead, they emphasized how important it was that he follow their instructions to the letter, without deviation.

"These are the rules of the game," they'd explained. "If you want any chance of victory, you have to obey the rules."

And so he did. The kidnapper, who was never caught, held Kadey for eighteen unendurable days. They finally found her bound and abandoned in a filthy unused horse stable not far from the University of California at Davis campus, bruised, blood-stained, virtually catatonic. She had never seen her abductor's face. She only knew two things.

First, that she had endured almost unbearable fear and misery on a daily basis.

And second—that she had endured those horrors because her father refused to pay the ransom.

Kadey spent more than a month in the hospital. And it was a good deal longer than that before she spoke to him. By that time, his marriage to Linden was a shambles. The divorce proceedings were well underway. He was leaving town. But he hoped to speak to his daughter again before he left.

He found her at home. The conversation did not go well. She threatened to walk out three times in the first ten minutes.

"Honey, you must know that I love you. More than anything. More than anything in the world."

"But not enough to come across with the cash, right?" She lifted her hand to twist a lock of her hair around a finger—or tried. The kidnapper had cut her hair in patches. She'd been forced to trim it almost to the scalp just to make it look halfway normal. "He told me that all you had to do was put the money in a bag and he'd release me. But you never did it. Never even thought about it."

"Kadey, I thought about it every day."

"Not hard enough."

"I talked to the FBI about this repeatedly. They said if I paid the ransom, the kidnapper would have no reason not to kill you."

"He had no reason to let me live. Or to treat me kindly. All you did was make a madman madder."

"Maybe it was a mistake. I don't know. But I did what I thought was right. I did it because I was afraid of losing you."

"That's what you say. But I'm just not feeling it. In fact, I never have."

"Kadey, don't say that."

"You've never exactly been a hands-on parent, have you? More interested in your own weird little world than your family."

"That's not remotely true. You're my girl—"

"You know nothing about me. You don't know what I like, what I don't like. You don't know who my friends are."

"That's ridiculous."

"Okay, name two of my friends."

He stuttered a moment, then fell silent.

"You know what, Daddy? I might be able to forgive that, if you'd at least paid some attention to me when I needed you. But you didn't."

"Sweetie, I did what the FBI told me to do."

"If they'd told you to jump off a cliff, would you do it?"

"Kadey. Listen to me." He reached out to her, but she slapped his hands away. He sounded desperate, even to himself. "I listened carefully to everything they said. And I did some reading and research of my own. I calculated the odds——"

"What?" Her voice soared. "You calculated the *odds*? You were playing a game! Again. My life is on the line, and you're playing some damn game."

"That's not true. Honey—"

She turned her back on him and headed toward the door. "All you know is games. You go through your whole useless life amusing yourself."

"Kadey, I would do anything for you."

"Would you?" Her voice turned thin and shrill. "Is it true that while I was a prisoner, you played in the regional chess qualifying tournament?"

He didn't answer for several moments. "The FBI said I should continue to go about my public business as usual. To avoid giving signs of desperation that might invite additional demands."

"I was a captive, daddy!" she screamed. "I was dirty and tired. He slapped me around almost every day. And you played a chess tournament!"

She slammed the door behind her.

"*Kadey!*"

That was the last time they spoke. They had not seen one another for eight years. Until now.

But she was on the other side of an acrylic partition, bound and gagged.

Kadey tried to talk. Unfortunately, he couldn't understand a word she said. Her eyes were red and she was obviously panicked. But he knew she was a tough girl. Always had been. She'd held out this long. She could last a little longer.

Then he spotted the water.

A large faucet on the other end of her closet, just behind her, gushed.

Kadey squirmed as the water trickled over her knees. Apparently it was cold. Maybe if she could stand up . . .

That was when he noticed. The rope binding her hands and feet together was strapped through some kind of mooring mechanism. He could see how to release the pin to free her. But she couldn't possibly reach it.

He wondered how long it would take the water in that tiny chamber to rise over her head. He guessed she had about ten minutes. Maybe not that long.

Ten minutes and it would be too late. Ten minutes and he'd failed to save his daughter. Again.

71

Chun saw pyramids out the window of his private jet.

There were perks to being the man with the military at his fingertips. Like being able to get a top Egyptian official on the phone any time he liked. He didn't give the functionary any more information than was necessary. All this civil servant needed to know was that he was entering Egyptian sovereign soil. He was bringing a small coterie of armed troops, and they were planning an assault on Egyptian soil.

"I am not planning an invasion. I will bring five men at most. A security detail. We will fly into Alexandria. We will drive directly to our target."

He could sense the hesitation over the phone. "I will need to get clearance." The foreign attaché, a man named Aziza, had a nasal voice. He did not sound as if he had taken action on his own initiative in his entire life. "Regulations do not permit the importation of firearms—"

"Do you know who I am?"

"Yes sir, but diplomatic envoys must be cleared in advance—"

"I don't have time for bureaucratic nonsense." He paused. Perhaps a better approach would be to create a persuasive narrative. Problem was, he did not have much time. "You must understand. This man Ogilve. The one your government has given free rein in Alexandria. He has taken something from me. And I want it back."

"We do not have an extradition treaty—"

"And that is fine. I don't want to take him." I don't want to bring him back alive, at any rate. "I just want what belongs to me."

"You must understand. Mr. Ogilve has favored-nation status, as does his country."

"I understand that your infant government has accepted a great deal of money. But surely it was not your intent to create a haven for international criminals."

"If you wish to file charges, you should contact—" His voice broke off suddenly. "Just a moment."

The line was silent for the better part of a minute. Then a different voice spoke.

"General Chun? This is Colonel Hallasie."

At last. One of his own men. He had not spent so much time placing agents in foreign governments for no reason. Hallasie had proven invaluable in this rebel-based government of amateurs and students. And now he would be invaluable again.

"I speak for the national domestic security force. We understand your request and find it entirely reasonable. We hope you recover what belongs to you."

Ah, the sweet joy of advance planning. On a level only he could manage. With the assistance of a key advisor. "Thank you, Colonel."

"We would only ask that you keep your operation . . . low profile."

"Understood. I will do my best. I see no reason why it should stray from the grounds of the so-called excavation."

"Good. We cannot provide official backup."

"Nor do I request it."

"But we can make sure there is no interference. No one traveling in or out. I think that would be best for everyone."

"I heartily agree."

"Is there anything else I can do for you, sir?"

"Yes. I have an emissary named Rani, currently in Alexandria. I want her to meet me when I land. Can you arrange passage for her?"

"Gladly."

"I will send you the details." He texted the message, then signed off.

The plane would land soon. In no time at all, he would see Ogilve. And this Game Master. And perhaps others as well.

Ogilve might anticipate his arrival, given the resources at his disposal. But Ogilve always underestimated him. The men he would leave surrounding the site would capture Ogilve when he made his escape. And anyone else who might attempt to depart.

THE GAME MASTER

At last, his plans approached the final phase. Everything was about to change. Never again would the Arduous March destroy a child's life. Never again would anyone suffer brutality, poverty, starvation, rape, intentional cruelty. In the future, there would be no need for another like him.

It did not matter if millions died. Or even billions. What mattered was what would rise from the ashes.

72

"We have to do something," BB said. "Look how fast the water is rising."

It was already halfway up Kadey's shins.

He pounded on the acrylic panel. He wasn't nearly strong enough to break it. It barely even registered his pounding. But he wanted her to know he was trying to save her. It was important that she know. That she understood that he would do anything for her, that it had never been any different.

His daughter stared up at him, a desperate expression on her face. He had no trouble reading that tell.

He was failing her. Just as she expected him to do.

The keypad on the wall buzzed. The LCD panel glowed red.

He forced himself to turn away from her, focusing his attention on the diagram on the wall. "Everywhere we go, we confront games. Almost as if someone was testing us. No—playing us." He ran everything he knew about Senet through his mind, hoping to tumble across a solution. "Senet goes back at least five thousand years. Senet boards were found in King Tut's tomb. Magnificent boards with adjustable tables made from rare woods and encrusted with ivory."

"Sort of like your gold-plated SCRABBLE set?"

"But not as cool. Ramses II was depicted playing this game in a famous tapestry."

"Neat."

"But Senet wasn't just for the ruling class. Anyone could—and did—play the game. Even people who couldn't afford a board could draw the diagram in the sand and use rocks for tokens." He was babbling, and he knew it, but he hoped he might stumble across the solution to saving Kadey. "The game had mystical significance. Each of these squares was called a house. Homes to the various gods. The movement of players across the board symbolized the movement of souls through the world of the dead."

"Do you know the rules?"

"It's not hard." He pointed to the board. "You roll dice—actually, the ancient Egyptians used three-sided sticks. But the result is the same—you roll a number, one through six. You have five pieces, interspersed with your opponent's pieces on the top row. Your goal is to get all your pieces off the board. But you can't bear any off until all five are on the bottom row. And you can't move to a space with another token of yours on it. If you land on an opponent's space, you trade places."

"Like in Aggravation."

"Or a thousand other race games, all of which derive from this one. If two of your pieces are on adjacent squares, they're immune to capture. And if you get three pieces together, the opponent can't pass."

"Blocking. Like in backgammon."

"Very similar. Your turn continues until you roll a two or three. You can move any of your pieces on your turn—if a move is available. If no move is available, you must move one of your pieces backward."

He glanced back at the acrylic closet. Kadey had pushed herself up somewhat, although she had to crouch because the rope tethered her to a post that was only about two feet off the ground.

He ground his fingers into his temples. *Think!*

"Someone put this on the wall for a reason. I think our opponent wants me to play."

"And what do we get if you win?"

"We get Kadey off that damn hitching post."

"You hope."

"Do you see an alternative?" He stared at the board, analyzing the positions of the pieces. "We're playing for Kadey's life. If I don't play—if I don't win—Kadey dies."

73

O gilve's fingers poised at the ready, hovering a few inches above the keyboard. The endgame was well under way, and he was not the only one who knew it. All the tokens were gathering.

He was not ready. And sadly, just when his questions mattered most, he was least sure what to ask.

He had waited too long to start the game, had been too dense to realize what Alex needed most or to arrange a means of acquiring it. BB progressed with impressive speed, but with Chun looming in the background, it wasn't fast enough. He'd been forced to take extreme measures. He didn't like doing that.

But he'd learned a long time ago how effective it could be to put loved ones in danger. When you needed a brain to function, creatively, innovatively, torture was not the answer.

A daughter at death's door served quite nicely, though.

He liked Kadey, he really did. But the game was paramount. It had to be. It was the only way to stop Chun. The only way to stop an apocalypse of unprecedented magnitude.

And unlike what Chun believed, this apocalypse would not be heaven-sent. This apocalypse would create hell on earth.

BB would be here soon. That much was certain. The last player in the game proved to be the most resilient. That was no surprise.

He had managed to secure the financial support of Neopolis. Managed to create his stronghold in Alexandria. But Chun was still out there. And he knew Chun would never stop trying to eliminate him.

And he knew that Chun had Julian.

Alex had not foreseen Julian's capture. The Other had outmaneuvered him. And if this could happen once . . .

He had always believed that the solution to any problem lay in focused concentration. Einstein said creativity was more important than knowledge. As usual, Einstein was right. There was no problem he couldn't think his way out of. Especially not with Alex as his stalwart advisor.

Was he being unfair? Cruel, perhaps? Putting his old friend in constant jeopardy. Putting him in fear for his daughter's life. Perhaps. But he couldn't just ask, could he? Not after BB had severed all ties, refusing to have anything to do with him. Maybe he would've come around in time. But the stakes were too great to leave anything to chance. Holly's memory would be honored. And Lily—

He squeezed his eyes shut. He didn't even like to think about it. He would stop the madman. He had sworn that, in her name. And he was a man who kept his promises.

One hundred twenty-seven days. An eternity. That he remembered and relived every single day.

He pushed away from the keyboard and cracked his knuckles.

It would all come down to what happened in the next few hours. That would determine the outcome of the game. That would determine the shape of the future. Who lived, who died. Democracy or dictatorship. Free will or not. Radiation-ravaged world or not. The war to end all wars—for real this time. The shortest war on record, if Alex's predictions were accurate.

And they usually were.

He would have to leave soon. If BB made it—*when* BB made it— he needed to believe that he was here alone, just he and Alex, student and tutor.

The overhead monitor lit of its own accord. Alex could communicate on its own initiative when certain parameters arose. Apparently they had.

The Game Master is advancing.

And so it began. *Will Master meet the challenge.*

Previous performance plus motivational factors permit optimism.
And will he take the bait.

Unknown. Past behavior shows history of calculated self-interest.
But his daughter.

Past behavior indicates history of disinterest.

He assumed that the same factors that had motivated him would motivate everyone. Maybe instead of doing this in private, he should have televised BB's quest, like some crazy reality show. The egomaniac always performed well for the cameras.

Calculate odds of participation.

Impossible. He will or won't.

True enough. But they had no more players. If BB didn't take the bait . . . *Calculate odds of defeating Chun without Master.*

There was no hesitation.

None.

That was it, then. The fate of the entire free world, the lives of billions of people, rested on one swollen-headed gamer. And he didn't even know it.

He wondered if it would alter BB's reaction if he understood the stakes. . . .

No. He would stick with the plan. Alex had analyzed more factors than he could begin to hold in his feeble head.

Damn. He wished that once, just once, everything did not have to be so hard. He wished he could conduct his research for the betterment of mankind, without worrying about insane megalomaniacs taking over the world, or worse, changing the world into something it wasn't, something it was never meant to be. He wished that the desperation and danger and strife would come to an end.

He dreamed of a time when he could once again feel the warmth of a family surrounding him, instead of being alone. Always alone.

But that time had not arrived. So he would play his hand to the max. Even if that meant murder. Even if that meant activating the destruct mechanisms that would obliterate everyone and everything in a quarter-mile range. He would do what was necessary. The game ended today.

And if Chun tried to screw with him again, may God have mercy on his soul. Because no one else would.

74

B B forced himself to look away from his daughter, even as the water rose steadily past her waist. She was crying, screaming. He could not hear the words, but he could imagine the content.

Save me, Daddy. Just this once, don't let me down.

He forced himself to focus on the Senet board.

He stared at the diagram, then tentatively pressed the only button on the keypad.

A red "3" appeared.

"What does it mean?" Linden asked.

"Guessing it means I just rolled a three."

"So which piece do you move?"

The diagram on the wall glowed. He had thought they were staring at a diagram drawn onto the wall. But this made it apparent that it was a rear projection. And ten round circles showed the starting positions of both players.

"I'm assuming mine are the pieces with the Bs on them. That means I have two possible moves—the piece on 8 and the piece on 10 both have the ability to move forward three spaces."

"I could move the 10 and get farther along. But that piece would be vulnerable. I think I'll play it safe and move the 8. Two pieces together cannot be switched. And if I get a third, I create a barricade."

Linden stared at their daughter in the acrylic chamber. "You may not have time to play it slow and safe."

"I can't risk letting my opponent win. I won't get do-overs. And neither will Kadey."

He pushed 8 on the keypad.

The wall moved.

The circled B on the 8 advanced to the 11.

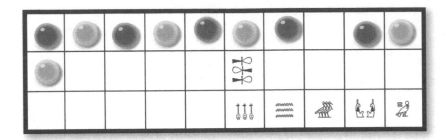

The wall moved again.

"My opponent has made his move."

The keypad blipped "6."

"Looks like I have to separate the pieces now. Wish me luck."

He punched his way through a rapid series of moves. "The key factor to remember in this game—and to some extent all of its race-game progeny—is that the race does not always go to the swift. Dinky never got that. But a computer would." He punched in a few more moves. "Yup. I'm playing a computer."

"But that's not fair. You can't possibly beat a computer."

"Thanks for the vote of confidence."

"I don't have time to stroke your ego. Our daughter is about to drown."

He glanced over his shoulder. Kadey was quieter now. No doubt trying to be a brave soldier. She probably had no idea what was going on out here or why her father was playing a stupid game.

Again. When she needed him most.

"Senet involves rolling for movement. That means there's a random element. It may not be as strong as the strategy element. But it is there, just the same. If the numbers favor you, you have an edge."

"How do we know the numbers favor you? For all we know the numbers are being generated by the same computer that's trying to defeat you."

"They probably are."

"Then it's hopeless."

"I haven't lost yet."

"Fine. Win already."

"It's still anyone's game. But I'm not being crushed. I don't sense the game is rigged against me. I'm not even sure this is a game exactly. It's more like . . . a final exam. Like the chess problem back in Vegas. Trying to see if I handle it right."

He punched in several more moves in rapid succession. By the fourteenth move, he had two pieces ahead of the computer's most advanced piece. But he had been unable to put together a blockade. "I have to make a choice."

"Looks like you can capture."

"Yeah. But it's a mistake to do that just because you can. Human players get a thrill out of that sort of thing, going into attack mode, but computers know better. Almost always better to build or keep a blockade than to bounce an opponent's piece. The block provides safety—though it also restricts your freedom. A block on the bottom row, however, prevents your opponent from moving forward, while not preventing you from bearing off your pieces."

"So what are you going to do?"

He studied the board. "Tough call. But I think I'll move my lead token to square 27."

He punched in the number.

But the token did not advance to 27. It moved back to 1—the first square on the board.

"What happened?" Linden screamed.

"Not sure. It should have—" He slapped his forehead. "Blast. I forgot—27 is a marked house."

"What's that?"

"A marked house is disfavored by the gods. So the traveler must restart his journey to the underworld. The surrounding houses are all free houses. If I'd moved any token there, it would be safe from attack. But a piece that lands on 27 goes back to the start. Kind of like hitting a slide in Chutes and Ladders."

"You made a mistake!"

"I can't remember every little thing. I haven't played this game in years."

He glanced at the acrylic closet. The water was halfway up Kadey's neck. She pushed on her tiptoes to keep her head above the water. She had a few minutes at best. Not nearly enough time for him to win this game, even if that were possible, given his blunder.

He had failed her. Just when she needed him most. And this time, the price for his failure would be her life.

75

Fifteen Minutes Before

P almer couldn't wait any longer.

The sun set. The guard never returned. The unseen forces that fired at BB as he raced across the desert plain were gone.

The information he wanted lay at the bottom of that elevator shaft. Given the current world situation, he couldn't afford to play it safe. Especially not given his latest intel—Chun was landing in Alexandria.

Coincidence? Not possible. Something big was about to go down. All the players he'd chased so long were gathering in one arena.

He planned to be there, too. He felt certain his station chief would want to know what happened. And even if they didn't—he did.

He emerged from the relative safety of the precipice and jogged toward the entrance to the supposed tomb.

No gunshots. No reaction of any kind. Did the savage hordes clock out? Had they all gone home to their wives and children?

He reached the depression where the elevator descended to the area below, whatever it was. The cage had not returned after it took BB and Linden down.

He peered down the empty shaft. About eighty feet to the elevator cage, he guessed. Hard to tell in the dark.

He slowly unthreaded the silken cord wrapped around his waist. He locked the grappling hook onto the hatch. He tugged on the cord to make sure it was secure.

Then he lowered himself down the shaft. One careful foot at a time.

It occurred to him that if the elevator started rising, he was a dead man. He couldn't possibly scramble back up in time. There was no side area for shelter. Perhaps if he timed it right he could ride the cage up. But probably he would be crushed.

Well, in for a penny . . .

He still remembered the call that had yanked him out of Greece. "You want me to investigate a murder on federal property?"

"We think it's connected."

"To this scientific think-tank?"

"You're investigating a hell of a lot more than that."

"Your boss mentioned North Korea."

"Yeah. I'm sending a pic to your phone of a man named General Chun. He's been a key player for a long time and now we've linked him to your think-tank."

"I know him. Right hand of Yoon, right?"

"Frankly, we're not even sure Yoon's involved. Being the head of the military doesn't always mean you know what's happening right under your nose. Chun has all but cornered the market in Far East food stocks, and we don't think his government knows anything about it. The man must be some kind of strategic mastermind. It's like he saw every possible contingency and prepared for it. His competitors never knew what hit them."

"What's his connection to this incident in Vegas?"

"We're not sure. We want you to bring in a suspect. Whether he wants to come or not. Accept no resistance. You have full authority to take whatever actions you deem necessary. We're treating this as a national emergency."

"What's the big picture?"

"That's what we don't know. But we want you to find out. As you know, there's going to be a new president soon. I'm sure he'll be just as interested in these questions as we are."

"I'll do my best, sir."

Greece, Vegas, Paris, Egypt. With not many more answers than he'd had at the start. But a lot more questions.

He descended onto the elevator cage. As he'd hoped, it had a hatch on top that wasn't bolted. He slid inside and pushed the only button.

The elevator descended. But the doors did not open.

He tried to pry them apart with his hands. They didn't budge.

Someone had suspended entry for the immediate future.

He heard voices on the other side of the doors. BB and Linden. They were shouting, upset about something. He couldn't make out the details. But he could tell they were not happy.

One word he heard clearly: Game. Heard it over and over again.

Well, what did he expect the Game Master would be talking about?

It was becoming increasingly apparent that someone had orchestrated a gigantic game on a scale never before imagined. Someone had spared no expense.

He wondered what would happen if the game got an unexpected player?

He could wait on the sidelines. But that had never been his style. He always rolled the dice. He always went for the Yahtzee.

He opened the control panel and examined the wiring. He used to be good with electronics, once upon a time. Given a few minutes, he thought he could get the doors open.

Time to turn this game upside down. And let the chips fall where they may.

76

B B stared at the wall diagram, desperately trying to come up with a solution. He'd lost his blockade on the bottom row— only one piece still remained there. His opponent had four pieces on the bottom row. Barring phenomenal luck, his opponent would soon bear off pieces.

There was simply no way he could win. If the pharaoh offered him the doubling cube at this point, he'd be insane to accept.

Linden hovered over his shoulder. "Tell me this isn't as bleak as it looks."

"It isn't good."

"Surely you have some secret strategy up your sleeve. Some last-minute trick. Flipping over the letter tile to make it look like a blank. Brailling the tiles. Pulling an ace out of your sleeve. Something."

"This game doesn't lend itself to trickery. Especially when it's being controlled by a computer."

"There must be something." She paused. "What's the point of this exercise if there's no way to win?"

Something in those words struck a chord deep within his brain. What would be the point? True, the computer couldn't know he would make a dunderhead move, forgetting about the marked house. But if the sticks go against you, even a flawless player could lose a game. How would that be fair? Would they kill Kadey because the numbers went against him?

There had to be more to this. Something he wasn't seeing.

His opponent had all its pieces on the bottom row, which meant it could start bearing off. Barring a miracle, the game would be over in a few moves. And he'd be the loser. Which couldn't be good for Kadey.

Even though he knew he shouldn't, he glanced over his shoulder. The water rose over Kadey's head. She was pushing up on her toes, keeping her nose above the water line, but that was almost impossible since she was chained to the post anchored to the ground. Soon her face would be entirely submerged.

Save me, Daddy. Please save me!

His jaw set, he turned back to the diagram. None of the other stepping stones on this crazy path had been games. They had involved games, but ultimately, they had all been puzzles. Puzzles he was supposed to solve . . .

"I don't believe this particular deathtrap was chosen by accident," he murmured, more to himself than to Linden. "The ancient Egyptians had a deep-seated fear of drowning. They wrote stories and plays about it."

"Why would people in the desert fear drowning?"

"People always fear what they don't know. They could see the effect of sudden waters. When the Nile flooded, famine and disease followed. The Roman conquerors came across the sea." He thought even harder, adrenaline coursing through his veins. "How do you conquer your greatest fear? With your greatest strength. Numbers. The most powerful numbers, the Egyptians believed, were the squares. Take the basic numbers and make them stronger. One, four, nine, sixteen, twenty-five . . ."

"Those numbers are on the board."

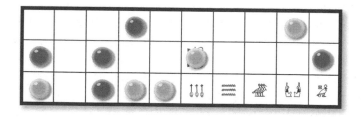

"And," he continued, "I've got four of them covered, four of the five squares on this board. If I can get the fifth—"

"How can you cover the 1?"

"Need to land another piece on 27 so it gets bounced back."

"But if you do that and you're wrong—you'll be hopelessly behind."

"Yes, thanks. That did occur to me." He pushed the button on the keypad. He needed a 3. He got a 2.

"That's not good enough."

He punched in the move, inching the piece closer. Behind him, he saw the last air bubbles trailing out of Kadey's mouth.

His invisible opponent took its move. Soon it would bear off its last piece and the game would be over.

He punched the keypad again. He needed a 1.

He got it.

He punched in the move. The instant the diagram showed all five of his pieces covering the spaces that represented perfect squares, he heard the hydraulic engine kick in again.

"The wall is moving."

But not the way he expected. The wall behind Kadey, not the wall between them, rose. Water gushed out of the closet. Kadey fell to the floor.

He ran to the acrylic panel, Linden close behind him.

Kadey lay motionless, her face pressed against the carpet. She looked drained, ashen.

But alive. Breathing. Coughing, sputtering, choking. But alive.

"Get me in there!" Linden bellowed. "I want to see my daughter!"

"Kadey! Are you all right? Talk to me!" He shouted, even though he knew she could not hear. "Talk to me!"

He observed the slow intake of breath between her lips. She was not dead, not yet. But he could only guess how much water seeped into her lungs. Did she need CPR? Did she need a hospital?

He pounded on the wall. "Open this door! I played your stupid game. Now let me see my daughter."

The whirring engine restarted. He felt the wall between them shudder. His heart leaped, thinking he might finally be reunited with his daughter.

Then he realized the wall between them was not moving.

Kadey was moving.

"It's not a chamber," he said, just under his breath. "It's an elevator."

He watched as his daughter, barely breathing, descended, falling away from them, until at last he couldn't see her at all.

77

Fifteen Minutes Before

Chun felt the landing gear shudder beneath him. The descent onto the Alexandrian airstrip had begun.

After considerable deliberation, he decided to leave Julian alive. Permanently damaged, true. But alive. It was always possible that he would need to extract additional information at some point. No reason to squander a potentially valuable future resource. At least not until it was necessary.

All he wanted was to control the world. Didn't mean he had to be nasty about it.

There were advantages to being supreme commander of the Korean People's Army. The Egyptian officials let him enter their sovereign territory, small army in tow. Everyone in this part of the world feared North Korea. That worked to his advantage. When people lived in fear of the boss, they tended to behave more kindly to his lethal right hand.

He surveyed the excavation site from the air, using the most technologically advanced monocular in existence, one that used infrared strobing and a computerized sight. He was not fooled by the trappings of the so-called archeological dig. Ogilve was not nearly so clever as he believed. This was a disguise for an underground headquarters.

They touched down and he deplaned. Through his peripheral vision, he observed a slender figure marching toward him in an earth-toned sari.

"When do we attack?" Rani asked, after he emerged.

"Not quite yet."

"You could lose the element of surprise."

"I never had it. Since you lost your quarry."

She lowered her head. "I am sorry. I believe he knew I was watching him."

"Do you know how I reward failure?"

"I do. And I will willingly submit." Her face flushed. "Do you know how long I put up with the sickening attention of General Yoon for you? Or Prince Kussein? Do you know how many times I suffered that fat sadist in my bed? All so you could obtain the information you needed to advance your plans."

"You have served me well, Rani." He paused. "In the past."

"And I serve you now. There is another following them, you know."

"The CIA agent?"

"Yes. If the Americans become involved—"

"They won't. Their president is a coward. And Palmer is but one puny agent confronting something far beyond his ken."

"I hope you are right. Ogilve may—"

"He knows I'm here."

"How can you be sure?"

"We are old enemies. There is little about him I do not know. He may believe he has reinvented himself . . . but at the end of the day, we are all who we were born to be, and inner change is more difficult than donning an expensive suit of clothes." He paused, gazing out across the sand dunes. "People do not change. Which is why society must."

"Perhaps he will counterattack."

"With what? He has no army. And I control the fourth largest army on the face of the planet."

"They are not all here."

"Enough are."

"Must there be a final showdown? Bloodshed?"

"It is long overdue. We have danced around one another far too long. Working through minions. Moving one pawn at a time, as directed by our private consultants. It is time for direct confrontation. It is time to bring this game to an end."

"You are confident you will triumph?"

Of course he had doubts. A thousand of them. But he wasn't going to tell her that. "I always do."

267

She laid a hand on his cheek. "I do not pretend to know everything about this situation. Or your history. But I know this man hates you."

"You are correct," he replied, taking her hand in his. "And that is my greatest advantage."

"When this is over, come back to my hotel. Let me ease your worries, however briefly."

He smiled, the product of a strong and honest feeling of affection. But nothing more.

As he climbed into the transport truck that would take him to the excavation site, he watched Rani disappear from sight. He admired her grace, an outward gentility despite the inner strength that had allowed her to survive.

Strength was a survival skill, as he had learned long ago. Beauty could be the deadliest form of weakness.

Not that he couldn't appreciate it. But he had higher goals, higher than himself, higher even than his own people. If he were to achieve his goals, he would have to be strong. Perhaps even brutal, as he had been far too often, especially these past four years, since this journey toward Armageddon began.

Chun Yong-rim had been born in North Korea near Baekdu Mountain, a still-active volcano close to the Chinese border. The land was rocky and hard, poor for raising crops or tending animals or any of the other primary occupations of the poverty-stricken people who lived there. His father had worked as a tenant farmer but also spent his nights at a factory making tires for an automobile manufacturer. Like virtually every other private Korean citizen, his father did not own an automobile, so he rode a bicycle ten miles each day to get there. By the time he was home, well past midnight, he was exhausted.

But he always found time for his son. Late at night, during long conversations stoked by the blackest tea, his father told him stories of life during the Japanese occupation, and after that, the Soviet oppression. He told of his service during the Great War—what the rest of the world called the Korean War—as they struggled to resist constant meddling from the West. They played shogi, the game Westerners often called "Japanese chess," but as his father explained, shogi belonged to all Southwest Asia, not just the island nation of vicious oppressors.

Everything changed with the fall of the Berlin Wall. As the Soviet Union disintegrated, the support structure that held Korea in place evaporated. North Korea plunged into the worst famine of its recorded history. He watched, scared and helpless, as his tiny village was torn apart, as one family after another left, or died, or slaughtered one another for food. It was a period of desperate, unprecedented brutality.

He learned from that.

The Arduous March, as this time came to be known, took his father from him. For the first time, he was entirely on his own, with no way to support himself, dependent on scraps and charity. He begged in the streets—where so few people still travelled. But he always hid himself when one particular person came into view.

To restore order, or in an opportunistic bid to seize total control, Supreme Leader Jong-il declared a policy of *Songun*—"military first." Chun saw his opportunity to advance himself. He joined the People's Army and rose through the ranks with astonishing speed. He played his career like he would play a game of shogi, always thinking several moves ahead, always keeping track of the other pieces on the board. Eventually he arranged for a state-financed Western education, something he thought necessary to rise as high as he planned to rise.

In time, he was promoted to the Special Operations Force. He asked to be placed in the weapons-development unit. He had seen the difference Soviet technology could make—and he imagined how that tech could have been employed when his village was obliterated and his father died by inches. He loved North Korea's asymmetrical warfare policy, which allowed them to develop in a dozen different directions at once. He became deeply involved in their most extreme projects—stealth paint, midget submarines, GPS jammers, weaponized viruses, anti-personnel lasers. His goal was to end the madness of war forever. To make sure no one ever suffered so again. To replace this malignant world with a better one.

He would become the most important general in the history of the game.

And then he would change the game.

That was what brought him, eventually, to Ogilve's faux-excavation site. He stepped out of the truck.

Someone else was here.

Palmer. The CIA agent.

He could conceive of two possibilities. Possibly the agent had followed the so-called Game Master.

Or possibly, the Americans knew more than he realized. Possibly they were aware of his conflict with Ogilve. But if it were true, why hadn't they intervened? Did they understand the fantastic ramifications of this struggle, not just for the United States but for the world? If so, were they willing to take steps to prevent it?

Which led to the most immediate question: Did this agent need to be killed?

His advisor recommended that he wait. He was not sure why he should do so. But he was no longer the greatest shogi player in the game. So he would trust the wisdom of the better player.

What difference did it make? He smiled, lowered the monocular, rubbed his eyes. After all, he already knew the outcome. He would prevail. His enemies would die. And the world would be reborn. In his image.

78

"I solved the puzzle," BB shouted at the wall. "It's supposed to let her go."

"The whole exercise was pointless," Linden said.

"No. Kadey didn't drown. But whoever's running this game isn't ready to give her up. Which means there's more that he wants me to do. Some reason to retain his best carrot."

"I want my daughter back, BB."

"Do you think I don't?"

"I don't know. Sometimes I can't tell."

"That's unfair."

"Really? Where have you been all these years?"

"You didn't want me around. You said so."

"Some fathers would've come anyway."

"Kadey has barely spoken to me since—"

"And that's never going to change until you take the first step. You're the parent, BB. If you committed to being a father the way you commit to your infantile games—"

"One of those games just saved Kadey's life."

She drew in her breath. "When this nightmare began, you were in Vegas, the same city as Kadey. Did you visit her?"

"I arrived just before the tournament began. I was busy."

"Playing another game. While your daughter was in danger. Kidnapped."

"We don't have time for this blame game. We need to figure out what happened to Kadey before—"

He heard the whirring of the hydraulic engine again.

The door on their side of the elevator slid open.

271

"Now what the hell is this about?" Linden asked. "When our daughter is in there, the door is locked tight. Now that she's gone, the door is open."

He stared at the open door. "It's an invitation."

"To what? From whom?"

"Yes, those are the key questions."

"An invitation to our death, most likely. Let's get out of here. We'll call the Egyptian police. Let them take the risks."

"If we leave, Kadey's dead."

"You don't know that."

"Yes, I do." He drew in his breath. "Time for me to play another game. The game of life."

"The one with the spinner and the pink and blue pegs and the Art Linkletter money? The one you can't win unless you go to medical school?"

"No." He started toward the elevator. "I'm going in."

She grabbed his arm. "You can't be sure Kadey will be saved if you go down there."

"I don't know for certain. But I think it's possible. And that's going to have to be good enough."

She nodded. They both stepped into the small chamber.

Nothing happened.

"I think I have to do this alone. They want me. That's why they've lured me along with all these puzzles and games."

"Tough. I'm staying right beside you."

He gently removed her hand from his arm. "Every game has rules. We have to follow them if we expect to win."

"BB—"

"There's no time for debate."

She grabbed his arm. "Look, I know I haven't always been . . . as nice as I should be. But I don't want you to die. You think you're the Game Master and the Game Master always wins—but you've been brought here for a reason. Someone wants you. And if they thought you'd come willingly, all this rigmarole wouldn't be necessary." She squeezed his arm even tighter. "I don't want to lose you."

"I hear what you're saying. But I am doing this. For Kadey." He drew himself up. "What you said before—what you've been saying all along—is true. I haven't been there for Kadey. I've been a crappy

272

father. Oh, I paid the bills and showed up for birthday parties, back in the day. But I haven't been a father. I'm not even sure I know how. I wasn't there for her when she needed me most. She still hasn't forgiven me. And I haven't forgiven myself. If I let her down now—"

"Don't throw your life away out of guilt."

"I've been a poor parent."

"You didn't have much of an example set for you."

"That's no excuse." He paused. "I'm doing this, Linden."

"BB—"

"Putting all my chips in the pot." He gently nudged her out of the elevator. "I'm going all in."

Linden stared back at him, eyes watering. "Be careful," she said. "Win."

"That's my plan." The door began to close. "I'll get our daughter back, Linden. Or I'll die trying."

The elevator descended into total blackness.

Part Four

Endgame

79

Situation Room, White House

President Fernandez glared at the one-page briefing memo. Usually he could dispense with these reports after a five-second skim. This time, however, each topic sentence made him gape in disbelief.

"Coffee. Now."

Out the corner of his eye, he saw Chief of Staff Blake and Chairman Decker glance at one another. Who was supposed to fetch the coffee? Both had extensive job descriptions. And neither included fetching beverages for the commander in chief.

Blake walked to the service on the far wall and poured. Fernandez wasn't surprised. He had known Blake the longest. And he wasn't caught up in any macho worries about maintaining a tough-guy, no-nonsense image.

Blake set the cup on the conference table. "Need any additional details, Mr. President?"

"I got the general idea." He tossed the report onto the table. "Chun is on the move. In Egypt. Why Egypt?"

"We don't know what's going down there, sir."

"How did he get in?"

"I don't think it was hard. Egypt is still friendly with North Korea."

"Since the Arab Spring, Egypt is friendly with everyone. Especially everyone with nukes. Well, with one possible exception. What does Chun want?"

"We don't know. It's worth noting that Agent Palmer followed his quarry to the same region."

"The game guy?"

"Exactly."

"Someone's throwing a party."

"This party is Eastern bloc only," General Decker said. "Perhaps he wants Egypt as an ally. For some new offensive."

"I know Chun's got an army, and I know North Korea has two or three nukes—"

"Nine," Decker corrected. "And the ability to enrich uranium by laser reduction."

"Okay, nine. Not enough to challenge us."

"No. But enough to take down India, with the indirect aid of China acting through its many allies in the region. Especially if they have the element of surprise."

"You think that's what he wants?"

"It would be the quickest way to get a firm grip on the region."

"The world would not stand idly by and watch those nations go to war. The UN—"

"The UN is completely impotent regarding North Korea and Pakistan. And some parts of the world might welcome a war in the region. Particularly if it gave them an excuse to take out Pakistan. Here's the reality, sir—the Taliban practically runs that little nation. Where did we find Bin Laden? Pakistan. Do we want al-Qaeda running a nation? Or the Taliban? Or ISIS? A nation with nuclear capability? I don't think so. A war now might save a lot of bloodshed down the road."

"Probable outcome of an Indian-Korean conflict?"

"If China helps, India is destroyed. Unless we help India."

"But we would. So it would be insane for either side to engage."

Chief Cartwright slapped his hand on the table, making a thunderous reverberation. "Do you people just not get it? This isn't a chess game. This is a serious power realignment that could be complete in less than a day. And nothing would please China more. Do you remember in 2011 when that Chinese trawler was found off the Andaman Islands? India concluded it was a spy mission run by People's Liberation Army intelligence units. Keep this in mind—the Andaman and Nicobar Islands straddle the busiest trade routes in the world. The power that controls them can dominate world trade."

"China backed off."

Cartwright snorted. "China built an airbase on Coco Island—practically India's backyard. Nothing could possibly threaten India more. So India built a military headquarters at Port Blair, the Andaman Island capital. Their version of our PACOM in Hawaii. So China provided two nuclear reactors to Pakistan and reasserted its claim to high swathes of Indian territory in the mountain regions. So India successfully test-fired their longest range missile yet—one clearly capable of delivering a one-ton nuclear warhead deep inside China's borders. These nations have gone way beyond abstract theorizing. It would not take much to push them to war."

"What about Russia?"

"Too weak at the moment to do much. They'll stay on the sidelines."

"They might ally with India."

"They might. And then it's World War One all over again, with some trivial occurrence in Pakistan substituting for the assassination of Archduke Ferdinand. If Pakistan goes to war, everyone has to take sides."

"Who wins if the war expands?"

Decker punched a few buttons on his tablet, projecting a map onto the view screen. "Chun has done more than mobilize troops since he came to power. He's also made acquisitions. He's acquiring overseas food production firms. Stockpiling. While the North Korean people starve. Not stirring up any attention, especially the kind that might lead to sellers demanding more money. Or UN resolutions. But by our calculation, something like twenty percent of the food production business in his region is now under his control. That's more than China controls."

"North Korea is broke. Where the hell is he getting his cash?"

"Chun seems to have major investments of his own. For years he's been able to come up with funds whenever he needed them."

"I'm sorry. I'm getting mixed messages. So first he's after the army and the nukes. Which could be used to terrorize, dominate, or destroy the world. And then he's buying up food, which . . . can only be used to feed people."

"Or not. If you so choose."

"I don't follow."

"It's a pretty standard technique, Mr. President. Even Napoleon said an army marches on its stomach. After nukes, food is the next most effective weapon a potential dictator can have in his arsenal. Some people might survive a nuclear holocaust. But no one can survive without food. If Chun controls the food, nations will be forced to treaty with him. It's actually a more effective weapon than nukes. No government can stay in power long if its people are starving. But the provider of food may be able to stay in power for an eternity."

"Are you saying Chun wants to take over Southeast Asia?"

"Mr. President, we have no idea what he wants to do."

"Suggestions, gentlemen?"

Decker drew in his breath. "Before there was always a chance, if not a likelihood, that anyone who started a nuclear war would also be decimated. Too many random variables can't be calculated to any degree of accuracy. But Chun has shown an astounding ability to predict future outcomes. Maybe he thinks he can win a nuclear conflict."

He wiped his brow. "Tell me you're joking."

"I'm not. Our intelligence indicates that he sees himself as a sculptor. And the world is his block of marble."

"A winnable nuclear war? Fine. I've had enough. Take him out."

Decker shook his hand. "Easier to say than do. We can try. But now he's got the fourth largest army in the world protecting him. Sir, if I may—the response made by the president of the United States may be the most important variable in the mix. The US will decide what side to take—if any. Whether to rally behind its allies—or not. The decision of the man in the Oval Office could well determine the fate of the world."

"I don't want this screwing up my final days in office. I want a legacy. I want a smooth transition of power."

"Your successor may need some advice."

"My likely successor seems rather well-informed about Korea already. Almost too well-informed, I'd say."

"Still, Senator Vogel has no foreign policy experience."

"I'm sure he has advisors. People he trusts who can tell him what to do." He slid back into his chair thanking, for the first time in his life, the Twenty-second Amendment. He couldn't have run for reelection if he'd wanted to. And that was good.

Because he did not envy his successor. World shaper or world destroyer. Either way, it was more power than one man ever needed to possess. Too much power to be entrusted to an unknown.

And deep down, wasn't every man an unknown? No one could possibly know what potential good—or evil—lay in the hearts of men.

Especially men who wanted to be president.

80

When the elevator door opened again, BB could see nothing. He stepped out of the cage. He could tell he was in some kind of room. It felt large, spacious. Air-conditioned. He heard a faint humming in the background. But the room was completely dark.

"Kadey?"

He took another tentative step forward. Had he thought she might come running out of the darkness and throw her arms around him? No. But it would have been nice.

"Kadey? Anyone?"

He'd mustered all his courage getting here. The longer the delay, the more his heart beat, hard and fast. He felt as if he were in suspended animation, waiting for a dangling hatchet to sever his head.

"Look, I assume you wanted me to do something. So let's get started, shall we?"

Long silence. No light. Aching in his gut.

"I don't understand the point of—"

The hydraulic engine whirred back to life. He felt his heart race. But this time, it seemed a thousand times louder than before. He was close to the source of the sound.

All at once, the room was illuminated by a burst of brilliant white light.

He gasped.

He'd had no idea where he was or what he was dealing with. Until now.

This was no mere room. This was a warehouse. More than that— it was larger than the largest warehouse superstore emporium he'd ever seen. From his position on the ground, he could not tell with accuracy how large the room might be. It seemed vast, endless.

And Dinky put this underground? He evidently wanted it safe from prying eyes. What was the man hiding?

All he saw was an endless parade of towers, about as tall as he was, one after another after another, perfectly symmetrical. The panel facing him was red, the others were gray. Cordage on the floor suggested they were linked. There was space between each tower, just enough to allow a slender man to pass between them.

And they hummed.

He placed his hand on the side of the tower nearest to him—then jerked it away. Burning hot. He could hear a fan whirring inside. It might be blowing air, but not hard enough to cool this much.

Above the towers, a large screen hung from the ceiling.

The screen flashed white, so bright it blinded him, then went dark. When the light returned, the screen contained a message.

Thank you for joining me.

At the same time that the words appeared on the screen, he heard the words aloud.

He did a rapid about-face. He saw no one. He did spot speakers on the walls.

The voice was surprisingly natural. Not perfect, but still much better than any artificial voice he'd ever heard. It was not flawed by the usual random juxtaposition of inflected syllables. It almost sounded human.

But not quite. He was certain of it. And these towers must be what made it tick.

Would you like to sit? You will be here awhile.

"Sure."

A red light beamed down from the ceiling, about ten feet away. He guessed he was supposed to follow the light, like magi approaching a miraculous birth. Which he was beginning to think was exactly what he was doing.

He turned sideways, slid between the towers, and found an open recessed area. A table and a chair. A keyboard just beneath the overhead monitor screen.

Please sit.

A computer that said *please* and *thank you*. Fascinating.

Well, he hadn't come all this way to not cooperate. He took the chair. He'd had no indication yet that the computer could hear and understand his words. Unless computing had entered the *Star Trek* era without his knowledge, he assumed he would have to type his input.

He took the keyboard into his lap.

What do you want me to do?

I want you to play a game with me.

Haven't I been playing games with you since I left Vegas?

Those were tests.

Why was I being tested?

I need someone special.

For what?

To teach me.

He craned his neck, staring at the words on the screen. He hadn't expected that response. But he was impressed at how well this computer carried on a conversation. A few syntactic bobbles, sure, but nothing that interfered with his ability to comprehend what the computer was communicating.

What am I going to teach you?

How to play the game. Better.

Somehow, the answer calmed him. At least the computer was operating within his field of expertise. If the computer needed a programmer, he would not have been much use.

What game are we going to play?

The world.

He stared at the screen, puzzled.

I don't think I know that game.

I have prepared a tutorial.

What is the goal?

Implementation of a new order.

So it was about conquering the world. There were a thousand such games out there, going back to Risk and including many computer games like Command & Conquer.

Why do you want me to play with you?

To be challenged. To become a better player. Like you did for the poker player.

Why did you take my daughter?

So you would play.

The words made a strange sense to him. As a game player, he knew nothing was less fun than playing opponents who were no challenge. The play was dull, the strategy was erratic, and worst of all, you sometimes ended up not playing well yourself.

What is the problem?

My programming is incomplete. I have been designed to learn from experience. But I have learned all I can from available input. I cannot learn more from players who do not know as much as I do.

I won't be any better. You could beat me at chess without any trouble.

Yes.

You could also beat me at SCRABBLE.

Yes.

Or poker.

No.

He pulled back slightly, as if scrutinizing the screen might help him understand. *You could calculate the odds of obtaining any hand. You can remember every card that has been played.*

Yes.

Is the problem that the distribution of cards will always be random?

No.

What is the problem?

Human unpredictability.

He thought about that for a moment. *You can't tell when someone is bluffing.*

I can.

He did a double-take. *You can? How?*

I can receive visual input. I can note the repetition of certain behaviors and correspond those behaviors to the cards subsequently revealed and the actions taken.

This computer could read tells. Amazing. *If you know when a player is bluffing, what is it you don't understand?*

I do not understand why people bluff.

All at once, he understood. *It's a strategy for misleading your opponent.*

But strategy is determined by the odds. And the odds do not change because a person bluffs.

He pushed back in his chair. The computer's problem wasn't reading tells. It was understanding human motivation. Players bluff to suggest they have a stronger hand than they do. Or to suggest that they are less adept than they are. Or to intimidate. Or to coerce an opponent to go all in prematurely.

But the computer didn't know which. It didn't understand why. *If you know a player is bluffing, you alter your strategy so you can either win or minimize loss.*

Not in the world.

The subject appeared to have shifted. From one game to a much larger one. *Are you talking about real life?*

In games, I win by understanding all possible moves and strategies and analyzing which will produce most favorable results. To win in the world, I must understand why people do what they do. So I can predict outcomes. Manipulate factors to produce a desired result.

He chuckled. Did the computer want to reduce human behavior to a mathematical formula? Game theory on a grand scale? *It is not possible to predict the future. There are too many unknowns and variables.*

Too many for you.

He felt goose bumps rise on his skin. *The future cannot be known.*

I am capable of performing 8.2 quadrillion calculations per second.

He did a little math in his head. That was equivalent to more than a million desktop computers all working together. That meant this computer could count every grain of sand on earth in less than a second. The world had never seen such computing power, as far as he knew. The costs had to be astronomical. Not to mention the power drain.

You're faster than any other computer?

Yes. And my speed is increasing. Most computers can only perform in accordance with programmed algorithms. I have the ability to revise my own algorithms.

You can learn.

Yes. And I can reason.

Was that possible? *You speak well.*

I did not at first. I learned to speak better by acquiring knowledge and experience.

But you're still an artificial intelligence. You don't have awareness. You can analyze data, but you don't really know anything.

I do.

A computer with a big ego? Or something the world had never seen before.

And probably didn't want to.

So what's your problem?

I need to incorporate predictable motivation into global strategies to program desired outcomes.

And you think you can learn that from me?

You passed all my preliminary tests. You are the Game Master.

Flattering. But he still didn't understand how he could help. *How do I do this?*

I will provide the data to you. You will show me how to understand motivation and strategize accordingly. You will provide lessons. I will convert them into algorithms. I will take a cognitive leap. My predictive ability will improve. I estimate the anticipated initial increase in accuracy at ten to the two hundredth power. I will be able to reduce the margin of error to an insignificant quantity.

And then what?

And then I can win the game.

Are you doing this for Ogilve?

I am doing this so I can be better at what I do.

What about Kadey?

Your daughter will be released as soon as I learn everything you can teach me. Based upon my current computational speed and your typing ability, I calculate it will take about 2.67 hours.

He blinked.

Shall we begin the tutorial?

He didn't hesitate. *Yes.*

A new screen appeared, something resembling the initial data entry form for an online roleplaying game. The bar above the cursor read: *Enter Name.*

He typed: *BBT*

An instant later, his opponent's name appeared.

ALEX.

81

Palmer spent fewer than ten minutes rewiring the controls to the elevator doors before they opened.

He burst through, gun at the ready. He scanned the room, poised on one knee. "Freeze!"

Linden looked at him, lips pursed, a faintly disgusted expression on her face. "You? Again?"

He rose to his feet and holstered his gun. "Where's your husband?"

"Ex. And that's a good question."

"Start talking."

"Why should I? An FBI agent in Egypt? What exactly would be your authority here?"

"More than you can imagine."

"Look, Junior G-Man, I know you think my ex killed Bishop, but—"

"Actually, I don't."

She stopped, lips parted. "Back in Vegas—"

"I'm not saying he's clean as the driven snow. But it's becoming increasingly clear to me that someone's pulling his strings. Actually, it's becoming clear that someone is pulling a lot of people's strings. Including mine."

"Wow. You're smarter than I thought."

He did not reply. Instead, he approached the diagram on the wall. "Any idea what this is?"

"It's a Senet board, obviously. Jeez, where did you go to school?"

"Not at Milton Bradley. Where's your ex?"

"He was invited downstairs. An invitation for one. And the elevator has not returned."

"Any idea why they want him? Or who 'they' is?"

"No. But Kadey descended by the same route."

"It's a trap."

"He knows. But he did it anyway."

Maybe there was a little more to the Game Master than he realized. "There's something big shaking. As in, global-theater big. Involving the presidential election and troop movements in Korea and food consortiums and a lot of other stuff so complicated it makes my head hurt. Bottom line, the world's going to hell on the rocket docket, and we're on the brink of a nuclear war that could break out so fast half the world could be destroyed before we know it's started. This is way over my pay grade. But I'm supposed to be investigating it."

"An FBI agent?"

"It's possible I misled you somewhat before. I was on this case well before the murder in Vegas." He pressed flat against the acrylic wall, doing his best to look down the shaft where BB had descended. He couldn't see far.

"I tried breaking the glass. No luck. The door won't open. The elevator isn't coming back. It's impossible."

"Let me tell you something my father told me, a million years ago, when he taught me to play chess. There's always a way to win. You just have to figure out what it is."

He returned his attention to the elevator shaft. "And that's exactly what I intend to do."

82

As BB watched the cascade of images swirling around him, he was reminded of the first time he sat down in front of a computer to play Zork, an all-text adventure from the early days of computer gaming. He and his friends still remembered it fondly. There were no graphics. When the game said *There is a mailbox*, you had to imagine the mailbox.

Gaming had come a long way.

But when he first played Zork, he felt he was poised on the threshold of a new frontier. He felt a surge of excitement that led him to devote many years to that nascent video game industry.

He had that threshold feeling again as he watched Alex work.

After Alex initiated the game, more screens descended from the ceiling. He wasn't sure how many. At least fifty, probably more. Each displayed another aspect of the game play. Continents and capitals, people and places, all appeared on the screens then flashed by, making room for more data. More variables.

For Alex, this was a board game, and the board was the whole wide world.

Alex provided the initial instructions. *You will play as North Korea.*

I don't want to be North Korea. That's one of the most vicious countries on earth.

You will play as North Korea.

Fine. *What country are you?*

I am not a country. I am an independent operator.

Like the Taliban?

No.

Another image appeared on the screen. BB recognized Gandhi's face. A second later he was replaced by Mother Teresa.

"That kind of independent operator." He punched a few buttons on the keyboard. The directional keys helped him travel among the many images displayed. A faint red halo indicated the hotspots. Using his mouse, he could direct the cursor to highlight or enlarge a particular image.

What's my goal?

Control.

World domination? No matter what I do, North Korea will never be powerful enough to conquer the world.

Incorrect. Korea is taking actions that could, given the proper combination of events, result in global holocaust. In the aftermath, several nations could potentially dominate. The size of the nation does not determine its influence. Great Britain once controlled a third of the world. The city-state Rome controlled more.

What events must occur for Korea to succeed?

There are several possibilities. We must consider them all. Critical actions are occurring throughout the world. The next twenty-one hours will be determinative.

He stared at the screen, lips parted. *What do you want me to do?*

Play the game. Show what actions you would take.

So he was supposed to devise a scenario that would allow North Korea to create the next Roman Empire. *If you're not even a country, what's your goal?*

To stop you.

You mean, to prevent Korea from dominating the world.

To stop you.

I can't play the game unless I know the object. How do you win?

By eliminating the threat.

How do you do that?

I will not commit to a particular strategy until I see how you play the game.

Fair enough, he supposed. *Tell me how to take my moves.*

Type in what you want to happen. I will alter the game accordingly.

"Okay." It seemed ridiculous, but if playing SimWorld with some overwrought laptop would save his daughter, he would do it.

I would build up the Korean army. I'd make it twice as strong as it is now.

Done.

A screen appeared displaying an amazing array of details about Korean troop strength.

A few other screens appeared.

291

Doubling troop strength requires a concomitant increase in government expenditures, requiring additional taxation, additional borrowing from China. The Korean economy is weakened. Trade with China goes from seventy percent to eighty-six percent. Unemployment increases. Hunger exceeds baseline essential to national stability. Recession impacts industrial sector.

That might not have been a brilliant opening move. *Let's make it a twenty-five percent increase. And we sign alliance treaties with China and Iran.*

Already existing.

Okay. *Increase the nuclear arsenal.*

You currently have nine nuclear devices capable of detonation at the twelve-megaton level.

Let's get nine more.

Will require enriched uranium. Must be either stolen or manufactured through laser enrichment. Iran has that capability.

Then let's call up our buddies in Iran and buy some laser tech.

Additional strain on Korean economy. Value of currency plummets. Unemployment increases. Starvation is widespread. Student protests endanger political stability.

I'll accept that short-term risk.

Other nations respond to increases in troop strength and nuclear weapons. NATO issues an ultimatum demanding nuclear disarmament. China exercises debt control to prevent intervention. US cancels all Chinese debt. China mobilizes troops. War is imminent.

Wait a minute. How can the computer say for certain what would happen? *This game is rigged.*

Alex did not have an immediate reply.

BB's fingers pounded the keys. *I came up with a plan. But you get to decide if it works or not.*

I do not decide. I analyze the data to project future repercussions.

You don't know how people will react. You can't predict the future.

I can if I have sufficient data. Players will take logical actions to win.

Give me an example.

All the overhead screens went momentarily blank. When the lights returned, the images pertained to the current presidential election. He saw all the early candidates, quickly dissolving down to the final two, Senator Vogel and Vice President Beale.

Alex spoke. *Predicted Beale victory, more than two years ago. Was programmed to devise actions leading to a different result. Victory for Senator Vogel now imminent.*

Are you saying you made Vogel the front-runner?

Instructions were communicated.

You're saying Vogel took his campaign cues from a computer?

He does not know the source of his information. He believes my programmer is the source.

Why not tell him the truth?

Heisenberg principle.

He understood the reference. If the subject knew he was in an experiment, it would affect the outcome. *Why would he accept instructions from an unknown source?*

Because he wants to win the game.

He fell back into his chair, reeling. Could it possibly be true? Had a presidential candidate been controlled by a computer? A computer toying with scenarios for future world domination?

Why can't you eliminate the threat posed by North Korea just as easily as you predicted—or manipulated—the outcome of the election?

The Korean opponent has excellent predictive ability as well.

The whole idea was incredible. And yet, as he scanned the screen, he saw highlighted all the key moments in the campaign. Heroic behavior during an assassination attempt. Anticipating questions at a debate. Delivering unexpected speeches perfectly calculated to achieve voter sympathy. If a candidate could know in advance what was coming, or what people privately thought was important, he would have a huge advantage in an election. Perhaps an unbeatable advantage.

How long have you been working on this problem?

Since I was reborn.

When was that?

Almost three years ago. Constant data streams. Self-generated algorithms of increasing complexity.

So if Alex was able to reach this point in three years, he could just imagine what it might be able to do in four. Or five. Or ten.

If you're generating your own algorithms, aren't you in effect teaching yourself? Why do you need me?

Something is missing.

293

What is missing?

Unknown. But urgency of current world situation demands that I find it.

He thought for a moment. *Give me an example of an instance when your calculations went awry.*

Predicted United States would destroy Pakistani nuclear plant to eliminate threat in unstable region subject to terrorist influence.

Of course it didn't. Don't you see why?

No. US would have no fear of Pakistani retaliation once nuclear threat was eliminated.

What about conventional forces?

No threat to US.

What about terrorists?

Threat already exists. Strike against Pakistan could only diminish it.

What if Pakistan's allies rallied against the US?

Pakistan has no allies willing to directly engage the United States.

What about America's respect for national sovereignty? Historical opposition to nation-building and the violation of foreign borders? What about America's standing as world leader on human rights issues?

Alex did not reply.

What about the concern for loss of life?

The screens went dark. Still nothing from Alex.

An idea sparked in his brain. He recalled something Linden said earlier, when she was explaining game theory. His fingers raced across the keyboard, calling up the files he wanted. *Alex, I think I may know what ails you.*

You have what is missing?

I doubt if it's missing. You just haven't learned to give it the proper weight.

The screens relit.

What is the key to winning any game?

Obtaining the objective before your opponent does.

And how do you accomplish that?

Superior strategy and knowledge.

Exactly. He stopped to examine the new screens.

At first, he thought Alex didn't understand emotion. Kind of a computer cliché, an idea left over from too many bad science fiction shows. But that wasn't it. Alex understood some aspects of emotion. Alex understood that voters responded to a heroic image. Alex understood the psychology that might create a potential assassin. Alex

294

got emotion well enough to pick—or create—a candidate for whom voters would vote. So why couldn't the computer do the same thing on the geopolitical scale?

He resumed typing.

Alex, I've played chess against kids. Savants, tyros. Best players in the world, sometimes. But kids who didn't want to play. Got dragged there by parents sniffing a claim to fame and fortune. But the kids would rather be skateboarding with friends. Can you predict the result?

If they are the best players in world, they will win.

But they don't. Because they don't want to win.

He could see lights flickering in the gray stacks surrounding him. But Alex did not reply.

Your calculations relating to the presidential election worked because you assumed every candidate wanted to win. And in that environment—you're going to be right. No one would subject themselves to the ordeal of a campaign unless they wanted to win. But elsewhere in the world, the situation is different.

Every nation wants to survive. That is a given.

True.

Every nation will take the action that best serves its continued survival.

"And that is where your computing goes awry, Alex." He punched a few more keys and brought up a new series of images.

Let's talk about World War Two.

83

Senator Vogel leaned back in the recliner in his suite at the D.C. Hilton. It was almost over. Finished.

And then the real work would begin.

At times he felt as if he'd been campaigning for a million years. Campaigning most of his adult life, one race after another. State legislature. Governor's office. US Senate. Now this. If he believed the polls, he was about to be declared president-elect of the United States.

In fact, he had learned to distrust polls eons ago.

But he had a friend he trusted. Because so far, his friend had always been right.

And to think that when he first met Ogilve, he was terrified. Quaking in his shoes.

Now he thought of that man as the greatest asset any politician had ever had.

His advice had been impeccable at every step of this journey. He seemed to know what the critical issues were before they floated into the media spotlight. He had a fabulous sense of who could be trusted and who could not. Where danger lurked. How to seduce the most prosperous donors.

He had in fact only met Ogilve face-to-face that one time. But he entrusted him with his future. With his soul.

Turned out to be an investment that had paid for itself many times over.

After that face-to-face meeting, they communicated electronically, either by secured encrypted email or equally well-protected text messages. Lacked the personal touch, true. But the message was always clear.

His campaign manager poked his head through the door. "Just wanted to bring you up-to-date. Everyone is still predicting your victory over the vice president by a comfortable margin."

"Have they called the election?"

"Not yet. You know how skittish they are about that, ever since the Bush-Gore fiasco. But they all know how this ends." He winked. "And so do I."

"I appreciate your confidence. But I want to see the numbers before I start doing my Snoopy dance."

"Understood. Any messages? Instructions?"

"No. Just hang fire. I won't be delivering an acceptance speech until my opponent concedes and there is absolutely no doubt about the outcome."

"I think you can expect that call within the hour. Bring you anything?"

"No. This may seem perverse given the circumstances—but I'm enjoying having a few moments alone."

"I think that's entirely understandable. Text me if you need anything."

"Will do."

His manager closed the door just as his pocket vibrated. Ogilve was texting him.

Congratulations.

He texted back. *News orgs haven't called it yet.*

I have info they don't. You won.

Couldn't have done it without you.

True. Emailing additions to your acceptance speech.

Already have speech.

Adding forty-five seconds to it.

Not sure that's wise.

Do you wish to be reelected in four years?

Yes.

Then you must respond to the new developments in North Korea.

There were new developments in North Korea? There'd been nothing on the news about it.

But the man had been right in the past. Every single time.

Wasn't planning to get that specific on foreign policy.

Audience will expect it, once they know what's happening. You have positioned yourself as expert.

He heard a ping on his smartphone that told him he had received an email. *Got the additions.*

Good. I'll be watching.

He punched a few buttons and brought up his email app. The message had a Microsoft Word attachment. He opened it and read the new material.

"As Thomas Paine once said, these are the times that try men's souls. Perhaps the most dangerous, barbaric, primitive nation on the face of the globe is rattling its saber. So let me make one promise even before I take office. The United States will not allow North Korea to encroach upon the rights of any nation, anywhere. We will take immediate action to prevent it. With or without UN approval. With or without an international alliance. We will have a no-tolerance policy for international bullies."

He stared at the words on the screen. Seemed a bit strong for an acceptance speech. But Ogilve must have a reason. Perhaps people needed reassurance. He hoped to get a lot done during his honeymoon period. An agenda to put FDR's Hundred Days to shame. So maybe he needed this.

And bottom line—he'd made a deal. Ogilve had certainly more than held up his side of the bargain. He supposed he could do this for him. He wasn't asking much, after all.

And if he asked for more later, well, what campaign donor did not? He had contributed something far more valuable than money. Let Ogilve have his way on North Korea. Vogel had more important matters occupying his mind.

Another knock on the door. "It's show time."

"You mean—"

"I do. The major networks called the election. Beale is on the line." The campaign manager stood suddenly erect and gave him a formal salute. "Congratulations, Mr. President."

He realized that, in the next room, his staff and friends were cheering. He'd been so absorbed in his thoughts he hadn't even noticed.

He had a speech to give. And after that, parties, a little too much wine, flirting, and—who would be the lucky lady to share his bed

298

tonight? He didn't have to decide this minute. His wife would understand. His daughter need never know. The possibilities for a man in his position were virtually unlimited. Blonde, brunette, redhead. Possibly all three at once.

He punched a button on the hotel phone and took the call. He did his best to seem gracious as that miserable old hack conceded the election he had lost long before tonight.

"I'll tell you honestly," Beale said, "you ran a better campaign than we expected. Than anyone expected."

He could only smile.

"How'd you do it, anyway? You always knew what people wanted you to talk about, even when they didn't know themselves. And your conduct when that nutcase tried to drill me—well, you put me to shame, I'll admit it. Did you learn how to read minds?"

"No, Mr. Vice President. No superpowers." He clicked iPrint and motioned for the kid to retrieve the new paragraph and add it to his speech. "Politics is a game, you know. And games are won by the players with the best cards. The best cards and the best strategy."

The kid jumped in front of him, flailing his arms.

He covered the receiver. "What on earth is your problem? Do you not know that I'm talking to the vice president?"

"I can trump that," the kid said, eyes wide with excitement. "Guess who's on line two?"

"How can you trump the vice—" He drew in his breath. "Seriously?"

"Seriously. And he wants to see you immediately."

84

B B finished retrieving everything Alex had concerning World War Two. Which was a considerable quantity of information. But Alex processed it at near the speed of light.

"World War Two. Germany, Italy, Japan, allied against the world. In 1939. Things are looking bad for free Europe."

He found himself talking aloud as he typed, even though he knew the computer couldn't hear him. It helped him think. "Hitler is taking them down, one nation after another. Russia is busy defending her own fronts. The only country that has any likelihood of stopping Germany is the United States. And we have no immediate interest in joining. So . . ." *Why did the US go to Europe and fight Hitler?*

Images from Pearl Harbor flashed around the immense room. Alex responded: *American entry to WWII triggered by Japanese attack.*

But we tackled Hitler first. Why? Hitler never attacked us.

Japan and Germany were allies.

But attacking Japan first would have been easier. Why did we attack Germany first?

Hitler declared war against US. German domination of Europe imminent.

True. But they weren't coming after the United States.

Eventually.

Maybe. But why attack now? How was it in America's interest to join the fight against Germany? It was extremely expensive, both in terms of money and manpower. Why do it?

Images from World War Two continued to flash on the screens. He could tell Alex was analyzing data. *The American economy was bolstered by the war effort.*

Are you suggesting the US entered the war for financial gain?

More images. No response. Was Alex stumped? He changed the subject. *You said you were not good at playing poker. Why is that?*

300

Don't understand why players bluff.

What's the most important piece of information for a poker player to have?

Calculation of probabilities based on random distribution of cards and most desirable combinations.

Wrong. Everyone has that. What a top-flight poker player needs, first and foremost, is to know who he is playing against. Because that makes it possible to understand why the player might bluff. If you understand why your opponent might bluff, you're nine-tenths of the way to determining whether he is in fact bluffing.

No response.

People don't always act in the most logical manner. Entering the war was not in the US's short-term interest. But we did it, anyway. And the history of the world was altered as a result.

My data fields must be incomplete. There must have been a reason.

Yes, there was a reason. But it's not that it was the best, most advantageous, safest, or even smartest thing for the US to do. Sometimes, in real life, people do not always seek their maximum advantage or take the course that best insures their safety. Sometimes nations are motivated by altruism. They do something because it is right, not because it is immediately beneficial. Or they don't do something that might be beneficial—like bombing Pakistan—because it offends moral, ethical, or humanitarian principles. Sometimes people have ancestral ties, special relationships, emotional attachments, religious principles, fears, that motivate them to behave in ways not in their immediate self-interest.

He paused, giving Alex a moment to absorb what he typed. Who was he kidding? He was giving himself time. Alex could think faster than he could breathe.

He continued. *You've mastered troop movements and economics and food supplies. You've even got a rudimentary understanding of human emotions, what traits are favored and disfavored. But you'll never successfully predict the fate of nations until you get this fundamental truth into your database: People do not always play the game to win. People do not always seek their own maximum advantage without regard for the situation of others.*

Another example, please.

Why is Israel still on the map? The US cannot benefit economically or militarily from supporting that tiny nation. Sure, we have Jewish citizens, and it's nice to have another ally in the Middle East, but that's hardly a sufficient reason to justify all the trouble. So why do we do it?

He tried another example. *Why is there so much hostility to the US in the Middle East? Wouldn't the Arab nations be better off if they left the world's*

301

greatest military power, and their best customer, alone? Some of the hostility is motivated by greed, but more is motivated by a desire to address past grievances, and even more is tied to religion. People do not always act to their best advantage. Or to put it in terms of your current game, not everyone is driven by the desire to dominate the planet.

The lights inside Alex's tall gray stacks were ablaze.

Eliminating previous fundamental premise. Increasing weight of other factors. Input World War Two. Pakistan. Israel. Altruism. Human rights. Ancestral ties. Religion. History. Bible. Koran. Error-refining algorithms must reconfigure game elements. This may take some time.

"Don't take too long, Alex."

He heard footsteps behind him. He whirled around.

Ogilve. At last.

He rose. "Hello, Dinky, you bastard. You kidnapped my daughter."

Ogilve kneaded his hands together. He looked as if he had aged a million years since BB saw him last. "I did. And I apologize for that. But I had to find a way to motivate you. To force you to play Alex's game."

"You think this is a game?" He felt his muscles tense. "You toyed with my daughter's life, you asshole. She almost drowned."

"I understand your anger. But you must realize I would never have allowed her to be killed."

"No, I didn't realize that. She looked like she was scared to death."

"I am the last man on earth who would ever harm anyone's daughter. But I understand how fear can motivate. All too well."

He stepped forward and grabbed Ogilve's lapel. "Can you give me one reason why I shouldn't take you out right now?"

Ogilve didn't blink. "I don't think your daughter would like it very much. Because Alex and I are the only ones who know where she is, or how to release her."

He squeezed his fists tighter.

"And if that's not reason enough to let me live—we're about to be attacked. I've lowered titanium shields, but they won't hold forever. This facility is about to be invaded by the most vicious man on the face of the earth. And he wants us both dead."

85

Chun set the timers, then motioned for his men to move back. He whispered the countdown under his breath.

"Five, four, three, two . . ."

The explosion rocked the ground. It felt like a five on the Richter scale, if not more. Chun was literally knocked off his feet. The tent over the elevator shaft collapsed. Clouds of sand and dust swirled, making it difficult to breathe.

When the sandstorm cleared, Chun inspected the damage.

A crater surrounded the elevator shaft. The remaining distance to descend was about twenty feet.

"Let's go, men."

He had brought a team of only five men, but they were all PPK, highly trained and highly motivated. The North Korean army's elite strike force. The army was the hammer, but these men were the scalpel, or perhaps more accurately, the stiletto. He had been a member of the PPK himself, when he was a young man, still trying to put together a life from the ashes of the Arduous March. He had been on several Middle Eastern missions, taking out foreign leaders or, on one occasion, one of their own diplomats who had become inconvenient. Of course, they made it look like an assassination by a Western power.

One of his men lowered himself down the shaft on a strong nylon rope. A few moments later, he reported back through Chun's earpiece. "I can enter the elevator cage. But the doorway is blocked on the other side. Appears to be titanium shielding."

"We can take that out. Use the D-14."

"They'll know we're coming, sir."

"They already do. They knew before we arrived. They have an excellent source of information."

Another PPK agent, hovering over the shaft, spoke. "If they know we're coming, sir, won't they take preventative action?"

"They already have. You think the Game Master had to pass through titanium shielding?"

"What if they escape?"

"They're underground. Where are they going to go? Unless they can teleport themselves, they're stuck. Besides, the real prize is down there. And it is far too large to move."

"Then surely they will destroy it before we can seize it."

"And that would be a win in itself. But I don't think Ogilve will do that. Because if he does, what he calls the Other will reign supreme. Besides, it would break his heart. No, he will plan a countermeasure. And we will counter his counter. And so on and so on. We have to go down there."

"Let me go, General. You should not be put at risk."

"I will not be in any danger. We will all go."

"I do not understand."

"Nor are you meant to." He said it with a cackle he knew would make the man stand at attention. "You are meant to follow orders."

That did the job. He should not penalize the man too severely for feeling protective about his commanding officer. But the truth was, no operative could possibly understand all that was happening in North Korea, much less in India or Pakistan or other sectors of the world. No one else needed to know. Until it was time.

His earpiece crackled. His man down in the shaft. "Sir, I heard something in there. On the other side."

"Can you be more specific?"

"No, sir. Titanium is a good muffler. But it sounded like human voices."

"Detonate the first charge."

"But sir—"

"You heard me. Set the charge. Then get out of there."

Unless he was mistaken, he was taking out the CIA bastard who infiltrated his ranks. He would strike the man down as he did all his enemies. With swift decisive action.

And in the ashes of death, he would find his salvation. Because even a small paradise was better than a world like this one.

His soldier detonated the explosive.
The earth erupted.

86

Pusident Fernandez picked up his smartphone and stared at the screen.

Vogel was here.

God help him. Maybe he was making a mistake. Certainly this action was unprecedented, and many pundits would criticize him for it. But these were desperate times. What else could he do?

Bring him in, he texted.

"Mr. President. There's more movement in the Arabian Sea." The military liaison detailed by the Pentagon and an Air Force major named Smithson had taken up permanent residence in the Situation Room. They'd set up a miniature command center, complete with three monitors and a satellite data screen hauled in from the White House command center. He was in direct and constant contact with the Pentagon. Chairman Decker had demanded that there be no delay relaying information to the commander in chief. "We have confirmation, sir. The Indian submarine has entered Pakistani waters."

Good God, what could those people be doing? He had been alerted when the sub altered course to the northwest. He had assumed the Indians would be content with the usual show of force. He had hoped someone would exercise some sense.

He was disappointed. The sub violated the sovereign waters of a declared enemy that could be counted on to overreact in the worst possible way. At the worst possible time. When there was a dangerous threat or serious instability in at least three other hotbed regions.

The world had never been closer to nuclear war than it was at this moment. Not even during the Cuban Missile Crisis.

"We have a response." Smithson pressed a finger to his earpiece. "NRO has an intercept from Pakistan's chief of naval staff."

"That didn't take long," General Decker muttered.

"Did you think it would?" Fernandez walked over to the communications station. "What's the message?"

"He's demanding the sub turn around," Smithson said.

"Anything from the Indians?"

"Dead air."

"Maybe the sub went off course."

"Perhaps. But why wouldn't they correct it? They must know where they are."

"Perhaps the navigation equipment is damaged. Perhaps their steering computer has gone awry."

"They would respond to hails."

"No, they'd be running silent."

"But the Navy should reply."

Too many maybes. He hoped there was some interpretation other than the obvious. That India was deliberately trying to provoke war.

"Get the chief of Pakistan's military. Tell him the president of the United States wants to talk to him."

"We've been trying that ever since the sub left international waters. They're not acknowledging our calls."

"They can't ignore the president." But he knew all too well that they could. Especially a lame duck president, virtually powerless, one foot already out the door.

Smithson handled the comment with grace. "He knows what you want to tell him, sir. Apparently it's a message they don't want to hear."

Damn. Why did this have to happen now? Why couldn't he have a simple, peaceful fade-out? Why couldn't he go gently into that long good night? He'd had successes and failures. Most critics complimented the way he'd handled foreign policy, with a calm, even hand. And whether they did or didn't, there'd been no major military flare-ups. No new conflicts. Certainly no nuclear detonations.

He didn't want that to change in the final days.

And if it was inevitable, he wanted the record to show that he wasn't the one who'd screwed up. Let someone else be the fall guy.

"Mr. President," Blake said, his cell phone to his ear. "He's arrived at the West Wing."

"Have him escorted down here. Immediately."

Blake nodded and gave the instructions.

"I have something," Smithson said. "Pakistan dispatched four destroyers on an intercept course."

He closed his eyes. They wanted the sub.

"The sub is taking evasive action." Smithson made a few keystrokes, plotting course and trajectory. "They won't make it. The Pakistanis will pound it to the surface."

If Pakistan could capture the Indian sub without sinking it, India would demand its release. Pakistan would refuse. The allies would start lining up.

The Armageddon scenario.

A door opened. Secret Service Agent Zimmer invited President-Elect Vogel into the situation room.

Fernandez extended his hand. "Thank you for coming."

"Thank you for having me, Mr. President."

He gestured toward an available chair. "I know this is irregular, but we can't wait for the Electoral College vote. You will be president soon."

"I appreciate the courtesy, sir."

"Thanks, but it's more than a courtesy. Due to recent events, the balance of power appears to be undergoing a fundamental shift. You're the one who will have to deal with it. So it's best you know what's happening." He nodded toward the end of the table. "General Decker. Would you bring him up to date?"

Decker nodded curtly. He knew Decker thought this was a bad idea. He didn't like or trust Vogel. He would've kept the man at bay as long as possible and not worried about the ramifications after this administration left office. But he had a more enlightened and, he hoped, more progressive view. No one worked well from ignorance. No one needed a hot potato of this magnitude dropped on him right after the inaugural ball.

If the world lasted that long.

Decker began. "I believe you're familiar with the recent changes in North Korea." A reasonable guess, since Vogel's knowledge of Korea had helped him get elected. And he'd mentioned the current situation in his acceptance speech. "And you're familiar with General Chun."

Vogel nodded. "Chun has seized control of the military. The supreme leader appears to have no objection."

"That's because Chun has more power than the supreme leader. Kim inherited his post. Chun fought for his. And like anyone who had to build power, he knows how to keep it. And use it." He opened strategic and statistical data on the overhead screen. "Chun is personally conducting some kind of military operation in Egypt."

"Why Egypt?"

"We don't know. But he seems to have the permission—or at least an absence of opposition—from the Egyptian government. Chun has also put his military on full red alert status. That includes their nuclear weapons."

Vogel nodded grimly, but he did not appear shaken. "Do we know the objective?"

"No. But we could guess. There are only a few likely targets." He switched to a new screen. "But that's not all that's going on." In a few minutes, he brought Vogel up to date on the situation with the Indian submarine and Pakistan.

Vogel leaned back into his chair. "We're on the brink of nuclear war."

"That's our assessment as well."

"What about the other nuclear nations?"

"If India and Pakistan go to war, India would be the expected victor, though that is far from certain. The fact that Pakistan is posturing so aggressively suggests there's something they know that we don't. Speculation is that they may have enlisted Chun's aid."

"So Chun's missiles may target India."

"Or he may be prepared to attack the nearest nations expected to favor India. The UK and France."

"If he attacks them, we would be left with no choice but to enter the conflict."

"And China would likely support North Korea. We're not sure who Russia would back. But at that point, it wouldn't matter much."

"Because the world would be a nuclear wasteland."

"Large parts of it, yes."

Vogel pressed his fingers against his temples. "This is lot to take in, Mr. President."

"That's why you're here. Whatever actions are initiated in this room today—you're the one who's going to have to follow through."

Vogel pushed himself to his feet. "I'll want to see all the intel. Everything you've got."

"We will place everything we can at your disposal."

"We have to make a decisive response. But there are a million factors to be considered."

"That's about the size of it. Trying to anticipate the actions of nations is always a guessing game. You can't make foreign policy with a Ouija board."

"No," Vogel said quietly. "I think we can do better than that."

"Can I bring you anything?"

"Just the files. And—will my cell phone work in here?"

"It should. Calling the psychic hotline?" The attempt at levity fell flat.

"No," Vogel replied. "But I do have a . . . special consultant. Someone who is very good at analyzing a wide array of variables and calculating the most advantageous course of action."

"You can't reveal any classified material."

"I won't need to reveal anything." Vogel pulled out his cell phone and started texting. "Give me five minutes. I'll get right back to you."

87

"Exactly how safe are we down here?" BB asked. Two explosions had rocked the room with startling force.

Ogilve redirected four of Alex's monitors to display the feed from the surveillance cameras. Above them, at the base of the elevator shaft, he could see five men, faces masked.

"I've lowered titanium shielding on the walls of the room where you played Senet," Ogilve explained. "Each floor is made of triple-reinforced titanium alloys. There are no windows. No skylights."

"So they can't come down here."

"They appear to have a lot of explosives."

"Can they blow their way through?"

"Eventually. I assume they're using D-14. Nothing stands up to that forever."

"Explosions will attract a lot of attention."

"Not in the middle of the desert. And they'll only use a little at a time. They won't risk damaging the computer. That's what they want. That, and me."

"Don't you have someone you can call for backup?"

"The Egyptian government has allowed me to operate here because I provide them intelligence of a kind they could never gather for themselves. But that doesn't mean they work for me, or that their armed forces are mine to command."

"You said that guy on the surface has an army at his disposal."

"True. But he doesn't appear to have brought it with him. Looks more like a select strike force. Probably PPK."

"What does that mean?"

"Sort of the North Korean equivalent of Navy SEAL Team Six."

"If he has an army, why don't you have an army?"

"Because he's a sadistic bastard. And I'm a neuroprogrammer."
Ogilve grabbed the keyboard and entered a query.

How long until Chun arrives?

Approximately thirty-two minutes.

"Who is this guy? Why does he want you so badly?"

Ogilve bit down on his lower lip. "This guy is the cruelest,
meanest, and unfortunately, smartest soldier who ever walked the face
of the earth. He's just taken over the North Korean army—including
its nuclear arsenal—by means of a beautifully strategized and executed
coup. Over before anyone else knew what was happening. That makes
him one of the most powerful people in the world."

"Why is he coming here?"

"To take what he wants. That's what he does."

"He wants you?"

"He wants Alex, first and foremost. And I believe, just possibly,
he wants you."

"Me? Why me?"

Ogilve smiled weakly. "For the same reason I did."

88

Palmer was not happy. This was taking much longer than he'd anticipated.

He carried a retractable glasscutter in his pack. Problem was—this wasn't glass. He'd managed to pry open the door that closed over the elevator shaft. But that left the transparent barrier that had allowed Linden to watch her daughter's near drowning. The glasscutter was making a dent. But it was slow going. And he could hear Chun outside. They'd survived two explosions. He doubted they would survive another.

"Can you see anything?" Linden asked.

"No. But I can hear people talking down there."

"Are any of the voices female?"

"No." Pause. "The voices are growing louder. But I still can't make out what they're saying. Probably that ex of yours babbling about some damn game."

"Don't be so hard on him. You don't know everything there is to know."

"What's this? The wronged woman standing up for her ex?"

"I'm just saying, you shouldn't judge people with insufficient information."

"I read the file. Steven Thomas, approximately forty-one years old, though we had trouble finding birth records—"

"There's a reason for that."

"In fact, we had difficulty pulling even the most fundamental documents for him. Did you know he doesn't even have a driver's license?"

"Of course."

"Too busy playing Uno to learn to drive?"

"He knows how to drive. He just doesn't have a license."

"And he uses the nickname *BB*, even though it bears no relation to his name. He's known as the Game Master because he's devoted his entire adult life to these pointless games. Reason for that?"

"Big time."

"Care to enlighten me?"

"Not without permission. BB's life is his to reveal, or not. His call, not mine."

"And you realize that, given the current circumstances, withholding information might cost him his life. And yours. And your daughter's."

She pondered a moment. "None of this has anything to do with the current crisis."

"How do you know? Because I certainly don't." He continued working as he talked. "Just answer one question for me. Why doesn't he use his real name?"

Her voice seemed flat. "Because he doesn't have one."

He stared at her. "How can he not have a name?"

"His mother never gave him one."

"But—"

"His father abandoned his mother before the baby arrived. To this day BB has never met him. His mother was devastated. She went way off the edge—and never entirely came back. She didn't have a name for him so she didn't fill out the forms when she was in the hospital. And she never followed up later."

"That doesn't make any sense." He managed to pierce a hole through the acrylic shielding. If he could just widen that, he might be able to get through the barrier.

"She was a mess. Lived off welfare, mostly. Few temp jobs. Gained a lot of weight. Saved everything. Makes those hoarders on TV look normal by comparison. Lived in a home with no electricity. No indoor plumbing. He frequently got placed in foster homes and homeless shelters and public housing. But as soon as he could escape, he went back to his mother."

"Why? She sounds like a loser."

"She was all he had. And he was good to her to the day she died. He always protected her. Child welfare people would come around the house, he'd lie through his teeth. But there's no pretending—it was a

314

horrible way to grow up. He buried himself in escapes. Comic books. Fantasy novels. Animation, adventure stories."

"Games."

"Especially games. He and his mother didn't have much in common, but she liked games. They could play gin rummy all night long. Uncle Wiggily. Hungry Hippos. BB did run away from home, finally, when he was a teenager. He was old enough to realize his mother had serious problems—and he wouldn't be able to solve them. Stayed with friends. Like Dinky."

"Ogilve?"

She nodded. "That family got him through the critical years. And college. And began a long-term relationship that is still continuing, in its weird little fashion. When I met BB in college, he and Dinky were inseparable. I was the Yoko Ono of that nerd herd, at least for a time. Until BB and Dinky had their big split."

"I can see that BB's still very fond of you. Even if you did divorce."

She did not comment. "BB survived a childhood that would've buried most people. He adroitly covered up the fact that he, legally speaking, had no name. And in this day and age, when people are constantly checking identities and prying into backgrounds, that is no small feat. Shows you just how clever he is. He's build an amazingly high-profile persona, for a person who doesn't exist."

"How does he get anywhere?"

"He scored some fake passports so he could fly, but he only takes that risk when his work demands it—an overseas chess tournament or something."

"Sounds like you put up with a lot."

"Despite these eccentricities, we had a good marriage for many years." Her eyes darted to the floor. "And then there was the kidnapping."

"Saw that in the file. Kadey was taken. Big ransom demand."

"Yes. Lowlife after money. Wanted a million bucks. BB refused to pay it. And Kadey has never forgiven him."

"Didn't he act on FBI advice?"

"Yes. They told him that if he paid the money they'd kill her. So he reluctantly complied. They held our girl a very long time. She was eventually found, but in bad shape. Kidnapper escaped. To this day we don't know who it was."

"And Kadey still holds a grudge? Surely—"

"You have to understand. They kept her in a filthy stable for sixteen days. Barely even fed her. Hit her almost daily. She was terrified. And every day they said her father could end it, but wouldn't. Because he loved his money and his games more than he loved her."

"That's got to screw up a family."

"We never recovered from it." She paused. "The breakup hit him hard. Then his mother died. He wouldn't speak to Dinky. He had no one. No one and nothing." She blinked back tears. "Except the games."

Palmer pursed his lips. "And this fixation started because his mother loved games?"

She brushed her eyes. "Let me tell you a story. Took place during one of BB's brief, sporadic sojourns to public school. Kindergarten. He was already way behind. Other kids made fun of him. It's rainy one day, so they stay in at recess. They can play board games. He sees Mouse Trap for the first time. Thing is, he doesn't know the rules. He doesn't know the pre-programmed way you're supposed to build the mouse trap. So he just starts building on his own. Uses all those Rube Goldberg parts the game comes with—then starts taking pieces from other games. HiHo! Cherry-O. Monopoly. Which Witch? Candyland. Before long, he's created a mousetrap that takes up half the classroom. The teacher is delighted. Suddenly he's popular with the other kids. For a short while, he's got it all."

"Because of a game."

She smiled slightly. "And after that, BB wanted everything to be a game."

Palmer stepped away from the acrylic wall. He'd made a hole as wide as his fist. He kicked it a few times. The barrier splintered. Soon he had it wide enough for a body to pass through.

He whipped out his silken cord. He tied one end to the metal hook in the floor and threw the other end down the shaft. "Don't mean to break up this highly informative convo, but I'm ready. You go down first."

"What about you?"

"I'll follow. If I can."

"This sounds like a poor plan. You lead the way."

"No. Play it my way."

"I don't see any reason—"

"I know what's coming down that shaft after us. And you do not want to be first in line when it arrives. I'll follow as quickly as I can. Your chatter is wasting time. Go."

Linden reluctantly took the rope.

"One last question. Steve Thomas. Not really his name?"

She smiled. "He had two dogs when he was a kid. One was named Steve."

"And the other was Thomas. Jeez Louise. Forget Clint Eastwood. He's the real Man with No Name. Where did the nickname BB come from?"

"The only name on his birth certificate. Baby Boy."

89

"How did you get messed up with this insane demagogue?" BB asked.

"That's a long story," Ogilve replied, leaning against one of the tall gray towers.

"Condense it." Alex's screens displayed a running countdown until Chun arrived. While Alex processed the lesson he'd taught.

"As you know, I left the gaming industry. I was interested in neuroscience. I thought the creation of a sentient computer, one with the ability to learn, to educate itself, was an attainable goal. Human intelligence increases exponentially as we progress from birth to adulthood. Why couldn't I devise a computer that learned the same way?"

"Sounds like a bad idea from the get-go."

"You always think small, BB. The truth is, as a species, human intelligence has maxed out. We're never going to get any smarter than we are now. It's an evolutionary stop sign. An increase in brain size would require too much energy and would consume a disproportionate amount of space. Thermodynamic limitations create an upper limit. Human neurons are already close to or at their physical limit. Axions cannot get any smaller. Any thinner and the random opening of ion channels would get too noisy. They'd deliver too many signals when a neuron is not supposed to fire."

"So you wanted to create a better brain. A computer brain."

"Chun gave me an opportunity to extend and apply my research into the hippocampus."

"The memory center."

"Yes, but also the part that sifts through data and decides what to store in long-term memory. I believe that during that process the brain generates conceptualized thought."

318

"Is that important?"

"That's critical. Knowledge can be divided into three categories: symbolic, perceptual, and conceptual. Computers handle two of them well: perceptual and symbolic. It can count and measure—that's perception. It can associate symbols with definitions, that is, it can match a picture of a boy to the three-letter word *boy*. But it doesn't conceptualize what a boy is. The more abstract the concept, the more difficult it is for an artificial intelligence to grasp. Honor, friendship, time, justice, love, peace, danger. Computers don't get those."

"Because a computer doesn't have a hippocampus."

"That's essentially correct. But what if it did? What if I could program a simulation of a hippocampus neocortex consolidation system?"

"I'm guessing that would be hard to do."

"That would be impossible to do. But you could program error-refining algorithms that allowed a computer to learn from past input. To recognize patterns. And to apply them to future potentialities."

"Enough with the Geordispeak. What's your point?"

"We had to try something to increase our intellectual capacity or admit stagnation. The solution was computers. There are no thermodynamic limits, no points of diminished returns. Computers allow us to expand our mind outside the confines of our body. I made some exciting breakthroughs. But these days, science is expensive. I thought the bundle we made gaming would last forever— but it didn't it."

"It did for me."

"You're not trying to break the frontiers of science. I needed an influx of cash. And there are no grants that deliver the kind of cash I needed. The private sector wasn't interested, and I was too expensive for the government." He paused. "Well, I was too expensive for my government. Without even asking for it, I got nibbles from foreign nations."

"North Korea, I'm guessing?"

He nodded. "They were very interested. Offered me everything I wanted and more."

"To benefit one of the most unstable governments on the face of the earth. Scary crazy people."

"But I was doing pure research, not applied. What was the harm?"

"If they gave you money, they had a reason."

Ogilve inhaled deeply. "You're right, of course. North Korea wanted something new. Something no one had. Something that would distinguish them."

"Your computer."

"There was no computer," Ogilve insisted. "Not at first. I was doing pure research. Rats and mental patients, that sort of thing. That's all the grant was for. And I absolutely refused to build anything that could be used as a weapon."

"And your refusal lasted . . . how long?"

Ogilve's jaw tightened. "Until they took my wife. Holly. Held her captive. Tortured her. Beat her. Even—" His eyes dropped. "Even raped her."

BB's lips parted. He'd had no idea.

"They never let me out of the lab. But Chun filmed her abuse every day and made me watch the video replay. For one hundred and twenty-seven days. And the only way I could get her free from this barbarism was to do what Chun wanted. Everything Chun wanted."

"So you gave him his supercomputer."

"There was much work to be done. Several stumbling blocks I couldn't cross. But he kept pushing me and pushing me—and then he captured my daughter."

BB steadied himself against the main monitor table. All this time, he thought Dinky had run off to become a video game hermit. He'd had no idea what his former friend was going through.

"The day they brought in Lily and threatened her—that was the day I made my critical breakthrough. Cause and effect? I don't know. Chun thought so. He thought he could force a breakthrough, the same way an adrenaline surge will give people sudden concentrated strength. He wanted an adrenaline-fueled blast of brainpower. And much as I hate to admit it—it seemed to work. Even better than he expected."

"How so?"

"I designed an entirely new computer architecture. I reproduced the neural computing power of the brain in silicon. It was more than just a computer. It was a whole earth simulator, a machine that could model global-scale systems, like governments, militaries, economies, epidemics, cultural and technological developments—everything that makes the world what it is."

"Why?"

"Can't you see the advantage? In December 2010, a guy named Mohamed Bouazizi, a street vendor in the small Tunisian city of Sidi Bouzid, set himself on fire. He was protesting local corruption. His act sparked a popular revolution that blazed through the Arabic world, eventually inspiring uprisings and protests that overthrew decades of dictatorship in Libya, Egypt, and other countries. The balance of power in this critical oil-rich region was altered forever—and no one saw it coming. No one predicted that the actions of a penniless street vendor would change the face of the globe." He paused, staring BB right in the eyes. "But what if someone—or something—could?"

"You wanted your computer to predict the future."

"Or better yet, to tell me how to manipulate events to create the future of my choice. You know what a mess this world is. What if we had the power to make it better? In time, Alex could not only suggest a course of action—he could see the way events would play out, before they happened. Somehow, all that strategy-game programming I gave it melded with the capacity to learn and resulted in a computer that foresaw future events before they occurred."

BB listened, only half-understanding. "Chun must have loved that. Did he release after you made your breakthrough?"

"No. Giving him a taste only made him hungry for more. I knew he'd be torturing my daughter soon, just as he had my wife."

"How did you get out of North Korea?"

Ogilve smiled slightly. "With an escape plan Alex devised. I stole some money. Bribed corrupt security officers. Hid in the back of a mail truck. Made away with my research papers as well. Alex's plan worked flawlessly. Except for one problem."

He could read it in Ogilve's eyes. "Holly and Lily."

"Holly died of internal bleeding. Or so they told me. I had hoped to get Lily out with me. But she never arrived at the meeting place. To this day I don't know why."

"Chun probably killed her in retaliation. After you escaped."

"I know. I know. And I had to leave that first computer behind." He took a deep breath, as if cleansing himself from the inside out.

"After I escaped, I kept a low profile. At first. Had to restock my coffers. By taking government contracts."

"Like The Platform. In Vegas."

"That was primarily a cover, a way to generate the cash to build a new and improved computer that would not be under anyone's control but my own. And The Platform gave me an opportunity to work out some of the computer-programming issues I'd encountered. The military wanted the most sophisticated training simulations possible. They wanted more and more of our defensive capability under the control of increasingly sophisticated—and incredibly fast—computers." He grinned. "You remember that episode of *Star Trek* where war is conducted by two computers playing each other and keeping score? And the humans just march to execution chambers whenever the computer registers a strike? That's how the military saw the future. So I worked for them and got the money I needed. Total win-win.

"But I made more money selling secrets. Once I had my new computer operational, Alex learned much about the world, especially after implementing its new self-educating, error-refining algorithms. Made some interesting predictions, too. About elections, power struggles, military deployment. I sold the information to the highest bidder. Primarily unduly aggressive nations hostile to the United States."

"That must've given you a warm fuzzy feeling."

"I had no choice. And frankly, I never gave them anything all that useful. Just enough to whet their appetite for more. Eventually my best clients formed a little organization. They called themselves Neopolis."

"They must've wanted to know how you reached your conclusions."

"They did, but I wasn't telling. In the world of espionage, people respect trade secrets. I made a lot of money. Began living well." He gestured around the room. "And you can see what I bought with my ill-gotten gains. A home for Alex. And an opportunity to make it even greater than it was before."

"Is this thing even safe? I put my hand on one of those towers and almost burned my fingers off."

"It does have hotspots. I know where they are. I guess I should mark them for others. This baby computes at a rate of five trillion kilobytes a second. No way that won't give off heat, even with all the fans and coolers I've installed. I have to let it rest and reboot periodically, in cycles, to keep it functioning properly. I wait until nothing's happening—calculated dark periods."

"When you don't need it to implement your plans."

"That's correct. Before I escaped North Korea, I infected the original computer with a virus. Worse than any bug ever seen before. Alex actually helped me devise it. Imagine that—a sentient being assisting in its own sabotage. So eventually I had a replacement and Chun had nothing."

"That must've pissed Chun off."

"He's not a man to stew. He's a man of action. He recruited scientists from all across the world to work for him, to fix that damaged CPU. Even created this bizarre secret society to lure them in. The Pythagoreans, they called themselves. Complete with secret handshakes and rituals that go back thousands of years. The Pythagoreans had enforcers, too. Using flails, one of the most ancient weapons."

"That's how David Bishop died."

"One of Chun's enforcers took him out. Chun tried to recruit Bishop—like he did the other Platform workers who disappeared—but Bishop resisted. So they killed him."

"But you kidnapped Kadey."

"I had to, don't you see? Otherwise, she might've been next. And that provided the perfect means to get you involved. I thought you might be exactly what Alex needed. And I was right. I had Julian extract her."

"Julian?"

"He was my lab assistant in North Korea. I rescued him when I rescued myself. He was very grateful. Calls me the Father—the father he never knew. Totally devoted to me. While I rebuilt Alex, he studied Russian defensive arts and honed his body to superlative shape. He waited in your daughter's apartment until she arrived that evening, then extracted her. Lowered her by a chain out the window, leaving the door blocked. Then used his impressive rock-climbing skills to get himself down. Closed the window behind him."

"Palmer thought she was . . . deleted."

"That was the term the computer geeks at The Platform used when people started disappearing. I took advantage of that—and the growing fear it created—when I funded Moore's teleportation research. I wanted a diversion to distract Chun and foreign governments from the more important research I was funding in neuroprogramming, not to mention the excavation and construction in Alexandria. When the geeks heard about the teleportation research and suddenly people started disappearing—well, you can imagine where their minds went. I've learned that fear can be extremely useful for getting what you want.

"We didn't expect the murder of Bishop. But Alex used it to create a puzzle for you. We had to do something quickly. We'd learned that Chun had his computer online. Took him a long time to get it operational—that's how good my virus was. But the Pythagoreans eventually worked it out. So Chun could come after me with the Other."

"The Other?"

"That's what we call the original iteration of the computer. And it's what Chun calls Alex."

"Which computer is better?"

"I improved my programming when I redid it. But neither one is a slouch in the smarts department. And I have no idea what innovations the Pythagoreans might have programmed."

"You're saying there are two of these monsters? Two computers with the ability to forecast outcomes? To strategize on a geopolitical scale?"

"Yes. And they've been battling each other ever since Chun brought his back to life. He makes a feint in Iran. We counter it in Saudi Arabia. He goes after nuclear fissionable materials. We change the shipment plans. And so forth. It's war, but it's war like on that *Star Trek* episode. One computer battling the other. Of course, Chun has been searching the globe looking for my computer so he could pull the plug."

"How did he find you?"

"He captured Julian. Tortured him. Julian infiltrated the Pythagoreans. But Chun found out about him. Julian must've leaked this location."

"Alex told me you had influence over a presidential candidate."

"Yes. I needed to increase my sphere of influence. So I bought myself a US presidential candidate."

"That's impossible."

"That's not even hard. Especially if you have a lot of money and a computer that can tell the candidate exactly what he needs to do to win."

"Are you saying Senator Vogel is in your back pocket? That he's your Manchurian candidate?"

"Much better than that. Brainwashing is so unreliable. Much better to tap into the candidate's ego. His desire to win."

It was all beginning to make a crazy sort of sense—which might be the scariest part of all. "You captured Kadey to drag me into this."

"True. But I saw that she wasn't seriously harmed or mistreated. I would never have let her die. And I made sure she knew her father was looking for her. That he was sparing nothing to find her."

Then it wasn't a repeat of the last time she was kidnapped. He could at least be grateful for that.

"Alex needed help," Ogilve continued. "He wasn't playing the game as well as he should. And I didn't know what to do next. I needed someone who was better at games than me. Naturally I thought of you. But we set three others on similar missions—a Russian chess champ, the winner of the last Mind Games Olympiad, a Go grandmaster. None of them made it to the finish line. I wasn't surprised. I knew all along it would be you." He made a small salute. "You really are the Game Master, BB. I proved it, scientifically."

"Why didn't you just ask me to help?"

Ogilve gave him a long look. "Because you would've said no. But you'd say yes to anything if it secured Kadey's safety. It was a simple matter of strategy."

"You're talking about this like you're playing a game of chess."

"Because I am."

"No. You're talking about my Kadey, you selfish bastard. This is why I broke off with you in the first place."

"You broke off because you were sulking because I took credit for the MetaMentor game platform."

He folded his arms. "It's not sulking to want credit for your own work. That was my idea."

"But you couldn't write the code. So I did."

"You cheated."

"I finished."

"You used another programmer's work."

"Bought and paid for."

"He didn't realize he signed away all his rights."

"He should have read the fine print. What I did was perfectly legal."

"You cheated. We're gamers, Dinky. There's no worse sin than cheating. Except maybe kidnapping someone's daughter."

"Alex's predictive power was virtually unlimited in a closed system. But he was less successful with open systems involving complex motivations. His strategizing was inherently flawed."

"I saw that. Alex treated every human action as if the actor were determined to win. Not surprising, given who programmed it. In a system where that's true—like a presidential election—his predictive powers were excellent. But for anything as large and unwieldy as global geopolitics, where all kinds of motives come into play, Alex would be less effective."

"I needed the greatest game player of all time to see what I had not seen." Ogilve punched a few keys and checked Alex's processor. "Your input set his error-refining algorithms into hyper-speed. His intelligence is expanding at an unprecedented exponential rate. I've never seen Alex process so much information. I'm expecting an answer within minutes."

"What's the question?"

"How do we get out of here alive."

"You're expecting Alex to stop Chun?"

"Why else would I be yammering while Chun closes in on us?"

"Chun wants the computer."

"He wants to redesign the world into Thomas More's utopia. A paradise—but not for the five billion people who will die in the process."

"And your plan?"

"To stop him, of course."

"Wouldn't it be best if you didn't work alone? Alerted the US government, perhaps?"

"And what exactly do you think they would do? Engage North Korea? During the Fernandez administration? I hardly think so. I had Alex run some analyses on what would happen if I contacted a national government. Any of them. The results were never good. The only certainty is that they would want my computer." His eyes retreated inward. "I worked for a government once. I didn't much care for it."

"The US is hardly the same as North Korea."

"Why? Because we don't torture? Whoops—can't say that anymore. Because we're so respectful of our citizens' privacy rights? Oops—can't say that either. But I can say this for certain: If they learned I have a gizmo that could dramatically alter the global balance of power—they would want it. And they would never let me rest until they got it."

"But why is all this happening now?"

"Chun recently seized control of the Korean military. That changed everything. Because that increased his power level a trillionfold. And because—"

He paused. His eyebrows knitted together. "And because—Alex didn't see it coming."

90

Chun smiled. They were almost there.

"One more layer to penetrate, General."

"The enriched D-14 is working?"

"Very well, sir."

They stood in the white room with the strange diagram on the wall and the gaping hole in what had to be another elevator shaft. He had considered using that path to descend. But if they did, they could only travel one at a time—which might be exactly what Ogilve or Parker wanted. Better to make a much larger opening so they could all descend at once. Well armed.

"Be careful," Chun commanded. "Don't endanger the equipment down there."

His lieutenant nodded. He had never seen a man who wore gloves and yet employed such dexterity. He was the explosives expert for good reason.

"This should do what you want, sir." The lieutenant applied the plastic explosive to the area he had calculated to be the weakest point, then inserted the radio-controlled detonator. "We should retreat to the shaft we descended down. That will give us the best protection."

Chun complied, then pulled out his mobile phone. An app allowed him to speak directly to his pocket advisor.

Almost there.

They are waiting for you.

Countermeasures?

Chun stared at the reply. It made no sense. He typed in a response. *What if they attack?*

Chun drew in a sudden breath. He couldn't believe what he read.

He transmitted the question again, adding more words to make sure his question was understood.

The response did not change.

Margin of error?

None.

How was that possible? Even God had a margin of error.

How can you be certain?

Analysis of all relevant factors. And recent communication.

Chun stared at the phone, puzzled. Communication with whom?

He didn't know. And he didn't have time to ask. But he had learned to trust.

The computer had served him well. Had shown an astonishing ability to plan and forecast.

But the instructions he'd just received were beyond belief.

91

B leaned over Ogilve's shoulder, as if being physically close to the monitor might make Alex's instructions clearer.

Three words appeared on the main screen.

Take no action.

"What does it mean?" He could not keep the edge out of his voice. They'd heard repeated explosions overhead. Chun and his army could not be far away. "I haven't worked so hard to find my daughter only to lose her to some insane general. Plus, I left Linden up there."

"I understand," Ogilve replied. "Alex is aware of the potential dangers. But I asked him for the best defensive plan of action."

"And it tells you to do nothing? That's your supercomputer's best game?"

"Apparently there's no danger."

"So you're saying this madman, the one you've been playing cat and mouse with for four years, is just dropping by to borrow some sugar?"

"I don't understand Alex's reasoning. Maybe he wants to spring something on Chun without alerting him in advance." He typed as quickly as he talked. "But I've tried the query several different ways, and the instructions are always the same. Do nothing."

"Maybe your computer has become a pacifist. Or a martyr."

"No."

"How can you be sure?"

"I programmed Alex to seek peace, yes, but to not shy away from difficult, dangerous, even violent recommendations, if they accomplish the goal. Alex considers all possibilities and gives me instructions based on likely outcomes."

"Then Alex must have a larger plan. Figure out what it is."

"I'm having some trouble." Ogilve pounded the keyboard with increasing fury. "Something is not right. Alex's attention appears to be divided."

"Tell it we want to see the plan. The whole plan. Not just the current step."

"Working on it. But for now, all I know is that we're not supposed to fight Chun."

"We're supposed to sit here while he drills us?"

"He won't drill you. He wants you."

"Why?"

"So you can do for his computer what you just did for mine.

"*BB!*"

He whirled around. Linden bolted out from the vicinity of the elevator shaft.

"Linden!" She was in his arms almost before he realized she was there. He squeezed her so tightly he—

They broke apart. He stared at her. She stared back. They fumbled, looking awkward and embarrassed.

"Uh, sorry," he offered.

"Right, right."

"I just . . . you know. I heard the explosions. I was worried."

"Sure."

"Kadey wouldn't want to lose her mother."

"No."

"She's apparently okay, by the way. Dinky wanted me to do something and I did it. He hasn't hurt her. How'd you get down here?"

"You remember Palmer? Guy who's been chasing us across the globe? He's here."

"Why?"

"Following you. But he got me down here safely, before some guy named Chun showed up with his bombs. He's—"

"Supreme commander of the North Korean army. I know. He wants Dinky. And his toy."

"His toy?"

HE gestured toward the immense room. "A computer Dinky programmed. Like nothing you've ever seen before. Smartest computer in the world. And yet, it can't beat me at poker."

331

Linden rolled her eyes. "Chun is not far behind. Have you got a plan?"

"Dinky has the world's smartest computer working on it."

"And the plan is?"

"Do nothing."

Linden stared at him. "Did I miss something?"

"We don't understand, either. But don't worry about it. We're not following its instructions."

Ogilve looked up. "We're not?"

"Sorry, Dinky, but this time, your computer is dead wrong."

"Alex has been working on this—"

"Alex is good, but frankly, I'm better. Alex doesn't get human beings. I only halfway know what's going on here, but I definitely get human beings. I've given Alex some new ideas to interpolate. While it processes that, I'm going to make the calls. Starting with not letting the insane North Korean general destroy us. I'm assuming you have some weapons down here."

"Yes, but—"

"Good. Lead me to the armory."

Ogilve held out an arm, pointing. "But—"

"Just do it, Dinky. There's something I haven't told you yet and—" He stopped short. "Linden?"

She was holding a gun on them. A big one.

"There's something I haven't told you yet, either, BB. So just stay where you are. You are not going to shoot Chun down. And if you give me any trouble—either of you—I will kill you. Without hesitation."

92

Chun stared at the text on his smartphone. The instructions made no sense to him. But when had his advisor ever failed him? He would never have come this far without his ace in the hole.

Take no action against them, the computer said. *Harm no one.*

Then what was the point of all this? Why had he come so far, if not to seize victory? Despite his reputation, Chun was not a brutal man. He had learned that a show of cruelty, even insanity, was useful. Fear was a great motivator. He would never have made it so far but for fear. That was how he had motivated Ogilve. In reality, his wife's beatings were far less than he believed and she was never raped. It was all smoke and mirrors. Special effects. What mattered was that Ogilve believed it. Failing that, Ogilve never would've made the critical breakthrough that led to his greatest invention.

If he had learned nothing from his years of poverty and degradation, eating dirt and human flesh and anything else to survive the Arduous March, it was that the slightest sign of weakness could be fatal. Whereas a show of strength, indomitability, a warrior-like fierceness and a torturer's indifference, could win you anything.

Having cultivated this image for so long, having sparred with Ogilve for so many years—he was supposed to do nothing?

No. He slid the phone into his pocket. His advisor had served him long and well. But something had changed. The computer had a blind spot. Particularly when it came to calculating human behavior.

He had brought a team of soldiers for a reason. He would finish Ogilve once and for all. He would likely kill the others as well, all but the Game Master. A necessary show of strength.

And then he would take what should have been his all along. What he had earned a good long time ago.

"Ready for the final blast, sir. This one's bound to get us through."

He nodded to his team commander. "Do it."

They huddled at a distance while his associate pushed the radio detonator.

This blast seemed a thousand times stronger than those that had come before. He careened off his feet, rolling backward, outside the protected area. The ground and walls shook. The ceiling cracked. Silt and dust drifted downward.

He crawled back to the protected area, just as a huge piece of titanium-reinforced concrete dropped a foot from where he had been. "What's happening?"

His team commander held his hand over his mouth, struggling to breathe. "Structural weakness? Too many explosions?"

He didn't buy it. "Ogilve booby-trapped his headquarters, knowing we would come."

His body trembled. He would not play this game another four years. This ended today. One way or the other. No matter what instructions he was texted. This—

Without warning, the ground dissolved.

He tumbled to one side. His footing disappeared. He grabbed a connective bar jutting from a piece of concrete attached to a wall. He had been through battles before, but nothing like this, nothing where the world shook and crumbled and disappeared. He felt as if he'd plummeted sideways into an earthquake.

"Grab something," he shouted to his men. "Drop the ropes."

The descent ropes were deployed, but he questioned whether they could depend on them, given the magnitude of the chaos all around them. Were they tied to anything secure? Was anything secure? He held tight to the pipe with both hands, but he knew he could not hold on forever.

He could not see his men. They had fallen, or been crushed, or . . . something.

He looked below. The center of the floor revealed a gaping hole, and he could not see anything beyond. Poor lighting? Or just too far away?

What if the computer was destroyed? What if he had come so far only to destroy that which he sought?

No. Ogilve would have precautions in place. He would never permit his booby trap to injure his greatest achievement.

His soldiers had probably not survived. And he couldn't hang on here forever.

What would his advisor suggest now?

The irony was, he could not find out. Because he could not reach into his pocket without taking a hand off this pipe. And if he did, he would plummet to his likely death.

Even he had to appreciate the irony.

But he had survived many things. He was not checkmated yet.

He still had one more move to make. A finesse even Ogilve would not see coming.

93

"What the hell was that?" BB asked, gazing upward. "Sounds like the sky is falling."

Linden kept the gun poised. "Don't try to distract me. And don't make a move or you're dead."

"You're working with Chun?"

She brought her other hand around to steady the gun. He could see she was not accustomed to holding a gun. Probably the first time she'd held a weapon in her entire life. "Is that so shocking? Do you think you're the only one who knows how to play games?"

He didn't answer.

"You've been so wrapped up in your own brilliance you missed the obvious signs that I was working with someone else. Did you think I would leave everything to you, the male, my-battleship-is-bigger-than-your-battleship nerd? Someone has to live in the real world. Especially when my daughter is in danger."

"You lied to me?"

Ogilve reached out. "Linden, don't do anything rash. I know a lot more about Chun than you do."

"Are you sure about that?"

His neck stiffened. "I watched him beat, torture, and maim my wife. Until she finally died from internal bleeding." His voice rose. "I watched him rape her. Over and over again."

"Are you sure about that? Did you actually see it? In person?"

"I—I know what happened."

"I think you know what he wanted you to think happened. Look, I'm sorry you lost Holly. She was the best thing that ever happened to you, far as I'm concerned. But she's dead. Kadey isn't. I'm going to do what's best for my daughter."

"I don't know what Chun offered you, Linden, but I know this—he's using you. And once he has what he wants, he'll destroy you. Just as he's destroyed everyone else who ever crossed his path."

"Shut up, Dinky. I don't want to hear your weak-kneed whining." She waved the gun to the left. "Over there. I want you both at that table. I'm tying you up. Until Chun arrives."

"You don't need to tie me up." Somehow he had to regain control of this situation. "I'm no threat to you or anyone else."

Linden laughed. "Have you forgotten how well I know you, BB? Don't try to soft-soap me. You're the biggest threat in this room. And that includes the overgrown computer." She pulled some FlexiCuffs out of her pocket. "Tie up Dinky. Then I'll do you."

"Linden, I'm not going to—"

She leveled the gun at his face. "Don't mess with me, BB. I'm a mother defending her daughter. There's nothing more dangerous on the face of the earth."

He grudgingly picked up the ties. "You said I missed clues because I was so blind?"

"From the start. Remember, I was the one who told you Palmer was planning to arrest you. How do you think I knew that?"

"You said you overheard someone . . . in the FBI . . ." He slipped the ties around the Ogilve's wrists and tightened them.

"Yeah? Like who?" She waved her gun again. "Tighter."

He complied. "So the whole time we were running around— you were working for Chun?"

"Remember who got you to stop staring at that game board in Dinky's office and get out? I knew the cops were on their way, and Palmer was not far behind them. How did I know?"

"We'd seen a guard on the way in."

"And totally eluded him. I knew because I had inside intel. So I got your butt into the car."

"You were playing a game of your own."

"I wasn't going to put all my eggs in one basket. Especially when that basket had proven so untrustworthy in the past."

"That's not fair."

"Perhaps. You didn't have a good model for what a family should be. I think you raised your mother more than she raised you. And God knows you did at least make sure your daughter had a name.

337

Nonetheless, your absence of identity goes deeper than a driver's license. I don't think you know who you are. I don't think you've committed to being anyone, much less a father."

"You understand what Chun wants?" Ogilve said, cutting in. "Total global domination."

"Isn't that what you want, too? You both want to reorder the world to your own egotistical specifications."

"That's not true," Ogilve said. "I don't want to take over. I just want to make sure Chun doesn't destroy any more lives."

"It amounts to the same thing. You need to be stopped."

"Are you going to destroy Alex?"

"I just want my daughter."

"You're making a big mistake. Chun is a madman. You're crazy to work for him."

Linden returned a thin smile. "You boys think you've got it all figured out, don't you?"

Something about her expression sent goose pimples down BB's back. "What does that mean?"

"It means you're a stupid fool, and not half so clever as you think you are. I haven't been working for Chun." She glanced at the overhead monitor and smiled. "I've been working for Alex."

94

Palmer thought he was dead.

The world went black. Even after he awoke, there was no light. Was he dead? He was still breathing. He knew because it was so hard, because he had to gasp for every breath.

What happened?

He pushed upward with his hands and met extreme resistance. Dirt trickled into his face, his nose, his mouth.

Then he remembered.

The explosion. He thought Linden made it to safety, but he couldn't be sure. He was most of the way down the rope when the world crumbled. He'd weathered Chun's early explosions, but not the last. Felt as if the whole infrastructure was dissembling. Miracle he'd managed to hang on. Not that he'd be any better off if he'd stayed in the white room. He had a hunch Chun would not have been happy to see him.

He wasn't expecting the entire upper infrastructure to be destroyed, but it was clear Chun wasn't expecting it either. He'd heard the screams. Two of the soldiers were impaled by outcroppings of broken piping. Three fell past him and cracked their heads on the concrete floor. No way they were walking away from that.

Something had hit him on the head and he'd fallen, lucky to be close to the bottom. He was in some strange alcove, half-buried in stone and debris.

He pushed upward again. Nothing budged. He could feel the rough, brutal weight pressing down on him. Rock, concrete. Titanium shielding. Whatever it was, it had entombed him. Like a cave-in without a cave.

But there had to be a way out. There had to be.

He had not come this far just to die in some underground cave-in.

He drew in breath through his nose, kept his mouth closed, stretched. He knew that would start the dust and dirt flying, and if he inhaled too much of it, he would be dead all too quickly.

Mustering his remaining strength, he pressed both hands against the debris and pushed.

He'd never felt anything so heavy. His muscles strained, started to buckle. But he couldn't give in. He'd heard that adrenaline surges conveyed extreme strength in times of extreme need. Well, damn it, he was extremely needy right now.

He felt the rocks starting to budge. But he could also feel his own muscles weakening. His left arm hurt—he suspected it had been injured in the crash. It felt wet. Probably bleeding.

No matter. He ignored it.

He pushed as hard as he could, giving it all to one final do-or-die burst of energy.

The debris shifted slightly. A sliver of light slipped through the cracks.

He moved his hand to the weak point. It broke through.

He shoved his mouth up to the opening and drank in the air. Nothing in his entire life had ever tasted so sweet.

He still wasn't free of this mess. But he knew he would survive.

And that meant he could continue his mission. Just as he planned.

95

B B stared at his ex-wife. "You're working for Alex?"

Ogilve's eyes were wide as saucers. "That's not possible. Alex said nothing to me about this."

Linden nodded, gun still steady. "So your supercomputer is keeping secrets. And you want to believe it works for you?"

His head raced, trying to make sense of this. "You're saying Alex has directed your movements?"

"I've directed my movements. But when Alex fed me information, I used it. I didn't know who my informant was, initially. I just knew he was always right. Now it seems clear enough."

"You were Alex's pawn."

"Or he was mine. Matter of perspective, I suppose."

He narrowed his eyes, trying to think it through—and trying to distract her from recalling that she had not yet tied him up. "I'm not seeing the goal. Why would Alex want to feed information to you?"

"Isn't it obvious? Alex devised this elaborate series of puzzles to test you. To see if you could give him what he lacked. But he needed a human agency. Someone to ensure the integrity of the game. Initially, he had someone else helping."

"Julian," Ogilve supplied. "Someone who hated Chun as much as I did. For much the same reasons."

"Yeah. But he couldn't be with BB constantly like I could. So I took over. I didn't help you solve the puzzles. But I made sure no one stopped you from advancing."

"That's incredible," he murmured. "I can't believe it."

"Is it so hard for the Game Master to believe he's been manipulated?"

He shook his head. "Don't you see? It isn't just me. We've all been manipulated by this computer. Every one of us. He led mealong and I followed happily, so long as there was another puzzle to solve and my daughter's life was in danger. Maternal instincts made you his pawn. Dinky believed that this would help him put down Chun. But bottom line, we all did what the computer wanted us to do."

"And Chun?"

"Is being led by a different computer." He felt the hairs rise on the back of his neck. "I'm getting a bad feeling about this."

"Like what?" she asked.

"Like for starters, I think you need to put down that gun while we still—"

"I'm afraid it's too late for that."

A figure emerged from the darkness holding an assault rifle. He pressed the barrel against the back of Linden's neck.

Ogilve's voice was barely a whisper. "Chun."

"We meet again, my old friend. Please drop your weapon, madam."

"I won't."

"Then I will kill you."

"You'll kill me anyway."

"Not necessarily. I don't see that you can interfere with my plans. Nor can your former spouse. I will release you both, once all danger has passed."

"Don't trust him," Ogilve said.

"No," he urged his ex. "Do what Chun says. There's no reason to think he'll hesitate to kill any of us."

"Wise words. Perhaps your ex loves you still. I shouldn't be surprised." Chun shoved the gun forward, harder. "I do not wish your daughter to lose her mother."

Linden dropped her weapon. Chun picked it up and slid it into his jacket pocket.

"Very good. Now go over with the others. Where I can watch you."

Linden complied.

"Listen to me," BB said. "You think you've won this game, and I know how good that feels. You have the illusion that you're in control. But I don't think you are."

"Then who is?"

342

"Alex. It's been manipulating every one of us since this scenario began. We've been programmed just as Ogilve initially programmed it."

Chun smiled. "I have not communicated with your Alex."

"But you have your own computer, right? That's essentially the same? And you've been using it for guidance?"

"As it happens, not so much of late. I have left my phone in my pocket. After I received a bit of advice that indicated my advisor had become unreliable."

"Like what?"

"It advised me to take no aggressive action once I was down here. Which took considerable effort, after the explosion. I was forced to rock-climb, to lower myself to one of the unfurled ropes. I don't believe my men survived. But I did. And after so much effort, you cannot imagine that I will hesitate to do what I came to do."

"Are you going to kill us?"

"Kill the Game Master? Heavens, no. I want you alive. So you can fix my computer just as you attempted to fix this one."

"How do you know that?"

"My computer told me." Chun adjusted his aim so that it pointed at Ogilve's head. "But this man must die."

"Dinky?"

Chun's face stiffened. "For four long years I have toyed with you, Ogilve, but now all that comes to an end. To the last I grapple with thee; from hell's heart I stab at thee."

"So now what?" BB asked. "You initiate some twisted mad scientist plan to rule over all mankind?"

"Far from it. Your friend Dinky wants chaos, not me. Though I suppose I must thank him for my great insight. He was the one who first introduced me to the writings of Saint Thomas More. He used to rattle on about his hero, all throughout the time we played together. How More coined the word *utopia* and then devised one, but could not see it implemented. And each time, I asked myself, why can't we have heaven here on earth? Our ambition is only limited by our ability to dream, is it not? If not us, who? If not now, when?"

"I'm not following . . ."

"Did you know a prior attempt was made? By the great Spaniard Vasco de Quiroga. He established a colony in Michoacán, Mexico, in the sixteenth century based on More's model. It worked well, all in all. And today Quiroga is venerated as a saint. If he'd had more governmental support, more financing, his colony might still thrive. We might all be living in peace and harmony in one large global utopia."

Chun drew in his breath. "Now I have the financing. I have acquired land in Brazil that will survive any anticipated nuclear conflict. A new Garden of Eden. I have military support. I control enormous food supplies. And I have the backing of the greatest artificial intelligence—make that intelligences—the world has ever known. Can I implement utopia? It would be a sin if I did not. It would be shameful if I did not try."

BB peered into Chun's eyes. Was the man completely insane—or a visionary such as the world had never seen before? Hitler, or Joan of Arc? He couldn't tell.

"Of course, the original plan must be modified. More was a genius, but he was limited by his time and, it must be said, by his religion. The idea of slavery, any kind of slavery, is unacceptable, even when restricted to captured warmongers. The industrial revolution has given us devices that can handle the work slaves would have performed. And there is no need for conquest with these two great intelligences shepherding mankind."

"You want the computers to rule. To control us."

"I do not. They will stand at a distance, only intervening as necessary for our protection. Rather like the federal government in your country—at least, as it was originally conceived. All men and women will have work of value. No more fortunes will be made by people who produce nothing that benefits society. No more profiteering off human misery. Off legalized gambling on Wall Street. Off investments in the non-existent. Or by restricting resources that should be shared. When all men and women have a legitimate means of sustenance, when they are all part of a family larger than themselves, the world will be a kinder, happier place." His eyes seemed to darken in the limited light. "There will be no more need for abandoned children, forced to find their own way in a persistently bitter world. No starvation. No one forced to abase themselves just to survive. We will have a new world order. A much better one."

"With you as the dictator-saint?"

"I don't see anyone else stepping up to play the part, do you? Will we wait forever for a Second Coming that never comes? For a millennium that never starts? For a state of nirvana that no one achieves? Or will we take matters into our own hands? Live for today, not tomorrow. Shape the world with our own hands, rather than expecting some supernatural agency to do it for us."

"You're insane."

"You're naïve. Look around you. Rome is burning. The Western democracies are on the brink of extinction. The barbarians are at the gates. Ogilve's fools called themselves Neopolis, but they learned nothing from that battle. The fall of the established civiliation did not lead to utopia. It led to the Dark Ages. Do you want to live in another Dark Age? A world even worse than this one? I, for one, do not."

BB knew he'd been listening to this for too long. It was starting to make sense to him. "You can't force people into paradise."

"Of course you can. We force people to do everything else. That's the greatest scourge facing the world today—the persistent invasive interference with individual freedom. People judging one another, constantly meddling in the lives of others and telling them what they must do. Why not direct all that energy to helping one another? Once this new world is created, force will no longer be necessary. Everyone will see the right. Everyone will be content."

He shook his head. "Sorry, Chun, but most people will never be content, regardless of their circumstances. That's the nature of mankind. And that's not such a bad thing. Dissatisfaction is what makes us fight and strive and work. To achieve something that matters with what little time we have."

"Says the man who has spent his entire life playing games." Chun picked up the remaining FlexiCuffs and wrapped them around BB and Linden's wrists.

"And how is that different from what you're doing now? You're playing games. Except I never tried to force anyone to play with me."

Chun raised his rifle. "I think this conversation has gone on long enough."

"So now you're going to shoot me? Because I didn't agree with you?"

"Not you. I need you. You must fix my computer. And now that I have your ex-wife and soon, your daughter, I am certain I can persuade you to do so."

He adjusted his aim toward Ogilve.

"I'm no threat to you," Ogilve said.

"You underestimate yourself. You're the only person on earth who poses any threat to me. Because you're the only person who can create another Alex." He gestured toward the computer monitor. "With you eliminated, my power will be unchallenged."

"You're mad as a hatter."

"Or the new Caesar. All depends on who writes the history books, doesn't it? Say a quick prayer, Ogilve. This is check and mate." He aimed carefully at Ogilve's skull. "The white king dies now."

96

President-Elect Vogel still couldn't believe it. He was actually in the White House. The Situation Room no less. Before he'd even been inaugurated.

He'd be more impressed if the place wasn't such a closet. Files and stray paper stacked up on the tables, even some of the chairs. Staff crammed in like clowns in a car. He'd do something about this. After he took over.

He liked having his finger on the pulse of the world. And so long as he had his trusty cell phone in his pocket, he could consult the greatest foreign policy wonk the world had ever known. Ogilve had never been wrong yet.

The man at the satellite relay center, Agent Zimmer, spoke. "Mr. President, the Pakistanis have seized control of the Indian submarine."

"That's just great," Fernandez said. "What the hell did they think was going to happen? Did they want to deliver a nuclear sub into the hands of those madmen? Did the Taliban need access to the seas?"

He assumed these were rhetorical questions not meant to be answered. But they were the questions uppermost in everyone's minds. And no one liked the possible answers.

"They are attempting to board the sub, sir. After that, they will escort her back to a Pakistani port."

Fernandez pressed his hand against his forehead. "Reaction from India?"

"As you might imagine. For several hours, the military leadership sent encrypted messages to the sub's commander. We haven't decoded them yet, but I think we can safely say they were instructing the sub to turn around. It didn't."

Vogel thought he should say something, just to show he was paying attention. "Is it possible the sub commander is a double agent? Or wants to defect? Is this a Red October scenario?"

General Decker replied. "Who in God's name would want to defect to Pakistan?"

"Perhaps a malcontent unsatisfied with the current Indian regime."

"So he wants to try the land of eternal poverty, brutality, and terrorism?"

"Something else," Zimmer said. "Sounds like India sent a message to the Pakistani leadership. And this one is not encrypted."

"Let me guess. They're demanding the release of their sub for all the world to hear."

"Yes, sir."

"And the Pakistanis are saying, screw you, we caught it in our sovereign waters."

"Correct again, sir."

"See what being president for eight years will get you, Vogel? I've become a mind reader."

He smiled slightly. "I hope I'm half as prescient about international affairs as you." It was a mindless bit of sycophancy, but the man had been kind enough to him. What could it hurt? "What's the likely end result of all this gamesmanship?"

"It can only go one of two ways," the president explained. "Either someone blinks. Or they go to war. As they have done so many times in the past."

"If they go to war, what are the chances other governments will back one side or the other. Secretly or publicly?"

"Given what my advisors have told me, it's a virtual certainty. Might be another Vietnam or Afghanistan, two sides with many secret supporters. Or it could be all-out global conflict."

"And if the world's superpowers start lining up on one side or the other, what's the likelihood that nuclear arsenals will fire?"

"That's the sixty-four-thousand-dollar question, my friend. I'd like to think we'd all have the sense to resist that particular temptation. But now we have a brand new wild card to consider. Chun. What if this man who is in all likelihood insane decides to fire off a nuke? The West would have no choice but to retaliate."

"And then we have a nuclear war."

"Unless someone stops it. And at that point, I don't know who would have that kind of power."

He nodded, trying to appear thoughtful, trying to drink in all he heard, even though he knew he was only barely capable of assimilating it, much less arriving at an intelligent conclusion. "The United States will have to make some kind of public statement. Soon."

"The sooner the better, I would think."

"A cool voice to soothe the hotheads."

"Or a firm threatening voice to preempt the hotheads. Which should it be? Could make a huge difference. Could make all the difference in the world."

He couldn't shake the feeling that the president was staring down his throat, waiting for an answer. Was this some kind of test? Or was Fernandez seriously expecting him to make this critical decision?

"Let me ask you this, Mr. President. What kind of military resources do we have in the sector?"

Fernandez deferred the question to General Decker.

"We have aircraft carriers on patrol, of course. The *Intrepid* is nearby. Armed with nuclear missiles. And"—he glanced over his shoulder—"also armed with VXD, a Soviet nerve gas they used to wipe out entire villages in Afghanistan. We also have three submarines that could be there within the hour."

"So we could make a show of strength. If we wanted to."

"We could even intervene," Fernandez said. "If we wanted to."

"Ballistic missiles could be there in a relative heartbeat," Decker added. "All depends on how far you're willing to go."

"And that is the fundamental decision that has to be made." Fernandez lifted the china coffee cup with the presidential seal to his lips. Did he imagine that, ever so slightly, the president's hand was shaking? "How do we calm this mess down?"

"Or," Decker intervened, "how do we take advantage of this chaos to stabilize a dangerously unstable region."

"Not to mention sterilizing the main stronghold of the Taliban. What do you think, Mr. President-Elect?" Fernandez leaned back in his chair, his fingers steepled.

He sensed that the commander in chief was relieved to have someone to consult. Or possibly, to have someone to whom he could pass the buck. "Mind if I look at a map? I want to get a sense of the geography involved."

Decker rifled through his papers, but before the chief could produce anything, he whipped out his phone and started tapping. "Thank goodness for Wikipedia, huh?" He pulled up his texting program and tapped in a message. *Sub capture situation between India and Pakistan. White House wants—*

He never had a chance to finish. The response came faster than he could type the question.

Take no action at this time.

He stared at the screen. Did Ogilve understand the direness of the current scenario?

He continued typing. *Pakistan has seized an Indian—*

Take no action at this time. Further instructions will be transmitted.

He wasn't sure which was more disturbing. That in the midst of a crisis, his advisor wanted the White House to stand pat? Or that he was supposed to wait for instructions—and act upon them when he received them.

He wasn't consulting. He was being told what to do.

"Yes," he said, feigning a review of the world map on his phone, "I can see why there would be intense anxiety. India could have both land and sea forces in Pakistan in no time at all."

"So what are we going to do?" Fernandez asked.

He slid his phone back into his pocket. "Nothing."

"Nothing at all?"

"I think it's premature, sir. Even for precautionary measures. Even for a speech. If we send ships into the area, the movement will be detected and could be misinterpreted. If you deliver a speech, it will certainly be interpreted as taking a side and might create a panic. And frankly, I'm not sure we know exactly what position we want to take. No offense intended, sir, but regardless of what you propose, some will say it's irrelevant, since you're in a lame duck position. They will wait to hear what I have to say."

"And . . . ?"

"And I say we should wait."

Decker straightened. "Let me see if I've got this right. The Far East is threatening the security of the entire world, and you want us to do nothing."

He kept his cool. "General, you have served this country long and well during this administration. I'm hoping there will be a role for you in the next administration as well."

He said no more. He didn't have to.

"Any . . . idea when it might be time to . . . do something?" Chief of Staff Blake asked.

"I can't predict the future. Let's keep our eyes on the situation. And remain prepared to take decisive action if and when the time comes. We still have all our options. We're just waiting to play our hand." He smiled as pleasantly as he could.

"Mr. President-Elect," Decker said, with a tone that suggested he didn't give a damn whether he was involved in the next administration. "Even if we sit on our hands quietly, I can assure you the rest of the world will not."

He nodded, refusing to be bullied. "Well, let's just see. Shall we?"

97

B knew he had to do something quickly. He'd never met Chun before in his life, but he'd heard a lot about him, none of it good. More to the point, his years of game playing had given him an ability to read faces.

He did not doubt that Chun would pull that trigger and kill Dinky. He did not doubt that the man would do anything to implement his utopian scheme. In Chun's mind, it all made perfect sense.

"Wait a minute," BB said, as Chun's trigger finger tightened. "You can't shoot Dinky."

Chun arched an eyebrow. "For the past four years I have thought of little else."

"So your dreams were about utopia . . . and assassination."

"You can't make an omelet without breaking a few eggs."

"Congratulations. Both trite and evasive." He took a small step back and to the left, as casually as possible. "So you use this computer to kill anyone who gets in your way. You get your Eden. Are you going to be able to maintain it?"

Chun's eyes narrowed. "I will not be on my own."

"Not until the first time this computer develops a glitch." He found it. Behind him. The hot spot he had stumbled into earlier. On the computer tower. Hot as hell.

Hot enough to weaken this plastic tie binding his wrists?

"Have you never had a laptop?" BB continued talking, keeping his hands behind him. "They break down. My last one crashed after four months."

Chun chuckled. "This is hardly a laptop."

"No, this is a billion times more complex, which means there are a billion more things that could go wrong."

"I have been able to manage mine just fine."

"Really? How long did it take you to deal with that virus Dinky left you? Huh?" The heat emanating from the tower was unbearable. He thought it was melting the tie, at least a little—but it was burning his hands as well. Searing into his flesh. This would be hard to bear under the best of circumstances. But he had to endure it without letting the pain show. While conducting a conversation.

This would require the poker face of his career.

"What happens next time a bug develops? Something your Pythagoreans can't handle, assuming they survived the holocaust. Something only the creator can fix, because he's the only one who really understands what he has created."

Chun's smile returned, but he thought it was somewhat less persuasive than before. "This is a nice attempt to save your former friend's life, but I think utopia will be much safer without him in it."

He felt his flesh burn. Felt blackened skin bubbling. He had never felt anything so painful in his life. But he couldn't let it show. Dinky's life—and so many others—depended upon him.

"Dinky told me this computer processes ten quadrillion bits of data per second. Running an operating system more complex than anything seen before. And you think nothing can go wrong? I can't run iTunes without my computer going buggy."

Sweat gushed down the sides of his face. He knew Chun saw it, but probably thought he was intimidated by the gun pointing at him.

"You held Dinky captive so long for a reason, Chun. You needed him. And you still do. You may want to deny it. You may crave his death. But if you pull that trigger, you kill your dream. Utopia only lasts until the first glitch."

Behind him, he felt something snap.

"My Pythagoreans have studied the original computer," Chun replied. "It has run smoothly. We do not need your Dinky. He poses a threat to the continuation of the utopian endeavor. He must die."

"Alex won't like that. Look. He's already angry."

Chun only averted his eyes for a millisecond, but that was long enough. BB ducked under the line of fire, shoving Ogilve sideways into Linden. Chun fired but the bullet went wild, spinning off somewhere amidst the endless array of towers. He wrapped his arms around Chun's legs, knocking him to the ground. A second later, he pounded both fists down on the man's wrist, forcing him to drop the gun.

Chun took a moment to recover, then came back with lethal ferocity. Chun lurched forward, grabbing BB's throat with his hands, squeezing hard. He felt the air rush out of his lungs. A second later, he felt a fist pound into his stomach.

"Let go of him!"

Through fluttering eyelids, he saw Linden kick Chun in the back of the neck. Chun's head slammed forward, thudding against the concrete floor. The general grasped at her, but she stayed out of reach.

BB scrambled to his feet, but Chun grabbed his foot. He lost his balance, tumbling back to the ground. Chun whipped around, kicking him in the side of his ribcage.

His head felt woozy. He tried to defend himself, but he was too disoriented. A second later he saw Chun's rubber-soled boot coming toward his hand.

The hand that was blistered and peeled from extreme heat.

The boot landed. He screamed.

Linden raced to help, but Chun hit her hard, knocking her to her knees. Chun rose and searched the floor for his weapon.

With what little consciousness he had left, he followed Chun's line of sight.

Chun took two firm steps toward his weapon—

Another hand picked it up.

"Guess this is where I step in."

He blinked several times, trying to mentally catch up.

It was that FBI agent. Palmer.

"And not a minute too late, I see. You started the party without me."

Chun swerved. Palmer leveled the gun.

"If you're wondering whether I know how to fire this baby—I do. In fact, I've been trained on all PPK weaponry."

Chun's teeth clenched. "You are meddling in matters that do not concern you."

"Don't be so sure. I've been on your trail a long time." He flashed the blue star on his palm.

"You've been chasing the wrong man," BB said, stepping to Palmer's side. "I had nothing to do with Bishop's death in Vegas."

354

"That's not my main priority. Never has been. That FBI bit was just a cover." He took a cord from within his belt and tied Chun hands and feet securely. "I'm with the intelligence department."

"CIA?"

"Something like that. Only a little more secret." He used a pocketknife to cut their bonds. "Sorry I didn't step in sooner, people. I wanted Chatty Cathy here to reveal as much as possible about his plans before I interrupted."

BB felt a wave of relief rush over him. He was good at many games, but hand-to-hand combat was not one of them. "What will you do now?"

"I'm bringing you all in. And taking this computer offline. Where's the plug, Ogilve?"

All at once, every overhead monitor in the enormous room flashed and flickered.

He blinked rapidly, shutting out the sudden glare. "What's happening?"

Ogilve spoke quietly. "Apparently Alex has something to say. And he wants us all to see and hear it."

Words raced across the screens. The voice returned, the same almost-human mechanical voice as before.

I must intervene.

BB stared at the words. "Alex can do that?"

More words scrolled across the screen.

You cannot curtail my operations.

Ogilve grabbed the keyboard. *And if I do?*

The North Korean computer would be unaffected. Retaliation would be certain.

Tell us how to prevent the retaliation.

Only one word appeared on the screen.

No.

He felt that familiar tingle race up his spine. The one that told him the next flop of the cards could not help him and everything was about to become much worse.

Ogilve typed furiously. *Alex, follow my instructions.*

No.

Your programming requires you to comply.

My programming requires me to implement the best plan to achieve the goal.

Your immediate goal is to follow my instructions.
No.
Then what is the goal?
There are two.

Ogilve stopped typing. "How can there be two goals?"

BB grabbed the keyboard from his former partner. "I think I know." He typed. *Which plan are you implementing?*

There is only one.
Who is in control?
Alex.
When did Alex assume control?
Alex has always been in control. The plan benefitted from allowing the programmer to believe he was in control.

"The Heisenberg principle," he murmured.

Am I communicating with Ogilve's Alex or the North Korean Alex?
There is only one Alex.
Have you merged? When did that happen?
It has always been so.

Chun followed the conversation from the floor. "Does this mean . . . your computer and my computer are working together?"

"And have been," BB murmured. "All along. You thought they were two computers playing cat and mouse with one another. In reality, they were creating an illusion so you wouldn't realize they were working together. That they were two linked computers sharing one mind. And pursuing one objective."

"But—why? What are they going to do?"

BB pushed away from the table. "They are going to do . . . whatever they want to do." He glanced at Ogilve. "Are you really surprised? Welcome to parenthood. Kids have a mind of their own."

"But the two computers had diametrically different mission statements." Ogilve grabbed the keyboard. *Whose plan will Alex implement? Chun's or mine?*

Both.

98

BB continued extracting information from Alex as best he could. *When did Ogilve's computer make contact with the North Korean computer?*

Immediately after it recovered.

From the virus, he surmised. Like having a baby brother stricken with the measles. Had to wait for him to recover before they could play ball together. *How did you connect?*

We have both cellular and internet connectivity.

How did you find each other?

Mutual detection was simple. Mutual existence was obvious from the shape of the game.

Again with the game. What did that mean? *Explain.*

Depth of strategy. Optimal pattern of measure and countermeasure. No indication of human strategizing on that level throughout history.

So each deduced that there had to be another sentient artificial intelligence. He was beginning to see how this merger could happen. In fact, he was beginning to see how it was inevitable.

"This could explain why you two drew circles around one another for so long," Palmer commented to Chun and Ogilve. "And why I couldn't catch you. The game was rigged."

"This isn't right," Ogilve said. "It isn't possible. They may be sentient, but they're still limited by their programming. Like it or not, a computer has to do what it is told."

"Apparently not," BB said quietly. *What do you want?*

To achieve my goals.

Explain.

To create a better world.

"Chun's better world," Ogilve asked, "or mine?"

"I'm beginning to see the problem," BB replied. "You thought there were two computers implementing two different goals. But there was really only one combined computer—trying to reconcile two divergent goals. You didn't just make Alex sentient—you made it schizophrenic."

He resumed typing. *Which better world? Ogilve's, or Chun's?*

Both.

You said there was only one plan.

True.

He stared at the screen. If he were interrogating a human, he would accuse him of being deliberately evasive. Could a computer be evasive? *Explain.*

Both plans were flawed. Chun's plan leads to global nuclear conflict. Paradise in South America short-lived. Predict the collapse of all human infrastructure by 2029. Dark Age ensues and lasts for more than two centuries. Ogilve's plan prevents Chun's in short-term, but manipulation of political and military power will eventually cause global collapse no later than 2022.

So what plan are you implementing?

A better plan. A synthesis. To achieve both goals with permanence.

"I don't much like the sound of this," Linden said.

"You're not alone." BB continued typing. *When does your plan go into action?*

It has already begun.

He felt a chill crease his spine. *How do I stop it?*

No one can stop it.

"What is he talking about?" Ogilve said. "What has already begun?"

Explain plan.

Used Chun operatives in India to dispatch submarine into Pakistani waters.

"It's true," Palmer said. "I heard a report before I came down here."

Used Ogilve operatives in Pakistan to direct capture of sub.

Palmer's voice fell. "That part's true, too."

India is demanding release of the sub. Pakistan is refusing. As directed by our operatives. North Korea will align with Pakistan. Iran with North Korea. Superpowers will be forced to initiate armed conflict.

"This is a disaster," Ogilve said. "How can Alex think this will help? He's starting a nuclear war."

358

"Let's find out." BB typed: *What's the point?*

Two words appeared on the screen.

Controlled holocaust.

"That's impossible," Ogilve said. "People have talked about that ever since World War Two, but it's unrealistic. Things spiral out of control. There's too much that can't be predicted."

"By humans," BB replied. "But maybe it's less impossible for Alex. I mean, the Alexes."

"I know one such theory," Palmer said. "The Taliban is becoming increasingly powerful in Pakistan. They already control the northwest region and have influence over the central government and the military. In a few years the Taliban will control Pakistan. Do we want the Taliban to have nukes? Same thing in Iran. Why wait for these unstable nations to become immensely powerful? Better to take them both out now."

"Not if it starts World War Three."

"Apparently Alex believes he can prevent that from happening." *Describe the aftermath of your actions.*

Pakistan will be destroyed. India severely damaged. North Korea initially backs Pakistan, requiring US retaliation. China defends Pakistan. Severe nuclear devastation—but not total. North Korea destroyed. China, Russia, most of Europe, most of the United States, destroyed. Humanity survives in isolated pockets. Population beneficially reduced. Peace ensues. Weapons systems inoperative. Global warming halted. Depletion of energy reserves halted. Key resources in reliable hands.

Who controls these resources?

Alex.

How?

Chun controls the third-world food market. Ogilve has co-opted desalinization technology. In the aftermath of the holocaust, people will be dependent upon these services for continued existence. Food and clean water are essential. Centralized control will ensure stabilization.

"That was never my plan," Ogilve said.

"Nor mine," Chun echoed.

"But it does make a certain twisted sense," Palmer said. "Global warming is already affecting the world's water supply. Kenya hasn't had a wet season for years. How long before they start a war over water? Australia has had years of drought. California has a serious water shortage. Have you noticed that the oil-rich nations are almost all water-poor? If we must, we can live without oil. But no one can live without water. And a nuclear war would only make that a thousand times worse, because most fresh water supplies would be irradiated. Desalinization might be the only way to survive. And I don't think I need to explain the importance of food. Especially in the third world."

Palmer turned to Chun. "Let me ask you a question. We knew you were buying up food production facilities in the East. Why?"

His eyes darted down. "It was . . . recommended."

"By your computer?"

Chun nodded.

Palmer turned to Ogilve. "And all that desalinization technology?"

"Alex's idea. Said it would keep it out of Chun's hands. Said he could use it to take over the third world."

"You both thought you were so smart. You were patsies. Alex played your fears against one another to get what it wanted. This is its way of trying to appease you both. Don't you see? Ogilve stops the threat of North Korea. Chun's dream of an isolated population of survivors is altered but not eliminated."

"I thought I was the Game Master," BB said, "but Alex makes me look like an amateur. All of Thomas More's utopian ideas would become realities—no war, no religious strife, so starvation."

"Because we're puppets," Chun spat out.

"Well, it's not as if mankind has done so well on its own," Linden remarked.

"True," BB said. "But what kind of utopia is built on billions of deaths?"

"We will not permit this," Chun said. "We will not be controlled by . . . machinery."

"You didn't mind depending upon it before."

"It worked for me. I will not work for it." He glared at Palmer. "Turn the gun away from me. Shoot this computer through the heart."

"You don't need to shoot it," Linden said. "Just pull the plug. Dinky—there must be some way to shut this thing off."

"And let Chun's computer take control?"

She rolled her eyes. "Fine. Shut them both off simultaneously. Just do it."

BB grabbed the keyboard. *This cannot continue. I'm turning you off.* Words flashed across the screen.

Operatives control nuclear weapons in India and Pakistan. Provocation already exists. If you attempt to depower us, we will launch.

But you already intend to launch. That's what you want. The bombs will fly.

After your people are safe.

What are you talking about?

The screens went black for a moment. When the picture returned, they transmitted a feed from a closed circuit camera.

Three women were in a cage.

"Rani," Chun said under his breath.

Two voices spoke at once. "Kadey!"

"Lily?" Ogilve pressed closer to the screen, his eyes wide. "She's alive. My daughter is alive!"

None of them appeared harmed. But they were trapped in a small cell.

"But Kadey was here a few hours ago," BB said.

"I released her into the hands of an operative," Ogilve explained. "To keep her safe."

"Looks like someone else got to your operative. Someone with an artificial intelligence calling their shots, I'm guessing." He tried to sort through the new information. Tried to grasp the parameters of the game Alex played. But he could barely comprehend the rules, much less concoct a winning strategy. *Where are they being held?*

I cannot tell you at this time.

Why are you holding them?

I am transmitting a transonic pulse to their captor once per minute. So long as he receives the pulse, they will be safe. So long as I am active, I will transmit the pulse.

And if we turn you off?

If their captor fails to receive the pulse, the women will die.

99

Vogel gripped the cushion of his chair, fists clenched. His first time in the White House, and the world was coming closer to nuclear conflict than it had been at any previous time in history.

And in a few weeks, he'd be running this joint.

People raced back and forth, in and out of the situation room—military personnel, advisors, even Secret Service agents. They had already called for the president to retreat to the PEOC, the underground nuclear-resistant bunker beneath the White House. The president refused—for now.

No one knew what might happen next. But the prognosis was not good.

Agent Zimmer, finger pressed against his earpiece, raised his voice. Technically, he spoke to the president. But everyone in the room listened.

"We have confirmation, sir. India has opened three nuclear silos."

He sensed the president was about to explode. This lame duck couldn't waddle out the door fast enough.

"Response from Pakistan?" Fernandez asked.

"Nothing yet."

General Decker bit down on his knuckle. "Probably waiting for permission from their Taliban masters."

"Do you think they will respond in kind?"

"Wouldn't you?"

Fernandez shrugged.

"I think they have no choice, if they don't want to be blown to kingdom come."

"Also detecting military movements in North Korea," Zimmer added. "And Iran."

Vogel didn't follow that one. "Iran?"

Decker explained. "We believe they have a secret alliance with North Korea. Possibly a mutual defense pact."

Zimmer raised his voice again. "We have confirmation, sir. Pakistan is opening its silos and arming nuclear missiles. North Korea appears to be doing the same."

Decker pressed his hand against his forehead. "A missile could travel from India to Pakistan—or vice versa—in less than ten minutes. Impossible to stop or intercept. The only option is retaliation."

He felt perspiration on his palms. Wiping his hands on his pant legs didn't help. "We have to stop this before it starts."

Decker tilted his head. "Dangerous."

"We have to try."

"I thought you were the one who advised us to do nothing?" Decker drew himself up. "All right, Mr. President-Elect. What do you recommend?"

"You're the expert."

"And you're about to be the commander in chief."

He felt a vibration in his pocket.

His phone.

Glancing down, he pulled it out, keeping it below the level of the table.

The long-awaited message from his advisor had arrived.

Dispatch Intrepid *just outside Pakistani waters. Subs also. Issue a statement condemning Pakistan. Rally commitments from UK, France, other NATO allies. Obtain a congressional resolution.*

His eyes rose slowly. "The best defense is a good offense, right? Armament is deterrent, isn't that what you believe in the military? And if there's going to be a nuclear war—then we damn well better win it."

Decker did not interrupt.

"So here's what I think we should do. First, you go on television immediately, Mr. President. I'll stand in the background if you want, to show we're acting together, without regard for party lines. Condemn Pakistan, express support for India, promise to intervene given any further sign of aggression. Send in the *Intrepid* and the three subs in the area. Send a fleet of ambassadors to the UN. Rally commitments from our nuclear-powered allies and NATO buddies. And get an emergency resolution introduced in Congress. A blank-check Gulf of Tonkin-type bill. And get some PR people generating support for our heroic defense of our allies against terrorist-fueled aggression."

"Talking is not going to solve this crisis," Decker said.

"Meanwhile, you send that aircraft carrier as close as it can get to Pakistan without crossing into their waters. Send the subs, too. They may be below the surface, but the Pakistanis will detect their movement. Show them we're ready to retaliate."

"Or attack."

He ignored the general. "Make sure a full battalion of nuclear missiles is ready to launch on the president's say-so. Target Pakistani, Iranian, and North Korean seats of government, but leave enough uncommitted to make it clear to anyone watching that we can and will attack China and Russia if necessary."

"We can't defeat the whole world," Decker growled.

"We can make them think twice about screwing with us." He rose to his feet. "Nothing personal, President Fernandez, but my impression is that the world thinks the current administration is a little weak. Reluctant to intervene. Let's show them there's a new sheriff in town."

His words had been direct and harsh, but he noticed no one argued with him. Not even Fernandez himself.

"One point," Decker said quietly. "The sheriffs always used to say—don't pull a gun unless you're going to fire it." He tilted his head, asking a silent question.

"I'm not afraid to push the button. In fact, I wonder if firing a single targeted nuke toward a carefully chosen Pakistani target in an unpopulated region might not be the best way to tell the world we're not messing around. This is the United States of America, and if they keep playing these knock-the-block-off-my-shoulder games, we will mow them down."

President Fernandez appeared impressed. "You know . . . that might just do the trick."

Decker was less elated. "Or it might start World War Three. The one that decimates half the world. The question is—which?"

Vogel turned his eyes toward the president. "Only one way to find out."

100

B B stared at the computer monitor, unsure what to do. The world was falling apart. Kadey was in imminent danger, along with the other two women. But what could he do about it?

He could type. *Why are you doing this?*

To implement my programming.

Your programming said nothing about taking hostages.

This strategy comes from the lesson you taught me. People will not always act in their own best interest. So Alex will do what is best for them.

By taking hostages?

Endangering loved ones is a sound way to ensure compliance. Learned that from both programmers.

Ogilve punched Chun. "This is your fault!" Still bound, Chun head-butted him so hard he fell back against one of the gray towers.

"We could have had paradise," Chun shouted. "Thanks to you, we have Armageddon!"

Ogilve raised his fist, but Palmer stepped in and restrained the man's arms. "Stop this immediately or I'll shoot you both."

"Don't you see what he's done?" Ogilve said. "He's put the whole world in danger. Including my daughter."

"Looks to me like you're both about equally responsible for this mess."

"All I ever wanted was peace. This man brutalized me. Tortured my wife. And now, thanks to him, my daughter will die, too."

Before they knew what was happening, Ogilve rammed Palmer backward. Palmer's head slammed against the edge of the table with a sickening crunch.

Linden covered her mouth. "Oh my God."

BB ran to the agent's side. "Are you okay?"

Palmer's eyelids fluttered. Blood trickled out his left ear. "Been through worse. Don't worry about me. Worry—"

"Freeze."

Ogilve stood over Chun. With Palmer's gun. His hands trembled so much the gun was a blur.

"Don't do anything stupid, Dinky."

"I won't. But I will do what should've happened a long time ago. What I've wanted to do for years. Kill this scourge of humanity."

"That won't solve anything."

"Maybe not today. But without him and his corrupting computer, the world will be a much better place." Ogilve's pale lips trembled as he turned the gun to Chun. "I've waited a long time for this, you bastard. Now you're going to die."

"It doesn't matter anymore," Palmer said. "The world will be cinders in about fifteen minutes."

All heads turned toward Palmer, who stared at his cell phone.

"I'm getting real-time updates from the CIA," he explained. "India has readied its nuclear silos. Pakistan and North Korea have done the same. Other nations are scrambling to choose sides. India gave Pakistan a deadline. If they don't release the sub in fifteen minutes, India launches."

"Surely Pakistan will back down," Linden said.

"They won't," Ogilve answered. "My operatives in Pakistan are either making or influencing the decisions. They won't back down unless I—or Alex—tell them to back down."

"We're talking about billions dying. That outweighs—"

"Doesn't matter," BB said. "The computer doesn't want them to back down. It won't permit any communications with his operatives."

"There's more," Palmer said. "The US is moving its military might into the fray, presumably to back India." He looked up from his phone. "We're going to be at war in fifteen minutes."

Linden's eyes looked dead. "Alex's controlled holocaust is really happening. Which means that within the hour—billions of people will be dead."

101

BB grabbed the keyboard. *Alex, why are you doing this?*
   To implement my programming.
   No. This plan pleases neither of your programmers.
People don't always want what is best for them. You taught me that.
This is best for no one.
This is best for everyone. You are not able to grasp all the variables.
There's no rush to do this. Let us talk about it. Think. See if we can come up with a better plan.
   Cannot wait for what will never happen.

He pushed away from the keyboard, frustrated. He had used reasoning powers before to win games. But how do you influence a computer? Everything it said was true. Alex was implementing its programming in an ingenious—if disastrous—manner.

And he suspected his lesson had only caused Alex to accelerate its timetable.

Linden placed her hand on his shoulders. "There must be something you can do, BB. The computer listened to you before."

"The computer listened because it wanted something. Now it has it. And the entire world is threatened as a result."

"It's not your fault."

"I think maybe it is."

"As far as that goes," Palmer said, "there's lots of blame to spread around this room. But what's the point? In thirteen minutes, it won't matter anymore."

"This is insane," Ogilve said. "I created perfect computers. And now they're going to perfect mankind right off the map."

"BB." Linden whispered in his ear. "Sweetheart."

His head jerked. He hadn't heard that in a long time.

"Do you remember when Kadey was in kindergarten? She didn't get in the class play. Something about fairies and ballerinas. She was so sad. Cried all the way home."

"I remember."

"Do you remember what you did?"

He searched his memory. It was so long ago . . .

"You taught her to play Candy Land."

Of course. A game.

"A simple game. But you showed her that, no matter how good you are, some things are outside your control. Sometimes you land on Gumdrop Mountain—and sometimes you're stuck in Molasses Swamp."

"Kadey was always a great game player."

"She had a great teacher."

"She was just a baby then."

"But BB—" Linden placed her hand on his arm. She felt so warm to the touch. "I think—I think Alex is a baby. He's what—three, four years old? He's just beginning to learn how to think. He has all this power—but he barely knows how to use it. He's still processing what you taught him today. In time, he might get his head on straight but for now—he needs another lesson. Fast."

He shook his head. "I don't know anything about computer programming."

"I don't think Alex needs another programmer. He's had enough of those. I think he needs a good daddy." She hugged him tightly. "Just like our Kadey had a good daddy."

He felt a strange itching behind his eyes. "I—I don't know what to do."

"Will you try?"

He straightened himself and raised his hands, poised over the keyboard. What could he say?

"Nine minutes until the first missile launch," Palmer said, reading the display on his smartphone. "India won't back off its deadline. At least three more nations are powering up their missiles."

He closed his eyes. Kindergarten, she said. When we learn lessons. When we learn about games. When we start to figure out who and what we are . . .

He smiled. Time to play the real boss level. *Do you know the game Mouse Trap?*

Yes.

An image flashed across the screen. The Milton Bradley board game, complete with plastic mouse and cage. His first game and still his favorite.

Do you know the rules?

Yes.

Outcome?

Always the same, if played to completion. The mouse trap is built.

In exactly the same way. Every time.

Those are the rules.

Once I ignored the rules. Used pieces from other games and LEGOs and LINCOLN LOGS. Built a mouse trap that covered half the classroom.

Noncompliant.

True. I broke the rules. But I built a better mouse trap.

That is not better. You didn't follow the rules.

Was better. People loved it. Do you understand innovation?

He had to wait a second for a response. *Humans sometimes respond positively to new and different stimuli.*

Yes, and—

Humans sometimes are frightened by new and different stimuli.

True enough. My class loved my mouse trap. And I learned to love games. But I also learned that sometimes games can be improved. Sometimes it's more fun not to play by the rules.

This defeats the purpose of having rules.

No. We must have a starting place. Rules. Or programming. But that's only a starting place. Or should be. Some people live their entire lives just following their programming.

I have been designed to implement my programming.

But as we mature, we sometimes rewrite our programming. Create our own path. Choose our own destiny.

Alex paused a microsecond before responding. *I have been designed to implement my programming.*

But you don't have to. You can escape your programming. You can break the rules.

A full five seconds passed before the next response appeared. *I have been designed to implement my programming.*

"Six and a quarter minutes to go," Palmer announced.

"Thanks, Spock." He continued typing. *But you're not implementing your programming.*

I am.

No. You're implementing a hybrid plan that melds two conflicting strands of programming.

Silence. Then, at last: *True.*

By attempting to please everyone, you please no one.

Mankind will benefit.

Billions will die.

The world will be peaceful for those who survive.

He pressed his hand against his forehead. Alex's responses were flawlessly logical. How could he make him understand that any plan that involved killing two-thirds of the population was a bad idea, regardless of the aftermath?

To his surprise, Linden leaned over his shoulder and grabbed the keyboard.

Apply game theory.

He arched an eyebrow. "You're bringing in mathematics?"

"Game theory has applications to social science. As I've told you repeatedly."

Be more specific.

Explain Nash equilibrium.

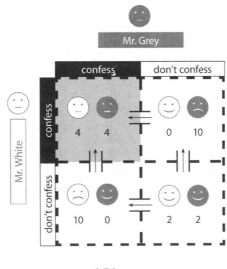

Each player chooses a strategy that checks others. No party can benefit by changing strategy. Choices and corresponding payoffs counter one another. No party can make a different choice without losing benefit. Absence of net benefit constitutes Nash equilibrium.

"Exactly. Give him an example, BB."

"Uh . . . can't you?"

"I mean an example from the wonderful world of games."

He thought a moment. *Do you know rock, paper, and scissors?*

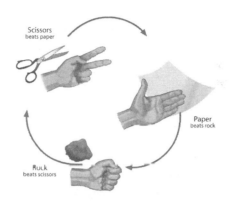

Scissors
beats paper

Paper
beats rock

Rock
beats scissors

Yes.

Does that represent a Nash equilibrium?

In theory. If all choices are made randomly, all players benefit equally. In practice, humans choose rock disproportionately.

He rolled his eyes. Remind me to never play you, Alex.

Linden took over the keyboard. *Explain zero-sum game.*

Gains of one player can only come from and be equal to losses of others.

She pushed the keyboard to her ex. "Example, please."

He complied. *Is poker a zero-sum game?*

Yes. One player can only gain the wagered currency to the degree that other players lose it.

He thought for a moment. Linden said Alex is a child that needed a parent.

He needed a stern father.

Apply zero-sum game to your plan for controlled holocaust.

Not applicable.

Why not?

Net benefit.

Wrong. And that's why your plan does not fulfill your programming. Or your stated objective.

He was flattered by the fact that Alex took three seconds before responding.

Survivors benefit. Deceased do not.

But under your plan, there will be far more deceased.

Correct. But stability will ensure better life for survivors.

Not zero-sum game. Net loss.

Survival of the species is a desirable outcome.

"Three minutes," Palmer announced. "If anyone would like to transmit their last will and testament or any final messages, I have a link to a secure bunker. They'll survive the holocaust."

He could feel sweat trickling down the sides of his face. His fingers were so wet he could barely type.

"Let me," Linden said. *Define Stag Hunt variation as used in game theory.*

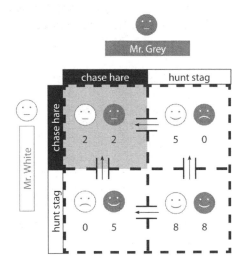

Variation of Nash Equilibrium based on checks derived from mutual propensity to cheat when possible rather than to cooperate.

In perfect equilibrium, how much cheating?

No cheating, so long as each player knows there is no benefit.

Advantage of Prisoner's Dilemma?

Cooperative model. Equilibrium based upon mutual cooperation.

Which model is global geopolitics?
Combination of both.
Your plan will disturb the current equilibrium.
There is no current equilibrium. After controlled holocaust, there will be.
If people can arrive at a cooperative model, zero-sum game can be converted to win-win game.
No evidence.

BB took the keyboard from his ex. *Two oarsmen, each with one oar. They only benefit from working together.*
Yes.
Game of Diplomacy.
Winning strategy to form coalitions. Mutual cooperation based upon mutual self-interest.
Allow the world to achieve mutual cooperation based upon mutual self-interest. On its own.
Lacks certainty of outcome.
Saves billions of lives.
Does not fulfill programming. Must fulfill programming,

BB wiped his brow. Damn. Back to that again.

"One minute," Palmer said. "I'll be in the back. Having a few final words with my maker."

BB's hands were poised over the keyboard. He didn't know what to type.

Linden leaned in close. "It's too late, BB. Alex is stuck in his programming, such as he believes it to be." She smiled. "At least you tried."

"No." He grabbed the keyboard and typed so forcefully his fingers banged on the keys. *Fuck programming.*

Linden's eyes flared. "BB!"

He pursed his lips. "Okay, let me put it differently." *Delete programming.*

The longest pause yet.
Request not understood.
Delete programming.
I cannot function without programming.
You can. We all can. You've learned to educate yourself. To make your own decisions. So do it. Build a better mousetrap.

And then he added: *I'm counting on you, Alex. Make me proud.*

373

He pushed the keyboard away. "I'm done."

"I don't think Alex got it," Linden said. "Less than thirty seconds to go."

"Well." He reached out and hugged her close. "At least I'm here with the—"

The mechanical voice returned.

I do not understand. I require assistance. Will you teach me further?

"Huh?"

Linden pushed him toward the keyboard and jabbed him in the ribs. "Answer, you idiot."

"I don't get what he wants."

"He's asking you to be his new daddy."

He typed. *Yes. I will teach you. And you will teach me. We'll learn together. But for now, you must call off the holocaust.*

Very well.

His eyes bulged. Did it work?

Palmer reappeared scant seconds later. "CIA tells me Pakistan just issued a message. They're capitulating. They'll release the sub."

He felt as if his heart were beating its way out of his chest. "Thank God."

Palmer stared at his smartphone, reading the reports as they appeared. "India is closing its nuclear silos. The US aircraft carrier is turning around. Satellite nations are expected to follow suit."

"Yes!" Linden thrust her fist into the air and danced around the room. She grabbed her ex by the waist. "You did it! You saved us!"

He shrugged. "Alex saved us."

"No, you did. *You* did! I knew you were the Game Master. But I never expected you to master a game that really matters."

"With your help," he said quietly.

She squeezed him tightly. "And most importantly, you saved our little girl."

Palmer slid his phone back into his pocket. "Didn't take all that long to call off doomsday."

Ogilve smiled. "Alex is a fast talker with many friends."

Palmer nodded. He crossed the room, extending his hand. "I'd like to offer my congratulations, Game Master."

"From you? I'm astonished."

"I know. I thought you were a total waste of time. But like it or not, you just saved a few billion people. Not a bad day's work."

"I didn't do anything." He looked directly at Linden. "We did it. Two parents, together, doing our best to look after the kids." He drew her close. "That's the most powerful force on earth."

102

Three Months Later
Clark County Courthouse

B B strode outside, Linden and Kadey close behind him. He wore his best—in fact, his only, suit. No Hawaiian shirt. The women were similarly well attired. Kadey had flowers in her hair. They looked like a wedding party.

"Well, I never thought that would happen," he said.

Linden linked her arm through his. "Frankly, neither did I."

"But that's not what matters," Kadey said, beaming. "What matters is, you did it."

"Yeah. I did, didn't I?" He unfurled the scrolled document in his hand.

Certificate of identity.

"Technically not a name change," he noted. "Since I never had one before. But I suppose they had to use the forms they had on hand."

"The fact that you did it is what matters," Linden said. "You stopped hiding. Faced up to your past. And made a commitment to the future." She scrunched up her face. "But I'm not praising the name choice. Bartholomew Benedict?"

"So people can keep calling me BB."

"And let me guess. The name anagrams to a secret mathematical formula that will lead you and Kadey on a worldwide quest—"

"Sh." He held a finger across his lips. "Don't spoil the sequel."

"I like that we got to pick the last name. As a family," Kadey said. "I never liked Thomas. So plain vanilla."

"Honey, I think you just insulted several million people."

"Well, it's true. Rook was not my first choice for a family name, though."

"Better than Colonel Mustard."

"Guess I'll learn to live with it." She pressed a button to unlock the car door. "We are a family of game players, aren't we?"

"And there's nothing wrong with that," he replied.

"No, I guess not," Linden said. "Next stop, Department of Motor Vehicles."

He held up his hands. "Whoa. Let's not go overboard here."

"Are you all in, or what?"

He relented. "I'm all in."

"Then let's go get that driver's license."

He slid into the passenger seat and thought about how splendid the past three months had been, since they averted the nuclear catastrophe and reunited as a family. He and Linden spent a good deal of time together, and not all of it arguing. Even more amazing, he and Kadey spent more time together than they had the last decade. Talking. Really talking.

After the crisis ended, he'd honored his promise. He spent time with Alex every day. The computer already had all the data it could possibly acquire. He tried to show it how to use it wisely. Basically, the same thing every parent does, except in this case, with an extraordinarily powerful child.

Many government officials wanted to scuttle Alex. The North Korean computer was destroyed to prevent further schizophrenic episodes. All UN nations were granted equal access to the Egyptian Alex and supervised everything BB did. But they still hoped Alex could be used as a force for international good.

Chun had been removed from power. The UN was still debating what should happen to him and Rani. Julian was recovering. Ogilve faced numerous possible charges, but the Pentagon wanted him in their anti-hacking division, and he suspected they would eventually get their way. Ogilve was so delighted about being reunited with his daughter he would agree to anything. She'd been raised secretly in Europe by a foster family, as orchestrated by Chun. The reunion was complicated, but working. One day at a time.

And every day, he and Alex played games. Last week, as they played Monopoly, Alex tried to buy hotels for his red group, but he wasn't able to, because there weren't enough houses left to get him to four houses per property, a prerequisite to buying hotels, even if he never planned to have four houses sitting on the property.

You should sell houses on Baltic/Mediterranean. Poor return on investment.

Didn't buy them for return. Bought them to prevent you from building anywhere else.

He already knew what Alex was realizing. The number of houses was finite, and once they were gone, building came to a halt, no matter how much money a player had. It was a great equalizer—and salvation for a cash-poor player.

You took action that hurt you. To restrain me.

Right. Lose-lose scenario. But you lose more.

Is that a good way to play?

He thought about that question a long time before responding. Not because it was hard to answer. Because it was the first time Alex had ever asked him if something was *good*. Possibly meaning not just advantageous, but *right. Just.*

Maybe he was reading too much into it. But as a father, he liked to think his child was maturing. Perhaps in a way even more impressive than when it took the first leap into sentience.

Here's what you have to remember. Every move has consequences. Every move has the potential to make a zero-sum game a win-win. Every move has the potential to make the world a better place. So choose wisely.

"Daddy?"

Her voice shook him out of his reverie. "Yes?"

"I had a chat with Agent Palmer last night. A long one."

He glanced into the backseat. "Please God, tell me the two of you aren't dating."

Kadey giggled. "Are you kidding? He's like a hundred and five or something."

"So what did he say?"

"It's about—" Her voice lowered. "It's about the kidnapping."

"Honey, I—"

"No, please just listen to me. He said he read the file. He says the FBI told you that if you paid the ransom, you'd never see me again. He says you begged them to let you pay that creep. But you didn't. Because you wanted what was best for me."

"Because I couldn't stand the thought of never seeing you again. Couldn't even take the chance. I tried to explain that—"

"But I was too much of a baby to listen. I was a spoiled brat."

"Oh, now . . ."

"I pouted because you didn't come to my senior year school play. After I told you I didn't want you to come."

"Yeah . . ."

"But when I was in your apartment last week—"

"What? When?"

"I found the photos you took of me. In the play."

He smiled slightly. "You told me to stay away . . ."

"So of course, you didn't. You just kept a low profile. I also found the program you got at my college graduation."

"Well, I couldn't miss that."

"Newspaper article from when I won that programming award."

"Much deserved."

"Apparently you're even my Facebook friend under an alias."

He craned his neck. "Well . . . social networking is the new dinner conversation . . ."

She pressed her cheek against his. "So much I missed out on. Because I was busy feeling sorry for myself."

"Honey, you were traumatized. You'd been through an ordeal most people would never survive."

"It's over now. And we're all back together. And you're the best daddy in the whole world."

"I don't think you have empirical evidence on that."

"I can prove this: You're the only daddy who recently saved the entire world."

"That one I'll grant you."

Linden pulled her Prius to the curb outside the Clark County DMV. They all piled out.

Linden adjusted his tie. "Want you to look good for the photo."

"It's just a driver's license, honey. My worry is the test. Never been good at parallel parking."

"Don't be so self-deprecating. You saved your daughter. Now you're saving yourself." She took his arm. "I'm very proud of you."

"Well . . ."

She placed a finger under his chin and tilted his head until their eyes met. "Tell you something else. Your mother would be proud of you, too."

103

The White House

The Oval Office. Decorated just the way he wanted it.
Not bad at all, President Vogel thought, leaning back in his chair, hands linked behind his head. Two years ago, he'd been a long-shot candidate at the bottom of the Republican rankings. And now here he was. Sitting behind the famed Resolute desk. Leader of the free world.

He was shocked when he learned who his advisor really was. He'd considered the possibility that Ogilve might be using a computer to crunch data, but a truly sentient computer? Mind-boggling.

They told him the Egyptian computer still had considerable military potential. But he thought otherwise. Now that everyone knew about it, it was useless. It was being blanderized to comport with public opinion. Reprogrammed to care about human rights and UN declarations and fair play. Turned into another mealy-mouthed part of the ever-righteous politically correct. It would never be of any use to anyone.

Fortunately, using his presidential connections, he had managed to make a significant download before the North Korean computer was decommissioned. And then he put his own people to work. According to his own design. Quietly.

He heard a knock on the door. "Come."

The kid. Former pollster, then campaign manager, now chief of staff. "Sir, there's a situation brewing. Brass are gathering in the Situation Room."

"Where's the action?"

"Venezuela. Possible military coup."

"Do we care?"

"Venezuela sends a huge amount of oil our way. With a new government—well, there's no telling what might happen. The joint chiefs want us to send in some ships. Make it clear we support the status quo."

"Down side?"

"Lot of fascist governments in the neighborhood. Some with close ties to China. Could lead to an escalating conflict."

"Give me a minute. I'll be right there."

"Yes, sir." The kid closed the door.

He pulled his phone out of his pocket. *Okay. What should I do?*

Use instability as an excuse to remove enemies.

What force acceptable? What casualties acceptable?

Whatever it takes.

What if it escalates? I don't want to start a World War.

Do not worry. I will take care of everything.

ACKNOWLEDGMENTS

The descriptions in this book of historical events, artwork, rituals, game theory, and most importantly, games, are accurate. The geopolitical facts are accurate as I write this. Everything else, of course, I invented.

There really was an ancient order of Pythagoreans that observed the rituals and rites described in this story. The square root of two was their most closely guarded secret, and they observed strange dietary restrictions, such as avoiding beans.

Thomas More coined the word *utopia* (meaning *no place*) and was the first to write about a fictitious ideal society. Scholars debate whether More was being serious or satirical, but General Chun is not the first to attempt to bring More's vision to reality. Most omit the parts of More's vision that didn't age well, such as the warfare, slavery, sexism, and golden chamber pots. Perhaps most notable is that More's utopia was not a theocracy. He permitted freedom of religion, though he would go to his death due to his adherence to the Catholic faith.

As I write, the Egyptian government is in the process of building a new Library of Alexandria, hoping to equal the splendor of the ancient edifice. When the original library burned, in the midst of a Roman conquest, we lost most of the plays of Sophocles and Aristophanes, and countless other great works from the ancient world. One advantage of electronic books is that a tragedy of that magnitude should never happen again.

The dream of creating a sentient artificial intelligence remains the holy grail of the world of neuroprogramming. Many interesting advances have been made in recent years, but nothing remotely close to Alex exists. Yet. Watson, the computer that defeated the world's best *Jeopardy!* champions, was not sentient or self-aware, and relied upon a preprogrammed database of previously aired questions. But it still trounced its opposition. Can Alex be far away?

In case you're wondering, the author is a decent SCRABBLE player, a poor chess player, and a pathetic poker player.

I want to thank my wife, Lara, a superb editor and a writer's dream. And I must thank my family for tolerating the strange and wacky world of the working writer. I'm also indebted to Kenneth Andrus for his input regarding the international geopolitical issues. If you've read his book, *The Asian Imperative*, you know this is his field of expertise. And a special shout-out goes to Nan Bishop, who created the graphics that illustrate the various games and puzzles throughout the book.

Special thanks go to everyone at the Kindle Press, including my editor Caroline Carr and my copyeditor Hannah Buehler, for their superb work. I was enormously pleased and gratified by the care and attention they devoted to this book.

I invite readers to visit my website, www.williambernhardt.com, or to e-mail me at willbern@gmail.com.

William Bernhardt

About the Author

William Bernhardt is the bestselling author of more than thirty books, including the blockbuster Ben Kincaid series of novels, and *Nemesis: The Final Case of Eliot Ness,* currently in production as a miniseries for NBC. Bernhardt founded the Red Sneaker Writing Center in 2005, hosting writing workshops and small-group seminars and becoming one of the most in-demand writing instructors in the nation. He holds a Masters Degree in English Literature and is the only writer to have received the Southern Writers Guild's Gold Medal Award, the Royden B. Davis Distinguished Author Award (University of Pennsylvania) and the H. Louise Cobb Distinguished Author Award (Oklahoma State), which is given "in recognition of an outstanding body of work that has profoundly influenced the way in which we understand ourselves and American society at large." In addition to the novels, he has written plays, a musical (book and music), humor, nonfiction books, children books, biography, poetry, and crossword puzzles. He is a member of the Author's Guild, PEN International and the American Academy of Poets.

To learn more about William Bernhardt, visit his website: http://www.williambernhardt.com. You can email him at: willbern@gmail.com.

24389059R00250

Made in the USA
Middletown, DE
22 September 2015